Praise for beloved romance author Betty Neels

D0528921

Romance readers around the world were sad to note the passing of **Betty Neels** in June 2001. Her career spanned thirty years, and she continued to write into her ninetieth year. To her millions of fans, Betty epitomized the romance writer, and yet she began writing almost by accident. She had retired from nursing, but her inquiring mind still sought stimulation. Her new career was born when she heard a lady in her local library bemoaning the lack of good romance novels. Betty's first book, *Sister Peters in Amsterdam*, was published in 1969, and she eventually completed 134 books. Her novels offer a reassuring warmth that was very much a part of her own personality. She was a wonderful writer, and she is greatly missed. Her spirit and genuine talent live on in all her stories.

BETTY NEELS

The Right Kind of Girl
& Pineapple Girl

HARLEQUIN® SPECIAL RELEASE

ISBN-13: 978-1-335-04515-7

The Right Kind of Girl & Pineapple Girl

Copyright © 2019 by Harlequin Books S.A.

The publisher acknowledges the copyright holder of the individual works as follows:

The Right Kind of Girl
Copyright © 1995 by Betty Neels

Pineapple Girl
Copyright © 1977 by Betty Neels

Recycling programs for this product may not exist in your area.

Printed in U.S.A.

HARLEQUIN®
www.Harlequin.com

CONTENTS

Chapter 1

Mrs Smith-Darcy had woken in a bad temper. She reclined, her abundant proportions supported by a number of pillows, in her bed, not bothering to reply to the quiet 'good morning' uttered by the girl who had entered the room; she was not a lady to waste courtesy on those she considered beneath her. Her late husband had left her rich, having made a fortune in pickled onions, and since she had an excellent opinion of herself she found no need to bother with the feelings of anyone whom she considered inferior. And, of course, a paid companion came into that category.

The paid companion crossed the wide expanse of carpet and stood beside the bed, notebook in hand. She looked out of place in the over-furnished, frilly room; a girl of medium height, with pale brown hair smoothed into a French pleat, she had unremarkable features, but her eyes were large, thickly lashed and of a pleasing hazel. She was dressed in a pleated skirt and a white blouse, with a grey cardigan to match the skirt—sober clothes which failed to conceal her pretty figure and elegant legs.

Mrs Smith-Darcy didn't bother to look at her. 'You can go to the bank and cash a cheque—the servants want their wages. Do call in at the butcher's and tell him that I'm not satisfied with the meat he's sending up to the house. When you get back—and don't be all day over a couple of errands—you can make an appointment with my hairdresser and get the invitations written for my luncheon party. The list's on my desk.'

She added pettishly, 'Well, get on with it, then; there's plenty of work waiting for you when you get back.'

The girl went out of the room without a word, closed the door quietly behind her and went downstairs to the kitchen where Cook had a cup of coffee waiting for her.

'Got your orders, Miss Trent? In a mood, is she?'

'I dare say it's this weather, Cook. I have to go to the shops. Is there anything I can bring back for you?'

'Well, now, love, if you could pop into Mr Coffin's and ask him to send up a couple of pounds of sausages with the meat? They'll do us a treat for our dinner.'

Emma Trent, battling on her bike against an icy February wind straight from Dartmoor and driving rain, reflected that there could be worse jobs, only just at that moment she couldn't think of any. It wasn't just the weather—she had lived in Buckfastleigh all her life and found nothing unusual in that; after all, it was only a mile or so from the heart of the moor with its severe winters.

Bad weather she could dismiss easily enough, but Mrs Smith-Darcy was another matter; a selfish lazy woman, uncaring of anyone's feelings but her own, she was Emma's daily trial, but her wages put the butter on the bread of Emma's mother's small pension so she had to be borne. Jobs weren't all that easy to find in a small rural town, and if she went to Plymouth or even Ashburton it would mean living away from home, whereas now they managed very well, although there was never much money over.

Her errands done, and with the sausages crammed into a pocket, since Mr Coffin had said that he wasn't sure if he could deliver the meat before the afternoon, she cycled back to the large house on the other side of the town where her employer lived, parked her bike by the side-door and went into the kitchen. There she handed over the sausages, hung her sopping raincoat to dry and went along to the little cubby-hole where she spent most of her days—making out cheques for the tradesmen, making appointments, writing notes and keeping the household books. When she wasn't doing that, she arranged the flowers, and answered the door if Alice, the housemaid, was busy or having her day off.

'Never a dull moment,' said Emma to her reflection as she tidied her hair and dried the rain from her face. The buzzer Mrs Smith-Darcy used whenever she demanded Emma's presence was clamouring to be answered, and she picked up her notebook and pencil and went unhurriedly upstairs.

Mrs Smith-Darcy had heaved herself out of bed and was sitting before the dressing-table mirror, doing her face. She didn't look up from the task of applying mascara. 'I have been buzzing you for several minutes,' she observed crossly. 'Where have you been? Really, a great, strong girl like you should have done those few errands in twenty minutes...'

Emma said mildly, 'I'm not a great, strong girl, Mrs Smith-Darcy, and cycling into the wind isn't the quickest way of travelling. Besides, I got wet—'

'Don't make childish excuses. Really, Miss Trent, I sometimes wonder if you are up to this job. Heaven knows, it's easy enough.'

Emma knew better than to answer that. Instead she asked, 'You wanted me to do something for you, Mrs Smith-Darcy?'

'Tell Cook I want my coffee in half an hour. I shall be out to lunch, and while I'm gone you can fetch Frou-Frou from the vet. I shall need Vickery with the car so I suppose you had better get a taxi—it wouldn't do for Frou-Frou to get wet. You can pay and I'll settle with you later.'

'I haven't brought any money with me.' Emma crossed her fingers behind her back as she spoke, for it was a fib, but on several occasions she had been told to pay for something and that she would be reimbursed later—something which had never happened.

Mrs Smith-Darcy frowned. 'Really, what an incompetent girl you are.' She opened her handbag and found a five-pound note. 'Take this—and I'll expect the correct change.'

'I'll get the driver to write the fare down and sign it,' said Emma quietly, and something in her voice made Mrs Smith-Darcy look at her.

'There's no need for that.'

'It will set your mind at rest,' said Emma sweetly. 'I'll get those invitations written; I can post them on my way home.'

Mrs Smith-Darcy, who liked to have the last word, was for once unable to think of anything to say as Emma left the room.

It was well after five o'clock when Emma got on to her bike and took herself off home—a small, neat house near the abbey where she and her mother had lived since her father had died several years earlier.

He had died suddenly and unexpectedly, and it hadn't been until after his death that Mrs Trent had been told that he had mortgaged the house in order to raise the money to help his younger brother, who had been in financial difficulties, under the impression that he would be repaid within a reasonable time. There hadn't been enough money to pay off the mortgage, so she had sold the house and bought a small terraced house, and, since her brother-in-law had gone abroad without leaving an address, she and Emma now managed on her small pension and Emma's salary. That she herself was underpaid Emma was well aware, but on the other hand her job allowed her to keep an eye on her mother's peptic ulcer...

There was an alley behind the row of houses. She

wheeled her bike along its length and into their small back garden, put it in the tumbledown shed outside the kitchen door and went into the house.

The kitchen was small, but its walls were distempered in a cheerful pale yellow and there was room for a small table and two chairs against one wall. She took off her outdoor things, carried them through to the narrow little hall and went into the sitting-room. That was small too, but it was comfortably furnished, although a bit shabby, and there was a cheerful fire burning in the small grate.

Mrs Trent looked up from her sewing. 'Hello, love. Have you had a tiring day? And so wet and cold too. Supper is in the oven but you'd like a cup of tea first...'

'I'll get it.' Emma dropped a kiss on her mother's cheek and went to make the tea and presently carried it back.

'Something smells heavenly,' she observed. 'What have you been cooking?'

'Casserole and dumplings. Did you get a proper lunch?'

Emma assured her that she had, with fleeting regret for most of the sausages she hadn't been given time to eat; Mrs Smith-Darcy had the nasty habit of demanding that some task must be done at once, never mind how inconvenient. She reflected with pleasure that her employer was going away for several days, and although she had been given a list of things to do which would take at least twice that period it would be like having a holiday.

She spent the next day packing Mrs Smith-Darcy's

expensive cases with the clothes necessary to make an impression during her stay at Torquay's finest hotel—a stay which, she pointed out to Emma, was vital to her health. This remark reminded her to order the central heating to be turned down while she was absent. 'And I expect an accurate statement of the household expenses.'

Life, after Mrs Smith-Darcy had been driven away by Vickery, the chauffeur, was all of a sudden pleasant.

It was delightful to arrive each morning and get on with her work without having to waste half an hour listening to her employer's querulous voice raised in criticism about something or other, just as it was delightful to go home each evening at five o'clock exactly.

Over and above this, Cook, unhampered by her employer's strictures, allowed her creative skills to run free so that they ate food which was never normally allowed—rich steak and kidney pudding with a drop of stout in the gravy, roasted potatoes—crisply brown, toad-in-the-hole, braised celery, cauliflower smothered in a creamy sauce and all followed by steamed puddings, sticky with treacle or bathed in custard.

Emma, eating her dinners in the kitchen with Cook and Alice, the housemaid, savoured every morsel, dutifully entered the bills in her household ledger and didn't query any of them; she would have to listen to a diatribe about the wicked extravagance of her staff from Mrs Smith-Darcy but it would be worth it, and Cook had given her a cake to take home, declaring that she had made two when one would have done.

On the last day of Mrs Smith-Darcy's absence from

home Emma arrived in good time. There were still one or two tasks to do before that lady returned—the flowers to arrange, the last of the post to sort out and have ready for her inspection, a list of the invitations accepted for the luncheon party...

She almost fell off her bike as she shot through the gates into the short drive to the house. The car was before the door and Vickery was taking the cases out of the boot. He cast his eyes up as she jumped off her bike.

'Took bad,' he said. 'During the night. 'Ad the doctor to see 'er—gave her an injection and told 'er it were a bug going round—gastric something or other. Alice is putting 'er to bed, miss. You'd better go up sharp, like.'

'Oh, Vickery, you must have had to get up very early—it's only just nine o'clock.'

'That I did, miss.' He smiled at her. 'I'll see to yer bike.'

'Thank you, Vickery. I'm sure Cook will have breakfast for you.'

She took off her outdoor things and went upstairs. Mrs Smith-Darcy's door was closed but she could hear her voice raised in annoyance. She couldn't be very ill if she could shout like that, thought Emma, opening the door.

'There you are—never where you're wanted, as usual. I'm ill—very ill. That stupid doctor who came to the hotel told me it was some kind of virus. I don't believe him. I'm obviously suffering from some grave internal disorder. Go and phone Dr Treble and tell him to come at once.'

'He'll be taking surgery,' Emma pointed out reasonably. 'I'll ask him to come as soon as he's finished.' She studied Mrs Smith-Darcy's face. 'Are you in great pain? Did the doctor at Torquay advise you to go to a hospital for emergency treatment?'

'Of course not. If I need anything done I shall go into a private hospital. I am in great pain—agony...' She didn't quite meet Emma's level gaze. 'Do as I tell you; I must be attended to at once.'

She was in bed now, having her pillows arranged just so by the timid Alice. Emma didn't think that she looked in pain; certainly her rather high colour was normal, and if she had been in the agony she described then she wouldn't have been fussing about her pillows and which bed-jacket she would wear. She went downstairs and dialled the surgery.

The receptionist answered. 'Emma—how are you? Your mother's all right? She looked well when I saw her a few days ago.'

'Mother's fine, thanks, Mrs Butts. Mrs Smith-Darcy came back this morning from a few days at Torquay. She wasn't well during the night and the hotel called a doctor who told her it was a bug and that she had better go home—he gave her something—I don't know what. She says she is in great pain and wants Dr Treble to come and see her immediately.'

'The surgery isn't finished—it'll be another half an hour or so, unless she'd like to be brought here in her car.' Mrs Butts chuckled. 'And that's unlikely, isn't it?' She paused. 'Is she really ill, Emma?'

'Her colour is normal; she's very cross...'

'When isn't she very cross? I'll ask Doctor to visit

when surgery is over, but, I warn you, if there's anything really urgent he'll have to see to it first.'

Emma went back to Mrs Smith-Darcy and found her sitting up in bed renewing her make-up. 'You're feeling better? Would you like coffee or tea? Or something to eat?'

'Don't be ridiculous, Miss Trent; can you not see how I'm suffering? Is the doctor on his way?'

'He'll come when surgery is finished—about half an hour, Mrs Butts said.'

'Mrs Butts? Do you mean to tell me that you didn't speak to Dr Treble?'

'No, he was busy with a patient.'

'I am a patient,' said Mrs Smith-Darcy in a furious voice.

Emma, as mild as milk and unmoved, said, 'Yes, Mrs Smith-Darcy. I'll be back in a minute; I'm going to open the post while I've the chance.'

There must be easier ways of earning a living, she reflected, going down to the kitchen to ask Cook to make lemonade.

She bore the refreshment upstairs presently, and took it down again as her employer didn't find it sweet enough. When she went back with it she was kept busy closing curtains because the dim light from the February morning was hurting the invalid's eyes, then fetching another blanket to put over her feet, and changing the bed-jacket she had on, which wasn't the right colour...

'Now go and fetch my letters,' said Mrs Smith-Darcy.

Perhaps, thought Emma, nipping smartly downstairs once more, Dr Treble would prescribe something which would soothe the lady and cause her to doze off for long periods. Certainly at the moment Mrs Smith-Darcy had no intention of doing any such thing.

Emma, proffering her post, got the full force of her displeasure.

'Bills,' said Mrs Smith-Darcy. 'Nothing but bills!' And went on that doubtless, while her back was turned, those whom she employed had eaten her out of house and home, and as for an indigent nephew who had had the effrontery to ask her for a small loan... 'Anyone would think that I was made of money,' she said angrily— which was, in fact, not far wrong.

The richer you are, the meaner you get, reflected Emma, retrieving envelopes and bills scattered over the bed and on the floor.

She was on her knees with her back to the door when it was opened and Alice said, 'The doctor, ma'am,' and something in her voice made Emma turn around. It wasn't Dr Treble but a complete stranger who, from her lowly position, looked enormous.

Indeed, he was a big man; not only very tall but built to match his height, he was also possessed of a hand-some face with a high-bridged nose and a firm mouth. Pepper and salt hair, she had time to notice, and on the wrong side of thirty. She was aware of his barely con-cealed look of amusement as she got to her feet.

'Get up, girl,' said Mrs Smith-Darcy and then added, 'I sent for Dr Treble.' She took a second look at him and altered her tone. 'I don't know you, do I?'

He crossed the room to the bed. 'Dr Wyatt. I have taken over from Dr Treble for a short period. What can

I do for you, Mrs Smith-Darcy? I received a message that it was urgent.'

'Oh, Doctor, I have had a shocking experience—' She broke off for a moment. 'Miss Trent, get the doctor a chair.'

But before Emma could move he had picked up a spindly affair and sat on it, seemingly unaware of the alarming creaks; at the same time he had glanced at her again with the ghost of a smile. Nice, thought Emma, making herself as inconspicuous as possible. I hope that he will see through her. At least she won't be able to bully him like she does Dr Treble.

Her hopes were justified. Mrs Smith-Darcy, prepared to discuss her symptoms at some length, found herself answering his questions with no chance of embellishment, although she did her best.

'You dined last evening?' he wanted to know. 'What exactly did you eat and drink?'

'The hotel is noted for its excellent food,' she gushed. 'It's expensive, of course, but one has to pay for the best, does one not?' She waited for him to make some comment and then, when he didn't, added pettishly, 'Well, a drink before I dined, of course, and some of the delightful canapés they serve. I have a small appetite but I managed a little caviare. Then, let me see, a morsel of sole with a mushroom sauce—cooked in cream, of course—and then a simply delicious pheasant with an excellent selection of vegetables.'

'And?' asked Dr Wyatt, his voice as bland as his face.

'Oh, dessert—meringue with a chocolate sauce

laced with curaçao—a small portion, I might add.' She laughed. 'A delicious meal—'

'And the reason for your gastric upset. There is nothing seriously wrong, Mrs Smith-Darcy, and it can be easily cured by taking some tablets which you can obtain from the chemist and then keeping to a much plainer diet in future. I'm sure that your daughter—'

'My paid companion,' snapped Mrs Smith-Darcy. 'I am a lonely widow, Doctor, and able to get about very little.'

'I suggest that you take regular exercise each day—a brisk walk, perhaps.'

Mrs Smith-Darcy shuddered. 'I feel that you don't understand my delicate constitution, Doctor; I hope that I shan't need to call you again.'

'I think it unlikely; I can assure you that there is nothing wrong with you, Mrs Smith-Darcy. You will feel better if you get up and dress.'

He bade her goodbye with cool courtesy. 'I will give your companion some instructions and write a prescription for some tablets.'

Emma opened the door for him, but he took the handle from her and ushered her through before closing it gently behind him.

'Is there somewhere we might go?'

'Yes—yes, of course.' She led the way downstairs and into her office.

He looked around him. 'This is where you work at being a companion?'

'Yes. Well, I do the accounts and bills and write

the letters here. Most of the time I'm with Mrs Smith-Darcy.'

'But you don't live here?' He had a pleasant, deep voice, quite quiet and soothing, and she answered his questions readily because he sounded so casual.

'No, I live in Buckfastleigh with my mother.'

'A pleasant little town. I prefer the other end, though, nearer the abbey.'

'Oh, so do I; that's where we are...' She stopped there; he wouldn't want to know anything about her—they were strangers, not likely to see each other again. 'Is there anything special I should learn about Mrs Smith-Darcy?'

'No, she is perfectly healthy although very over-weight. Next time she overeats try to persuade her to take one of these tablets instead of calling the doctor.' He was writing out a prescription and paused to look at her. 'You're wasted here, you know.'

She blushed. 'I've not had any training—at least, only shorthand and typing and a little bookkeeping—and there aren't many jobs here.'

'You don't wish to leave home?'

'No. I can't do that. Is Dr Treble ill?'

'Yes, he's in hospital. He has had a heart attack and most likely will retire.'

She gave him a thoughtful look. 'I'm very sorry. You don't want me to tell Mrs Smith-Darcy?'

'No. In a little while the practice will be taken over by another doctor.'

'You?'

He smiled. 'No, no. I'm merely filling in until things have been settled.'

He gave her the prescription and closed his bag. The hand he offered was large and very firm and she wanted to keep her hand in his. He was, she reflected, a very nice man—dependable; he would make a splendid friend. It was such an absurd idea that she smiled and he decided that her smile was enchanting.

She went to the door with him and saw the steel-grey Rolls-Royce parked in the drive. 'Is that yours?' she asked.

'Yes.' He sounded amused and she begged his pardon and went pink again and stood, rather prim, in the open door until he got in and drove away.

She turned, and went in and up to the bedroom to find Mrs Smith-Darcy decidedly peevish. 'Really, I don't know what is coming to the medical profession,' she began, the moment Emma opened the door. 'Nothing wrong with me, indeed; I never heard such nonsense. I'm thoroughly upset. Go down and get my coffee and some of those wine biscuits.'

'I have a prescription for you, Mrs Smith-Darcy,' said Emma. 'I'll fetch it while you're getting dressed, shall I?'

'I have no intention of dressing. You can go to the chemist while I'm having my coffee—and don't hang around. There's plenty for you to do here.'

When she got back Mrs Smith-Darcy asked, 'What has happened to Dr Treble? I hope that that man is replacing him for a very short time; I have no wish to see him again.'

To which remark Emma prudently made no answer. Presently she went off to the kitchen to tell Cook that her mistress fancied asparagus soup made with single cream and a touch of parsley, and two lamb cutlets with creamed potatoes and braised celery in a cheese sauce. So much for the new doctor's advice, reflected Emma, ordered down to the cellar to fetch a bottle of Bollinger to tempt the invalid's appetite.

That evening, sitting at supper with her mother, Emma told her of the new doctor. 'He was nice. I expect if you were really ill he would take the greatest care of you.'

'Elderly?' asked Mrs Trent artlessly.

'Something between thirty and thirty-five, I suppose. Pepper and salt hair...'

A not very satisfactory answer from her mother's point of view.

February, tired of being winter, became spring for a couple of days, and Emma, speeding to and fro from Mrs Smith-Darcy's house, had her head full of plans— a day out with her mother on the following Sunday. She could rent a car from Dobbs's garage and drive her mother to Widecombe in the Moor and then on to Bovey Tracey; they could have lunch there and then go on back home through Ilsington—no main roads, just a quiet jaunt around the country they both loved.

She had been saving for a tweed coat and skirt, but she told herself that since she seldom went anywhere, other than a rare visit to Exeter or Plymouth, they could wait until autumn. She and her mother both needed a day out...

The weather was kind; Sunday was bright and clear, even if cold. Emma got up early, fed Queenie, their elderly cat, took tea to her mother and got the breakfast and, while Mrs Trent cleared it away, went along to the garage and fetched the car.

Mr Dobbs had known her father and was always willing to rent her a car, letting her have it at a reduced price since it was usually the smallest and shabbiest in his garage, though in good order, as he was always prompt to tell her. Today she was to have an elderly Fiat, bright red and with all the basic comforts, but, she was assured, running well. Emma, casting her eye over it, had a momentary vision of a sleek Rolls Royce...

They set off in the still, early morning and, since they had the day before them, Emma drove to Ashburton and presently took the narrow moor road to Widecombe, where they stopped for coffee before driving on to Bovey Tracey. It was too early for lunch, so they drove on then to Lustleigh, an ancient village deep in the moorland, the hills around it dotted with granite boulders. But although the houses and cottages were built of granite there was nothing forbidding about them—they were charming even on a chilly winter's day, the thatched roofs gleaming with the last of the previous night's frost, smoke eddying gently from their chimney-pots.

Scattered around the village were several substantial houses, tucked cosily between the hills. They were all old—as old as the village—and several of them were prosperous farms while others stood in sheltered grounds.

'I wouldn't mind living here,' said Emma as they passed one particularly handsome house, standing well back from the narrow road, the hills at its back, sheltered by carefully planted trees. 'Shall we go as far as Lustleigh Cleave and take a look at the river?'

After that it was time to find somewhere for lunch. Most of the cafés and restaurants in the little town were closed, since the tourist season was still several months away, but they found a pub where they were served roast beef with all the trimmings and home-made mince tarts to follow.

Watching her mother's pleasure at the simple, well-cooked meal, Emma promised herself that they would do a similar trip before the winter ended, while the villages were quiet and the roads almost empty.

It was still fine weather but the afternoon was already fading, and she had promised to return the car by seven o'clock at the latest. They decided to drive straight home and have tea when they got in, and since it was still a clear afternoon they decided to take a minor road through Ilsington. Emma had turned off the main road on to the small country lane when her mother slumped in her seat without uttering a sound. Emma stopped the car and turned to look at her unconscious parent.

She said, 'Mother—Mother, whatever is the matter…?' And then she pulled herself together—bleating her name wasn't going to help. She undid her safety-belt, took her mother's pulse and called her name again, but Mrs Trent lolled in her seat, her eyes closed. At least Emma could feel her pulse, and her breathing seemed normal.

Emma looked around her. The lane was narrow; she would never be able to turn the car and there was little point in driving on as Ilsington was a small village—too small for a doctor. She pulled a rug from the back seat and wrapped it round her mother and was full of thankful relief when Mrs Trent opened her eyes, but the relief was short-lived. Mrs Trent gave a groan. 'Emma, it's such a pain, I don't think I can bear it...'

There was only one thing to do—to reverse the car back down the lane, return to the main road and race back to Bovey Tracey.

'It's all right, Mother,' said Emma. 'It's not far to Bovey... There's the cottage hospital there; they'll help you.'

She began to reverse, going painfully slowly since the lane curved between high hedges, and it was a good thing she did, for the oncoming car behind her braked smoothly inches from her boot. She got out so fast that she almost tumbled over; here was help! She had no eyes for the other car but rushed to poke her worried face through the window that its driver had just opened.

'It's you!' she exclaimed. 'Oh, you can help. Only, please come quickly.' Dr. Wyatt didn't utter a word but he was beside her before she could draw another breath. 'Mother—it's Mother; she's collapsed and she's in terrible pain. I couldn't turn the car and this lane goes to Ilsington, and it's on the moor miles from anywhere...'

He put a large, steadying hand on her arm. 'Shall I take a look?'

Mrs Trent was a nasty pasty colour and her hand, when he took it, felt cold and clammy. Emma, half-in, half-out of the car on her side, said, 'Mother's got an ulcer—a peptic ulcer; she takes alkaline medicine and small meals and extra milk.'

He was bending over Mrs Trent. 'Will you undo her coat and anything else in the way? I must take a quick look. I'll fetch my bag.'

He straightened up presently. 'Your mother needs to be treated without delay. I'll put her into my car and drive to Exeter. You follow as soon as you can.'

'Yes.' She cast him a bewildered look.

'Problems?' he asked.

'I rented the car from Dobbs's garage; it has to be back by seven o'clock.'

'I'm going to give your mother an injection to take away the pain. Go to my car; there's a phone between the front seats. Phone this Dobbs, tell him what has happened and say that you'll bring the car back as soon as possible.' He turned his back on Mrs Trent, looming over Emma so that she had to crane her neck to see his face. 'I am sure that your mother has a perforated ulcer, which means surgery as soon as possible.'

She stared up at him, pale with shock, unable to think of anything to say. She nodded once and ran back to his car, and by the time she had made her call she had seen him lift her mother gently and carry her to the car. They made her comfortable on the back seat and Emma was thankful to see that her mother appeared to be dozing. 'She'll be all right? You'll hurry, won't you? I'll drive on until I can turn and then I'll come to the hospital—which one?'

'The Royal Devon and Exeter—you know where it is?' He got into his car and began to reverse down the lane. If the circumstances hadn't been so dire, she would have stayed to admire the way he did it—with the same ease as if he were going forwards.

She got into her car, then, and drove on for a mile or more before she came to a rough track leading on to the moor, where she reversed and drove back the way she had come. She was shaking now, in a panic that her mother was in danger of her life and she wouldn't reach the hospital in time, but she forced herself to drive carefully. Once she reached the main road and turned on to the carriageway, it was only thirteen miles to Exeter...

She forced herself to park the car neatly in the hospital forecourt and walk, not run, in through the casualty entrance. There, thank heaven, they knew who she was and why she had come. Sister, a cosy body with a soft Devon voice, came to meet her.

'Miss Trent? Your mother in is Theatre; the professor is operating at the moment. You come and sit down in the waiting-room and a nurse will bring you a cup of tea—you look as though you could do with it. Your mother is in very good hands, and as soon as she is back in her bed you shall go and see her. In a few minutes I should like some details, but you have your tea first.'

Emma nodded; if she had spoken she would have burst into tears; her small world seemed to be tumbling around her ears. She drank her tea, holding the cup in both hands since she was still shaking, and presently, when Sister came back, she gave her the details she needed in a wooden little voice. 'Will it be much longer?' she asked.

Sister glanced at the clock. 'Not long now. I'm sure you'll be told the moment the operation is finished. Will you go back to Buckfastleigh this evening?'

'Could I stay here? I could sit here, couldn't I? I wouldn't get in anyone's way.'

'If you are to stay we'll do better than that, my dear. Do you want to telephone anyone?'

Emma shook her head. 'There's only Mother and me.' She tried to smile and gave a great sniff. 'So sorry, it's all happened so suddenly.'

'You have a nice cry if you want to. I must go and see what's happening. There's been a street-fight and we'll be busy...'

Emma sat still and didn't cry—when she saw her mother she must look cheerful—so that when somebody came at last she turned a rigidly controlled face to hear the news.

Dr Wyatt was crossing the room to her. 'Your mother is going to be all right, Emma.' And then he held her in his arms as she burst into tears.

Chapter 2

Emma didn't cry for long but hiccuped, sniffed, sobbed a bit and drew away from him to blow her nose on the handkerchief he offered her.

'You're sure? Was it a big operation? Were you in the theatre?'

'Well, yes. It was quite a major operation but successful, I'm glad to say. You may see your mother; she will be semi-conscious but she'll know that you are there. She's in Intensive Care just for tonight. Tomorrow she will go to a ward—' He broke off as Sister joined them.

'They're wanting you on Male Surgical, sir—urgently.'

He nodded at Emma and went away.

'Mother's going to get well,' said Emma. She heaved a great sigh. 'What would I have done if Dr Wyatt hadn't been driving down the lane when Mother was taken ill? He works here as well as taking over the practice at home?'

Sister looked surprised and then smiled. 'Indeed he works here; he's our Senior Consultant Surgeon, although he's supposed to be taking a sabbatical, but I hear he's helping out Dr Treble for a week or two.'

'So he's a surgeon, not a GP?'

Sister smiled again. 'Sir Paul Wyatt is a professor of surgery, and much in demand for consultations, lecture-tours and seminars. You were indeed fortunate that he happened to be there when you needed help so urgently.'

'Would Mother have died, Sister?'

'Yes, love.'

'He saved her life...' She would, reflected Emma, do anything—anything at all—to repay him. Sooner or later there would be a chance. Perhaps not for years, but she wouldn't forget.

She was taken to see her mother then, who was lying in a tangle of tubes, surrounded by monitoring screens but blessedly awake. Emma bent to kiss her white face, her own face almost as white. 'Darling, everything's fine; you're going to be all right. I'll be here and come and see you in the morning after you've had a good sleep.'

Her mother frowned. 'Queenie,' she muttered.

'I'll phone Mr Dobbs and ask him to put some food outside the cat-flap.'

'Yes, do that, Emma.' Mrs Trent closed her eyes.

Emma turned at the touch on her arm. 'You're going to stay for the night?' A pretty, young nurse smiled at her. 'There's a rest-room on the ground floor; we'll call you if there's any need but I think your mother will sleep until the morning. You can see her before you go home then.'

Emma nodded. 'Is there a phone?'

'Yes, just by the rest-room, and there's a canteen down the corridor where you can get tea and sandwiches.'

'You're very kind.' Emma took a last look at her mother and went to the rest-room. There was no one else there and there were comfortable chairs and a table with magazines on it. As she hesitated at the door the sister from Casualty joined her.

'There's a washroom just across the passage. Try and sleep a little, won't you?'

When she had hurried away Emma picked up the phone. Mr Dobbs was sympathetic and very helpful—of course he'd see to Queenie, and Emma wasn't to worry about the car. 'Come back when you feel you can, love,' he told her. 'And you'd better keep the car for a day or two so's you can see your ma as often as possible.'

Mrs Smith-Darcy was an entirely different kettle of fish. 'My luncheon party,' she exclaimed. 'You will have to come back tomorrow morning and see to it; I am not strong enough to cope with it—you know how delicate I am. It is most inconsiderate of you...'

'My mother,' said Emma, between her teeth, 'in case you didn't hear what I have told you, is dangerously ill. I shall stay here with her as long as necessary. And you are not in the least delicate, Mrs Smith-Darcy, only spoilt and lazy and very selfish!'

She hung up, her ear shattered by Mrs Smith-

Darcy's furious bellow. Well, she had burnt her boats, cooked her goose and would probably be had up for libel—or was it slander? She didn't care. She had given voice to sentiments she had choked back for more than a year and she didn't care.

She felt better after her outburst, even though she was now out of work. She drank some tea and ate sandwiches from the canteen, resisted a wish to go in search of someone and ask about her mother, washed her face and combed her hair, plaited it and settled in the easiest of the chairs. Underneath her calm front panic and fright bubbled away.

Her mother might have a relapse; she had looked so dreadfully ill. She would need to be looked after for weeks, which was something Emma would do with loving care, but they would be horribly short of money. There was no one around, so she was able to shed a few tears; she was lonely and scared and tired. She mumbled her prayers and fell asleep before she had finished them.

Sir Paul Wyatt, coming to check his patient's condition at two o'clock in the morning and satisfied with it, took himself down to the rest-room. If Emma was awake he would be able to reassure her...

She was curled up in the chair, her knees drawn up under her chin, the half of her face he could see tear-stained, her thick rope of hair hanging over one shoulder. She looked very young and entirely without glamour, and he knew that when she woke in the morning she would have a job uncoiling herself from the tight ball into which she had wound herself.

He went and fetched a blanket from Casualty and laid it carefully over her; she was going to be stiff in the morning—there was no need for her to be cold as well. He put his hand lightly on her hair, touched by the sight of her, and then smiled and frowned at the sentimental gesture and went away again.

Emma woke early, roused by a burst of activity in Casualty, and just as Sir Paul Wyatt had foreseen, discovered that she was stiff and cramped. She got up awkwardly, folding the blanket neatly, and wondered who had been kind during the night. Then she went to wash her face and comb her hair.

Even with powder and lipstick she still looked a mess—not that it mattered, since there was no one to see her. She rubbed her cheeks to get some colour into them and practised a smile in the looking-glass so that her mother would see how cheerful and unworried she was. She would have to drive back to Buckfastleigh after she had visited her and somehow she would come each day to see her, although at the moment she wasn't sure how. Of one thing she was sure—Mrs Smith-Darcy would have dismissed her out-of-hand, so she would have her days free.

She drank tea and polished off some toast in the canteen, then went to find someone who would tell her when she might see her mother. She didn't have far to go—coming towards her along the passage was Sir Paul Wyatt, immaculate in clerical grey and spotless linen, freshly shaved, his shoes brilliantly polished. She wished him a good morning and, without waiting for him to answer, asked, 'Mother—is she all right? May I see her?'

'She had a good night, and of course you may see her.'

He stood looking at her, and the relief at his words was somewhat mitigated by knowing that her scruffy appearance seemed even more scruffy in contrast to his elegance. She rushed into speech to cover her awkwardness. 'They have been very kind to me here...'

He nodded with faint impatience—of course, he was a busy man and hadn't any time to waste. 'I'll go to Mother now,' she told him. 'I'm truly grateful to you for saving Mother. She's going to be quite well again, isn't she?'

'Yes, but you must allow time for her to regain her strength. I'll take you up to the ward on my way.'

She went with him silently, through corridors and then in a lift and finally through swing-doors where he beckoned a nurse, spoke briefly, then turned on his heel with a quick nod, leaving her to follow the nurse into the ward beyond.

Her mother wasn't in the ward but in a small room beyond, sitting up in bed. She looked pale and tired but she was smiling, and Emma had to fight her strong wish to burst into tears at the sight of her. She smiled instead. 'Mother, dear, you look so much better. How do you feel? And how nice that you're in a room by yourself...'

She bent and kissed her parent. 'I've just seen Sir Paul Wyatt and he says everything is most satisfactory.' She pulled up a chair and sat by the bed, taking her mother's hand in hers. 'What a coincidence that he should be here. Sister told me that he's a professor of surgery.'

Her mother smiled. 'Yes, love, and I'm fine. I really am. You're to go home now and not worry.'

'Yes, Mother. I'll phone this evening and I'll be back tomorrow. Do you want me to bring anything? I'll pack nighties and slippers and so on and bring them with me.'

Her mother closed her eyes. 'Yes, you know what to bring...'

Emma bent to kiss her again. 'I'm going now; you're tired. Have a nap, darling.'

It was still early; patients were being washed and tended before the breakfast trolley arrived. Emma was too early for the ward sister but the night staff nurse assured her that she would be told if anything unforeseen occurred. 'But your mother is most satisfactory, Miss Trent. The professor's been to see her already; he came in the night too. He's away for most of the day but his registrar is a splendid man. Ring this evening, if you like. You'll be coming tomorrow?'

Emma nodded. 'Can I come any time?'

'Afternoon or evening is best.'

Emma went down to the car and drove herself back to Buckfastleigh. As she went she planned her day. She would have to go and see Mrs Smith-Darcy and explain that she wouldn't be able to work for her any more. That lady was going to be angry and she supposed that she would have to apologise... She was owed a week's wages too, and she would need it.

Perhaps Mr Dobbs would let her hire the car each day just for the drive to and from the hospital; it would cost more than bus fares but it would be much quicker. She would have to go to the bank too; there wasn't much money there but she was prepared to spend the lot if necessary. It was too early to think about anything but the immediate future.

She took the car back to the garage and was warmed by Mr Dobbs's sympathy and his assurance that if she needed it urgently she had only to say so. 'And no hurry to pay the bill,' he promised her.

She went home then, and fed an anxious Queenie before making coffee. She was hungry, but it was past nine o'clock by now and Mrs Smith-Darcy would have to be faced before anything else. She had a shower, changed into her usual blouse, skirt and cardigan, did her face, brushed her hair into its usual smoothness and got on to her bike.

Alice opened the door to her. 'Oh, miss, whatever's happened? The mistress is in a fine state. Cook says come and have a cup of tea before you go up to her room; you'll need all your strength.'

'How kind of Cook,' said Emma. 'I think I'd rather have it afterwards, if I may.' She ran upstairs and tapped on Mrs Smith-Darcy's door and went in.

Mrs Smith-Darcy wasted no time in expressing her opinion of Emma; she repeated it several times before she ran out of breath, which enabled Emma to say, 'I'm sorry if I was rude to you on the phone, Mrs Smith-Darcy, but you didn't seem to understand that my mother was seriously ill—still is. I shall have to go to the hospital each day until she is well enough to come home, when I shall have to look after her until she is quite recovered—and that will take a considerable time.'

'My luncheon party,' gabbled Mrs Smith-Darcy. 'You wicked girl, leaving me like this. I'm incapable...'

Emma's efforts to behave well melted away. 'Yes, you are incapable,' she agreed. 'You're incapable of sympathy or human kindness. I suggest that you get up, Mrs Smith-Darcy, and see to your luncheon party yourself. I apologised to you just now—that was a mistake. You're everything I said and a lot more beside.'

She went out of the room and closed the door gently behind here. Then she opened it again. 'Will you be good enough to send my wages to my home?' She closed the door again on Mrs Smith-Darcy's enraged gasp.

She was shaking so much that her teeth rattled against the mug of tea Cook offered her.

'Now, don't you mind what she says,' said Cook. 'Nasty old lady she is too. You go on home and have a good sleep, for you're fair worn out. I've put up a pasty and one or two snacks, like; you take them home and if you've no time to cook you just slip round here to the back door—there's always a morsel of something in the fridge.'

The dear soul's kindness was enough to make Emma weep; she sniffed instead, gave Cook a hug and then got on her bike and cycled home, where she did exactly what that lady had told her to do—undressed like lightning and got into bed. She was asleep within minutes.

She woke suddenly to the sound of the door-knocker being thumped.

'Mother,' said Emma, and scrambled out of bed, her

heart thumping as loudly as the knocker. Not bothering with slippers, she tugged her dressing-gown on as she flew downstairs. It was already dusk; she had slept for hours—too long—she should have phoned the hospital. She turned the key in the lock and flung the door open.

Professor Sir Paul Wyatt was on the doorstep. He took the door from her and came in and shut it behind him. 'It is most unwise to open your door without putting up the chain or making sure that you know who it is.'

She eyed him through a tangle of hair. 'How can I know if I don't look first, and there isn't a chain?' Her half-awake brain remembered then.

'Mother—what's happened? Why are you here?' She caught at his sleeve. 'She's worse...'

His firm hand covered hers. 'Your mother is doing splendidly; she's an excellent patient. I'm sorry, I should have realised... You were asleep.'

She curled her cold toes on the hall carpet and nodded. 'I didn't mean to sleep for so long; it's getting dark.' She looked up at him. 'Why are you here, then?'

'I'm on my way home, but it has occurred to me that I shall be taking morning surgery here for the next week or two. I'll drive you up to Exeter after my morning visits and bring you back in time for evening surgery here.'

'Oh, would you? Would you really do that? How very kind of you, but won't it be putting you out? Sister said that you were taking a sabbatical, and that means you're on holiday, doesn't it?'

'Hardly a holiday, and I'm free to go in and out as I wish.'

'But you live in Exeter?'

'No, but not far from it; I shall not be in the least inconvenienced.'

She looked at him uncertainly, for he sounded casual and a little annoyed, but before she could speak he went on briskly, 'You'd better go and put some clothes on. Have you food in the house?'

'Yes, thank you. Cook gave me a pasty.' She was suddenly hungry at the thought of it. 'It was kind of you to come. I expect you want to go home—your days are long...'

He smiled. 'I'll make a pot of tea while you dress, and while we are drinking it I can explain exactly what I've done for your mother.'

She flew upstairs and flung on her clothes, washed her face and tied back her hair. Never mind how she looked—he wouldn't notice and he must be wanting to go home, wherever that was.

She perceived that he was a handy man in the kitchen—the tea was made, Queenie had been fed, and he had found a tin of biscuits.

'No milk, I'm afraid,' he said, not looking up from pouring the tea into two mugs. And then, very much to her surprise he asked, 'Have you sufficient money?'

'Yes—yes, thank you, and Mrs Smith-Darcy owes me a week's wages.' Probably in the circumstances she wouldn't get them, but he didn't need to know that.

He nodded, handed her a mug and said, 'Now, as to your mother...'

He explained simply in dry-as-dust words which were neither threatening nor casual. 'Your mother will stay in hospital for a week—ten days, perhaps—then I propose to send her to a convalescent home—there is a good one at Moretonhampstead, not too far from here—just for a few weeks. When she returns home she should be more or less able to resume her normal way of living, although she will have to keep to some kind of a diet. Time enough for that, however. Will you stay here alone?' He glanced at her. 'Perhaps you have family or a friend who would come…?'

'No family—at least, father had some cousins somewhere in London but they don't—that is, since he died we haven't heard from them. I've friends all over Buckfastleigh, though. If I asked one of them I know they'd come and stay but there's no need. I'm not nervous; besides, I'll try and find some temporary work until Mother comes home.'

'Mrs Smith-Darcy has given you the sack?'

'I'm sure of it. I was very rude to her this morning.' Anxious not to invite his pity, she added, 'There's always part-time work here—the abbey shop or the otter sanctuary.' True enough during the season—some months away!

He put down his mug. 'Good. I'll call for you some time after twelve o'clock tomorrow morning.' His goodbye was brief.

Left alone, she put the pasty to warm in the oven, washed the mugs and laid out a tray. The house was cold—there had never been enough money for central heating, and it was too late to make a fire in the sitting-room. She ate her supper, had a shower and went to bed, reassured by her visitor's calm manner and his certainty that her mother was going to be all right. He was nice, she thought sleepily, and not a bit pompous. She slept on the thought.

It was raining hard when she woke and there was a vicious wind driving off the moor. She had breakfast and hurried round to Dobbs's garage to use his phone. Her mother had had a good night, she was told, and was looking forward to seeing her later—reassuring news, which sent her back to give the good news to Queenie and then do the housework while she planned all the things she would do before her mother came home.

She had a sandwich and a cup of coffee well before twelve o'clock, anxious not to keep the professor waiting, so that when he arrived a few minutes before that hour she was in her coat, the house secure, Queenie settled in her basket and the bag she had packed for her mother ready in the hall.

He wished her a friendly good morning, remarked upon the bad weather and swept her into the car and drove away without wasting a moment. Conversation, she soon discovered, wasn't going to flourish in the face of his monosyllabic replies to her attempts to make small talk. She decided that he was tired or mulling over his patients and contented herself with watching the bleak landscape around them.

At the hospital he said, 'Will half-past four suit you? Be at the main entrance, will you?' He added kindly, 'I'm sure you'll be pleased with your mother's progress.' He got out of the car and opened her door, waited while she went in and then, contrary to her surmise, drove out of the forecourt and out of the city. Emma, unaware of this, expecting him to be about his own business in the hospital, made her way to her mother's room and forgot him at once.

Her mother was indeed better—pale still, and hung around with various tubes, but her hair had been nicely brushed and when Emma had helped her into her pink bed-jacket she looked very nearly her old self.

'It's a miracle, isn't it?' said Emma, gently embracing her parent. 'I mean, it's only forty-eight or so hours and here you are sitting up in bed.'

Mrs Trent, nicely sedated still, agreed drowsily. 'You brought my knitting? Thank you, dear. Is Queenie all right? And how are you managing to come? It can't be easy—don't come every day; it's such a long way...'

'Professor Wyatt is standing in for Dr Treble, so he brings me here after morning surgery and takes me back in time for his evening surgery.'

'That's nice.' Mrs Trent gave Emma's hand a little squeeze. 'So I'll see you each day; I'm so glad.' She closed her eyes and dropped off and Emma sat holding her hand, making plans.

A job—that was the most important thing to consider; a job she would be able to give up when her mother returned home. She might not be trained for anything much but she could type well enough and she could do simple accounts and housekeep adequately enough; there was sure to be something...

Her mother woke presently and she talked cheerfully about everyday things, not mentioning Mrs Smith-

Darcy and, indeed, she didn't intend to do so unless her mother asked.

A nurse came and Emma, watching her skilful handling of tubes and the saline drip, so wished that she could be cool and calm and efficient and—an added bonus—pretty. Probably she worked for the professor— saw him every day, was able to understand him when he gave his orders in strange surgical terms, and received his thanks. He seemed to Emma to be a man of effortless good manners.

Her mother dozed again and didn't rouse as the teatrolley was wheeled in, which was a good thing since a cup of tea was out of the question, but Emma was given one, with two Petit Beurre biscuits, and since her hurried lunch seemed a long time ago she was grateful.

Her mother was soon awake again, content to lie quietly, not talking much and finally with an eye on the clock, Emma kissed her goodbye. 'I'll be here tomorrow,' she promised, and went down to the main entrance.

She had just reached it when the Rolls came soundlessly to a halt beside her. The professor got out and opened her door, got back in and drove away with nothing more than a murmured greeting, but presently he said, 'Your mother looks better, does she not?'

'Oh, yes. She slept for most of the afternoon but she looks much better than I expected.'

'Of course, she's being sedated, and will be for the next forty-eight hours. After that she will be free of pain and taking an interest in life again. She's had a tiring time...'

It was still raining—a cold rain driven by an icy wind—and the moor looked bleak and forbidding in the early dusk. Emma, who had lived close to it all her life, was untroubled by that; she wondered if the professor felt the same. He had said that he lived near Exeter. She wondered exactly where; perhaps, after a few days of going to and fro, he would be more forthcoming. Certainly he was a very silent man.

The thought struck her that he might find her boring, but on the following day, when she ventured a few remarks of a commonplace nature, he had little to say in reply, although he sounded friendly enough. She decided that silence, unless he began a conversation, was the best policy, so that by the end of a week she was no nearer knowing anything about him than when they had first met. She liked him—she liked him very much—but she had the good sense to know that they inhabited different worlds. He had no wish to get to know her—merely to offer a helping hand, just as he would have done with anyone else in similar circumstances.

Her mother was making good progress and Emma scanned the local paper over the weekend, and checked the advertisements outside the news agents in the hope of finding a job.

Mrs Smith-Darcy had, surprisingly, sent Alice with her wages, and Emma had made a pot of coffee and listened to Alice's outpourings on life with that lady. 'Mad as fire, she was,' Alice had said, with relish. 'You should 'ave 'eard 'er, Miss Trent. And that lunch party—that was a lark and no mistake—'er whingeing away about servants and such like. I didn't 'ear no kind words about you and your poor ma, though. Mean old cat.' She had grinned. 'Can't get another companion for love nor money, either.'

She had drunk most of the coffee and eaten all the biscuits Emma had and then got up to go. 'Almost forgot,' she'd said, suddenly awkward, 'me and Cook thought your ma might like a few chocs now she's better. And there's one of Cook's steak and kidney pies—just wants a warm-up—do for your dinner.'

'How lucky I am to have two such good friends,' Emma had said and meant it.

Going to the hospital on Monday, sitting quietly beside Sir Paul, she noticed him glance down at her lap where the box of chocolates sat.

'I hope that those are not for your mother?'

'Well, yes and no. Cook and Alice—from Mrs Smith-Darcy's house, you know—gave them to me to give her. I don't expect that she can have them, but she'll like to see them and she can give them to her nurses.'

He nodded. 'I examined your mother yesterday evening. I intend to have her transferred to Moretonhampstead within the next day or so. She will remain there for two weeks at least, three if possible, so that when she returns home she will be quite fit.'

'That is good news. Thank you for arranging it,' said Emma gratefully, and wondered how she was going to visit her mother. With a car it would have been easy enough.

She would have to find out how the buses ran—probably along the highway to Exeter and then down

the turn-off to Moretonhampstead halfway along it—
but the buses might not connect. She had saved as much
money as she could and she had her last week's wages;
perhaps she could get the car from Mr Dobbs again and
visit her mother once a week; it was thirty miles or so,
an hour's drive...

She explained this to her mother and was relieved to
see that the prospect of going to a convalescent home
and starting on a normal life once more had put her in
such good spirits that she made no demur when Emma
suggested that she might come only once a week to
see her.

'It's only for a few weeks, Emma, and I'm sure I
shall have plenty to keep me occupied. I've been so well
cared for here, and everyone has been so kind. Everything's all right at home? Queenie is well?'

'She's splendid and everything is fine. I'll bring you
some more clothes, shall I?' She made a list and observed, 'I'll bring them tomorrow, for the professor
didn't say when you were going—when there's a vacancy I expect—he just said a day or two.'

When she got up to go her mother walked part of
the way with her, anxious to show how strong she had
become. By the lifts they said goodbye, though, 'I'm a
slow walker,' said Mrs Trent. 'It won't do to keep him
waiting.'

For once, Emma was glad of Sir Paul's silence, for
she had a lot to think about. They were almost at Buckfastleigh when he told her that her mother would be
transferred on the day after tomorrow.

'So tomorrow will be the last day I go to the hospital?'

'Yes. Talk to Sister when you see her tomorrow; she will give you all the particulars and the phone number. Your mother will go by ambulance. The matron there is a very kind woman, there are plenty of staff and two resident doctors so your mother will be well cared for.'

'I'm sure of that. She's looking foward to going; she feels she's really getting well.'

'It has been a worrying time for you—' his voice was kind '—but I think she will make a complete recovery.'

Indoors she put the pie in the oven, fed an impatient Queenie and sat down to add up the money in her purse—enough to rent a car from Mr Dobbs on the following weekend and not much over. She ate her supper, packed a case with the clothes her mother would need and went to put the dustbin out before she went to bed.

The local paper had been pushed through the letter-box. She took it back to the kitchen and turned to the page where the few advertisements were and there, staring her in the face, was a chance of a job. It stated:

Wanted urgently—a sensible woman to help immediately for two or three weeks while present staff are ill. Someone able to cope with a small baby as well as normal household chores and able to cook.

Emma, reading it, thought that the woman wouldn't only have to be sensible, she would need to be a bundle of energy as well, but it was only for two or three weeks and it might be exactly what she was looking for. The phone number was a local one too.

Emma went to bed convinced that miracles did happen and slept soundly.

In the morning she waited with impatience until half-past eight before going round to use Mr Dobbs's phone. The voice which answered her was a woman's, shrill and agitated.

'Thank heaven—I'm at my wits' end and there's no one here. The baby's been crying all night...'

'If you would give me your address. I live in Buck-fastleigh.'

'So do I. Picket House—go past the otter sanctuary and it's at the end of the road down a turning on the left. You've got a car?'

'No, a bike. I'll come straight away, shall I?'

She listened to a jumble of incoherent thanks and, after phoning the surgery to cancel her lift with Sir Paul, hurried back to the house. Queenie, having breakfasted, was preparing to take a nap. Emma left food for her, got into her coat, tied a scarf over her head and fetched her bike. At least it wasn't raining as she pedalled briskly from one end of the little town to the other.

Picket House was a rambling old place, beautifully maintained, lying back from the lane, surrounded by a large garden. Emma skidded to the front door and halted, and before she had got off her bike it was opened.

'Come in, come in, do.' The girl wasn't much older than Emma but there the resemblance ended, for she was extremely pretty, with fair, curly hair, big blue eyes and a dainty little nose. She pulled Emma inside and then burst into tears. 'I've had a dreadful night, you have no idea. Cook's ill with flu and so is Elsie, and the nurse who's supposed to come sent a message to say that her mother's ill.'

'There's no one who could come—your mother or a sister?'

'They're in Scotland.' She dismissed them with a wave of the hand. 'And Mike, my husband, he's in America and won't be back for weeks.' She wiped her eyes and smiled a little. 'You will come and help me?'

'Yes—yes, of course. You'll want references...?'

'Yes, yes—but later will do for that. I want a bath and I've not had breakfast. To tell the truth, I'm not much of a cook.'

'The baby?' asked Emma, taking off her coat and scarf and hanging them on the elaborate hat-stand in the hall. 'A boy or a girl?'

'Oh, a boy.'

'Has he had a feed?'

'I gave him one during the night but I'm not sure if I mixed it properly; he was sick afterwards.'

'You don't feed him yourself?'

The pretty face was screwed up in horror. 'No, no, I couldn't possibly—I'm far too sensitive. Could you move in until the nurse can come?'

'I can't live here, but I'll come early in the morning and stay until the baby's last feed, if that would do?'

'I'll be alone during the night...'

'If the baby's had a good feed he should sleep for the night and I'll leave a feed ready for you to warm up.'

'Will you cook and tidy up a bit? I'm hopeless at housework.'

It seemed to Emma that now would be the time to learn about it, but she didn't say so. 'I don't know your name,' she said.

'Hervey—Doreen Hervey.'

'Emma Trent. Should we take a look at the baby before I get your breakfast?'

'Oh, yes, I suppose so. He's very small, just a month old. You're not a nurse, are you?'

'No, but I took a course in baby care and housewifery when I left school.'

They were going upstairs. 'Would you come for a hundred pounds a week?'

'Yes.' It would be two or three weeks and she could save every penny of it.

They had reached the wide landing, and from somewhere along a passage leading to the back of the house there was a small, wailing noise.

The nursery was perfection—pastel walls, a thick carpet underfoot, pretty curtains drawn back from spotless white net, the right furniture and gloriously warm. The cot was a splendid affair and Mrs Hervey went to lean over it. 'There he is,' she said unnecessarily.

He was a very small baby, with dark hair, screwed up eyes and a wide open mouth. The wails had turned to screams and he was waving miniature fists in a fury of infant rage.

'The lamb,' said Emma. 'He's wet; I'll change him. When did he have his feed? Can you remember the time?'

'I can't possibly remember; I was so tired. I suppose it was about two o'clock.'

'Is his feed in the kitchen?'

'Yes, on the table. I suppose he's hungry?'

Emma suppressed a desire to shake Mrs Hervey. 'Go and have your bath while I change him and feed him. Perhaps you could start breakfast—boil an egg and make toast?'

Mrs Hervey went thankfully away and Emma took the sopping infant from his sopping cot. While she was at it he could be bathed; everything she could possibly need was there...

With the baby tucked under one arm, swathed in his shawl, she went downstairs presently. The tin of baby-milk was on the table in the kind of kitchen every woman dreamt of. She boiled a kettle, mixed a feed and sat down to wait while it cooled. The baby glared at her from under his shawl. Since he looked as if he would cry again at any minute she talked gently to him.

She had fed him, winded him and cuddled him close as he dropped off and there was still no sign of his mother, but presently she came, her make-up immaculate, looking quite lovely.

'Oh, good, he's gone to sleep. I'm so hungry.' She smiled widely, looking like an angel. 'I'm so glad you've come, Emma—may I call you Emma?'

'Please do,' said Emma. She had her reservations about feeling glad as she bore the baby back to his cot.

Chapter 3

By the end of the day Emma realised that she would have her hands full for the next week or two. Mrs Hervey, no doubt a charming and good-natured woman, hadn't the least idea how to be a mother.

Over lunch she had confided to Emma that she had never had to do anything for herself—she had been pampered in succession by a devoted nanny, a doting mother and father, and then an adoring husband with money enough to keep her in the style to which she had been accustomed. 'Everyone's ill,' she had wailed. 'My old nanny ought to be here looking after me while Mike's away, but she's had to go and look after my sister's children—they've got measles. And the mother of this wretched nanny who was supposed to come. Just imagine, Emma, I came home from the nursing home and Cook and Elsie got ill the very next day!'

'You were in the nursing home for several weeks? Were you ill after the baby was born?'

'No, no. Mike arranged that so I could have plenty of time to recover before I had to plunge into normal life again.'

Emma had forborne from telling her that most women plunged back into normal life with no more help than a willing husband. She'd said cautiously, 'While I'm here I'll show you how to look after the baby and how to mix the feeds, so that when Nanny has her days off you'll know what to do.'

'Will you? How sensible you are.'

'Hasn't the baby got a name?'

'We hadn't decided on that when Mike had to go away. We called him "Baby"—I suppose he'll be Bartholemew, after Mike's father, you know. He's very rich.'

It seemed a pity, Emma had reflected, to saddle the baby with such a name for the sake of future moneybags. 'May I call him Bart?' she'd asked.

'Why not?' Mrs Hervey had cast an anxious glance at Emma. 'You're quite happy here? It's a long day...'

As indeed it was.

After the first day, ending well after nine o'clock in the evening, Emma saw that she would have to alter things a bit. A little rearranging was all that was required. Bart needed a six o'clock feed, so she agreed to make it up the evening before for his mother to warm up.

'I'll come in at eight o'clock and get your breakfast,

and while you are having it I'll bath Bart and make up his feed for ten o'clock. When he's had his two o'clock feed I'll leave him with you—he'll sleep for several hours and you will be able to rest if you want to.

'I'd like to go home for an hour or two, to do the shopping and so on, but I'll be back in plenty of time to see to his evening feed and get your supper. I'll stay until nine o'clock, so that you can get ready for bed before I go, then all you need to do is feed him at ten o'clock. I'll make up an extra feed in case he wakes at two o'clock.'

Mrs Hervey looked at her with her big blue eyes. 'You're an angel. Of course you must go home—and you will stay until nine o'clock?'

'Yes, of course.'

'You'll have lunch and supper with me, won't you?'

'Thank you, that would be nice. How about shopping? It wouldn't hurt Bart to be taken for an airing in his pram.'

'I'd be scared—all the traffic, and it's so far to the shops. I've always phoned for anything I want.'

'In that case, I'll take him for half an hour in the mornings when the weather's not too bad.'

'Will you? I say, I've just had such a good idea. Couldn't you take him with you in the afternoons?'

Emma had been expecting that. 'Well, no. You see, it's quite a long way and I go on my bike—I haven't anywhere to put the pram. Besides, you are his mum; he wants to be with you.'

'Oh, does he? You see, I'm not sure what to do when he cries...'

'Pick him up and see if he's wet. If he is, change him, and give him a cuddle.'

'It sounds so easy.'

'And it will be very nice if you know how to go on, so that when the nanny comes you can tell her how you want things done.'

Mrs Hervey, much struck with this idea, agreed.

It took a day or two to establish some sort of routine. Mrs Hervey was singularly helpless, not only with her son but about the running of a household; she had always had time to spend on herself and this time was now curtailed. But although she was so helpless, and not very quick to grasp anything, she had a placid nature and was very willing to learn.

The pair of them got on well and Bart, now that his small wants were dealt with promptly, was a contented baby.

Emma phoned her mother during the week and was relieved to hear that she had settled down nicely, and when Emma explained that she had a job, just for a week or two, and might not be able to go and see her, she told her comfortably that she was quite happy and that Emma wasn't to worry.

It was on Saturday that Sir Paul Wyatt, on his way home from a conference in Bristol, decided to visit Mrs Trent. He had seen nothing of Emma in Buckfastleigh, and on the one occasion when he had given way to a wish to visit her the house had been locked up and there had been no sign of her. Staying with friends, probably, he'd decided, and didn't go again.

Mrs Trent was delighted to see him. She was making good progress and seemed happy enough. Indeed, he wondered if she might not be able to return home very shortly. Only her enthusiastic description of Emma's new job made him pause, for, if he sent her home, Emma would have to give it up, at least for a few weeks, and he suspected that the Trent household needed the money.

'Emma has a local job?' he asked kindly.

'Yes. She is able to cycle there every day. It's with a Mrs Hervey; she lives at the other end of Buckfastleigh— a very nice house, Emma says. There is a very new baby and Mrs Hervey's cook and maid are both ill and the nanny she has engaged was unable to come, so Emma's helping out until she turns up and the other two are back.'

'Mrs Hervey is a young woman, presumably?'

'Oh, yes. Her husband is away—in America I believe. Mrs Hervey seems quite lost without him.'

He agreed, that might be so.

'I'm keeping you, Professor,' she went on. 'I'm sure you want to go home to your own family. It was very kind of you to come and see me. I told Emma not to come here; from what she said I rather think that she has very little time to herself and I shall soon be home.'

'Indeed you will, Mrs Trent.'

They shook hands and she added, 'You won't be seeing her, I suppose?'

'If I do I will give her your love,' he assured her.

Fifteen minutes later he stopped the car outside his front door in the heart of Lustleigh village. The house was close to the church, and was a rambling thatched cottage, its roof at various levels, its windows small and diamond-paned. The door was arched and solid and its walls in summer and autumn were a mass of colour from the climbing plants clinging to its irregularities.

He let himself in, to be met in the narrow hall by two dogs—a Jack Russell with an impudent face and a sober golden Labrador. He bent to caress them as a door at the end of the hall was opened and his housekeeper came trotting towards him. She was short and stout with a round, pink-cheeked face, small blue eyes and a smiling mouth.

'There you are, then,' she observed, 'and high time too, if I might say so. There's as nice a dinner waiting for you as you'd find anywhere in the land.'

'Give me ten minutes, Mrs Parfitt, and I'll do it justice.'

'Had a busy day, I reckon. Time you took a bit of a holiday; though it's not my place to say so, dear knows you've earned it.' She gave an indignant snort. 'Supposed to be free of all that operating and hospital work, aren't you, for six months? And look at you, sir, working your fingers off to help out old Dr Treble, going to conferences...'

Sir Paul had taken off his coat, picked up his bag and opened a door. 'I'm rather enjoying it,' he observed mildly, and went into his study.

There was a pile of letters on his desk and the light on the answer-phone was blinking; he ignored them both and sat down at his desk and, lifting the phone's receiver, dialled a number and waited patiently for it to be answered.

* * *

Emma had soon discovered that it was impossible to get annoyed or impatient with Mrs Hervey. She had become resigned to the mess she found each morning when she arrived for work—the table in the kitchen left littered with unwashed crockery used by Mrs Hervey for the snack she fancied before she went to bed, the remnants of that snack left to solidify in the frying-pan or saucepan. But at least she had grasped the instructions for Bart's feeds, even though she made no attempt to clean anything once it had been used. She was, however, getting much better at handling her small son, and although she was prone to weep at the slightest set-back she was invariably good-natured.

Towards the end of the week Emma had suggested that it might be a good idea to take Bart to the baby clinic, or find out if there was a health visitor who would check Bart's progress.

'Absolutely not,' Mrs Hervey had said airily. 'They talked about it while I was in the nursing home but of course I said there was no need with a trained nanny already booked.'

'But the nanny isn't here,' Emma had pointed out.

'Well, you are, and she'll come soon—she said she would.' Mrs Hervey had given her a sunny smile and begged her not to fuss but to come and inspect various baby garments which had just arrived from Harrods.

By the end of the week Emma was tired; her few hours each afternoon were just sufficient for her to look after her house, do the necessary shopping, see to Queenie and do the washing and ironing, and by the time she got home in the evening she was too tired to do more than eat a sandwich and drink a pot of tea before tumbling into bed. She was well aware that she was working for far too many hours, but she told herself it was only for a few weeks and, with the first hundred pounds swelling the woefully meagre sum in their bank account, she went doggedly on.

All the same, on Saturday evening, as nine o'clock approached, she heaved a sigh of relief. Sunday would be a day like any weekday, but perhaps by the end of another week someone—the cook or the housemaid— would be back and then her day's work would be lighter. She had been tempted once or twice to suggest that Mrs Hervey might find someone to come in each day and do some housework, but this had been dismissed with a puzzled, 'But you are managing beautifully, Emma; you're doing all the things I asked for in the advert.'

Emma had said no more—what was the use? She only hoped that Mrs Hervey would never fall on hard times; her cushioned life had hardly prepared her for that.

She was about to put on her coat when Mrs Hervey's agitated voice made her pause. She took off her coat again and went back upstairs to find her bending over Bart's cot. 'He's red in the face,' she cried. 'Look at him; he's going to have a fit, I know it!'

'He needs changing,' said Emma.

'Oh, I'm so glad you're still here.' Mrs Hervey gave her a warm smile and went to answer the phone.

She came back a few moments later. 'A visitor,' she

said happily. 'He's on his way. I'll go and get the drinks ready.'

Emma, still coping with Bart's urgent needs, heard the doorbell presently, and voices. Mrs Hervey was laughing a lot; it must be someone she knew very well and was glad to see. She had, so far, refused all invitations from her friends and hadn't invited any of them to come to the house. 'I promised Mike that I'd stay quietly at home and look after Baby,' she had explained to Emma. 'As soon as Nanny is here and settled in then I shall make up for it.' Her eyes had sparkled at the thought.

Bart, now that she had made him comfortable once more, was already half-asleep; Emma was tucking him up when the door was opened and Mrs Hervey came in and, with her, Sir Paul Wyatt.

Emma's heart gave a delighted leap at the sight of him while at the same time she felt a deep annoyance; she looked a fright—even at her best she was nothing to look at, but now, at the end of the day, she wasn't worth a glance. What was he doing here anyway? She gave him a distant look and waited to see who would speak first.

It was Mrs Hervey, bubbling over with pleasure. 'Emma, this is Sir Paul Wyatt; he's a professor or something. He's Mike's oldest friend and he's come to see Bart. He didn't know that I was home—I did say that I would go to Scotland until Mike came home. Just fancy, he's turned into a GP, just for a bit while Dr Treble is away.' She turned a puzzled gaze to him. 'I thought you were a surgeon?'

'I am. This is by way of a change. Emma and I have already met; I operated upon her mother not so long ago.' He smiled at her across the room. 'Good evening, Emma. You are staying here?'

'No, I'm just going home.'

'Rather late, isn't it?'

'Oh, well, that's my fault,' said Mrs Hervey cheerfully. 'Bart went all red and was roaring his head off and Emma hadn't quite gone so she came back. I thought he was ill.'

He lifted an enquiring eyebrow as Emma said in a no-nonsense voice, 'He needed changing.'

He laughed. 'Oh, Doreen, when will you grow up? The sooner Mike gets back the better!' He had gone to lean over the cot and was looking at the sleeping infant. 'The image of his father. He looks healthy enough.' He touched the small cheek with a gentle finger. 'Why do you not have a nanny, and where are the servants?'

Mrs Hervey tugged at his sleeve. 'Come downstairs and have a drink and I'll tell you.'

Emma, longing to go, saw that Bart was already asleep.

'How do you get back?' he enquired of Emma.

'I bike—it's only a short way.' She added, in a convincingly brisk tone, 'I enjoy the exercise.'

He held the door open and she followed Mrs Hervey downstairs, got into her coat once again and heard him telling Mrs Hervey that he could spare ten minutes and no more. She wished them goodnight and then let herself out of the house and pedalled furiously home.

It was already half-past nine and, although she was

hungry, she was too tired to do more than put on the kettle for tea. She fed a disgruntled Queenie and poked her head into the fridge and eyed its sparse contents, trying to decide whether a boiled egg and yesterday's loaf would be preferable to a quick bath and a cup of tea in bed.

A brisk tattoo on the door-knocker caused her to withdraw her head smartly and listen. The tattoo was repeated and she went to the door then, suddenly afraid that it was bad news of her mother. She put up the new chain and opened the door a few inches, her view quite blocked by the professor's bulk.

He said testily, 'Yes, it is I, Emma.'

'What do you want?' The door was still on the chain but she looked up into his face, half-hidden in the dark night. 'Mother?' she asked in a sudden panic.

'Your mother is well; I have seen her recently. Now, open the door, there's a good girl.'

She was too tired to argue. She opened it and he crowded into the narrow hall, his arms full.

'Fish and chips,' said Emma, suddenly famished.

'A quick and nourishing meal, but it must be eaten immediately.'

She led the way into the kitchen, took down plates from the small dresser and then paused. 'Oh, you won't want to eat fish and chips...'

'And why not? I have had no dinner this evening and I am extremely hungry.' He was portioning out the food on to the two plates while she laid the cloth and fetched knives and forks.

'I was making tea,' she told him.

'Splendid. You do not mind if I join you?'

Since he was already sitting at the table there seemed no point in objecting, and anyway, she didn't want to!

They sat opposite each other at the small table with Queenie, aroused by the delightful smell, at their feet, and for a few minutes neither of them spoke. Only when the first few mouthfuls had been eaten did Sir Paul ask, 'How long have you been with Doreen Hervey?'

Emma, gobbling chips, told him.

'And what free time do you have? It seems to me that your day is excessively long.'

'I come home each afternoon just for an hour or two...'

'To shop and wash and clean and make your bed? You are too pale, Emma; you need fresh air and a few idle hours.'

'Well, I'll get them in a week or two; the nanny said it would be only a few weeks, and Mrs Hervey told me today that the housemaid is coming back in just over a week.'

'Of course you need the money.'

He said it in such a matter-of-fact way that she said at once, 'Yes, I do, I won't be able to work for a bit when Mother comes home.' She selected a chip and bit into it. She had small very white teeth, and when she smiled and wasn't tired she looked almost pretty.

It was surprising, he reflected, what fish and chips and a pot of tea did for one. He couldn't remember when he had last had such a meal and he was glad to see that Emma's rather pale cheeks had taken on a tinge of colour.

He got up from the table, took their plates to the sink and poured the water from the kettle into the bowl.

'You can't wash up,' said Emma.

'I can and I shall. You may dry the dishes if you wish.'

'Well, really...' muttered Emma and then laughed. 'You're not a bit like a professor of surgery.'

'I am relieved to hear it. I don't spend all day and every day bending over the operating table, you know. I have a social side to my life.'

She felt a pang of regret that she would never know what that was.

As soon as the last knife and fork had been put away he wished her a pleasant good evening and went away. She felt deflated when he had gone. 'Only because,' she explained to Queenie, for lack of any other listener, 'I don't get many people—well, many men.'

Half an hour later Sir Paul let himself into his house, to be greeted as he always was by his dogs and his housekeeper.

'Dear knows, you're a busy man, sir, but it's long past the hour any self-respecting man should be working. You'll be wanting your dinner.'

'I've dined, thank you, Mrs Parfitt. I would have phoned but there was no phone.'

'Dined? With Dr Treble?' She sniffed. 'His housekeeper is a careless one in the kitchen—I doubt you enjoyed your food.'

'Fish and chips, and I enjoyed every mouthful.'

'Not out of newspaper?' Mrs Parfitt's round face was puckered in horror.

'No, no. On a plate in the company of a young lady.'

Mrs Parfitt twinkled at him. 'Ah, I'm glad to hear it, sir. Was she pretty?'

'No.' He smiled at her. 'Don't allow your thoughts to get sentimental, Mrs Parfitt—she needed a meal.'

'Helping another of your lame dogs over the stile, were you? There's a pile of post in your study; I'll bring you a tray of coffee and some of my little biscuits.'

'Excellent. They should dispel any lingering taste of my supper.'

Mrs Parfitt was right; there were a great many letters to open and read and the answering machine to deal with. He was occupied until the early hours of the morning, when he took the dogs for a brisk walk, and saw them to their baskets and finally took himself off to bed. He hadn't thought of Emma once.

'Fancy you knowing Paul,' said Mrs Hervey, when Emma arrived in the morning. 'He's a stunner; if Mike hadn't turned up I could have fallen for him. Not that he gave me any encouragement.' She sighed. 'You see, he'll pick a suitable wife when he decides he wants one and not a minute sooner. I don't believe he's ever been in love—oh, he's dozens of girlfriends, of course, but it'll take someone special to touch his heart.'

Emma nodded. It would have to be someone like Mrs Hervey, pretty as a picture, amusing and helpless; men, Emma supposed, would like that. She thought with regret that she had never had the opportunity to be helpless. And she would never, she decided, taking a quick look in the unnecessary looking-glass in the nursery, be pretty.

That her eyes were large and thickly lashed and her hair, confined tidily in a French pleat, was long and silky, and that her mouth, though too wide, was gentle and her complexion as clear and unblemished as a baby's quite escaped her attention.

Sir Paul Wyatt, fulfilling his role of general practitioner in the middle of the following week, allowed his thoughts to dwell on just those pleasing aspects of Emma's person, only relinquishing them when the next patients came into the surgery.

Surgery finished, he went on his rounds; the inhabitants of Buckfastleigh were, on the whole, a healthy bunch and his visits were few. He drove himself home, ate his lunch, took the dogs for a walk and then got into the Rolls and drove back to Buckfastleigh again.

Emma was at home; her elderly bike was propped against the house wall and the windows were open. He knocked on the door, wondering why he had come.

She answered the door at once, an apron tied round her slender middle, her hair, loosed from its severe plait, tied back with a ribbon.

She stared up at him mutely, and he stared back with a placid face.

'Not Mother?' she said finally, and he shook his head.

'Is Mrs Hervey all right? Bart was asleep when I left.'

He nodded and she asked sharply, 'So why have you come?' She frowned. 'Do you want something?'

He smiled then. 'I am not certain about that... May I come in?'

'Sorry,' said Emma. 'Please do—I was surprised to see you...' She added unnecessarily, 'I was just doing a few chores.'

'When do you have to go back?' He was in the hall, taking up most of the space.

'Just after four o'clock to get Mrs Hervey's tea.'

He glanced at his watch. 'May we have tea here first? I'll go and get something—crumpets—while you do the dusting.'

Emma was surprised, although she agreed readily. Perhaps he had missed his lunch; perhaps surgery was earlier than usual that afternoon. She stood in the doorway and watched him drive away, and then rushed around with the duster and the carpet-sweeper before setting out the tea things. Tea would have to be in the kitchen; there was no fire laid in the sitting-room.

She fed Queenie, filled the kettle and went upstairs to do her face and pin her hair. Studying her reflection, she thought how dull she looked in her tweed skirt, blouse and—that essentially British garment—a cardigan.

She was back downstairs with minutes to spare before he returned.

It wasn't just crumpets he had brought with him—there were scones and doughnuts, a tub of butter and a pot of strawberry jam. He arranged them on a dish while she put the crumpets under the grill and boiled the kettle, all the while carrying on an undemanding conversation about nothing much so that Emma, who had felt suddenly awkward, was soothed into a pleasant feeling of ease.

They had finished the crumpets and were starting on the scones when he asked casually, 'What do you intend doing when you leave Doreen Hervey, Emma?'

'Do? Well, I'll stay at home for a bit, until Mother is quite herself again, and then I'll look for another job.'

He passed her the butter and the jam. 'You might train for something?'

'I can type and do shorthand, though I'm not very good at either, and people always need mother's helps.' She decided that it was time to change the conversation. 'I expect Mother will be on some kind of a diet?'

'Yes—small meals taken frequently, cut out vinegar and pickles and so on.' He sounded impatient. 'She will be given a leaflet when she comes home. The physicians have taken over now.' He frowned. 'Is it easy to get a job here?'

Her red herring hadn't been of much use. 'I think so. My kind of a job anyway.'

'You're wasted—bullied by selfish women and changing babies' nappies.'

'I like babies.' She added tartly, 'It's kind of you to bother, but there is no need—'

'How old are you, Emma?'

'Almost twenty-six.'

He smiled. 'Twenty-five, going on fifteen! I'm forty—do you find that old?'

'Old? Of course not. You're not yet in your prime. And you don't feel like forty, do you?'

'Upon occasion I feel ninety, but at the moment at least I feel thirty at the most!' He smiled at her and she thought what a very nice smile he had—warm and somehow reassuring. 'Have another doughnut?'

She accepted it with the forthright manner of a polite child. She was not, he reflected, in the least coy or self-conscious. He didn't search too deeply into his reasons for worrying about her future, although he admitted to the worry. It was probably because she was so willing to accept what life had to offer her.

He went presently, with a casual goodbye and no mention of seeing her again. Not that she had expected that. She cycled back to Mrs Hervey and Bart, reflecting that she was becoming quite fond of him.

It was the beginning of the third week, with another hundred pounds swelling their bank balance, when Mrs Hervey told her that the new nanny would be with them by the end of the week, and Cook and the housemaid would return in three days' time.

'And about time too,' said Mrs Hervey rather pettishly. 'I mean, three weeks just to get over flu...'

Emma held her tongue and Mrs Hervey went on, 'You'll stay until the end of the week, won't you, Emma? As soon as Cook and that girl are here I shall have a chance to go to the hairdresser. I'm desperate to get to Exeter—I need some clothes and a facial too. You'll only have Bart to look after, and Nanny comes on Friday evening. I dare say she'll want to ask your advice about Bart before you go.'

'I think,' said Emma carefully, 'that she may prefer

not to do that. She's professional, you see, and I'm just a temporary help. I'm sure you will be able to tell her everything that she would want to know.'

'Will I? Write it all down for me, Emma, won't you? I never can remember Bart's feeds and what he ought to weigh.'

Certainly, once the cook and housemaid returned, life was much easier for Emma. She devoted the whole of her day to Bart, taking him for long rides in his pram, sitting with him on her lap, cuddling him and singing half-forgotten nursery rhymes while he stared up at her with his blue eyes. Cuddling was something that his mother wasn't very good at. She loved him, Emma was sure of that, but she was awkward with him. Perhaps the new nanny would be able to show Mrs Hervey how to cuddle her small son.

It was on her last day, handing over to a decidedly frosty Nanny, that she heard Sir Paul's voice in the drawing-room. She listened with half an ear to the superior young woman who was to have charge of Bart telling her of all the things she should have done, and wondered if she would see him. It seemed that she wouldn't, for presently Mrs Hervey joined them, remarking that Sir Paul had just called to see if everything was normal again.

'I asked him if he would like to see Bart but he said he hadn't the time. He was on his way to Plymouth.' She turned to the nanny. 'You've had a talk with Emma? Wasn't it fortunate that she was able to come and help me?' She made a comic little face. 'I'm not much good with babies.'

'I'm accustomed to take sole charge, Mrs Hervey; you need have no further worries about Bart. Tomorrow, perhaps, we might have a little talk and I will explain my duties to you.'

It should surely be the other way round, thought Emma. But Mrs Hervey didn't seem to mind.

'Oh, of course. I'm happy to leave everything to you. You're ready to go, Emma? Say goodbye to Bart; he's got very fond of you...'

A remark which annoyed Nanny, for she said quite sharply that the baby was sleeping and shouldn't be disturbed. So Emma had to content herself with looking at him lying in his cot, profoundly asleep, looking like a very small cherub.

She would miss him.

She bade Nanny a quiet goodbye and went downstairs with Mrs Hervey and got on her bike, warmed by that lady's thanks and the cheque in her pocket. Three hundred pounds would keep them going for quite some time, used sparingly with her mother's pension.

When she got home, she took her bike round to the shed, went indoors and made some supper for Queenie, and boiled an egg for herself. She felt sad that the job was finished, but a good deal of the sadness was because she hadn't seen the professor again.

There was a letter from her mother in the morning, telling her that she would be brought home by ambulance in two days' time. How nice, she wrote, that Emma's job was finished just in time for her return.

Emma wondered how she had known that, and then forgot about it as she made plans for the next two days.

It was pleasant to get up the next morning and know that she had the day to herself. It was Sunday, of course, so she wouldn't be able to do any shopping, but there was plenty to do in the house—the bed to make up, wood and coal to be brought in, the whole place to be dusted and aired. And, when that was done, she sat down and made a shopping list.

Bearing in mind what Sir Paul had said about diet, she wrote down what she hoped would be suitable and added flowers and one or two magazines, Earl Grey tea instead of the economical brand they usually drank, extra milk and eggs—the list went on and on, but for once she didn't care. Her mother was coming home and that was a cause for extravagance.

She had the whole of Monday morning in which to shop, and with money in her purse she enjoyed herself, refusing to think about the future, reminding herself that it would soon be the tourist season again and there were always jobs to be found. It didn't matter what she did so long as she could be at home.

Her mother arrived during the afternoon, delighted to be at home again, protesting that she felt marvellous, admiring the flowers and the tea-tray on a small table by the lighted fire in the sitting-room. Emma gave the ambulance driver tea and biscuits, received an envelope with instructions as to her mother's diet and went back to her mother.

Mrs Trent certainly looked well; she drank her weak tea and ate the madeira cake Emma had baked and settled back in her chair. 'Now, tell me all the news, Emma. What was this job like? Were you happy? A nice change looking after a baby?'

Emma recounted her days, making light of the long hours. 'It was a very nice job,' she declared, 'and I earned three hundred pounds, so I can stay at home for as long as you want me to.'

They talked for the rest of that afternoon and evening, with Queenie sitting on Mrs Trent's lap and finally trailing upstairs with her to curl up on her bed.

Emma, taking her some warm milk and making sure that she was comfortable before she went to bed herself, felt a surge of relief at the sight of her mother once more in her own bed. The future was going to be fine, she told herself as she kissed her mother goodnight.

Chapter 4

Emma and her mother settled down into a quiet routine: gentle pottering around the house, short walks in the afternoon, pleasant evenings round the fire at the end of the day. For economy's sake, Emma shared her mother's small, bland meals, and found herself thinking longingly of the fish and chips Sir Paul had brought to the house.

There was no sign of him, of course, and it wasn't likely that she would see him again; the new doctor had come to take over from Dr Treble and the professor had doubtless taken up his normal life again. She speculated a bit about that, imagining him stalking the wards with a bunch of underlings who hung on to any words of wisdom he might choose to utter and watched with awe while he performed some complicated operation. And his private life? Her imagination ran riot over that—married to some beautiful young woman—she would have to be beautiful, he wouldn't look at anyone less—perhaps with children—handsome little boys and pretty little girls. If he wasn't married he would certainly have any number of women-friends and get asked out a great deal—dinner parties and banquets and evenings at the theatre and visits to London.

A waste of time, she told herself time and again—she would forget all about him. But that wasn't easy, because her mother talked about him a great deal although, when pumped by Emma, she was unable to tell her anything about his private life.

Mrs Trent had been home for a week when he came to see her. Emma had seen the Rolls draw up from her mother's bedroom window and had hurried down to open the door, forgetting her unmade-up face and her hair bunched up anyhow on top of her head. It was only as she opened the door that she remembered her appearance, so that she met his faintly amused look with a frown and her feelings so plain on her face that he said to her at once, 'I do apologise for coming unexpectedly, but I had half an hour to spare and I wanted to see how your mother was getting on.'

'Hello,' said Emma gruffly, finding her voice and her manners. 'Please come in; she will be glad to see you.'

She led the way into the little sitting-room. 'I was going to make Mother's morning drink and have some coffee. Would you like a cup?' She gave him a brief glance. 'Shall I take your coat?'

'Coffee would be delightful.' He took off his overcoat

and flung it over a chair and went to take Mrs Trent's hand, which gave Emma the chance to escape. She galloped up to her room, powdered her nose, pinned up her hair and tore downstairs again to make the coffee and carry it in presently, looking her usual neat self.

Sir Paul, chatting with her mother, looked at her from under his lids and hid a smile, steering the conversation with effortless ease towards trivial matters. It was only when they had finished their coffee that he asked Mrs Trent a few casual questions. He seemed satisfied with her answers and presently took his leave.

As he shook hands with the older woman she asked, 'Are you still working here as a GP? Has the new doctor arrived?'

'Several days ago; he will be calling on you very shortly, I have no doubt.'

'So we shan't see you again? I owe you so much, Sir Paul.'

'It is a great satisfaction to me to see you on your feet again, Mrs Trent. Don't rush things, will you? You're in very capable hands.' He glanced at Emma, who had her gaze fixed on his waistcoat and didn't meet his eye.

When he had driven away Mrs Trent said, 'I'm sorry we shan't see him again. I felt quite safe with him…'

'I expect the new doctor is just as kind as Dr Treble. I'm sure he'll come and see you in a day or two, Mother.'

Which he did—a pleasant, youngish man who asked the same questions that Sir Paul had asked, assured Emma that her mother was making excellent progress and suggested that she might go to the surgery in a month's time for a check-up.

'No need really,' he said cheerfully. 'But I should like to keep an eye on you for a little while.' As Emma saw him to the door he observed, 'I'm sure you're looking after your mother very well; it's fortunate that you are living here with her.' It was a remark which stopped her just in time from asking him when he thought it would be suitable for her to look for a job again.

The days slid past, each one like the previous; Mrs Trent was content to knit and read and go for short walks, and Emma felt a faint prick of unease. Surely by now her mother should be feeling more energetic? She was youngish still—nowadays most people in their fifties were barely middle-aged and still active—but her mother seemed listless, and disinclined to exert herself.

The days lengthened and winter began to give way reluctantly to spring, but Mrs Trent had no inclination to go out and about. Emma got Mr Dobbs to drive them to the surgery, when a month was up, after reminding her mother that it was time she saw the doctor again.

She had already spoken to him on Mr Dobbs's phone, voicing her vague worries and feeling rather silly since there was nothing definite to tell him, but he was kindness itself as he examined Mrs Trent.

He said finally, 'You're doing very well, Mrs Trent—well enough to resume normal life once more. I'll see about some surgical stockings for you—you do have a couple of varicose veins. Recent, are they?'

'Oh, yes, but they don't bother me really. I'm not on my feet all that much.' Mrs Trent laughed. 'I'm getting rather lazy...'

'Well, don't get too lazy; a little more exercise will do you good, I think. The operation was entirely successful and there is no reason why you shouldn't resume your normal way of life.' He gave her an encouraging smile. 'Come and see me in a month's time and do wear those stockings—I'll see you get them.'

'A nice young man,' declared Mrs Trent as they were driven home by Mr Dobbs and Emma agreed, although she had the feeling that he had thought her over-fussy about her mother. Still, he had said that her mother was quite well again, excepting for those veins...

It was several days later, as she was getting their tea, that she heard her mother call out and then the sound of her falling. She flew to the sitting-room and found her mother lying on the floor, and she knew before she picked up her hand that there would be no pulse.

'Mother,' said Emma, and even though it was useless she put a cushion under her head before she tore out of the house to Mr Dobbs and the phone.

An embolism, the doctor said, a pulmonary embolism, sudden and fatal. Emma said, in a voice which didn't sound like hers, 'Varicose veins—it was a blood clot.' She saw his surprised look. 'I've done my First Aid.' She raised anguished eyes to his. 'Couldn't you have known?'

He shook his head. 'No, there were no symptoms and varicose veins are commonplace; one always bears in mind that a clot might get dislodged, but there is usually some warning.'

'She wouldn't have known?'

'No, I'm certain of that.'

There was no one to turn to, no family or very close friends, although the neighbours were kind—cooking her meals she couldn't eat, offering to help. They had liked her mother and they liked her and she was grateful, thanking them in a quiet voice without expression, grief a stone in her chest.

They came to the funeral too, those same neighbors, and the doctor, Cook and Alice from Mrs Smith-Darcy's house, taking no notice of that lady's orders to remain away. Mrs Hervey was there too, and kind Mr Dobbs. The only person Emma wanted to see was absent— Sir Paul Wyatt wasn't there, and she supposed that he had no reason to be there anyway. That he must know she was certain, for the doctor had told her that he had written to him...

There was no money, of course, and no will. She remembered her mother telling her laughingly that when she was sixty she would make one, but in any case there was almost nothing to leave—the house and the furniture and a few trinkets.

Emma, during the next few empty days, pondered her future. She would sell the house if she could find a small flat in Plymouth, and train properly as a shorthand typist and then find a permanent job. She had no real wish to go to Plymouth but if she went to Exeter, a city she knew and loved, she might meet Sir Paul— something, she told herself, she didn't wish to do. Indeed, she didn't want to see him again.

A new life, she decided, and the sooner the better. Thirty wasn't all that far off, and by then she was determined to have built herself a secure future. 'At least

I've got Queenie,' she observed to the empty sitting-room as she polished and dusted, quite unnecessarily because the house was clean, but it filled the days. She longed to pack her things and settle her future at once, but there were all the problems of unexpected death to unravel first, so she crammed her days with hard work and cried herself to sleep each night, hugging Queenie for comfort, keeping her sorrow to herself.

People were very kind—calling to see how she was, offering companionship, suggesting small outings—and to all of them she showed a cheerful face and gave the assurance that she was getting along splendidly and making plans for the future, and they went away, relieved that she was coping so well.

'Of course, Emma has always been such a sensible girl,' they told each other, deceived by her calm manner.

Ten days after the funeral, her small affairs not yet settled, she was in the kitchen, making herself an early morning cup of tea and wondering how much longer she would have to wait before she could put the house up for sale. She would keep most of the furniture, she mused, sitting down at the kitchen table, only to be interrupted by a bang on the door-knocker. It must be the postman, earlier than usual, but perhaps there would be something interesting in the post. The unbidden thought that there might be a letter from Sir Paul passed through her mind as she opened the door.

It wasn't a letter from him but he himself in person, looming in the doorway and, before she could speak, inside the house, squashed up against her in the narrow little hall.

At the sight of him she burst into tears, burying her face in the tweed of his jacket without stopping to think what she was doing, only aware of the comfort of his arms around her.

He said gently, 'My poor girl. I didn't know—I've been in America and only got back yesterday evening. I was told what had happened by your doctor. He wrote—but by the time I had read his letter it was too late to come to you. I am so very sorry.'

'There wasn't anyone,' said Emma, between great heaving sobs. 'Everyone was so kind…' It was a muddled remark, which he rightly guessed referred to his absence. He let her cry her fill and presently, when the sobs became snivels, he offered a large white linen handkerchief.

'I'm here now,' he said cheerfully, 'and we'll have breakfast while you tell me what happened.' He gave her an avuncular pat on the back and she drew away from him, feeling ashamed of her outburst but at the same time aware that the hard stone of her grief had softened to a gentle sorrow.

'I'm famished,' said Sir Paul in a matter-of-fact voice which made the day normal again. 'I'll lay the table while you cook.'

'I must look a fright. I'll go and do something to my face…'

He studied her with an impersonal look which she found reassuring. Not a fright, he reflected, but the face far too pale, the lovely eyes with shadows beneath them and the clear skin blotched and pinkened with her tears. 'It looks all right to me,' he told her and knew that, despite the tearstains, she was feeling better.

'As long as you don't mind,' she said rather shyly, and got out the frying-pan. 'Will fried eggs and fried bread do?' she asked. 'I'm afraid there isn't any bacon...'

'Splendidly. Where do you keep the marmalade?'

They sat down eventually, facing each other across the kitchen table and Emma, who had had no appetite for days, discovered that she was hungry. It wasn't until they had topped off the eggs with toast and marmalade that Sir Paul allowed the conversation to become serious.

'What are your plans?' he wanted to know, when he had listened without interruption to her account of her mother's death.

'I'll have to sell this house. I thought I'd find a small flat in Plymouth and take a course in office management and then get a proper job. I've enough furniture and I'll have Queenie.'

'Is there no money other than the proceeds from the house?'

'Well, no, there isn't. Mother's pension won't be paid any more of course.' She added hastily, anxious to let him see that she was able to manage very well, 'I can put the house up for sale just as soon as I'm allowed to. There are still some papers and things. They said they'd let me know.'

'And is that what you would like to do, Emma?'

'Yes, of course.' She caught his eye and added honestly, 'I don't know what else to do.'

He smiled at her across the table. 'Will you marry me, Emma?'

Her mouth dropped open. 'Marry you? You're joking!'

'Er—no, I have never considered marriage a joke.'

'Why do you want to marry me? You don't know anything about me—and I'm plain and not a bit interesting. Besides, you don't—don't love me.'

'I know enough about you to believe that you would make me an admirable wife and, to be truthful, I have never considered you plain. As for loving you, I am perhaps old-fashioned enough to consider that mutual liking and compatibility and the willingness to make a good marriage are excellent foundations for happiness. Since the circumstances are unusual we will marry as soon as possible and get to know each other at our leisure.'

'But your family and your friends…?' She saw his lifted eyebrows and went on awkwardly, 'What I mean is, I don't think I'm used to your kind of life.' She waved a hand round the little kitchen. 'I don't expect it's like this.'

He said evenly, 'I live in a thatched cottage at Lustleigh and I have an elderly housekeeper and two dogs. My mother and father live in the Cotswolds and I have two sisters, both married. I'm a consultant at the Exeter hospitals and I frequently go to London, where I am a consultant at various hospitals. I go abroad fairly frequently, to lecture and operate, but at present I have taken a sabbatical, although I still fulfil one or two appointments.'

'Aren't you too busy to have a wife? I mean—' she frowned, trying to find the right words '—you lead such a busy life.'

'When I come home in the evenings it will be pleasant to find you there, waiting to listen to my grumbles if things haven't gone right with my day, and at the weekends I will have a companion.'

'You don't—that is, you won't mind me not loving you?'

'I think,' he said gently, 'that we might leave love out of it, don't you?' He smiled a tender smile, which warmed her down to the soles of her feet. 'We like each other, don't we? And that's important.'

'You might fall in love with someone…'

She wasn't looking at him, otherwise she would have seen his slow smile.

'So might you—a calculated risk which we must both take.' He smiled again, completely at ease. 'I'll wash up and tidy things away while you go and pack a bag.'

'A bag? What for?'

'You're coming back with me. And while Mrs Parfitt fattens you up and the moor's fresh air brings colour into your cheeks you can decide what you want to do.' When she opened her mouth to speak he raised a hand. 'No, don't argue, Emma. I've no intention of leaving you alone here. Later you can tell me what still has to be settled about the house and furniture and I'll deal with the solicitor. Are the bills paid?'

He was quite matter-of-fact about it and she found herself telling him that there were still a few outstanding. 'But everyone said they'd wait until the house was sold.'

He nodded. 'Leave it to me, if you will. Now, run along and get some things packed. Has Queenie got a basket?'

'Yes, it's beside the dresser.'

She went meekly upstairs, and only as she was packing did she reflect that he was behaving in a high-handed fashion, getting his own way without any effort. That, she reminded herself, was because she was too tired and unhappy to resist him. She was thankful to leave everything to him, but once she had pulled herself together she would convince him that marrying him was quite out of the question.

And, since he didn't say another word about it as he drove back to Lustleigh, she told herself that he might have made the suggestion on the spur of the moment and was even now regretting it.

It was a bright morning and cold, but spring was definitely upon them. Lustleigh was a pretty village and a pale sun shone on its cottages. It shone on Sir Paul's home too and Emma, getting out of the car, fell in love with the house at first glance.

'Oh, how delightful. It's all nooks and crannies, isn't it?'

He had a hand under her elbow, urging her to the door. 'It has been in the family for a long time, and each generation has added a room or a chimney-pot or another window just as the fancy took it.' He opened the door and Mrs Parfitt came bustling down the curving staircase at the back of the hall.

'God bless my soul, so you're back, sir.'

She cast him a reproachful look and he said quickly, 'I got back late last night and went straight to the hospital and, since it was already after midnight and I wanted to go to Buckfastleigh as early as possible, I didn't come home. They put me up there.' He still had his hand on Emma's arm. 'Mrs Parfitt, I've brought a guest who will stay with us for a little while. Miss Trent's mother died recently and she needs a break. Emma, this is my housekeeper, Mrs Parfitt.'

Emma shook hands, conscious of sharp, elderly eyes looking her over.

'I hope I won't give you too much extra work…'

Mrs Parfitt had approved of what she saw. All in good time, she promised herself, she would discover the whys and wherefores. 'A pleasure to have someone in the house, miss, for Sir Paul is mostly away from home or shut in that study of his—he might just as well be in the middle of the Sahara for all I see of him!'

She chuckled cosily. 'I'll bring coffee into the sitting-room, shall I, sir? And get a room ready for Miss Trent?'

Sir Paul took Emma's coat and opened a door, urging her ahead of him. The room was long and low, with small windows overlooking the narrow street and glass doors opening on to the garden at the far end. He went past her to open them and let in the dogs, who danced around, delighted to see him.

'Come and meet Kate and Willy,' he invited, and Emma crossed the room and offered a balled fist.

'Won't they mind Queenie?' she wanted to know.

'Not in the least, and Mrs Parfitt will be delighted; her cat died some time ago and she is always talking of getting a kitten—Queenie is much more suitable. I'll get her, and they can get used to each other while we have our coffee.'

While he was gone she looked around the room. Its walls were irregular and there were small windows on each side of the inglenook, and a set of heavy oak beams supporting the ceiling. The walls were white but there was no lack of colour in the room—the fine old carpet almost covered the wood floor, its russets and faded blues toning with the velvet curtains. There were bookshelves crammed with books, several easy-chairs, and a vast sofa drawn up to the fire and charming pie-crust tables holding reading lamps—a delightful lived-in room.

She pictured it in mid-winter, when the wind whistled from the moor and snow fell; with the curtains drawn and a fire roaring up the chimney one would feel safe and secure and content. For the first time since her mother's death she felt a small spark of happiness.

Sir Paul, coming in with Queenie under his arm, disturbed her thoughts and saw them reflected in her face. He said casually, 'You like this room? Let us see if Queenie approves of it... No, don't worry about the dogs—they'll not touch her.'

Mrs Parfitt came in to bring the coffee then, and they sat drinking it, watching the dogs, obedient to their master, sitting comfortably while Queenie edged round them and finally, to Emma's surprise, sat down and washed herself.

'The garden is walled—she won't be able to get out; she'll be quite at home in a few days. I've taken your bag upstairs; I expect you would like to unpack before lunch. This afternoon we'll walk round the village so that you can find your way about. I'll take the dogs for a run and see you at lunch.'

Emma, soothed by the room and content to have someone to tell her how to order her day, nodded. It was like being in a dream after the loneliness of the last week or two. It wouldn't last, of course, for she had no intention of marrying Sir Paul. But for the moment she was happy to go on dreaming.

She was led away presently, up the charming little staircase and on to a landing with passages leading from it in all directions.

'A bit of a jumble,' said Mrs Parfitt cheerfully, 'but you'll soon find your way around. I've put you in a nice quiet room overlooking the garden. Down this passage and up these two steps. The door's a bit narrow...'

Which it was—solid oak like the rest of the doors in the cottage and opening into a room with a large circle of windows taking up all of one wall. There was a balcony beyond them with a wrought-iron balustrade and a sloping roof. 'For your little cat,' explained Mrs Parfitt. 'I dare say you like to have her with you at night? I always had my Jenkin—such a comfort he was!'

'How thoughtful of you, Mrs Parfitt. I hope you'll like Queenie; she's really very good.'

'Bless you, miss, I like any cat.' She trotted over to another door by the bed. 'The bathroom's here and mind the step down, and if there's anything you need you just say so. You'll want to hang up your things now. Lunch is at one o'clock, but come downstairs when you're ready and sit by the fire.'

When she had gone Emma looked around her; the room had uneven walls so that the bay window took up the longest of them. There was a small fireplace in the centre of one short wall and the bedhead was against the wall facing the window. That was irregular too, and the fourth wall had a deep-set alcove into which the dressing-table fitted. She ran a finger along its surface, delighting in the golden brown of the wood.

It was a cosy room, despite the awkwardness of its shape, and delightfully furnished in muted pinks and blues. She unpacked her things and laid them away in the tallboy, and hung her dress in the cupboard concealed in one of the walls. She had brought very little with her—her sensible skirt and blouses, her cardigan and this one dress. She tidied away her undies, hung up her dressing-gown and sat down before the dressing-table.

Her reflection wasn't reassuring and that was partly her fault, for she hadn't bothered much with her appearance during the two weeks since her mother had died—something she would have to remedy. She did her face and brushed her hair and pinned it into its neat French pleat and went downstairs, peering along the various passages as she went.

It was indeed a delightful house, and although Sir Paul had called it a cottage it was a good deal larger than that. There was no sign of him when she reached the hall but Mrs Parfitt popped her head round a door. 'He won't be long, miss. Come into the kitchen if you've a mind. Your little cat's here, as good as gold, sitting in the warm. Taken to us like a duck to water, she has.'

Indeed, Queenie looked as though she had lived there all her life, stretched out before the Aga.

'You don't mind her being here? In your kitchen?'

'Bless you, miss, whatever harm could she do? Just wait while I give the soup a stir and I'll show you the rest of it…'

She opened a door and led the way down a short passage. 'This bit of the house Sir Paul's grandfather added; you can't see it from the lane. There's a pantry—' she opened another door '—and a wash-house opposite and all mod cons—Sir Paul saw to that. And over here there's what was the stillroom; I use it for bottled fruit and jam and pickles. I make those myself. Then there's this cubby-hole where the shoes are cleaned and the dogs' leads and such like are kept. If ever you should want a good thick coat there's plenty hanging there—boots too.'

She opened the door at the end of the passage. 'The back garden, miss; leastways, the side of it with a gate into the path which leads back to the lane.' She gave a chuckle. 'Higgledy-piggledy, as you might say, but you'll soon find your way around.'

As she spoke the gate opened and Sir Paul and the dogs came through.

'Ready for lunch?' he wanted to know, and swept Emma back with him to the sitting-room. 'A glass of sherry? It will give you an appetite.'

It loosened her tongue too, so that over Mrs Parfitt's delicious lunch she found herself answering his carefully casual questions and even, from time to time, letting slip some of her doubts and fears about the future, until she remembered with a shock that he had offered her a future and here she was talking as though he had said nothing.

He made no comment, but began to talk about the village and the people living in it. It was obvious to her that he was attached to his home, although according to Mrs Parfitt he was away a good deal.

He took her round the house after lunch. There was a small sitting-room at the front of the cottage, with his study behind it. A dining-room was reached through a short passage and, up several steps to one side of the hall, there was a dear little room most comfortably furnished and with rows of bookshelves, filled to overflowing. Emma could imagine sitting there by the fire, reading her fill.

There was a writing-desk under the small window, with blotter, writing-paper and envelopes neatly arranged upon it, and the telephone to one side. One could sit there and write letters in comfort and peace, she thought. Only there was no one for her to write to. Well, there was Mr Dobbs, although he was always so busy he probably wouldn't have time to read a letter, and she hardly thought that Mrs Hervey would be interested. Cook and Alice, of course, but they would prefer postcards...

Sir Paul had been watching her. 'You like this room?'

She nodded. 'I like the whole cottage; it's like home.'

'It is home, Emma.'

She had no answer to that.

* * *

She was given no time to brood. During the next few days he walked her over the moor, taking the dogs, bundling her into one of the elderly coats by the back door, marching her along, mile after mile, not talking much, and when they got home Mrs Parfitt had delicious meals waiting for them, so that between the good food and hours in the open air she was blissfully tired at the end of each day, only too willing to accept Sir Paul's suggestion that she should go early to bed—to fall asleep the moment her head touched the pillow.

On Sunday he took her to church. St John's dated from the thirteenth century, old and beautiful, and a mere stone's throw from the cottage. Wearing the dress under her winter coat, and her only hat—a plain felt which did nothing for her—Emma sat beside him in a pew in the front of the church, and watched him read the lesson, surprised that he put on a pair of glasses to do so, but enthralled by his deep, unhurried voice. Afterwards she stood in the church porch while he introduced her to the rector and his wife, and several people who stopped to speak to him.

They were friendly, and if they were curious they were far too well-mannered to show it. They all gave them invitations to come for a drink or to dine, promising to phone and arrange dates, chorusing that they must get to know Emma while she was in Lustleigh.

'We are always glad to see a new face,' declared a talkative middle-aged woman. 'And as for you, Paul, we see you so seldom that you simply must come.'

He replied suitably but, Emma noted, made no promises. That made sense too; their curiosity would be even greater if she were to return home and never be seen again there. Sir Paul would deal with that without fuss, just as he did everything else. She remained quiet, smiling a little and making vague remarks when she had to.

After Sunday lunch, sitting by the fire, the Sunday papers strewn around, the dogs at Sir Paul's feet and Queenie on her lap, Emma said suddenly, 'You have a great many friends…'

He looked at her over his glasses and then took them off. 'Well, I have lived here for a number of years, and my parents before me, and their parents before them. We aren't exactly cut off from the world but we are a close-knit community.' He added casually, 'I believe you will fit in and settle down very well here.'

His gaze was steady and thoughtful, and after a moment she said, 'I don't understand why you want me to marry you.'

'I have given you my reasons. They are sound and sensible. I am not a young man, to make decisions lightly, Emma.'

'No, I'm sure of that. But it isn't just because you're sorry for me?'

'No, certainly not. That would hardly be a good foundation for a happy marriage.'

He smiled at her and she found herself smiling too. 'We might quarrel…'

'I should be very surprised if we didn't from time to time—which wouldn't matter in the least since we are both sensible enough to make it up afterwards. We are bound to agree to differ about a number of things—life would be dull if we didn't.'

Early the following week he drove her to Buckfastleigh. 'You're having coffee with Doreen Hervey,' he told her. 'Unless you want to come with me to the solicitor and house agent. Will you stay with her until I fetch you?'

'Should I go with you?'

'Not unless you wish to. From what you have told me, everything is settled and you can sell your house. The solicitor has already been in contact with the house agent, hasn't he? It's just a question of tying up the ends. Would you like to go there and see if there's anything you want to keep? There's plenty of room at the cottage.'

'You're talking as though we are going to be married.'

For a moment he covered her clasped hands with one of his. He said quietly, 'Say yes, Emma, and trust me.'

She turned her head to gaze at his calm face. He was not looking at her, but watching the road ahead. Of course she trusted him; he was the nicest person she had ever met, and the kindest.

'I do trust you,' she told him earnestly, 'and I'll marry you and be a good wife.'

He gave her a quick glance—so quick that she hadn't time to puzzle over the look on his face. She dismissed it, suddenly filled quite joyously with quiet content.

Chapter 5

Emma and Paul had a lot to talk about as he drove back later that day. Everything, he assured her, was arranged; it was now only a question of selling the house.

He had settled the few debts, paid the outstanding bills and returned to Doreen Hervey's house, where he found Emma in the nursery, hanging over Bart's cot, heedless of Nanny's disapproval.

Mrs Hervey, sitting meekly in the chair Nanny had offered, had been amused. 'Wait till you've got one of your own,' she had said.

Emma had turned her face away, her cheeks warm, and listened thankfully to his easy, 'One would imagine that you were worn to a thread looking after Bart, Doreen. When will Mike be home?'

He had taken her to her house then, and helped her

decide which small keepsakes she wished to have—a few pieces of silver, some precious china, her mother's little Victorian work table, her father's silver tankard, photos in old silver frames.

Standing in the small sitting-room, she had asked diffidently, 'Would you mind if Mr Dobbs and Cook and Alice came and chose something? They were very kind to me and to Mother...'

'Of course. We'll take the car and fetch them now.'

'Mrs Smith-Darcy will never let them come.'

'Leave it to me. You stay here and collect the things you want while I bring them here.'

She didn't know what he had said but they were all there within twenty minutes, and she had left them to choose what they wanted.

'If I could have some of Mrs Trent's clothes?' Alice had whispered. Alice was the eldest of numerous children, whose wages went straight into the family purse. She had gone away delighted, with Cook clutching several pictures she had fancied. As for Mr Dobbs, he had had an eye on the clock in the kitchen for a long time, he had told her.

Sir Paul had taken them all back and mentioned casually on his return that he had arranged to send everything but the furniture to a charity shop. Emma had been dreading packing up her mother's clothes and the contents of the linen cupboard. She had thanked him with gratitude.

He had popped her back into the car then, taken her to Buckland in the Moor and given her lunch at the country hotel there. She had been conscious that her first sharp grief had given way to a gentle sorrow and she had been able to laugh and talk and feel again. She had tried to thank him then. 'I told you that I would never be able to repay you for all you did for Mother, and now I'm doubly in your debt.'

He had smiled his kind smile. 'Shall we cry quits? After all, I'm getting a wife, am I not? And I fancy the debt should be mine.'

That evening, as they sat round the fire, with the dogs and Queenie sprawling at their feet, he suggested that they might go to Exeter on the following day. 'You have plenty of money now,' he reminded her, and when she told him that she had only a few pounds he said, 'You forget your house. Supposing I settle any bills for the present and you pay me when it is sold?'

'I already owe you money for the solicitor and all these debts...'

'You can easily repay those also, but all in good time. I'm sure that the house will sell well enough.'

'Thank you so much, then; I do need some clothes.'

'I have yet to meet a woman who didn't. At the same time we might decide on a date for our wedding. There is no point in waiting, is there? Will you think about it and let me know what you would like to do?'

When she didn't reply he went on quietly, 'Supposing we go along and see the vicar? He can read the banns; that will give you three weeks to decide on a date. It will also give you a breathing-space to think things over.'

'You mean if I should want to back out?'

'Precisely.' He was smiling at her.

'I'll not do that,' said Emma.

She was uncertain what to buy and sat up in bed that night making a list. Good clothes, of course, suitable for the wife of a consultant surgeon and at the same time wearable each day in the country. 'Tweeds,' she wrote. 'Suit and a top-coat'—even though spring was well settled in it could be cold on the moor.

One or two pretty dresses, she thought, and undies, shoes—and perhaps she could find a hat which actually did something for her. She would need boots and slippers—and should she look for something to wear in the evenings? Did those people she'd met at the church give parties or rather grand dinners?

She asked Paul at breakfast. He was a great help.

'The dinner parties are usually formal—black tie and so on, short frocks for the ladies. I suppose because we tend to make our own amusements, celebrating birthdays and so on. But more often, as far as I remember, the ladies wear pretty dresses. You'll need a warm wrap of some kind, though, for the evening. It'll stay chilly here for some time yet.' He looked across at her list. 'Don't forget a warm dressing-gown and slippers.'

'I need rather a lot...'

'You have plenty of money coming to you.'

'How much should I spend?'

He named a sum which left her open-mouthed. 'But that's hundreds and hundreds!'

Poker-faced, he observed that good clothes lasted a long time and were more economical in the long run.

'You really don't mind lending me the money?'

'No. I'll come with you and write the cheques. If you outrun the constable, I'll warn you.'

* * *

Thus reassured, Emma plunged into her day's shopping. She would have gone to one of the department stores but Paul took her instead to several small, elegant and very expensive boutiques. Even with a pause for coffee, by lunchtime she had acquired a tweed suit, a cashmere top-coat—its price still made her feel a little faint—more skirts, blouses and sweaters, a windproof jacket to go with them, and two fine wool dresses.

When she would have chosen shades which she considered long-wearing he had suggested something more colourful—plaids, a dress in garnet-red, another in turquoise and various shades of blue, silk blouses in old rose, blue and green, and a dress for the dinner parties— a tawny crêpe, deceptively simple.

He took her to lunch then. Watching her crossing through her list, he observed, 'A good waterproof, don't you think? Then I'll collect the parcels and go to the car and leave you to buy the rest. Will an hour be enough?'

'Yes, oh, yes.' She paused, wondering how she should tell him that she had barely enough money to buy stockings, let alone undies and a dressing-gown.

'You'll need some money.' He was casual about it, handing her a roll of notes. 'If it isn't enough we can come again tomorrow.'

They bought the raincoat, and a hat to go with it, before he left her at a department store. 'Don't worry about the time; I'll wait,' he told her, and waited until she was inside.

Before she bought anything she would have to count the notes he had given her. There was no one else in the Ladies, and she took the roll out of her handbag. The total shocked her—she could have lived on it for months. At the same time it presented the opportunity for her to spend lavishly.

Which she did. Might as well be hung for a sheep as for a lamb, she reflected, choosing silk and lace undies, a quilted dressing-gown, and matching up stockings with shoes and the soft leather boots she had bought. Even so, there was still money in her purse. Laden with her purchases, she left the shop and found Paul waiting for her.

He took her packages from her. 'Everything you need for the time being?' he asked.

'For years,' she corrected him. 'I've had a lovely day, Paul; you have no idea. There's a lot of money left over...'

'Keep it. I'm sure you'll need it.' He glanced sideways at her. 'Before we marry,' he added.

It was at breakfast the next morning that he told her that he would be away for a few days. 'I have an appointment in Edinburgh which I must keep,' he told her. 'If you want to go to Exeter for more shopping ask Truscott at the garage to drive you there and bring you back here. I'll have a word with him before I go.'

'Thank you.' She was very conscious of disappointment but all she said was, 'May I take the dogs out?'

'Of course. I usually walk them to Lustleigh Cleave in the early morning. If it's clear weather you'll enjoy a good walk on the moor.'

'I can christen the new tweeds,' said Emma soberly.

He wouldn't be there to see them; she had been look-ing forward to astonishing him with the difference in her appearance when she was well-dressed. That would have to wait now. 'You're leaving today?'

'In an hour or so. Mrs Parfitt will look after you, Emma, but feel free to do whatever you like; this house will be your home as well as mine.'

He had gone by mid-morning, and when she had had coffee with Mrs Parfitt she went to her room with Queenie and tried on her new clothes.

They certainly made a difference; their colours changed her ordinary features to near prettiness and their cut showed off her neat figure. It was a pity that Paul wasn't there to see the chrysalis changing into a butterfly. She had to make do with Queenie.

She had to admit that by teatime, even though she had filled the rest of the day by taking the dogs for a long walk, she was missing him, which was, of course, exactly what he had intended.

Mrs Parfitt, when Emma asked her the next day, had no idea when he would be back. 'Sir Paul goes off for days at a time,' she explained to Emma. 'He goes to other hospitals, and abroad too. Does a lot of work in London, so I've been told. Got friends there too. I dare say he'll be back in a day or two. Why not put on one of your new skirts and that jacket and go down to the shop for me and fetch up a few groceries?'

So Emma went shopping, exchanging good morn-ings rather shyly with the various people she met. They were friendly, wanting to know if she liked the village and did she get on with the dogs? She guessed that there were other questions hovering on their tongues but they were too considerate to ask them.

Going back with her shopping, she reflected that, since she had promised to marry Paul, it might be a good thing to do so as soon as possible. He had told her to decide on a date. As soon after the banns had been read as could be arranged—which thought reminded her that she would certainly need something special to wear on her wedding-day.

Very soon, she promised herself, she would get the morning bus to Exeter and go to the boutique Paul had taken her to. She had plenty of money still—her own money too… Well, almost her own, she admitted, once the house was sold and she had paid him back what she owed him.

The time passed pleasantly, her head filled with the delightful problem of what she would wear next, and even the steady rain which began to fall as she walked on the moor with the dogs did nothing to dampen her spirits.

She got up early and took them out for a walk before her breakfast the next day and then, with Mrs Parfitt's anxious tut-tutting because she wouldn't get the taxi from the garage ringing in her ears, she got on the bus.

It was a slow journey to the city, since the bus stopped whenever passengers wished to get on or off, but she hardly noticed, and when it arrived at last she nipped smartly away, intent on her search for the perfect wedding-outfit.

Of course, she had had her dreams of tulle veils and elaborate wedding-dresses, but theirs wasn't going to be that sort of wedding. She should have something suitable but pretty, and, since she had an economical mind, something which could be worn again.

The sales lady in the boutique remembered her and nodded her head in satisfaction at the vast improvement in Emma's appearance now that she was wearing the tweed suit. The little hat she had persuaded her to buy had been just right… She smiled encouragingly. 'If I may say so, madam, that tweed is exactly the right colour for you. How can I help you?'

'I want something to wear at my wedding,' said Emma, and went delightfully pink.

The sales lady concealed a sentimental heart under her severely corseted black satin. She beamed a genuine smile. 'A quiet wedding? In church?'

Emma nodded. 'I thought a dress and jacket and a hat…'

'Exactly right, madam, and I have just the thing, if you will take a seat.'

Emma sat and a young girl came with the first of a selection of outfits. Very pretty, but blue would look cold in the church. And the next one? Pink, and with rather too many buttons and braid for her taste—it was too frivolous. The third one was the one—winter white in a fine soft woollen material, it had a short jacket and a plain white sheath of a dress.

'I'll try that one,' said Emma.

It fitted, but she had known that it would. Now that she was wearing it she knew that it was exactly what she had wanted.

The sales lady circled her knowingly. 'Elegant and feminine. Madam has a very pretty figure.'

'I must find a hat…'

'No problem. These outfits for special occasions I always team up with several hats so that the outfit is complete.' She waved a hand at the girl, who opened drawers and tenderly lifted out a selection and offered them one by one.

Emma, studying her reflection, gave a sigh. 'I'm so plain,' she said in a resigned voice, and removed a confection of silk flowers and ribbon from her head.

The sales lady was good at her job. 'If I may say so, madam, you have fine eyes and a splendid complexion. Perhaps something… Ah, I have it.'

It looked nothing in her hand—white velvet with a pale blue cord twisted round it—but on Emma's head it became at once stylish, its small soft brim framing her face.

'Oh, yes,' said Emma, and then rather anxiously, 'I hope I have enough money with me.'

The older woman waved an airy hand. 'Please do not worry about that, madam. Any money outstanding you can send to me when you return home.'

Emma took off the hat and, while it and the outfit were being packed up, counted the money in her purse. There was more than enough when she was presented with the bill. She paid, feeling guilty at spending such a great deal of money. On the other hand she wanted to look her very best on her wedding-day. They would be happy, she promised herself, and stifled the sadness she felt that her mother wouldn't see her wed.

There were still one or two small items that she needed. She had coffee and then bought them, and by that time she was hungry. She had soup and a roll in a small café tucked away behind the high street and then, since the bus didn't leave for another hour or so, wandered round the shops, admiring the contents of their windows, thinking with astonishment that, if she wanted, she could buy anything she desired, within reason. She would have plenty of money of her own when the house was sold; she would get Paul to invest it in something safe and use the interest. She need never ask him for a penny, she thought, and fell to wondering where he was and what he was doing.

Sir Paul, already on his way back from Edinburgh, had turned off the main road to pay a visit to his mother and father, and, as he always did, gave a smile of content as he took the Rolls between the gateposts and along the short drive which led to their home—an old manor-house built of Cotswold stone, mellow with age and surrounded by a large, rambling garden which even at the bleakest time of year looked charming.

One day it would be his, but not for many years yet he hoped, catching sight of his father pottering in one of the flowerbeds. He drew up before the door, got out and went to meet him and together they walked to the house, going in through the garden door. 'My dirty boots, Paul; your mother will turn on me if I go in through the front door.'

They both laughed. His mother, to the best of his knowledge, had never turned on anyone in her life. She came to meet them now. Of middle height, rather stout and with a sweet face framed by grey hair stylishly dressed, she looked delighted to see him.

'Paul—' she lifted her face for his kiss '—how lovely to see you. Are you back at work again? Going somewhere or coming back?'

'Coming back. I can't stay, my dear, I need to get home—but may I come next weekend and bring the girl I'm going to marry to meet you both?'

'Marry? Paul—is it anyone we know?'

'No, I think not. She has lived at Buckfastleigh all her life except for her time at boarding-school. Her mother died recently. I hope—I think you will like her.'

'Pretty?' asked his mother.

'No—at least, she has a face you can talk to— peaceful—and she listens. Her eyes are lovely and she is also sensible and matter-of-fact.'

He didn't look like a man in love, reflected his mother. On the other hand, he was of an age to lose his heart for the rest of his life and beyond; she only hoped that she was the right girl. He had from time to time over the years brought girls to his parents' home and she hadn't liked any of them. They had all been as pretty as pictures, but he hadn't been in love with any of them.

'This is wonderful news, Paul, and we will make her very welcome. Come for lunch on Saturday. Can you stay until Monday morning?'

'I've a teaching round in the afternoon. If we leave soon after breakfast I can take Emma home first.'

'Emma—that's a pretty and old-fashioned name.'

He smiled. 'She's rather an old-fashioned girl.'

Watching him drive away presently, his mother said, 'Do you suppose it will be all right, Peter?'

'My dear, Paul is forty years old. He hasn't married sooner because he hadn't found the right girl. Now he has.'

Emma got off the bus in the village, walked the short distance to Paul's house, went along the alley and in through the side-door. Mrs Parfitt would be preparing dinner and she didn't want to disturb her. She went through to the hall and opened the drawing-room door, her parcels clamped under one arm.

Sir Paul was sitting by the fire, with the dogs resting their chins on his feet and Queenie on the arm of his chair. Emma gave a squeak of delight, dropped her parcels and hurried across the room.

'Paul! Oh, how lovely; you're home. Don't get up…'

He was already on his feet, his eyes very bright, scanning her happy face. He said lightly, 'Emma, you've been shopping again.' And she pulled up short beside him, conscious that she had been quite prepared to fling herself into his arms. The thought took her breath so that her voice didn't sound quite like hers.

'Well, yes, my wedding-dress.' She added earnestly, 'I couldn't buy it the other day because you mustn't see it until we're in the church.'

'A pleasure I look forward to.' He picked up the box and parcels she had dropped. 'You'd like a cup of tea? I'll tell Mrs Parfitt while you take off your things.'

When she came down the tea-tray was on a little

table by the fire—tea in its silver teapot, muffins in their silver dish, tiny cakes.

She was pouring their second cups when he said quietly, 'Next Saturday we are going to my parents' home in the Cotswolds—just for the weekend.'

She almost dropped the pot. 'Oh, well, yes, of course. I—I hope they'll like me.' She put down the teapot carefully. 'I think that perhaps I'm not quite the kind of girl they would expect you to marry, if you see what I mean.'

'On the contrary. You will find that they will welcome you as their daughter.' He spoke kindly but she could sense that it would be of no use arguing about it.

She said merely, 'That's good. I'll look forward to meeting them.'

'If you've finished your tea shall we go along to the vicarage and discuss dates with the vicar? If you're not too tired we can walk.'

The vicarage was on the other side of the church. I suppose I shall walk to my wedding, thought Emma as Paul rang the bell.

The vicar was a man of Paul's age. 'I'll read the first banns this Sunday, tomorrow, which means that you can marry any day after the third Sunday. You've a date in mind?'

They both looked at Emma; who said sensibly, 'Well, it will have to fit in with Paul's work, won't it?' She smiled at him. 'I know I'm supposed to choose, but I think you had better...'

'Will the Tuesday of the following week suit you? I believe I'm more or less free for a few days after that.' He glanced at Emma, who looked back serenely.

'In the morning?' she asked.

'Whenever you like; since I chose the day you must choose the time.'

She realised that she had no idea if there would be anyone else there, and her face betrayed the thought so plainly that Sir Paul said quickly, 'There will be a number of guests at the reception.'

He was rewarded by the look of relief on her face. 'Eleven o'clock,' she said.

The vicar's wife came in then, with a tray of coffee, and they sat for a while and talked and presently walked back to the cottage.

'You said there would be guests,' observed Emma, in a voice which held a hint of coolness.

'It quite slipped my mind,' he told her placidly. 'I'm sorry, Emma. We'll make a list this evening, shall we?' He smiled at her and she forgot about being cool. 'Mrs Parfitt will be in her element.'

The list was more lengthy than she had expected—his parents, his sisters and their husbands, a number of his colleagues from Exeter, friends from London, friends in and around the village, Doreen Hervey and her husband. 'And we must ask Mr Dobbs—I take it there is a Mrs Dobbs?'

'Yes, I think they'd like to come. Shall I write to them?'

'I'll get some cards printed—no time to have them engraved—and I'll phone everyone and tell them the cards will arrive later.' He glanced at his watch. 'I can reach several friends after dinner this evening.'

They told Mrs Parfitt the wedding-date when she

came to wish them goodnight. 'The village will turn out to a man,' she told them happily. 'Been wanting to see you wed for a long time, sir. Your ma and pa will be coming, no doubt.'

'Indeed they are, Mrs Parfitt, and we hope you will be our guest too.'

'Well, now—that's a treat I'll enjoy. I'll need a new hat.'

'Then you must go to Exeter and get one. I'll drive you in whenever you wish to go.'

Emma saw very little of Paul until the weekend; he had consulting rooms in Exeter and saw his private patients there, and, in the evenings, although they discussed the wedding from time to time he made no mention of their future. All the guests were coming, he told her, and would she mind very much if he went to Exeter on the day after their wedding? He had promised to read a paper at a seminar; he had hoped to postpone it but it hadn't been possible.

'Well, of course you must go,' said Emma. 'May I come with you? I shan't understand a word but I'd very much like to be there.'

He had agreed very readily, but she wasn't sure if he was pleased about it or not.

They left early on Saturday morning and Emma sat silently beside him, hoping that she had brought the right clothes with her and that his parents would like her. She was then comforted by his quiet, 'Don't worry, Emma, everything will be all right.' And as though Willy and Kate had understood him, they had uttered gentle grumbling barks, and Willy had got down off the back seat and licked the back of her neck.

It was a day when spring had the upper hand and winter had withdrawn to the more remote stretches of the moor, and once they had bypassed Exeter and were racing up the motorway the country showed a great deal of green in the hedges. The car was blissfully warm and smelled of good leather, Paul's aftershave and the faint whiff of dog and, soothed by it, Emma decided in her sensible way that there was no point in worrying about something she knew very little about. So when Paul began a rambling conversation about nothing much she joined in quite cheerfully.

Just past Taunton he stopped for coffee and then turned off the motorway to drive across country—Midsomer Norton, Bath and then onwards towards Cirencester—to turn off presently into a country road which led them deep into the Cotswolds.

'Oh, this is nice,' said Emma. 'I like the houses—all that lovely pale yellow stone. Where are we exactly?'

'Cirencester is to the north-east, Tetbury is away to the right of us—the next village is where we are going.'

When he stopped the car in front of his parents' home, she sat for a moment, peering at it. 'It's beautiful,' she said softly. 'Do you love it very much?'

He said gravely, 'Yes, I do, and I hope that you will love it too. Come inside...' He took her by the elbow and went towards the opening door.

His mother stood there, smiling a welcome. She offered a cheek for his kiss and turned to Emma. 'Emma—such a pretty name—welcome, my dear.'

She shook hands and then kissed Emma's cheek and tucked her arm in hers. 'Come and meet my husband.' She paused a moment to look up at her son. 'Paul, you described Emma exactly.'

He smiled but didn't speak, and when they entered the drawing-room and his father came to meet them he shook hands and then drew Emma towards him. 'Father, this is Emma—my father, Emma.'

Mr Wyatt wore his years lightly, and it was obvious where his son had got his good looks. She put out a hand and he took it and then kissed her. 'Welcome, my dear. We are delighted to have you here with us.'

After that everything was perfect. Going to bed that night in the charming bedroom, Emma reflected that she had had no need to worry—Paul's mother and father had been kindness itself, and Paul had taken her round the house and the large garden while Willy and Kate and his father's elderly spaniel trotted to and fro, dashing off following imaginary rabbits and then coming back to trot at their heels.

It had been an hour she didn't think she would forget; they hadn't talked much but somehow there hadn't been the need for that. All the same, when they had gone back into the house for tea, she'd had the strange feeling that she knew Paul better than she had done.

In the evening, after dinner, they had sat talking about the wedding and who would be coming to it and Mrs Wyatt had admired her dress—one of the pretty ones Paul had persuaded her to have. 'You will make a charming bride,' she had told Emma. 'Paul is a lucky man.'

Emma, curling up in the comfortable bed, promised

herself that she would make sure that he was. Not loving him didn't seem to matter, somehow, and she supposed that he felt the same about her. They were friends and they liked each other; everything would be all right, and on this cheerful thought she went to sleep.

They all went to church the next morning, and Emma got stared at. Somehow the news had got around that Sir Paul had got himself engaged at last and everyone wanted to see the bride-to-be. Wedged between father and son, Emma did her best not to notice the interested stares, hoping that they wouldn't be disappointed that she wasn't a girl whose good looks would match her bridgegroom's. She peeped up at Paul's face and found him looking at her and took heart at his kind smile, knowing that he understood how she felt.

They left early on Monday morning, and his mother kissed her and gave her a little hug. 'My dear, we are so happy for you both. You are exactly right for Paul and we wish you every happiness. We shan't see you before your wedding-day—it's something we both look forward to. You'll meet the rest of the family then—they will love you too.'

Emma got into the car feeling a pleasant glow of content; she had been accepted by Paul's family—something which mattered to her.

They were home by lunchtime but he went back to Exeter directly after, saying that he might be late back and that she wasn't to wait up for him. He didn't say why he was going and she didn't ask, although she longed to. Instead she offered to take the dogs for their walk in the late afternoon.

'Yes, do that. But not after teatime, Emma. I'll give them a good run when I get home.'

He patted her shoulder in what she considered to be a highly unsatisfactory manner and got back into the Rolls and drove away. The day, which had begun so pleasantly, had turned sour, and although she told herself that she had no reason to complain, she felt ill done by. She sat still when he had gone, looking at her ringless hand. Had he forgotten that it was the custom to give one's intended bride a ring? Or perhaps he thought that the unusual circumstances of their marriage didn't merit one.

Moping about and feeling sorry for herself would do no good, she told herself, and, leaving Queenie by the fire, she took Willy and Kate for a long walk.

She was late getting back to the cottage and Mrs Parfitt said severely, 'Another ten minutes and I'd have been getting worried about you, miss. Sir Paul said most particular that you weren't to go out after teatime. And quite right too!'

It was a remark which cheered her up a little, and tea round the fire, with the lamps lighted against the gloomy day, restored her usual good spirits. She spent a careful half-hour writing her bread-and-butter letter to Mrs Wyatt, then stamped it and left it on the hall table. The postman would take it in the morning.

She lingered over dinner, helped Mrs Parfitt clear the table and, since there was no sign of Paul, went to bed with a book. She read for a long time, one ear cocked for the sound of his footfall, but by midnight she was half-asleep. She put the book down, telling herself that this was no way to behave—there would probably be years of similar evenings, and if she lay in bed worrying about him she would grow old before her time. Queenie, glad at last that the bedside lamp was out, crept up beside her and she fell asleep.

When she went down to breakfast the next morning, Paul was already at the table. His good morning was cheerful and friendly. 'You slept well?' he wanted to know.

'Like a top, whatever that means! What a nice morning it is…'

'Yes, indeed—a pity I have to go back to Exeter this morning. Unfinished business, I'm afraid.'

'Would you like me to take the dogs out?' She buttered toast, not looking at him.

'I'll take them before I go; I'm sure you have a lot to do here.'

What, in heaven's name? Mrs Parfitt got upset if she offered to help in the house, the garden was beautifully kept by the part-time gardener, but there was a chance that she could go to the village shop for Mrs Parfitt…

'Oh, yes, I've lots to do,' she told him serenely.

'You won't mind if I leave you?' And at her cheerful, 'Of course not,' he got up.

On his way to the door, though, he paused and came back to the table. 'I must beg your forgiveness, Emma.' He took a small box from a pocket. 'I have been carrying this round since we left yesterday and forgot all about it.'

He took a ring out of the box and held it in the palm of

his hand—sapphires and diamonds in an old-fashioned setting. 'It has been kept in the safe in father's study, waiting for the next bride in the family. It is very old and is handed down from one generation to the next.' He picked up her hand and slipped the ring on her finger.

'It fits,' said Emma.

'As I knew it would.' He bent and kissed her, a quick kiss which took her by surprise. 'That augers well for our future.'

Emma said, 'Thank you, Paul,' and, while she was still trying to think of something else to add to that, he patted her shoulder and was gone.

Chapter 6

Emma didn't see much of Paul during that week; he took her with him to Exeter one day, so that she might do some last-minute shopping, and once or twice he was home early so that they could walk the dogs together. On the Saturday he drove down to Buckfastleigh.

They had been invited by the Herveys to have drinks and at the same time they called at the house agent's. There were enquiries, they were told; it was certain that the house would sell, especially now that the warmer weather was coming.

'You don't mind waiting for the money?' asked Emma worriedly as they got back into the car.

'No, Emma, there's no hurry for that.' He turned to smile at her. 'There's time for us to get an armful of flowers and visit your mother's grave.'

She hadn't liked to ask but that was exactly what she wanted to do. He bought the flowers she chose—roses and carnations—and they took them to the quiet churchyard. Emma's sadness was mitigated by the feel of Paul's great arm round her shoulder and his unspoken sympathy.

The Herveys were delighted to see them and Emma was borne upstairs to see Bart, asleep in his cot. Emma was relieved to see that Nanny had been replaced by an older woman with a pleasant face and a ready smile.

'He's grown,' said Emma. 'He's perfect...'

'He's rather a duck,' said his mother fondly, 'and Nanny's splendid with him—and I'm getting better, aren't I, Nanny?'

On the way downstairs she took Emma's arm. 'Mike took one look at that other nanny and gave her notice,' she confided. 'Didn't fancy her at all—a regular sargeant major, he said she was. This one's an old dear, and she's taught me a lot—you know, how to hold Bart properly and what to do when he yells. I'm not afraid of him any more.'

She was quite serious; Emma murmured sympathetically, reflecting that it was fortunate that the Herveys could afford a nanny.

They had their drinks then, talking about the wedding and the baby and listening to Mike's amusing account of his trip to America. Then the two men went upstairs to see Bart and Mrs Hervey described in great detail what she intended to wear at the wedding.

Listening to her, Emma thought it likely that she

would outshine the bride. Not that she minded—she liked Doreen Hervey; she might be helpless and unable to do much for herself but she was kind and friendly and light-hearted, and she went into raptures over Emma's ring.

'It's a family heirloom, isn't it? You deserve it, Emma, for you're such a nice girl, and Paul's the nicest man I know—excepting Mike, of course. He's frightfully rich, of course, and awfully important—but you'd never know, would you? Never says a word about himself—never told anyone why he was knighted... I don't suppose you would tell me? I'll not breathe a word...'

'Well, no,' said Emma. 'He wants to keep it a private matter.'

So private, she thought, that he had never mentioned it to her. She would ask him...

Which she did as they were driving back to Lustleigh, and was thwarted by his placid, 'Oh, you know how it is—names out of a hat and I happened to be lucky.' Even though he sounded placid there was something in his voice which prevented her from asking any more questions. Perhaps, she thought wistfully, when they had been married for a long time and had got to know each other really well he would tell her.

They went to church in the morning and heard their last banns read, and after the service an endless stream of people stopped to wish them well. They all wanted to know the date of the wedding.

'It will be very quiet—just family and a few close friends,' said Paul and, when pressed, told them the day on which they were to marry, knowing that if he didn't tell them they would find a reason to call at the cottage and ask Mrs Parfitt.

If Emma had hoped to see more of Paul during the next week she was disapointed; even at the weekend he was called away urgently to operate on a road casualty so that her wedding-day loomed without her having had the chance to get to know him better. Indeed, suspicion that he was avoiding her lurked at the back of her head and became so urgent that on the evening before her wedding, left to her own devices while he worked in his study, she put down the book she was reading, thumped on the door and then entered the study before she could change her mind.

He got up as she went in. 'Emma—what's wrong? You look as though...' He paused and asked mildly, 'Something has upset you?'

'Yes—no, I'm not sure.' She gave him a worried look. 'Why don't I see you more often? You're always going somewhere, and even when you're at home you keep out of my way. Don't you want to marry me? It's quite all right if you've changed your mind; it isn't as if... I wouldn't like you to get married to the wrong person and be unhappy.'

He came round the desk and took her hands in his. 'Emma, my dear girl, what can I say to reassure you? Only that I want to marry you and that you are the right person. If you haven't seen much of me it is because I've had a good deal of work, and I'm afraid that is something you will have to learn to live with.' He smiled down at her, a tender smile which set her heart thumping. 'And I haven't changed my mind, nor will that ever happen.'

'I've been silly,' said Emma. 'I'm sorry—and I've interrupted your work.'

He turned her round and put an arm round her shoulders. 'We will sit down and go over the arrangements for tomorrow.' He was propelling her gently out of the study and back into the drawing-room. 'Are you feeling nervous? No need—you know almost everyone who'll be there. The car will fetch you tomorrow morning; I know it's only a few yards to the church but I can't have my bride walking there...'

'The car? But what about you?'

'I'm spending the night at Eastrey Barton—the family are already there. It is considered very bad luck, so I'm told, for the bride and groom to spend the night before their wedding under the same roof. Mrs Parfitt will look after you and I'll phone you in the morning.'

'Oh, I thought we'd just have breakfast together as usual and then walk to church.'

'I have neglected you shamefully, Emma—the truth is...'

'You forgot that you were getting married!' she finished for him, unaware that that hadn't been what he had been going to say.

She spoke matter-of-factly and Sir Paul gave a soundless sigh. Patience, he reminded himself—she wasn't ready to hear his reason for avoiding her company, and, when he was with her, treating her with a casual friendliness.

* * *

Dressed for her wedding, Emma took a final look at herself in the pier glass, and even to her critical eye she considered that she didn't look too bad. Not beautiful—brides were supposed to look beautiful—not even pretty, but the outfit suited her and the little hat framed her rather anxious face with its soft velvet brim.

She went downstairs to where Dr Treble, who was to give her away, waited, and was much heartened by his surprised admiration. He and Mrs Parfitt, who was on the point of leaving for the church, chorused their approval in no uncertain terms, so that she got into the car feeling more confident.

Her confidence faltered a little as they started down the aisle and she clutched the small bouquet of pink roses which Paul had given her in a nervous hand; she hadn't expected the church to be full of people—the entire village appeared to be in the pews, nodding and smiling at her as she passed them. When she reached the front pews Paul's mother looked round and smiled and nodded too, but Emma scarcely noticed her; her eyes were on Paul's broad back—if only he would turn round and look at her...

He did, smiling a little, and her heart gave a great jump against her ribs so that she caught her breath. Her thoughts were wild; it was a bit late in the day to fall in love with him, wasn't it? And not at all a good idea either, for now everything was going to be a bit complicated.

She stood beside him and the vicar began to speak the opening words of the service. She did her best to listen but odd thoughts kept popping in and out of her head. She had loved him for quite a while, she thought, only she hadn't known it, and if she had would she have married him?

The solemn words the vicar was speaking cut across her reflections at last and she listened then. Never mind the future. She would make her vows and keep to them; she would be a good wife, and if Paul didn't need her love, only her companionship, then she would do her best to be the kind of person he wanted. When the moment came, she spoke her 'I will' in a clear, steady little voice that everyone could hear, and then took comfort from Paul's deep voice, as assured and certain as hers had been.

They exchanged rings then and went to sign the register, and presently were walking down the aisle and out into the bright morning, but before they could get into the Rolls they were surrounded by guests with cameras poised and had to pass through a barrage of confetti and good wishes.

Paul had been holding her hand, and as they reached the car at last gave it an encouraging squeeze. 'So much for our quiet wedding,' he said. 'I'm enjoying it, aren't you?'

'Oh, yes,' said Emma. 'It's the most wonderful day of my life.' She spoke with such fervour that he looked down at her, but the little hat shaded her face from his as she got into the car.

The rest of the day was like a dream; the cottage was full of people laughing and talking and drinking champagne and eating canapés. Paul had Emma by the hand, and as various friends greeted him he introduced her.

His sisters had been the first to join them after his mother and father—handsome young women who kissed her warmly and listened smilingly as their husbands flattered her gently and congratulated Paul—and after them there were people she realised she would meet again—colleagues from the hospital, several from London, old friends with their wives and of course the Herveys and Mr Dobbs and his wife.

Mr Dobbs had given her a smacking kiss. 'Wait till I tell 'em all about this,' he said. 'I'll make sure that Mrs Smith-Darcy gets the lot. I've taken some photos too.' He transferred his beaming smile to Sir Paul. 'You are a lucky man, and no mistake,' he told him.

Since they weren't going anywhere, the guests lingered, renewing acquaintances, plying Emma and Paul with invitations, and then at last taking their leave. The cake had been cut, the last toast drunk and Emma longed to take off her new shoes. The moment the last guest had gone, she did so. 'You don't mind, do you? Just for a few minutes—they're new...'

'And very pretty. You look charming, Emma, and I do like that hat.' He took her arm as they went indoors to where his mother and father and sisters were waiting. 'We're going out to dinner—just the family—but we can sit around for a while and talk.'

'I'll get Mrs Parfitt to make a pot of tea...'

'A splendid idea, although I suspect she's already got the kettle on.'

As indeed she had, and presently she bustled in with

the tea-tray and a plate of cucumber sandwiches. 'After all that cake and bits and pieces,' she explained. 'Not but it wasn't a rare fine party.' Her eyes fell on the dogs, basking in the late afternoon sunshine. 'Queenie's in the kitchen having her tea.'

'And what about you, Mrs Parfitt?' asked Emma. 'You've worked so hard; you must have your tea too…'

'That I shall, ma'am—wetted it not five minutes ago with a nice boiled egg and a bit of toast.'

Emma, in bed that night, thought back over her wedding-day. It had ended on a light-hearted note at Eastrey Barton, where they had all dined splendidly with a great deal of talk and laughter, and she had been happy because Paul had given her a wedding-present—a double row of pearls which she had immediately worn.

When they had returned to the cottage he had kissed her goodnight—a quick, friendly kiss—almost a peck—she thought wistfully, but at least it was a kiss. It had been difficult not to kiss him back, but she hadn't. She would keep to her resolve of being a good companion, however hard it was, and perhaps in time he would come to love her. At least, she told herself stoutly, she had several advantages—she was his wife and she loved him.

The next day he took her to Exeter with him as he had promised, and she sat in the lecture hall and listened to him addressing a large and attentive audience. She understood very little of the lecture—that it was about bones went without saying, and some of it must have been amusing for the audience laughed quite often.

When he had sat down they clapped for a long time before someone on the platform got up and made a speech about him in glowing terms.

Emma, sitting at the back of the hall, beamed with pride and Sir Paul, who had seen her the moment he started his lecture, smiled—his dear little Emma…

They had tea with a number of his colleagues— several foreign surgeons and members of the hospital board—and Emma—being Emma—had little to say for herself but listened to the opinions of various learned gentlemen who were quick to observe to Sir Paul that his wife was a charming young lady and a splendid listener. 'Such beautiful eyes,' sighed an Italian surgeon, over in England to exchange ideas with his colleagues. 'I hope we shall meet again.'

Driving back to Lustleigh presently, Paul repeated this. 'How fortunate that I'm not a jealous husband,' he said lightly. 'You were a great success, Emma.'

'Oh, was I? I didn't understand half of what they were talking about but they were all very nice to me.' She turned to look at him. 'Perhaps it was because I'm your wife and they were being polite.'

'No, no. They all fell for you…' He was laughing and that hurt.

'I expect it was my new clothes,' said Emma.

'You enjoyed the lecture?' he asked her.

'Very much, although I didn't understand very much of it. Do you lecture a great deal?'

'From time to time. Sometimes I'm invited to other countries—you shall come with me.'

'Oh, may I? Don't you have a secretary with you?'

'Yes, if it's a long tour, but for the present I shall be in England.'

'Not always at Exeter?'

'No—but I'm usually only away for a day or two—not long.'

At dinner that evening he asked her if she would like to drive to Torquay in the morning. 'It's pleasant at this time of year—not too many people yet, and the dogs love the beach.'

She peeped at him over her glass. He looked tired and preoccupied—a carefree day by the sea would be pleasant. 'I'd love it,' she told him.

They left soon after breakfast, and since it was a clear day, Emma wore a skirt with a cashmere sweater and a velvet beret perched over one eye. 'Very fetching,' said Sir Paul. 'You are sure you'll be warm enough?'

He drove to the A38 and took the fork over Haldon to the coast and, as he had said, Torquay was not too crowded.

'Coffee first or walk the dogs?' he asked her.

'The dogs,' said Emma, conscious of two anxious, whiskery faces turned towards her. So they parked the car and took them down on to the beach and walked arm-in-arm for a mile or more, stopping every now and again to throw sticks for the dogs and look out to sea.

'It looks very cold,' said Emma, and then added, 'I expect you can swim…'

'Yes.' They were standing at the water's edge and he flung an arm around her shoulders. 'You don't?'

'Well, I tried—at school, you know—and once or

twice when I went on holiday with Mother and Father. I think I'm a coward.'

His arm tightened. 'Nonsense. You haven't had the chance to learn, that's all. I'll teach you. I've a small yacht which I keep at Salcombe; we'll go there when I'm free.'

'I've never been on a yacht.'

'I shall very much enjoy having you for my crew,' he told her.

He took her to the Imperial Hotel for lunch—lobster bisque and *boeuf en croute*, rounded off by a chocolate soufflé, and washed down by a claret handled by the wine waiter as though it were a precious baby rather than a bottle.

Emma, who knew almost nothing about wines, took a sip, then another. 'It's perfect—I've never tasted anything as heavenly.'

Sir Paul thought it unlikely that she had, but he expressed the view that it was considered a good wine and that he was glad that she enjoyed it.

The day was fine. They walked again after lunch, on the beach once more but this time in the opposite direction, with the dogs rushing about, barking at the water, begging for sticks to be thrown. Presently they turned back and got into the car and began to drive back to Lustleigh, stopping on the way at a tea-room in one of the villages. It was old-fashioned—a front room in a thatched cottage—but they had a splendid tea of muffins, oozing butter, and a large pot of strong tea, while the dogs sat under the table, gobbling the bits of muffin Emma handed them.

'You'll spoil them,' observed Sir Paul.

She said at once, 'Oh, I'm sorry, I shouldn't have done it.'

He frowned, annoyed with himself for sounding as though he was criticising her. She saw the frown and guessed quite wrongly that he was vexed with her so that she became ill at ease.

The day had been heavenly—just being with him had been wonderful—but now, in her efforts to behave as the kind of wife he had wished for, she drew back from the friendly rapport they had had, still making small talk, but keeping him at arm's length while willingly answering him when he spoke.

He, however, was practised in the art of putting patients at their ease, and by the time they reached home she was her usual, friendly self and they dined together in the easy companionship that he was so careful to maintain.

That, she was to discover, was to be the last of their days together for some time, for he left directly after breakfast each morning and was rarely home before seven or eight o'clock in the evening. She hid her disappointment and showed a bright face when he got back—ready to listen about his day, even though she understood very little of what he had been doing. She was also careful not to chat at breakfast while he was glancing through his post. True, they had been out to dine on several evenings, but she saw little of him then, though it was pleasant to meet the people he counted his friends.

She filled her days with walking the dogs, working

doggedly at a piece of tapestry she had begun with so much enthusiasm, not realising the amount of work and tiny stitches it required before it was finished. She was happy because she loved Paul, but she found herself counting the hours until he came home each evening.

They had been married for several weeks when he told her at breakfast that someone would deliver a Mini that morning. 'For you, Emma, so you can go wherever you want. I'll be home early today and you can take me for a drive in it.'

She smiled widely at him across the table. 'Paul, thank you—how perfectly splendid.' She added, 'I'll be very careful…'

He smiled. 'Keep to the roads around here until you're quite used to it. I'll be home before five o'clock so be ready for me.'

He dropped a kiss on her head as he went away.

The Mini, a nice shade of blue, arrived at lunchtime, and she got into it at once and drove to Bovey Tracey and back and then waited impatiently for Paul to come home. When he did she drove him to Moretonhampstead, very conscious of him sitting squashed up beside her.

'It's a bit small for you,' she said, driving carefully past the sheep wandering across the road.

'Indeed, but just right for you, I hope, Emma.'

'Yes, oh, yes. It's a wonderful present.'

Back home, as they sat at dinner he asked her, 'Do you find the days long, Emma?'

'Well, yes, a bit. You see, I've had to work all day

for quite a time and I'm not really used to having so much leisure.'

'Would you like a little job? Voluntary, of course. There is a nursery at Moretonhampstead. It takes unwanted babies and toddlers—most of them are orphaned or abandoned. Not ill, but neglected and very underfed. Diana Pearson, who is in charge, is an old friend of mine and she tells me that she needs more help urgently. Would you like to go there once or twice a week and give a hand? No nursing, just common sense and a liking for infants.'

He wanted her to say yes, she was sure—perhaps that was why he had given her the car. She didn't hesitate. 'Yes, I'd love to help,' she told him.

'Good. We'll go there on Monday; I'm not operating until the afternoon. Would you ask Mrs Parfitt to have lunch ready for us at one o'clock? I'll bring you back and have lunch here.' He added, 'One or two days a week and not more than four hours at a time, Emma. It has to be interesting, not tiring and demanding, and never at the weekends.'

The nursery was on the outskirts of the town—a long, low building, with cheerfully coloured walls and a large playroom and several nurseries. Sir Paul walked in as though he knew the place well and went straight to a door with 'Office' written on it.

The young woman who got up as he went in was tall and dark with almost black eyes in a lovely face. She was elegantly dressed and she smiled at him in a way which gave Emma food for thought. Her greeting was casual enough and when Paul introduced her she shook hands with a pleasant murmur and another smile—quite different from the first one, though.

It was obvious that she knew all about Emma, for she said pleasantly, 'We'd love to have you here; we're desperate for help. Paul said two days in a week and not more than four hours at a time.' She put a hand on his arm and smiled at Emma, who smiled back, knowing that she was disliked just as she disliked the speaker. 'Come and look around—there are a lot of small babies at the moment. The travellers bring them in for a week or two's feeding up—the little ones get cold and quickly ill; it's not really an ideal life for babies, although the children seem happy enough.'

They went round the place together, and Emma said she would come each Tuesday and Thursday in the mornings. 'Is nine o'clock too early?'

'We take over from the night staff at eight o'clock, but that'll be too early for you.' Diana stole a look at Paul. 'Won't it, Paul?' She smiled as she spoke, and Emma repressed a desire to slap her. If it hadn't been for Paul's obvious wish that she should have something to occupy her days she would have said there and then that she had changed her mind.

On the way back to the cottage Paul said carefully, 'You'll like Diana—she is a marvellous organiser. She has no need to work and it surprises me that she hasn't married—she's quite lovely, isn't she?'

'She's beautiful,' said Emma. 'Have you been friends for a long time?'

'Two or three years, I suppose. We met at a friend's house and found that we had a good deal in common.'

Emma kept her voice pleasant. 'Instant rapport—that's what it's called, isn't it? You meet someone and feel as though you've known them all your life...' She added before he could reply, 'I'm sure I shall enjoy giving a hand—thank you for thinking of it, Paul.'

'I wondered if you were becoming bored with life—I'm not at home much, am I?'

She said cheerfully, 'Well, I didn't expect you to be—doctors never are, are they?'

That evening he asked her if she would like to spend a weekend with his parents. 'Next weekend I'm free. We could drive up on Saturday afternoon and come back on the Sunday evening.'

'I'd like that.'

But first there was the nursery. She drove there in the Mini and within ten minutes, wrapped in a plastic pinny, she was bathing a very small baby in a room where five other babies were awaiting her attention.

Diana Pearson, elegant and beautiful, sitting behind her desk, had greeted her pleasantly but without warmth. 'Hello, Emma—so you have turned up. So many volunteer ladies change their minds at the last minute. Will you go to the end nursery and start bathings? Someone will be along to give you a hand presently.'

Emma had waited for more information but Diana had smiled vaguely and bent her head over the papers before her. At least she'd been credited with enough good sense to find her own way around, reflected

Emma, and anyway she'd met another girl on the way to the nursery, who'd shown her where to find a pinny before hurrying off in the opposite direction.

Emma, not easily flurried, had found the pinny, assembled all that she needed to deal with the babies and picked up the first one...

She had just picked up the second baby, a small, wizened creature, bawling his head off, tiny fists balled in rage, eyes screwed up tightly, when she was joined by a middle-aged woman with a sour expression.

'New, are you?' she wanted to know as she tied her pinny. 'What's yer name?'

Not a local woman, thought Emma, and said pleasantly, 'Emma—Emma Wyatt, and yes, I'm new. I hope you'll tell me when I do something wrong.'

'You bet I will. 'Ere, you that Professor Wyatt's wife?'

'Yes, I am.'

'Well, don't expect me ter call yer 'yer ladyship', 'cos I'm not going to.'

'I'd like it if you'd call me Emma.'

The woman looked surprised. 'OK, I'm Maisie.' She picked up the third baby and began to take off its gown with surprisingly gentle hands. 'He's the worst of the bunch you've got there,' she observed. 'Proper little imp, 'e is—always shouting 'is 'ead off.'

Emma looked down at the scrap on her lap; he had stopped crying and was glaring at her from bright blue eyes. 'He's rather sweet...'

Maisie gave a cackle of laughter. 'Your first day, isn't

it? Wait till you've been 'ere a couple of months—that's if you last as long as that.'

'Why do you say that?'

'You'll find out for yerself—Madam there, sitting in her office, doing nothin'—that is, until someone comes along. Pulls the wool nicely over their eyes, that she does. That 'usband of yours—she's 'ad her sights on 'im this last year or more. 'Ad her nose put out of joint and no mistake.' She was pinning a nappy with an expertise Emma envied. 'Better watch out, you 'ad.'

The baby, freshly bathed and gowned, looked up at Emma with interest; she picked him up and tucked his small head under her chin and cuddled him.

''Ere, there ain't no time for cuddling—leastways not in the mornings—there's the feeds to do next.'

So Emma put him back in his cot and set to work on the fourth baby, a placid girl who blew bubbles and waved her small arms at her. Maisie had finished before her; she was already feeding the first baby by the time Emma had tidied everything away and fetched her three bottles from the little pantry.

When the infants had been fed and lay sleeping it off, she and Maisie had to tidy the nursery, put everything ready for the afternoon and then go and have their coffee. They sat together in the small room set aside for them and Emma listened to Maisie's numerous tips about the work.

'Have you been here long?' she asked.

'Upwards of two years. It's a job, see. Me old man scarpered off and the kids are at school all day—keeps me mind off things.'

She blew on her coffee and took a gulp. 'You going ter stick it out? It's not everyone's cup of tea.'

'Well, I like babies,' said Emma, 'and my husband's away almost all day. He told me that Miss Pearson was short-handed and asked if I'd like to help out, so I'll stay for as long as I'm needed. I only come twice a week.'

Maisie eyed her thoughtfully over her mug. 'Persuaded 'im, she did? Men—blind as bats! Never mind the "lady this" and "lady that"—you're a nice young woman, so keep those eyes of yours peeled.'

'Thank you for your advice. Shall I see you on Thursday?'

'Yep. Me, I come every morning—oftener if it gets really busy. Some of the babies will be going back to their mums tomorrow—bin waiting for an 'ouse or flat or whatever, yer see.'

'I hope the same babies will be here when I come on Thursday.'

'Well, Charlie—that's the little 'owler—e'll be with us for a while yet. 'Is mum's in prison for a couple of months—won't 'ave 'im near 'er.'

'Why ever not?'

'Dunno; bit flighty, I dare say.' She put down her mug. 'We gotta bag the wash before we go.'

Diana came out of the office as Emma took off her pinny. 'Going? See you on Thursday and many thanks. Oh, would you ask Paul to call in some time? I need his advice about one of the toddlers—a congenital dislocation of the hip—I think the splint needs adjusting.'

'I'll tell him,' said Emma. 'I'm sure he'll come when he has the time.'

Diana laughed. 'He usually comes whenever I ask him to, whether he's busy or not—we're old friends.'

Emma dredged up a smile. 'That's nice—I'll see you on Thursday.'

She drove back home, ate the lunch Mrs Parfitt had ready for her and then took the dogs for a long walk. She had a great deal to think about.

'It's a good thing I'm married to him,' she told Willy, who was loitering beside her. 'I mean, it's an advantage, if you see what I mean—and I love him. The point is, does he love her? That's something I have to find out. But if he does why did he marry me?' She stopped and Kate came lumbering back to see why. 'If it was out of pity...?' She sounded so fierce that Willy gave a whimper.

Paul was home for tea, which surprised her. 'How nice,' she said, and beamed at him. 'Have you had a busy day?'

'I've beds at the children's hospital and an out-patients clinic at Honiton; I seem to have spent a lot of my time driving from here to there.' He bit into one of Mrs Parfitt's scones. 'Tell me, did you enjoy your morning?'

'Very much. I bathed three babies and fed them. There was someone else there in the nursery—a nice woman who was very friendly and helpful. Oh, and Diana says could you go and see the baby with the dislocated hip? She thinks the splint needs changing.'

'It'll have to be tomorrow evening. I've a list in the morning and a ward-round in the afternoon and a couple of private patients to see after that.'

'Where do you see them?'

'I've rooms in Southernhay. I'll phone Diana presently and tell her when I'll be free.'

'I'll ask Mrs Parfitt to make dinner a bit later, shall I?'

'Yes, do that if you will. Did you take the dogs out?'

'Yes, it was lovely on the moor. After all it is summer.'

'That doesn't mean to say we shan't get some shockingly bad weather.' He got up. 'I've some phoning to do, then I'll take the dogs for ten minutes.' He smiled at her. 'You must tell me more about the nursery when I get back.'

The following evening he phoned at teatime to say that he would be home later than he had expected and that she wasn't to wait dinner for him. 'I'll get something here,' he told her.

She gave him a cheerful answer and spent the rest of the evening imagining him and Diana dining together at some quiet restaurant. She knew it was silly to do so but she seemed unable to think of anything else.

Perhaps it wasn't so silly either, she told herself, lying in bed later, waiting for the sound of the car and dropping off to sleep at last without having heard it.

He was already at the table when she went down to breakfast. He wished her good morning. 'You don't mind if I get on? I've a busy day ahead.'

'Did you have a busy time last night?' She kept her voice casually interested.

'Yes. I trust I didn't disturb you when I got back?'

'Will you go and see the baby today? Do you want me to give Diana a message?'

He gave her a thoughtful look. 'No need. I saw her yesterday.'

'Oh, good,' said Emma, bashing her boiled egg, wishing it was Diana.

Chapter 7

Diana's greeting when Emma reached the nursery was friendly. It was as though she was trying to erase her rather cool manner towards her; she asked if she was quite happy with the babies, if she would like to alter her hours and expressed the hope that she wasn't too tired at the end of her morning's work. Emma took all this with a pinch of salt, not convinced by all this charm that Diana was going to like her—and, anyway, she didn't like Diana.

It was refreshing, after all that sweetness, to listen to Maisie's down-to-earth talk, which covered everything under the sun—the royal family, the government, the price of fish and chips and the goings-on of the young couple who had rented rooms beneath hers—and all the while she talked she attended to the babies, raising her voice above their small cries.

They had finished the bathing and were feeding them when she said, 'Your old man was 'ere yesterday—late too.'

Emma was feeding Charlie, who was content for once, sucking at his bottle as though it would be torn from him at any moment. 'Yes, I know,' she said quietly.

Maisie turned her head to look at her. 'You're a quiet one, but I bet me last penny you'll get the better of 'er.'

'Yes, I believe I shall,' said Emma, and smiled down at Charlie's small face. He wasn't a pretty baby—he was too pale and thin for that. It was to be hoped that when his mother claimed him once more—if she ever did— he'd look more like a baby and not a cross old man. She kissed the top of his head and gave him a quick cuddle and then put him over her shoulder so that he could bring up his wind.

It was after they had had dinner together that evening that Paul told her that he was going to Boston in two days' time.

Emma said, 'Boston? You mean Boston, USA?'

'Yes, and then on to New York, Philadelphia and Chicago. I shall be away for ten days, perhaps a little longer.' He said, carefully casual, 'I expect the trip would be a bit boring for you.'

She was quick to decide that he didn't want her with him. 'Yes, I think it might be,' she said. 'Will you be lecturing?'

She looked to see if he was disappointed but his face gave nothing away. 'If you need help of any sort, phone John Taggart, my solicitor; he'll sort things out for you. I've opened an account for you at my bank—I have also arranged for a joint account but I'd like you to have your own money. The house agent phoned to say that he has a possible buyer for your house; send everything to John—he'll deal with it.'

'The dogs will miss you,' said Emma. She would miss him too, but she wasn't going to tell him that. 'There's a card from the Frobishers—they've asked us to dinner. I'll write and explain, shall I?'

'Yes, do that. Suggest we take up their invitation when I get back.'

It was all very business-like and she did her best to match her manner to his. 'Shall I write to your mother and tell her that we shan't be coming for the weekend?'

'I phoned her last night. They are very sorry not to be seeing us.'

'I could drive myself...'

'I'd prefer you not to, Emma.'

The cottage seemed very quiet when he had gone. Emma couldn't bear to be in it and took the dogs for a long walk on the moor; they walked for miles and the austere vastness of it made his absence bearable. 'It's only for just over a week,' she told the dogs. 'But how shall I bear to be away from him for so long?'

A problem solved for her by Diana, who, when Emma went on Tuesday as usual, asked her if she could manage to help out for a third morning.

'We're so short of staff, I don't know which way to turn. I'm so glad that Paul didn't want you to go with him.' She laughed gently. 'Wives can be a bit of an encumbrance sometimes. It was so wise of him to marry someone like you, Emma.'

Emma asked why.

'Well, you're not demanding, are you? You're content to sit at home and wait for him to come back—just what he needed...'

Emma said, 'Yes, I think it is. He leads a busy life.'

Diana laughed again. 'Yes, but he always has time for his friends. He and I have such a lot in common.'

'I expect you have,' said Emma sweetly, 'but not marriage.' Her smile was as sweet as her voice. 'I'll get started on the babies,' she said.

Maisie, already at work with her three, looked up as she went into the nursery. ''Ello, Emma, what's riled you? 'As her 'igh and mightiness been tearing yer off a strip?'

'No—just a slight difference of opinion. I'm going to do an extra morning, Maisie; I hope you'll be here too.'

'Come every day, don't I, love? I'll be here. So'll Charlie there, from wot I 'eard. 'Is mum don't really want 'im, poor little beggar.'

'What will happen to him?' Emma was lifting him from his cot; he was bawling as usual.

'Foster-mum if they can find one, or an orphanage...'

'He's so small...'

'Plenty more like 'im,' said Maisie. 'Maybe there'll be someone who don't mind a bad-tempered kid.'

'Well, I'd be bad-tempered if I were he,' said Emma, smiling down at the cross little face on her lap. 'Who's a lovely boy, then?' she said.

She thought of Paul constantly, and when he phoned from Boston that night she went around in a cloud of content which was, however, quickly dispelled when she went into the nursery the next day.

'Heard from Paul?' asked Diana, with a friendly concern Emma didn't trust.

'Well, yes. He phoned yesterday evening…'

'He always does.' Diana smiled at Emma—a small secret smile, suggesting that words weren't necessary.

She had no right to be jealous, reflected Emma, bathing a belligerent Charlie, for she had no hold on Paul's feelings, had she? He had wanted a companion and the kind of wife to suit his lifestyle. He had never promised love…

That afternoon when she took the dogs on to the moor she saw the clouds piling up over the tors and felt the iciness of the wind. Bad weather was on the way, and even though it was summer the moor could be bleak and cold. She turned for home and was thankful for the bright fire in the drawing-room and the delicious tea Mrs Parfitt had ready for her.

Diana came out of her office as she arrived at the nursery on Thursday. 'Emma, I'm so glad to see you. You know the moor well, don't you? There's a party of travellers camping somewhere near Fernworthy Reservoir— one of them phoned me. We've one of their toddlers here already and he says there are several children sick—not ill enough for the doctor—colds, he thinks, and perhaps flu. He asked me to send someone with blankets, baby food and cough medicine. I wonder if you would go? It's not far but a bit out of the way. Perhaps you can get them to come off the moor until the weather gets warmer again.'

'Yes, of course I'll go. I'll phone Mrs Parfitt, though, so that she can take the dogs out if I'm not back.'

Mrs Parfitt didn't fancy the idea at all. 'Sir Paul would never allow it,' she demurred. 'You going off on your own like that.'

'I'll be gone for an hour or two,' said Emma. 'It's not far away, you know...'

Mrs Parfitt snorted. 'Maybe not, madam, but it's so isolated it could be the North Pole.'

It wasn't quite the North Pole but it was certainly isolated. Emma had a job finding the camp, tucked away from the narrow road which led to nowhere but the reservoir. When she found it eventually it took quite a time to unload the blankets and baby food and hand them over.

There were half a dozen broken-down buses and vans drawn up in a semicircle and their owners clamoured for her attention as she was led from one to another ramshackle vehicle. In one of them she found a sick baby—too ill to cry. 'She's ill,' she told the young woman who was with her. 'She needs medical attention—will you bring her to the nursery? I'll take you now...'

The girl needed a lot of persuading. ''Tis only a cold,' she told Emma. 'There's half a dozen kids as bad. Come in and look if you don't believe me.'

She was right. There were more than half a dozen, though—some of them small babies. Emma, although no nurse, could recognise the signs of whooping cough when she saw it. It would need several ambulances to take them to the nursery. 'Look,' she said to one of the older women, 'I haven't room to take them all, but I'll go back now and send an ambulance for them.'

They gathered round her, all talking at once, but at last she got back into the Mini, with the baby and its mother in the back, and began her journey back to Moretonhampstead. As Diana had said, it wasn't far, but the road was narrow and winding and little used and there were no houses or farms in sight. She was glad when they reached the nursery and she could hand the baby and mother over to Diana.

It was Maisie who led them away while Emma explained to Diana that there were more babies and toddlers needing help. 'An ambulance?' she suggested. 'They are really quite ill and it's so cold for them.'

Diana frowned. 'Wait here. I'll see if I can get help. Go and have a cup of coffee; you must need one.'

When Emma returned Diana shook her head. 'Would you believe it, there's nothing to be had until tomorrow morning—it's not urgent you see...'

'But they need more baby food and someone to clean them up—nappies and warm clothes.'

Diana appeared to think. 'Look, I wouldn't ask it of everyone but you're so sensible, Emma. If I get more stuff packed up would you take it back? Why not go back to Lustleigh and pack an overnight bag just in case you feel you can't leave them? I'll get a doctor to them as soon as I can and you can go straight home once he's got organised.'

'You're sure there's no one available?'

'Quite sure. There's a flap on with a major road accident—whooping cough just doesn't count.'

Emma was only half listening, which was a pity for then she might have queried that, but she was worried about the babies wheezing and gasping, so far from the care they needed. She said, 'All right, I'll go. I wish Paul were here...'

'Oh, my dear, so do I. He's such a tower of strength— we have been so close.' Diana's voice was soft and sad. 'We still are and I know you won't mind; it isn't as if you love each other.' She turned away and dabbed at a dry eye. 'You see, his work is all-important to him; he cannot afford to be distracted by the all-embracing love I—' She choked and took a long breath. 'Of course, he has explained all that to you—he told me how understanding you were.'

Emma said, 'I'd better be on my way,' and left without another word.

She went over the conversation word for word as she drove back to the cottage, and although she hated Diana she had to admit that it was all probably true. Paul didn't love her; he liked her enough to marry her, though, knowing that she would provide the calm background his arduous work demanded, whereas Diana's flamboyant nature would have distracted him.

It was well into the afternoon by now, and the sky was threatening rain. She hurried into the cottage, explained to Mrs Parfitt that she might not get back that night and ran upstairs to push essentials into a shoulder-bag. Mrs Parfitt came after her. 'You didn't ought to go,' she said worriedly. 'Whatever will Sir Paul say when he hears?'

'Well, he doesn't need to know. I'm only going to the reservoir, and don't worry, Mrs Parfitt, there'll be a doctor there tomorrow and I'll come home.' She turned to look at the faithful creature. 'Think of those babies—they really need some help.'

'Sir Paul wouldn't let you go, ma'am, but since you won't listen to me at least you'll have a bowl of soup and a nice strong cup of tea.'

Emma, who hadn't had her lunch, agreed, wolfed down the soup and some of Mrs Parfitt's home-made bread, drank several cups of tea and got back into the car. It was raining now and the wind had got up. She waved goodbye to Mrs Parfitt and Willy and Kate and drove back to the nursery.

It was amazing how much could be packed into the Mini; it was amazing too how helpful Diana was. 'Don't worry,' she told Emma. 'Someone will be with you just as soon as possible.'

She waved goodbye as Emma drove away, then went into the office and picked up the phone. 'There's no hurry to send anyone out to that camp on the moor. I've sent everything they need and the girl who is taking the stuff is sensible and capable. I'll let you know more in the morning!'

Emma was still a mile or so from the reservoir when she saw the first wisps of mist creeping towards her, and five minutes later she was in the thick of it. It was eddying to and fro so that for a moment she could see ahead and then the next was completely enshrouded.

She had been caught in the moorland mists before now; to a stranger they were frightening but she had

learnt to take them in her stride. All the same, she was
relieved when she saw the rough track leading to the
camp and bumped her way along it until the first of the
buses loomed out of the mist. The mist had brought Sty-
gian gloom with it and she was glad to see the lights
shining from the open doorways. As she got out several
of the campers came to surround her.

They were friendly—happy in the way they lived,
making nothing of its drawbacks—but now they were
anxious about the babies and Emma, taken to see them,
was anxious too. No expert, she could still see that they
were as ill as the one she had taken to the nursery. She
handed out the blankets, baby food and bags of nappies, drank the mug of strong tea she was offered and
prepared to return.

The mist had thickened by now and it was almost
dark—to find her way wouldn't be easy or particularly
safe; she would have to stay where she was until the
morning and, since there were hours to get through,
she could curl up in the back of the Mini for the night.
She helped with the babies, looking at their small white
faces and listening to their harsh breathing and hoping
that, despite the awful weather, an ambulance or at least
a doctor would come to their aid.

No one came, however, so she shared supper with
one of the families and, after a last worried look at the
babies, wrapped herself in a blanket and curled up on
the Mini's back seat. It was a tight fit and she was cold,
and the thin wails of the babies prevented her from
sleeping, and when she at last lightly dozed off she was

awakened almost immediately by one of the men with a mug of tea.

The mist had lifted. She scrambled up, tidied herself as best she could and got back into the car. If she drove round the reservoir and took the lane on the other side she would reach a hamlet, isolated but surely with a telephone. She explained what she was going to do and set off into the cold, bleak morning.

It was beginning to rain and there was a strong wind blowing; summer, for the moment, was absent. The lane was rutted and thick with mud and there was no question of hurrying. She saw with relief a couple of houses ahead of her and then a good-sized farm.

There was a phone. The farmer, already up, took her into the farmhouse when she explained, and shook his head. 'They'm foolish folk,' he observed. 'Only just there, I reckon. Leastways they weren't there when I was checking the sheep a few days ago.' He was a kindly man. 'Reckon you'd enjoy a cuppa?'

'Oh, I'd love one, but if I might phone first? The babies do need to go into care as quickly as possible.'

A cheerful West Country voice answered her. They'd be there right away, she was told, just let her sit tight till they came. Much relieved, she drank her tea, thanked the farmer and drove back to tell the travellers that help was on the way.

'Likely they'll move us on,' said one woman.

'It's common land, isn't it? I dare say they'll let you stay as long as the babies are taken care of. I expect they'll take them to hospital and transfer them to the nursery until they are well again. You'll be able to see them whenever you all want to. Some of you may want to go with them.' She looked around her. 'I can give three of you lifts, if you like.'

One of the younger women offered to go.

'How ever will you get back?' asked Emma.

'Thumb a lift and walk the last bit—no problem.'

The ambulance came then, and Emma stood aside while the paramedics took over. They lifted the babies into the ambulance presently, offered the young woman who was to have gone with Emma a seat, and drove away. That left her free to go at last. No one wanted a lift—they were content to wait and see what the young woman would tell them when she got back. Emma got into her car and drove home, to be met at the door by an agitated Mrs Parfitt.

'You're fit to drop,' she scolded kindly. 'In you come, madam, and straight into a nice, hot bath while I get your breakfast. Like as not you've caught your death of cold.'

Not quite death, as it turned out, but for the moment she was very tired and shivery. The bath was bliss, and so were breakfast and the warm bed she got into afterwards.

'I must ring the nursery,' she said worriedly, and began to get out of bed again, to Queenie's annoyance.

'I'll do that,' said Mrs Parfitt. 'No good going there for a day or two, and so I'll tell that Miss Pearson.'

'I'm not ill,' said Emma peevishly, and fell asleep.

She woke hours later with a head stuffed with cotton wool and a sore thorat and crept downstairs, to be instantly shooed back to her bed by Mrs Parfitt bearing hot lemon and some paracetamol.

'It's more than my job's worth, Lady Wyatt, to let you get up. Sir Paul would send me packing.'

Emma, aware that Mrs Parfitt only called her Lady Wyatt when she was severely put out, meekly got back into bed.

'Did you phone the nursery?' she croaked.

'I did, and there is no need for you to go in until you are free of your cold. You'd only give it to the babies.' Mrs Parfitt eyed her anxiously. 'I wonder if I should get the doctor to you, ma'am?'

'No, no—it's only a cold; I'll be fine in a day or two.'

Sir Paul, back from his travels, drove himself straight to the hospital, listened impatiently to his senior registrar's litany of things which had gone wrong during his absence and then, eager to get back home, phoned his secretary, who read out a formidable list of patients waiting for his services.

'Give me a day?' he begged her. 'I've a short list on the day after tomorrow. I'll come to my rooms in the afternoon—I leave it to you...'

He was about to ring off when she stopped him. 'Sir Paul, Miss Pearson phoned several times, and said it was most urgent that she should see you as soon as you got back.'

He frowned. 'Why didn't she speak to my registrar?'

'I don't know, sir; she sounded upset.'

'I'll call in on my way home.'

He was tired; he wanted to go home and see Emma, watch her face light up when she saw him. She might not love him but she was always happy to be with him. He smiled as he got out of the car and went along to Diana's office.

He might be tired but good manners necessitated his cheerful greeting. 'You wanted to see me; is it very urgent? I'm now on my way home.'

'I had to see you first,' said Diana. She was, for her, very quiet and serious. 'It's about Emma. Oh, don't worry, she's not ill, but I'm so upset. You see, she went dashing off; she simply wouldn't listen…'

Sir Paul sat down. 'Start at the beginning,' he said quietly.

Which was just what Diana had hoped he would say. She began to tell him her version of what had happened and, because she was a clever young woman, it all sounded true.

Sir Paul let himself into his house quietly, took off his coat and, since there were no lights on in the drawing-room, went to the little sitting-room at the back of the house. Emma was there, with Queenie on her lap and the dogs draped over her feet.

When he walked in she turned round, saw who it was, flew to her feet and ran across to him in a flurry of animals. 'Paul—you're back!' Her voice was still hoarse, and her nose pink from constant blowing, and it was a silly thing to say but she couldn't hide her delight.

He closed the door behind him and stood leaning against it, and it was only then that she realised that he was in a rage. His mouth was a thin hard line and his eyes were cold.

'What possessed you to behave in such a foolish manner?' he wanted to know. 'Why all the melodrama? What are the ambulances for? Or the police, for that matter? What in the name of heaven possessed you, Emma? To go racing off on to the moor in bad weather, sending dramatic messages, spending the night in a God-forsaken camp. Ignoring Diana's pleading to wait and give her time to phone for help. No, you must race away like a heroine in a novel, bent on self-glory.'

Emma said in a shaky voice, 'But Diana—'

'Diana is worth a dozen of you.'

It was a remark which stopped her from uttering another word.

'We'll talk later,' said Sir Paul, and went away to his study and sat down behind his desk, his dogs at his feet. He'd been too hard on her; he tried not to think of her white, puzzled face with its pink nose, but he had been full of rage, thinking of all those things which could have happened to her. 'The little idiot,' he told the dogs. 'I could wring her darling neck.'

Emma gave herself ten minutes to stop shaking, then went in search of Mrs Parfitt. 'Sir Paul's home,' she told her. 'Can we stretch dinner for three?'

Mrs Parfitt gave her a thoughtful look, but all she said was, 'I'll grill some more cutlets and shall I serve a soup first? No doubt he's hungry after that journey.'

'That would be fine, Mrs Parfitt. I dare say he's famished. Could we have dinner quite soon?'

'Half an hour, ma'am—gives him time to have a drink and stretch out in his study.'

Emma went to her room, re-did her face and pinned her hair back rather more severely than usual, and then practised a few expressions in the looking-glass—a look of interest, a cool aloofness—she liked that one best...

Downstairs again, in the drawing-room, she picked up her tapestry work and began poking the needle in and out in a careless fashion, practising cool aloofness. She succeeded so well that when Paul came into the room intent on making his peace with her he changed his mind at once—the look she cast him was as effective as a barbed wire fence.

All the same, after a moment or two he essayed some kind of a conversation while he wondered how best to get back on a friendly footing once more.

Emma, her hurt and anger almost a physical pain, had no intention of allowing him to do that. She sat, mangling her needlework most dreadfully, silent except when it was absolutely necessary to say yes or no.

They had their dinner in silence, and as they got up from the table Paul said, 'I think we should have a talk, Emma.'

She paused on her way to the door. 'No, I have understood you very well, Paul; there is no need to say it all over again.'

'Do I take it that you don't wish to work at the nursery any more?'

Her eyes were very large in her pale face. 'I shall go tomorrow morning as usual. Why not?'

His cold, 'Just as you wish,' was as icy as her own manner.

At breakfast she treated him with a frigid politeness which infuriated him—asking him if he would be late home, reminding him that they were due to attend a dinner party on the following evening and wishing him a cool goodbye as he got up to go.

When he had gone she allowed her rigid mouth to droop. She supposed that in a while they would return to their easy-going relationship, but it wouldn't be the same—he had believed Diana, he had mocked her attempts at helping the travellers and, worst of all, he hadn't asked her if any of the things Diana had told him were true. So, if his opinion of her was so low why had he married her? To provide a screen of respectability so that he and Diana could continue as they were? So why hadn't he married her?

Emma's thoughts swirled around in her tired head and didn't make sense. All she did know was that Diana had lied about her and Paul had listened willingly. She didn't think that Diana would expect her back but she was going. Moreover, she would behave as though nothing unusual had occurred, only now she would be on her guard. It was a pity that she had fallen in love with Paul but, since she had, there was nothing more she could do about it—only make sure that Diana didn't get him.

Her imagination working overtime, Emma took herself off to the clinic.

It was a source of satisfaction actually to see that Diana was actually surprised and a little uncomfortable when she walked in.

'Emma—I didn't expect you. You're sure you feel up to it? I heard that you had a heavy cold.'

'Not as heavy as all that. I'll wear a mask, shall I? Are there any new babies?'

Diana's eyes slid away from hers. 'Three from that camp. They're in isolation—whooping cough. They were in a pretty poor way, you know.' She added casually, 'I hear that Paul is back?'

'Yes, didn't he come to see you? I thought he might have popped in on his way home. He's got a busy day—I dare say he'll do his best to call in this evening. I'd better get on with the bathings or I'll have Maisie on my tail.'

Maisie was already busy with the first of her three babies. She looked up as Emma wrapped her pinny round her and got everything ready before picking up Charlie, who was bawling as he always did.

'I heard a lot,' said Maisie. 'Most of which I don't believe. You look like something the cat's dragged in.'

'As bad as that? And I don't think you need to believe any of it, Maisie.'

'You're a right plucky un coming back 'ere. I couldn't 'elp but 'ear wot madam was saying—being busy outside the office door as it were. And that 'usband of yours coming out like a bullet from a gun, ready to do murder. If 'e'd been a bit calmer I'd 'ave spoke up. But 'e almost knocks me over, sets me back on me feet and all without a word. 'E's got a nasty temper and no mistake.'

They sat in silence for a few minutes, then Maisie asked, 'Going to tell 'er awf, are yer?' She scowled. 'I could tell a few tales about 'er if you don't.'

'No—please, Maisie, don't do that. There's a reason...'

'Oh, yeah? Well, yer knows best, but if yer want any 'elp you just ask old Maisie.'

'I certainly will, and thank you, Maisie. I can't explain but I have to wait and see...'

'You're worth a dozen of 'er,' said Maisie, which brought a great knot of tears into Emma's throat, so that she had to bury her face in the back of Charlie's small neck until she had swallowed them back where they belonged.

Sir Paul came home late that evening and Emma, beyond asking politely if he had had a busy day, forbore from wanting to know where he had been. Anyway, Maisie, who was at the nursery for most of the day, would tell her soon enough if he had been to see Diana.

They exchanged polite remarks during dinner and then he went to his study, only coming to the drawing-room as she was folding away her tapestry. Sir Paul, a man of moral and physical courage, quailed under her stony glance and frosty goodnight.

Where, he asked himself, was his enchanting little Emma, so anxious to please, always so friendly and so unaware of his love? He had behaved badly towards her, but couldn't she understand that it was because he had been so appalled at the idea of her going off on her own like that? Perhaps Diana had exaggerated a little; he would go and see her again.

Emma wasn't going to the nursery the following morning. She took the dogs for a long walk and spent an agreeable half-hour deciding which dress she would wear to the dinner party. It was to be rather a grand affair, at one of the lovely old manor-houses on the outskirts of the village, and she wanted to make a good impression.

She had decided to wear the silver-grey dress with the long sleeves and modest neckline, deceptively simple but making the most of her charming shape. She would wear the pearls too, and do her hair in the coil the hairdresser had shown her how to manage on her own.

She had changed and was waiting rather anxiously for Paul to come home by the time he opened the door. She bade him good evening, warned him that he had less than half an hour in which to shower and change, and offered him tea.

He had taken off his coat and was standing in the doorway. 'Emma—I went to the camp this afternoon—'

She cut him short gently. 'You must tell me about it—but not now, you haven't time...'

He didn't move. 'I went to see Diana too.'

'Well, yes, I quite understand about that, but I don't want to talk about it, if you don't mind.' She added in a wifely voice, 'We're going to be late.'

He turned away and went upstairs and presently came down again, immaculate in his dinner-jacket, his face impassive, and courteously attentive to her needs.

They left the cottage, got into the car and drove the few miles to the party.

It was a pleasant evening; Emma knew several of the people there and, seated between two elderly gentlemen bent on flattering her, she began to enjoy herself. Paul, watching her from the other end of the table, thought how pretty she had grown in the last few weeks. When they got home he would ask her about her night in the camp.

The men and women he had talked to there had been loud in her praise.

'Saved the kids lives,' one young man had said. 'Acted prompt, she did—and gave an 'and with cleaning 'em up too. Didn't turn a hair—took our little un and 'er mum back with 'er and then came back in that perishing fog—couldn't see yer 'and in front of yer face. Proper little lady, she were.'

He bent his handsome head to listen to what his dinner partner was talking about—something to do with her sciatica. He assumed his listening face; being a bone man, his knowledge of that illness was rudimentary, but he nodded and looked sympathetic while he wondered once again if Diana had exaggerated and why Emma hadn't told him her side of the story.

He glanced down the table once more and squashed a desire to get out of his chair, pick her up out of hers and carry her off home. The trouble was that they didn't see enough of each other.

Chapter 8

'A very pleasant evening,' observed Sir Paul as they drove home.

'Delightful,' agreed Emma. It was fortunate that it was a short journey for there didn't seem to be anything else to say, and once they were at home she bade him a quiet goodnight and took herself off to bed. As she went up the stairs she hoped against hope that he would leap after her, beg her forgiveness... Of course he did no such thing!

In the morning when she went downstairs she found him on the point of leaving. 'I'll have to rearrange my day,' he told her. 'There's a patient—an emergency—for Theatre, so the list will run late. I'll probably be home around six o'clock, perhaps later. Don't forget that we are going to Mother's for the weekend.'

'Shall I take the dogs out?'

He was already through the door. 'I walked them earlier.' He nodded a goodbye and drove away as Mrs Parfitt came out of the kitchen.

'Sir Paul will knock himself out,' she observed, 'tearing off without a proper breakfast, up half the night working, and down here this morning before six o'clock, walking his legs off with those dogs.' She shook her head. 'I never did.'

Emma said, 'It's an emergency...'

'Maybe it is, but he didn't ought to go gallivanting around before dawn after being up half the night—he's only flesh and blood like the rest of us.' She bent her gaze on Emma. 'Now you come and have your breakfast, ma'am; you look as though you could do with a bit of feeding up.'

When Emma got to the nursery she found Diana waiting for her.

'Emma, did Paul remember to tell you that I am giving a little party next week? Tuesday, I thought—it's one of his less busy days.'

She smiled, and Emma said, 'No, but we were out to dinner until late and he left early for the hospital.'

'Yes, I know,' said Diana, who didn't but somehow she made it sound like the truth. 'He works too hard; he'll overdo things if he's not careful. I'll try and persuade him to ease off a bit.'

'I think you can leave that to me, Diana. You know, you're so—so motherly you should find a husband.' Emma's smile was sweet. 'Well, I'll get started.'

She wished Maisie good morning and Maisie said, 'You're smouldering again. Been 'aving words?'

'I'm afraid so. I'm turning into a very unpleasant person, Maisie.'

'Not you—proper little lady, you are. Don't meet many of 'em these days. Now, that young woman downstairs…' She branched off into an account of the goings-on of the young couple on the landing below her flat and Emma forgot her seething rage and laughed a little.

'Doing anything nice this weekend?' asked Maisie as they sat feeding the babies.

'We're going to spend it with my husband's parents.'

'Like that, will you?'

'Oh, yes, they're such dears, and it's a nice old house with a large garden. What are you going to do, Maisie? It's your weekend off, isn't it?'

'S'right.' Maisie looked coy. 'I got a bloke—'e's the milkman; we get on proper nice. Been courting me for a bit, 'e 'as, and we're thinking of having a go…'

'Oh, Maisie, how lovely. You're going to marry him?'

'I ain't said yes, mind you, but it'll be nice not ter 'ave ter come 'ere day in day out, with Madam looking down her nose at me.'

'You'll be able to stay home—oh, Maisie, I am glad; you must say yes. Does he got on well with your family?'

'They get on a treat. Yer don't think I'm silly?'

'Silly? To marry a man who wants you, who'll give you a home and learn to be a father to the children. Of course it's not silly. It's the nicest thing I've heard for days.'

'Oh, well, p'raps I will. Yer're 'appy, ain't yer?'

Emma was bending over Charlie's cot, tucking him in. 'Yes, Maisie.'

'Me, I'd be scared to be married to Sir Paul, that I would—never know what 'e's thinking. 'E don't show 'is feelings, do 'e?'

'Perhaps not, but they are there all the same.'

'Well, you should know,' said Maisie, and chuckled.

The weather was still bad later on, so Emma walked the dogs briefly and went home to sit by the fire. She had a lot to think about; Diana seemed very confident that Paul was in love with her and he had said nothing to give the lie to that, and there was that one remark that she would never forget—that she was worth twelve of Emma. 'Oh, well,' she told the dogs, 'we'll go to this party and see what happens.'

She was glad that they were going away for the weekend, for two days spent alone with Paul, keeping up a façade of friendliness, was rather more than she felt she could cope with. She packed a pretty dress, got into her skirt and one of her cashmere jumpers, made up her face carefully and declared herself ready to go directly after breakfast on Saturday.

It was easier in the car, for she could admire the scenery and there was no need to talk even though she longed to. She sat watching his hands on the wheel— large, capable hands, well-kept. She loved them; she loved the rest of him too and she wasn't going to sit back tamely and let Diana dazzle him...

His parents welcomed them warmly, sweeping them

indoors while the dogs went racing off into the garden. 'And where is Queenie?' asked Mrs Wyatt.

'She's happy with Mrs Parfitt and they're company for each other.'

'Of course. You're quite well again after that cold? We missed seeing you while Paul was away. Such a shame. Never mind, we'll make the most of you while you are here. Let Paul take your coat, my dear, and come and sit down and have some coffee.'

It was Mrs Wyatt who asked her how she had come to catch cold. 'Paul tells me that you work twice a week in a nursery in Moretonhampstead; I dare say you caught it there.'

Emma didn't look at Paul. She murmured something and waited to see if he would tell them how she had caught a cold. He remained silent. As well he might, she reflected crossly as he stood there looking faintly amused. Really, he was a most tiresome man; if she hadn't loved him so much she would have disliked him intensely.

There might have been an awkward pause if he hadn't, with the ease of good manners, made some trifling remark about the weather. Smooth, thought Emma, and went pink when her mother-in-law said, 'Well, cold or no cold, I must say that marriage suits you, my dear.'

Emma put her coffee-cup down with care and wished that she didn't blush so easily. Blushing, she felt sure, had gone out with the coming of women's lib and feminism, whatever that was exactly. Mrs Wyatt, being of an older generation, wasn't concerned with either and found the blush entirely suitable.

Paul found it enchanting.

The weekend passed too quickly.

No one would ever replace her mother, but Mrs Wyatt helped to fill the emptiness her mother had left, and if she noticed the careful way Emma and Paul avoided any of the usual ways of the newly wed she said nothing.

Paul had never worn his heart on his sleeve but his feelings ran deep and, unless her maternal instinct was at fault, he was deeply in love with Emma. And Emma with him, she was sure of that. They had probably had one of the many little tiffs they would have before they settled down, she decided.

'You must come again soon,' she begged them as they took their leave on Sunday evening.

It was late by the time they reached the cottage, which gave Emma the excuse to go to bed at once. Paul's 'Goodnight, my dear,' was uttered in a placid voice, and he added that there was no need for her to get up for breakfast if she didn't feel like it. 'I shall be away all day,' he said. 'I've several private patients to see after I've finished at the hospital.'

In bed, sitting against the pillows with her knees under her chin, Emma told Queenie, 'This can't go on, you know; something must be done.'

The Fates had come to the same conclusion, it seemed, for as Paul opened the front door the next evening, Emma, coming down the stairs, tripped and fell.

He picked her up within seconds, scooping her into his arms, holding her close.

'Emma—are you hurt? Stay still a moment while I look.'

She would have stayed still forever with his arms around her, but she managed a rather shaky, 'I'm fine, really...'

He spoke to the top of her head, which was buried in his waistcoat. 'Emma—you must tell me—this ridiculous business of spending the night at that camp. Why did you refuse to listen to Diana? She is still upset and I cannot understand...'

Emma wrenched herself free. 'You listened to her and you believed her without even asking me. Well, go on believing her; you've known her for years, haven't you? And you've only known me for months; you don't know much about me, do you? But I expect you know Diana very well indeed.'

Paul put his hands in his pockets. 'Yes. Go on, Emma.'

'Well, if I were you, I'd believe her and not me,' she added bitterly. 'After all, she's worth a dozen of me.'

She flew back upstairs and shut her bedroom door with a snap and when Mrs Parfitt came presently to see if she should serve dinner she found Emma lying on her bed.

'I have such a shocking headache,' sighed Emma. 'Would you give Sir Paul his dinner? I couldn't eat anything.'

Indeed she did look poorly. Mrs Parfitt tut-tutted and offered one of her herbal teas. 'You just get into bed, ma'am. I'll tell Sir Paul and I dare say he'll be up to see you.'

'No, no, there's no need. Let him have his dinner first; he's had a busy day and he needs a meal and time to rest. I dare say it will get better in an hour or two.'

The headache had been an excuse, but soon it was real. Emma got herself into bed and eventually fell asleep.

That was how Paul found her when he came to see her. She was curled up, her tear-stained face cushioned on a hand, the other arm round Queenie. He stood studying her for some minutes. Her hair was loose, spread over the pillows, and her mouth was slightly open. Her cheeks were rather blotchy because of the tears but the long, curling brown lashes swept them gently. When he had fallen in love with her he hadn't considered her to be beautiful but now he could see that her ordinary little face held a beauty which had nothing to do with good looks.

He went away presently, reassured Mrs Parfitt and went to his study. There was always work.

Emma went down to breakfast in the morning, exchanged good mornings with Paul, assured him that her headache had quite gone and volunteered the information that she was going to the nursery that morning. 'And I said I would go tomorrow morning as well—they're short-handed for a few days. Will you be home late?'

'No, in time for tea I hope. There's the parish council meeting at eight o'clock this evening.'

'Oh, yes. I am helping with the coffee and biscuits.'

He left then, and very soon after she got into the Mini and drove herself to the nursery.

''Ere,' said Maisie as she sat down and picked up the first baby, 'wot yer been up ter? 'Ad a tiff?'

'No, no, Maisie. I'm fine, really. How's your intended?'

It was a red herring which took them through most of the morning.

It was just as Emma was leaving and passing the office that Diana called to her. 'Emma, don't worry if Paul is late this evening—he's coming to check one of the babies from the camp—a fractured arm as well as whooping cough.'

Emma asked, 'Did he say he'd come? He's got a parish meeting this evening; he won't want to miss it.'

Diana smiled slowly. 'Oh, I'm sure it won't matter if he's not there.' She stared at Emma. 'As a matter of fact, he said he was coming to see me anyway.'

'That's all right, then,' said Emma. She didn't believe Diana.

She had lunch, then took the dogs for a long walk and helped Mrs Parfitt get the tea. Buttered muffins and cucumber sandwiches, she decided, and one of Mrs Parfitt's rich fruit cakes.

Teatime came and went, and there was no Paul. At last she had a cup of tea anyway, and a slice of cake, helped Mrs Parfitt clear away and went upstairs to get ready. She put on a plain jersey dress suitable for a parish council meeting.

When seven o'clock came and went she told Mrs

Parfitt to delay her cooking. 'Sir Paul won't have time to eat in comfort before eight o'clock. Perhaps we could have a meal when we get home?'

'No problem,' said Mrs Parfitt. 'The ragout'll only need warming up and the rest will be ready by the time you've had a drink.'

'You have your supper when you like, Mrs Parfitt.' Emma glanced at the clock; she would have to go to the meeting and make Paul's excuses.

The councillors were friendly and very nice about it. Doctors were never free to choose their comings and goings, observed old Major Pike, but he for one was delighted to see his little wife.

Emma smiled shyly at him—he was a dear old man, very knowledgeable about the moor, born and bred in Lustleigh even though he had spent years away from it. He thoroughly approved of her, for she was a local girl and looked sensible.

The meeting was drawing to a close when the door opened and Paul came in. Emma, sitting quietly at the back of the village hall, watched him as he made his excuses, exchanged a few laughing remarks with the rest of the council and sat down at the table. He hadn't looked at her, but presently he turned his head and gave her a look which shook her.

He was pale and without expression, and she knew that he was very angry. With her? she wondered. Had Diana been making more mischief between them? She hoped he would smile but he turned away and soon it was time for her to go and help the vicar's wife in the kitchen.

They made the coffee and arranged Petit Beurre biscuits on a plate and carried them through just as the chairman closed the meeting. Eventually goodnights were exchanged and everyone started to go home.

Emma, collecting cups and saucers, saw that Paul had stayed. Waiting for her, she supposed, and when she came from the kitchen presently he was still there.

He got up when he saw her, passed a pleasant time of day with the vicar's wife, helped them on with their coats, turned out the lights, locked the door and gave the key to the vicar, who had walked back for his wife. That done, he turned for home, his hand under Emma's elbow.

She sensed that it was an angry hand and, anxious not to make things worse than they apparently were, she trotted briskly beside him, keeping up with his strides.

In the drawing-room she sat down in her usual chair, but Paul stood by the door, the dogs beside him. Perhaps it would be best to carry the war into the enemy camp, Emma decided.

'You were very late; did you have an emergency?'

'No.'

'You went to see Diana…?'

'Indeed I did.'

Emma nodded. 'She told me that you would go and see her, and that you were going to see her anyway.'

'And you believed her?'

'Well, no, I didn't—but I do now.'

He said softly, 'And why do you suppose that I went to see her?'

Emma said carefully, 'Shall we not talk about that? Something has made you angry and you must be tired.

I'll tell Mrs Parfitt that we are ready for dinner, shall I? While you have a drink.'

She was surprised when he laughed.

It was while they were eating that Paul said quietly, 'I do not wish you to go to the clinic any more, Emma.'

She had a forkful of ragout halfway to her mouth. 'Not go? Why ever not?'

'Would it do if I just asked you to do as I wish? There are good reasons.'

Emma allowed her imagination to run riot. Diana would have convinced him in her charming way that she was no good at the nursery, that she was too slow, too independent too. She said slowly, 'Very well, Paul, but I should like to go tomorrow morning to say good-bye to Maisie. I have been working with her and she is getting married—I've a present for her. And I'd like to see Charlie—he's so cross and unloved...'

'Of course you must go. Diana won't be there, but you could leave a note.'

'Very well. I'll think up a good excuse.'

She wrote it later when Paul was in his study. Obviously Paul didn't want her to meet Diana again. Why? she wondered. Perhaps she would never know. It had been silly of her to refuse to talk about it; she hadn't given him a chance to explain why he was angry. She thought that he still was but he had got his rage under control; his manner was imperturbable.

He had looked, she reflected, as though he could have swept the extremely valuable decanter and glasses off the side-table. She sighed—everything had gone

wrong. Their marriage had seemed such a splendid idea
and she had been sure that it would be a success.

The mousy little woman who deputised for Diana
was at the nursery the next day.

'Is Diana ill?' asked Emma, agog for information.

'No, Lady Wyatt. She felt she should have a few days
off; she's been working hard just lately. You'll be sorry
to have missed her. I hear you're leaving us.'

'Yes, I'm afraid so. I shall miss the babies. May I go
and say goodbye to them and Maisie?'

'Of course. I'm sure Diana is grateful for your help
while you were with us.'

'I enjoyed it,' said Emma.

Maisie was on her own, and Emma resisted the urge
to put on her pinny and give her a hand. 'I'm leaving,
Maisie. I didn't want to but Sir Paul asked me to.'

'Did 'e now?' Maisie looked smug. She had been
there yesterday evening when Sir Paul had come to see
Diana and, although she hadn't been able to hear what
was said, she had heard Diana's voice, shrill and then
tearful, and Sir Paul's measured rumble. He had come
out of the office eventually, and this time Maisie had
been brave and stopped him before he got into his car.

'I don't know the ins and outs,' she had told him
briskly, 'but it's time you caught on ter that Diana telling great whoppers about that little wife of yours. Little
angel, she is, and never said a word, I'll bet. 'Oo pretended there weren't no doctors nor ambulances to go
ter the camp? Moonshine. I 'eard 'er with me own ears
telling 'em there weren't no need to send anyone. Sent

little Emma back into all that mist and dark, she did, and tells everyone she'd done it awf 'er own bat and against 'er wishes.' Maisie had stuck her chin out. 'Sack me if yer want to. I likes ter see justice done, mister!'

Sir Paul had put out a hand and engulfed hers. 'Maisie—so do I. Thank you for telling me; Emma has a loyal friend in you.'

'Don't you go telling her, now.'

He had kept his word. Emma obviously knew nothing about his visit. Now everything would be all right. 'I'll miss yer, but I dare say you'll 'ave a few of yer own soon enough.'

Emma had picked up Charlie. 'I do hope Charlie will be wanted by someone.'

'Now, as ter that, I've a bit of good news. 'E's ter be adopted by such a nice woman and 'er 'usband—no kids of their own and they want a boy. 'E'll 'ave a good 'ome.'

'Oh, lovely. Maisie, will you write and tell me when you're to be married? And here's a wedding-present.'

Emma dived into her shoulder-bag and handed over a beribboned box.

'Cor, love, yer didn't orter…'

Maisie was already untying the ribbons. Inside was a brown leather handbag and, under that, a pair of matching gloves.

'I'll wear 'em on me wedding-day,' said Maisie, and got up and offered a hand.

Emma took it and then kissed Maisie's cheek. 'I hope you'll be very happy, and please write to me sometimes.'

'I ain't much 'and with a pen, but I'll do me best,' said Maisie.

Back home again, Emma took the dogs for a walk, had her lunch and then went into the garden. She pottered about, weeding here and there, tying things up, examining the rose bushes, anxious to keep busy so that she didn't need to think too much. She supposed that sooner or later she and Paul would have to talk—perhaps it would be best to get it over with. He had said that he would be home for tea. She began to rehearse a casual conversation—anything to prevent them talking about Diana.

The rehearsal wasn't necessary; when Paul got home he treated her with a casual friendliness which quite disarmed her. It was only later that she remembered she had told him that she had no wish to discuss the unfortunate episode at the camp and Diana's accusations. Which, of course, made it impossible for her to mention it now. They spent the evening together, making trivial talk, so that by the time she went to bed she was feeling peevish from her efforts to think up something harmless to say.

Paul got up to open the door for her, and as she went past him with a quick goodnight he observed, 'Difficult, isn't it, Emma?'

She paused to look up at him in surprise.

'Making polite small talk when you're bursting to utter quite different thoughts out loud.' He smiled down at her—a small, mocking smile with a tender edge to it, but she didn't see the tenderness, only the mockery.

For want of anything better, she said, 'I've no idea what you mean.'

* * *

Over the next few days they settled down to an uneasy truce—at least, it was uneasy on Emma's part, although Paul behaved as though nothing had occurred to disturb the easy-going relationship between them.

He was due up in Edinburgh at the beginning of the following week, but he didn't suggest that she should go with him. Not that I would have gone, reflected Emma, all the same annoyed that he hadn't asked her.

He would be back in three days he told her. 'Why not call Father to take you up to the Cotswolds, and spend a couple of days with them?'

'Well, Mrs Parfitt did say that she would like a few days to visit her sister at Brixham. I thought I might drive her there and fetch her back. Willy and Kate can sit in the back and I can leave Queenie for most of the day.'

'You would like to do that? Then by all means go. I don't really like your being alone in the house, though, Emma.'

'It won't be the first time, and I have the dogs. I'm not nervous.'

'I'll leave my phone number, of course. Perhaps it would be better if Mrs Parfitt waited until I am back home.'

'No, it wouldn't. There's lots more to do around the house and more cooking when you're home.'

'A nuisance in my own house, Emma?' He sounded amused.

'No—oh, no, of course not. But I know she'd prefer to go away when you're not here.'

'As you wish. In any case, I shall phone each evening.'

Paul left soon after breakfast, so Emma was able to drive Mrs Parfitt to her sister's very shortly after that.

It was a pleasant drive and the morning was fine, and when she reached Brixham she delivered Mrs Parfitt and then drove down to the harbour, where she parked the car and took the dogs for a run. She had coffee in a small café near by and then drove back to Lustleigh. When she reached the cottage and let herself in she realised that she felt lonely, despite the animals' company.

She wandered through the house, picking things up and putting them down again and, since Mrs Parfitt had left everything in apple-pie order, there was nothing for her to do except get the lunch.

A long walk did much to dispel her gloom and took up the time nicely until she could get her tea, and then it was the evening and Paul had said that he would phone...

She wondered how long it would take him to get there; it was a long way and he might be too tired to ring up.

Of course he did, though; she was watching the six o'clock news when the phone rang and she rushed to it, fearful that he might ring off before she reached it.

Yes, his cool voice assured her, he had had a very pleasant drive, not all that tiring, and he had already seen two patients who needed his particular skills. 'I have a clinic tomorrow morning,' he told her, 'and then a lecture before dining with friends. I may phone rather later. You enjoyed your drive to Brixham?'

'Yes. We went for a long walk this afternoon; Willy got a thorn in his paw but I got it out. I'm getting their suppers...'

'In that case, don't let me keep you. Sleep well, Emma.'

He didn't wait for her answer but hung up.

An unsatisfactory conversation, thought Emma, snivelling into the dog food. He hadn't asked her if she was lonely or cautioned her kindly about locking up securely; indeed, he had asked hardly any questions about her at all.

She poked around in the fridge and ate two cold sausages and a carton of yoghurt, then took herself off to bed after letting the dogs out and then bolting and barring all the doors and the windows. She had no reason to feel nervous—it was a pity that she didn't know that the village constable, alerted by Sir Paul, had made it his business to keep an eye on her.

She lay awake for a long time, thinking about Paul. She missed him dreadfully; it was as though only half of her were alive—to have him home was all she wanted, and never mind if they no longer enjoyed their pleasant comradeship. She would have to learn to take second place to Diana and be thankful for that.

'But why he couldn't have married her and been done with it, I don't know,' Emma observed to the sleeping Queenie and, naturally enough, got no answer.

She walked to the village stores after breakfast, took her purchases home and went off for another walk with the dogs. The fine weather held and the sun shone, and out on the moors her worries seemed of no account.

They went back home with splendid appetites and, having filled the dogs' bowls and attended to Queenie's more modest needs, Emma had her own lunch. The day was half done, and in the evening Paul would phone again.

She was putting away the last spoons and forks when there was a thump on the door-knocker. She wiped her hands on her apron and went to open it.

Diana stood there, beautifully dressed, exquisitely made-up, and smiling.

'Emma—I've been lunching at Bovey Tracey and I just had to come and see you. I know Paul's in Edinburgh and I thought you might like a visit. I'm surprised he didn't take you with him. It's great for a professor's image to have a wife, you know.'

She had walked past Emma as she held the door open and now stood in the hall, looking round. 'Nothing's changed,' she observed and heaved a sigh. 'I never liked that portrait over the table, but Paul said he was a famous surgeon in his day and he wouldn't move him.'

She smiled at Emma, and Emma smiled back. 'Well, it is Paul's house,' she said pleasantly. 'Would you like a cup of coffee?'

'I'd love one.' Diana had taken off her jacket and thrown it over a chair. 'I had the most ghastly lunch at the Prostle-Hammetts and the coffee was undrinkable.'

It was the kind of remark Diana would make, thought Emma as she led the way into the drawing-room.

'Oh, the dogs,' cried Diana. 'We always had such fun together...'

Neither dog took any notice of her, which cheered Emma enormously—they were on her side.

'Do sit down,' she said. 'I'll fetch the coffee.'

'Can I help? I know my way around, you know.'

'No, no. Sit down here—you look a bit pinched. I expect you're tired.' She saw Diana's frown and the quick peek in the great Chippendale mirror over the fireplace.

In the kitchen she poured the coffee and wondered why Diana had come. To see how she had settled in as Paul's wife? Or just to needle her? Emma told herself stoutly that she wasn't going to believe anything Diana said. After all, so far she had done nothing but hint at her close friendship with Paul; all that nonsense about her love distracting him from his work had been nothing but moonshine. All the same, Diana had played a dirty trick on her when she had been at the nursery and she wasn't to be trusted.

She took the coffee-tray in, offered sugar and cream and sat down opposite her unwelcome guest. She didn't believe that Diana had called out of friendliness—it was probably just out of curiosity.

'Paul has a busy few days in Edinburgh,' said Diana. 'Patients yesterday and today after that long drive, and a clinic tomorrow. What a blessing it is that he has good friends—we always dined there...' She cast a sidelong look at Emma and gave a little laugh. 'Of course, everyone expected us to marry.'

'Then why didn't you?' Emma lifted the coffee-pot. 'More coffee?'

'No, thanks—I have to think of my figure.'

Emma said pertly, 'Well, yes, I suppose you do; we none of us grow any younger do we?'

Diana put her cup and saucer down. 'Look, Emma, you don't like me and I don't like you, but that doesn't alter the fact that Paul still loves me. He married you for all kinds of worthy reasons: you're an ideal wife for a busy man who is seldom at home; you don't complain; you're not pretty enough to attract other men. I dare say you're a good housewife and you won't pester him to take you out to enjoy the bright lights. As I said, you're an ideal wife for him. He's fond of you, I suppose—but loving you? I don't suppose you know what that means; you're content with a mild affection, aren't you? Whereas he…'

She had contrived to get tears in her eyes and Emma, seeing them, had sudden doubts.

'We love each other,' said Diana quietly. 'He has married you and he'll be a kind and good husband to you but you must understand that that is all he will ever be. I know you think I'm not worthy of him, and I know I'm not.' She blinked away another tear. 'He's not happy, you know, Emma.'

Emma said, 'You could go away—right away.'

Diana said simply, 'He would come after me—don't you know that? There's nothing I can do—I've talked and talked and he won't listen.' She looked at Emma. 'It is you who must go, Emma.'

Emma, looking at her and not trusting her an inch, found herself half believing her. She detested Diana, but if Paul loved her that didn't matter, did it? However, she didn't quite believe Diana; she would need proof.

Where would she get proof? It would have to be something that would hold water, not vague hints. She said, 'I don't intend to go, Diana.'

She got up to answer the phone and it was Paul. His quiet voice sounded reassuring to her ear. 'It will be late before I can phone you this evening so it seemed sensible to do so now. Is everything all right at home?'

'Yes, thank you—have you been busy?'

'Yes. I'll be here for another two days. Do you fetch Mrs Parfitt back tomorrow?'

'No, the day after.'

'You're not lonely?'

'No. Diana is here, paying a flying visit.'

She heard the change in his voice. 'I'll speak to her, Emma.'

'It's Paul; he'd like a word with you.' Emma handed the phone to Diana. 'I'll take the coffee out to the kitchen.'

Which she did, but not before she heard Diana's rather loud, 'Darling...'

Chapter 9

Emma hesitated for a moment; to nip back and listen at the door was tempting, but not very practical with the coffee-tray in her hands. She went to the kitchen, letting the door bang behind her, put the tray on the table and then returned noiselessly to the hall. The drawing-room door was ajar; she could hear Diana very clearly.

'I'll be at home until Friday. Goodbye, Paul.'

Emma retreated smartly to the kitchen and rattled a few cups and saucers and then went back to the drawing-room, shutting the baize door to the kitchen with a thump. Diana was putting on her coat.

'My dear, I must go. Thanks for the coffee, and I'm so glad to see that you've altered nothing in the cottage.' She paused, pulling on her gloves. 'Emma, you will think over what I have said, won't you? It sounds cruel but we are all unhappy now, aren't we? If you let Paul go then there would be only one of us unhappy, and since you don't love him you'll get over it quickly enough. He'll treat you well—financially, I mean.'

'I think you'd better go,' said Emma, 'before I throw something at you.' She went ahead of Diana and opened the cottage door. 'You're very vulgar, aren't you?'

She shut the door before Diana could reply.

She went back to the drawing-room and sat down; Queenie got on to her lap while Willy and Kate settled beside her. She didn't want to believe Diana but she had sounded sincere and she had cried. Moreover, she had told Paul that she would be at home until Friday. Why would she do that unless she expected him to go and see her? There was no way of finding out—at least, until Paul came home again.

He phoned the following evening. 'You're all right?' he wanted to know. 'Not lonely?'

'Not in the least,' said Emma airily. 'I had tea with the Postle-Hammets. I like Mrs Postle-Hammet and the children are sweet; I enjoyed myself.'

Largely because Mrs Postle-Hammet had been remarkably frank about her opinion of Diana, she thought. 'Cold as a fish and selfish to the bone and clever enough to hide it,' she had said—hardly information she could pass on to Paul.

'I should be home tomorrow evening, but if I should be delayed will you leave the side-door locked but not bolted? You'll fetch Mrs Parfitt tomorrow?'

'Yes, after lunch.'

'Good. I'll say goodnight, Emma. I've several more

phone calls to make.' One of them to Diana? she wondered, and tried not to think about that.

She had an early lunch the next day and drove to
Brixham through driving rain to fetch Mrs Parfitt, and
then drove home again, listening to that lady's account
of her few days' holiday. 'Very nice it was too, ma'am,
but my sister isn't a good cook and I missed my kitchen.
Still, the sea air was nice and there are some good shops.
You've not been too alone, I hope?'

'No, no, Mrs Parfitt. I've been out to tea and Miss
Pearson came to see me and Sir Paul has phoned each
evening, and of course there were the dogs to take out.
I had no time to be lonely—' Emma turned to smile at
her companion '—but it's very nice to have you back,
Mrs Parfitt. The cottage doesn't seem the same without
you. Sir Paul is coming back this evening.'

'He'll need his dinner if he's driving all that way.
Did you have anything in mind, ma'am?'

They spent the rest of the journey deciding on a menu
to tempt him when he got home. 'Something that won't
spoil,' cautioned Emma, 'for I've no idea exactly when
he'll be back.'

Mrs Parfitt took off her best hat and her sensible coat
and went straight to the kitchen. 'A nice cup of tea,' she
observed, 'and while the kettle's boiling I'll pop a few
scones in the oven.'

Emma went from room to room, making sure that
everything was just so, shaking up cushions, rearranging the flowers, laying the pile of letters on the table by
Paul's chair and, since it was going to be a gloomy eve-

ning, switching on lamps here and there so that there was a cheerful glow from the windows.

Satisfied that everything was as welcoming as she could make it, she went upstairs and changed into a patterned silk jersey dress, did her face with care and brushed her hair into a knot at the back of her head; it took a long time to get it just so but she was pleased with the result. Then she went downstairs to wait.

At ten o'clock she sent Mrs Parfitt to bed and ate a sketchy meal off a tray in the kitchen. When the long case clock in the hall chimed one o'clock she went to bed herself.

She was still awake when it chimed again, followed by the silvery tinkle of the carriage clock in the drawing-room. She slept after that but woke when it was barely light to creep downstairs to see if Paul was home. If he was, the back door would be bolted. It wasn't!

Emma stared at it for a long moment and then went to the phone and picked it up. The night porter answered it. Yes, Sir Paul had been in the hospital during the late evening and had left again shortly after—he had seen him leave in his car.

He sounded a little surprised at her query and she hastened to say that it was perfectly all right. 'Sir Paul said that he might do that. I'll ring him now. Thank you.'

She went to the kitchen then, and put on the kettle. She spooned tea into the pot, trying not to think about the previous evening, trying not to believe Diana's remarks but quite unable to forget them.

She was making tea when the kitchen door opened

and Paul walked in. Emma caught her breath and choked on a surge of strong feelings.

'A fine time to come home,' she snapped, rage for the moment overcoming the delight of seeing him again, and she made unnecessary work of refilling the kettle and putting it back on the Aga.

Sir Paul didn't speak, but stood in the doorway looking at her indignant back, and since the silence was rather long she asked stiffly, 'Would you like a cup of tea?'

'Er—no, thank you, Emma. I'm sorry if you were worried.'

'Worried? Why should I be worried?' said Emma at her haughtiest. 'I phoned the hospital early this morning and I was told that you had been in and gone again late last night.' She drew a long breath. 'So I had no need to worry, had I?'

When he most annoyingly didn't answer, she said, 'I knew where you were…'

'Indeed.'

She had her back to him, busy with mug and sugar and milk and pouring tea. 'Well, Diana came to see me—I told you that—you spoke to her…'

'Ah, Diana—of course. *Latet anguis in herba*!' murmured Sir Paul.

Emma's knowledge of Latin was sketchy and, anyway, what had grass got to do with it? For she had recognised the word *herba*, and if he was trailing a red herring she meant to ignore it. In any case her tongue was running on now, regardless of prudence.

'So of course I knew you'd go to her when you got

back. She was very—very frank.' She gave an angry snuffle. 'She was glad I hadn't altered the pictures or anything.' She wouldn't look at him. 'Would you like breakfast?'

'No, Emma, I'll shower and change and go to the hospital.'

'You'll be back later? Teatime?'

'Don't count on that.' He spoke quietly, and something in his voice made her turn to look at him. He looked very tired but he gave her a bland stare from cold eyes. She had no doubt that he was angry. She was angry too, and miserable, and she loved him so much that she felt the ache of it. The urge to tell him so was so great that she started to speak, but she had barely uttered his name when he went away.

He had left the house by the time she had dressed and gone back downstairs to find Mrs Parfitt in the kitchen.

'Gone again,' cried Mrs Parfitt. 'I saw him drive off not ten minutes ago. By the time I'd got downstairs he'd gone. He'll wear himself out, that he will. How about a nice leg of lamb for dinner this evening? He'll need his strength kept up.'

When Emma said that he had come home very early in the morning Mrs. Parfitt commented, 'Must have been an accident. Now you go and eat your breakfast, ma'am, for no doubt you've been worrying half the night. Who'd be a doctor's wife, eh?' She laughed, and Emma echoed it in a hollow way.

She took the dogs for their walk after breakfast while Mrs Parfitt took herself off to the village shop and paid a visit to the butcher. It was while she was drying the dogs in the outhouse by the kitchen that Mrs Parfitt joined her.

'Postie was in the stores—there's been a nasty accident on the M5 where it turns into the A38.' Mrs Parfitt paused for breath, bursting with her news. 'Nine cars, he said, all squashed together, and Sir Paul right behind them on his way back here. Goes back to the hospital and spends the night in the operating theatre, he does. He's back there now, no doubt, working himself to death. He didn't ought to do it. He didn't say nothing to you, ma'am? No—well, of course, he wouldn't; he'd have known how upset you'd have been.'

Emma had gone very pale. 'Not a word. He didn't want tea or his breakfast but he said he had to go back.' The full horror of what she had said to him dawned on her—she had accused him of being with Diana while all the time he had been saving lives. She hadn't even given him the chance to tell her anything. She felt sick at the thought, and Mrs Parfitt took her arm and sat her down by the table.

'There, I shouldn't have come out with it so quick; you're that pale—like a little ghost. You stay there while I fetch you a drop of brandy.'

Emma was only too willing to sit. It was chilly in the little room, and the dogs, released from the tiresome business of being cleaned up before going into the house, had slipped away to lie by the Aga.

Mrs Parfitt came back with the brandy. 'It don't do to give way, ma'am,' she urged Emma. 'He's safe and sound even if he's tired to his bones, but you must show a bright face when he gets home, for that'll be what he needs.'

Emma drank the brandy, although she thought he wouldn't care if her face was bright or not. He would be polite, because he had beautiful manners and they wouldn't allow him to be otherwise, but he would have gone behind the barrier she had always sensed was between them—only now that barrier was twice as high and she doubted if she would ever climb it.

She spent a restless day, dreading his return and yet longing for it, going over and over in her aching head the awful things she had said and rehearsing the humble speech she would offer him when he came home. Which he did just as Mrs Parfitt brought in the tea-tray, following her into the drawing-room.

'There,' said Mrs Parfitt. 'Didn't I bake that fruit cake knowing you'd be here for your tea? I'll fetch another cup and a sandwich or two.'

She trotted off; she firmly believed that the way to a man's heart was through his stomach, and his doubtless needed filling.

He thanked her quickly and stooped to fondle the dogs weaving around his feet. 'Hello, Emma,' he said quietly.

'Paul.' The strength of her feelings was choking her as she got out of her chair, spilling an indignant Queenie on to the carpet. She said stupidly, 'I didn't know...' Her tongue shrivelled under his cold stare; underneath his quietness he was furiously angry, and suddenly she was angry again. 'Why didn't you tell me?'

He sat down in his chair and the dogs curled up beside him. 'I don't believe that I had the opportunity,' he observed mildly.

'You could have—' Emma burst out, only to be interrupted by Mrs Parfitt with fresh tea, cup and saucer and a plate of sandwiches.

'Gentleman's Relish,' she pointed out in a pleased voice. 'Just what you fancy, sir, and cucumber and cress. I shall be serving dinner a bit earlier, ma'am? I dare say the master's peckish.'

Emma glanced at Paul, who said, 'That would be very nice, Mrs Parfitt.' He sounded like any man just home and sitting by his own fireside but Emma, unwittingly catching his eye, blinked at its icy hardness.

After Mrs Parfitt had gone Emma poured the tea, offered sandwiches and strove to think of something to say; she would have to apologise, and she wanted to, but for the moment the right words eluded her. All the same she made a halting start, only to have it swept aside as Paul began a conversation which gave her no chance to utter a word.

It was an undemanding and impersonal stream of small talk, quiet and unhurried. He could have been soothing a scared patient before telling her his diagnosis. Well, she wasn't a patient but she was scared, and the diagnosis, when it came, left her without words.

She was pouring his second cup of tea when he said casually, 'I've been offered a lecture tour in the States...'

He watched her pale face go even paler and saw the shock in it.

'The States? America? For how long?'

'Four months.'

She gulped back a protesting scream. 'That's a long time.'

'Yes. Time enough for us to consider our future, don't you agree?'

If only he wasn't so pleasant about it, Emma thought unhappily, and if only I could think of the right thing to say. After a minute she said, 'I expect you'd like to go?'

He didn't answer that so she tried again, asking a question her tongue uttered before she could stop it. 'Will you go alone?'

'Oh, yes.'

He didn't add to that, and she seized the opportunity and plunged into a muddled apology. None of the things she had meant to say came out properly. 'I'm sorry, Paul, I'm so very sorry; it was terribly stupid of me and unkind...'

He stopped her quite gently. 'Don't say any more, Emma. I thought that when we married...' He paused. 'You must see that if you don't trust me our marriage is going to be unhappy. That is why I shall go on this tour; you will have time to decide what you want to do with your future.'

She gave him a bewildered look. 'You mean, you don't want me to be your wife?'

'I didn't say that...'

'Well, no—but I think you meant that, only you are too polite to say so. I expect it's a good idea.'

At the end of four months, she thought sadly, he would come back, and they would separate without fuss and he would go his way and she would go hers. What about Diana? He hadn't mentioned her, had he? And she didn't dare to ask.

'I've made you very angry.'

'Indeed you have,' he agreed politely.

'I think it would have been better if you had shouted at me...'

'I could never shout at you, Emma.'

He smiled a little, thinking that he wanted to pick her up and shake her and carry her off somewhere and never let her go—his darling Emma.

Perhaps he was too old for her; perhaps she regretted marrying him. Certainly she had been a constantly good companion, and at times he had thought that she might become more than that, but once she had got over the shock she had given no sign that she didn't want him to go away. Indeed, she had taken it for granted that she would stay here.

He got up. 'I've one or two letters to write,' he told her. 'I'll go and do them before dinner—I can take the dogs out later.'

Emma nodded, and when he had gone carried the tray out to the kitchen. She stayed there for ten minutes, getting in Mrs Parfitt's way, and presently went back to the drawing-room and got out her embroidery. She wasn't being very successful with it and spent the next half-hour unpicking the work she had done the previous evening. It left her thoughts free and she allowed them full rein.

Somehow she must find a way to convince Paul that she was truly sorry. If he wanted to be free—perhaps to marry Diana—then the least she could do was to make it easy for him. She owed him so much that she could never repay him. She must find out when this lecture tour was to start; if she were to go away first, then he wouldn't need to go.

Her head seethed with plans; she could tell everyone that an aunt or uncle needed her urgently. That she had no relations of any kind made no difference—no one was to know that. She would do it in a way that would arouse no suspicions. Diana would guess, of course— she had suggested it in the first place—but she wasn't likely to tell anyone.

She would write a letter to Paul, saying all the things she wanted to say—that she loved him and wanted him to be happy and thanked him for his kindness and generosity. Her mind made up, she attacked her embroidery with vigour and a complete disregard for accuracy.

Out-patients' sister watched Sir Paul's vast back disappear down the corridor. 'Well, what's the matter with him?' she asked her staff nurse. 'I've never known him dash off without his cup of tea, and him so quiet too. Something on his mind, do you suppose? He's got that nice little wife to go home to and you're not telling me that they're not happy together. Mention her and his face lights up—looks ten years younger. Ah, well, he'll go home and spend a lovely evening with her, I dare say.'

Sir Paul drove himself to the nursery, got out of his car and walked into Diana's office. She was getting ready to go home but put her jacket down as he went in. 'Paul, how lovely to see you—it's ages.'

He closed the door behind him—a disappointment to

Maisie, who was getting ready to go home too, standing in the cloakroom near enough to the office to hear anything interesting which might be said.

'Perhaps you will spare me ten minutes, Diana?'

He hadn't moved from the door and she sat down slowly. 'All the time in the world for you, Paul.'

'You went to see Emma—why?'

She shrugged her shoulders. 'I thought she might be lonely.'

'The truth, Diana...'

Now Maisie edged nearer the door. She couldn't hear what was being said but she could hear Diana's voice getting more and more agitated, and Sir Paul's voice sounding severe and, presently, angry.

Sir Paul wasn't mincing his words. 'I have never at any time given you reason to believe that I was in love with you.' He added, with brutal frankness, 'Indeed, you are the last woman I would wish to have for a wife.'

Maisie, her ear pressed to the keyhole, just had time to nip back into the cloakroom as he opened the door.

He saw at once on his return home that this was not the right time to talk to Emma. She was being carefully polite and the expression on her face warned him not to be other than that; so the evening was spent in a guarded manner, neither of them saying any of the things they wanted to say, both waiting for some sign...

Emma went to bed rather early, relieved that she was alone and could grizzle and mope and presently go over her plans to leave. Just for a little while that evening, despite their coolness towards each other, she had wondered if she could stay, if they could patch things up between them. But trying to read Paul's thoughts was an impossible task; they were far too well hidden behind his bland face. He wasn't going to reproach her; he wasn't going to say another word about the whole sorry business. Presumably it was to be forgotten and they would go on as before, just good friends and then, when the right moment came, parting.

'I hate Diana,' said Emma, and kicked a cushion across the floor. 'I hope she makes him very unhappy.' It was a palpable lie which did nothing to restore her spirits.

She didn't sleep much—she was too busy making plans. Many were wildly unsuitable to begin with, but by the early morning she had discarded most of them in favour of one which seemed to her to be simple and foolproof.

She would give Mrs Parfitt a day off—it would have to be in two days' time, when Paul had his theatre list and a ward round, which meant he wouldn't be home before about six o'clock. Once Mrs Parfitt was out of the house she would pack a few things in a suitable bag, write a letter to Paul and one to Mrs Parfitt—the illness of a fictitious aunt would do very well—walk to Bovey Tracey, get a bus down to the main road and another bus to Plymouth.

She could lose herself there and get a job in a restaurant or a hotel—surely there would be temporary jobs in the tourist trade. She would have to buy some kind of a bag—a knapsack would do. In the morning she would take her car into Exeter and get one. It was morning already, she reminded herself, and got up and dressed and did the best she could to disguise her sleepless night.

Sir Paul bade her good morning in his usual manner, remarked on the fine day and studied her tired face. She looked excited too, in a secret kind of way, as though she were hatching some plot or other. He decided to come home early but told her smoothly when she asked if he would be home for tea that he thought it unlikely, watching the relief on her face.

It was easy to get Mrs Parfitt to take a day off; Emma knew that she wanted to go to Exeter and buy a new hat. 'Take the whole day,' she suggested. 'I might go over to Mrs Postle-Hammett's—it's a good walk for the dogs and she's very fond of them. I'm sure Sir Paul will give you a lift tomorrow morning.'

'Well, if you don't mind, ma'am. I must say I'd like a day to shop around.'

'I'm going to Exeter this morning,' said Emma. 'One or two things I want. Do we need anything for the house while I'm there?'

There was nothing needed. She went to her room and got into her jacket, found her car keys and drove herself to Exeter. She soon found exactly what she wanted in a funny little shop at the bottom of the high street, walked back to the car park in Queen Street and on the way came face to face with Maisie.

'Come and have a cup of coffee?' said Emma. She was glad to see her and steered her into a café. 'Aren't you at the nursery any more?'

'Leaving on Saturday,' said Maisie and looked coy. 'Getting married, yer see.'

'On Saturday? Oh, Maisie, I am glad; I hope you'll both be very happy. In church?'

'Baptist. Just the kids and 'is mum and dad.' Maisie sugared her coffee lavishly. 'Saw yer old man at the nursery—leastways, 'eard 'im. In a bit of a rage, it sounded like, and that Diana going 'ammer and tongs. Sounded all tearful she did—kept saying, "Oh, Paul, oh, Paul." Didn't come to work today neither. Nasty piece of work she is; turns on the charm like I switches on the electric.'

'She's very attractive,' said Emma, and felt sick. So, he was still seeing Diana; it was a good thing she had decided to go…

'Suppose so,' said Maisie. 'Leastways, to men. Good thing you're married to yer old man!'

She chuckled and Emma managed a laugh. 'Yes, isn't it? Tell me what you're going to wear…'

Which filled the next ten minutes very nicely before Maisie declared that she still had some shopping to do.

'We'll 'ave some photos,' she promised. 'I'll send you one.'

'Please do, Maisie, and it was lovely meeting you like that.'

They said goodbye and Emma went back to the car and drove home. The small hopeful doubt she had had about leaving had been doused by Maisie's news. Tomorrow she would go.

She was surprised when Paul came home at teatime, but she greeted him in what she hoped was a normal voice, and, when he asked her, told him that she had been to Exeter—'One or two things I wanted'—and had met Maisie. Maisie's approaching wedding made a good topic of conversation; Emma wore it threadbare and Paul, listening to her repeating herself, decided that whatever it was she was planning it wouldn't be that evening.

He went to his study presently and spent some time on the phone rearranging the next day's work. When his receptionist complained that he had several patients to see on the following afternoon he told her ruthlessly to change their appointments. 'I must have the whole of tomorrow afternoon and evening free,' he told her, and then spent ten minutes charming Theatre Sister into altering his list.

'I'll start at eight o'clock instead of nine,' he told her, and, since she liked him and admired him, she agreed, aware that it would mean a good deal of rearranging for her to do.

As for his registrar, who admired him too, he agreed cheerfully to take over out-patients once the ward-round was done.

Sir Paul ate his supper, well aware that he had done all he could to avert whatever disaster his Emma was plotting.

The cottage seemed very empty once Paul and Mrs Parfitt had gone the next morning. It was still early; she had all day before her. Emma took the dogs for a long walk, went from room to room tidying up, clearing the breakfast things Mrs Parfitt hadn't had the time to do, and then she sat down to write her letters.

This took her a long time, for it was difficult to write exactly what she wanted to say to Paul. She finished at last, wrote a letter to Mrs Parfitt about the sick aunt and went to pack her knapsack. Only the necessities went into it—her lavish wardrobe she left. She left her lovely sapphire and diamond ring too, putting it in its little velvet box on the tallboy in his dressing-room.

She wasn't hungry but she forced herself to eat some lunch, for she wasn't sure where she would get her supper. She had some money too—not very much but enough to keep her for a week, and as soon as she had a job she would pay it back; she had been careful to put that in her letter.

It was going on for three o'clock by then. She got her jacket, changed into sensible shoes, took the dogs for a quick run and then carefully locked up the house. It only remained for her to take her letter and leave it in Paul's study.

She left the knapsack in the hall with Mrs Parfitt's letter and went to the study. The letter in her hand, she sat for a moment in his chair, imagining him sitting in it presently, reading her letter, and two tears trickled down her cheeks. She wiped them away, got out of the chair and went round the desk and leaned over to prop the letter against the inkstand.

Sir Paul's hand took it gently from her just as she set it down, and for a moment she didn't move. The sight of the sober grey sleeve, immaculate linen and gold cufflinks, and his large, well-kept hand appearing from nowhere, had taken her breath, but after a moment she turned round to face him. 'Give it to me, please, Paul.' Her voice was a whisper.

'But it is addressed to me, Emma.'

'Yes, yes, I know it is. But you weren't to read it until after...'

'You had gone?' he added gently. 'But I am here, Emma, and I am going to read it.'

The door wasn't very far; she took a step towards it but he put out an arm and swept her close. 'Stay here where you belong,' he said gently and, with one arm holding her tight, he opened the letter.

He read it and then read it again, and Emma tried to wriggle free.

'Well, now you know,' she said in a watery voice. 'What are you going to do about it? I didn't mean to fall in love with you—it—it was an accident; I didn't know it would be so—so... What are you going to do, Paul?'

His other arm was round her now. 'Do? Something I wanted to do when I first saw you.' He bent and kissed her, taking his time about it.

Emma said shakily, 'You mustn't—we mustn't—what about Diana?'

'I can see that we shall have to have a cosy little talk, my darling, but not yet.' He kissed her again. 'I've always loved you. You didn't know that, did you? I didn't tell you, for I hurried you into marriage and you weren't ready for me, were you? So I waited, like a fool, and somehow I didn't know what to do.'

'It was me,' said Emma fiercely into his shoulder. 'I listened to Diana and I don't know why I did. I suppose it was because I love you and I want you to be happy, and I thought it was her and not me.' She gave a great sniff. 'She's so beautiful and clever and the babies were darlings and she told me to go to the travellers' camp...'

Sir Paul, used to the occasional incoherence of his patients, sorted this out. 'Darling heart, you are beautiful and honest and brave, and the only woman I have ever loved or could love.' He gave a rumble of laughter. 'And you shall have a darling baby of your own...'

'Oh, I shall love that—we'll share him. Supposing he's a girl?'

'In that case we must hope that we will be given a second chance.'

His arms tightened round her and she looked up at him, smiling. 'We'll start all over again—being married, I mean.'

He kissed her once more. 'That idea had occurred to me too.'

* * * * *

PINEAPPLE GIRL

Chapter 1

The ward was in twilight, the patients settling down for the night, those recently operated upon already sedated and made as comfortable as possible, while those ladies who were once more on their legs were putting in the last hair rollers, cleaning their teeth, and drinking the final dregs of the cocoa or Horlick's which the junior night nurse had been handing round. There were curtains round the bed by the door, though, and everyone was careful not to look in that direction. Mrs Peake, who had been in the ward for weeks now, was about to leave it. She had been quiet and uncomplaining and grateful for even the smallest service, and as Miss Crow, a convalescent appendix, remarked: 'It did seem 'ard to 'ave ter die all quiet-like.' Her listeners had nodded in agreement and one of them had whispered: 'Yer so right, dearie, but at least she's got our nice Staff with 'er.'

There was another round of whispered agreement. Eloise Bennett was liked by all her patients; she somehow managed to make a long night shorter, and the coming of morning something pleasant, even for those due for theatre that day. And she was a good nurse, too, seeing to uncomfortable pillows before the bed's occupant had time to complain, whisking sheets smooth, knowing when to be firm and when to sympathise, and over and above these things, she knew her work well— all the complications of drips and pumps, ventilators and tubes held no fears for her; sudden emergencies were dealt with with a calm born of experience and common sense, so that although she had only been qualified for a little more than a year, she had already been singled out by authority to be thrust into Sister's blue the moment a vacancy occurred.

She came from behind the curtains now, a tall girl, with a splendid figure and a wealth of nut-brown hair piled under her nurse's cap, and a face which could be considered plain but for a pair of large hazel eyes, richly fringed, for her nose was too short and her mouth far too wide and her brows, although nicely arched, were dark and thick. She smiled as she encountered the gaze of the little group of women still out of their beds, said in a pleasant voice: 'Ladies, you're missing your beauty sleep,' and went past them to start her evening round at the top of the ward.

The first three beds offered no hindrance to her progress; operation cases of that afternoon, they were al-

ready settled for the night and sleeping, so she merely
checked their conditions, studied their charts and moved
on down the ward. Old Mrs James was in the next bed,
elderly and crotchety and impatient of the major surgery she had undergone a few days previously; Eloise
stayed with her for a few minutes, listened to her small
grievances, promised sleeping pills very shortly and
went on to the next bed.

The ward was almost full, only one empty bed at the
end of the row stood ready to receive any emergency
which might arrive at a moment's notice. It would have
to be moved presently, thought Eloise as she sped past it,
for if anyone came in during the night the whole ward
would be awakened by the trundling of the trolley down
its length. She sighed a little, for the day staff could
have done it easily without disturbing anyone at all…

The first bed on the other side of the ward still had
its overhead light on, its occupant sitting up against her
pillows, reading. The new patient, admitted that day
for operation in the morning and according to the day
nurses, as tiresome a woman as one could wish not to
meet. Eloise stopped by the bed, said, 'Good evening,
Mrs Fellows,' in her nice quiet voice and pointed out
that bed lights had been due out ten minutes earlier.
'I'm going to give you something to make you sleep,'
she promised. 'You've had a drink, haven't you? Nurse
will bring you a cup of tea early in the morning and get
you ready for theatre.'

Mrs Fellows was aggressively blonde, extremely fat
and far from sweet-tempered. 'And who are you?' she
wanted to know, belligerently. 'I shan't sleep a wink, no

one knows how I suffer with my poor nerves—the least sound and I wake. I need the greatest care and attention—the very thought of my operation makes me feel faint!'

Eloise considered privately that fainting was the last thing that Mrs Fellows was likely to do; shout, scream, wake everyone up—yes, very probably; anything to focus attention on her plump person.

'Don't think about it,' she advised, 'there's no need, you know, because you'll know absolutely nothing about it...'

Mrs Fellows shot her a look of dislike. 'Easy to talk,' she sneered, 'a great hulking girl like you, as hard as nails and never a day's illness. You're all alike,' she added vaguely.

'I expect we seem like that to you,' conceded Eloise, 'but we're not really.' She stretched up and turned off the bed light. 'I'll be back presently with those pills.' She smiled kindly at the tiresome woman and turned to the occupant of the next bed, Mrs White, a small, wiry woman who was going home the next day and who greeted her with a smile. 'I'll miss yer, dearie,' she said softly. 'It'll be nice to get 'ome, but I'll miss yer... 'Ere, this is from me old man and me. Yer been an angel and we wants yer ter 'ave it.'

And Mrs White, with a swift movement worthy of a magician, heaved at something under the blankets and produced a pineapple.

'Oh!' said Eloise, startled, and then: 'Mrs White, what a simply lovely present—thank you, and your husband. I've—I've never had such a delightful surprise.' She clasped the fruit to her person and bent to kiss the donor. She was going to look a little strange finishing the round hugging it to her aproned bosom, but to do anything else would hurt Mrs White's feelings. She tucked it under one arm, where it got dreadfully in the way, until she was back at her desk once more, where she put it in a prominent position, mindful of her patient's watchful eye.

It stayed there for the rest of the night, while Eloise, with her junior trotting beside her, dealt with all the small emergencies which cropped up. She dealt with the inevitable admission too, a young girl who had got involved in a fight between her boyfriend and some other young man; she had been punched and knocked around and both hands had been cut where she had tried to take the knife away from one of them. She was still shocked when she was admitted; Eloise dealt with her gently, sedated her under the eye of the house surgeon on duty, and went back to her routine chores; they had to be fitted in however many times she was interrupted. And the girl was quiet, which was more than could be said for the two men admitted with her. Lucy Page, the staff nurse on Men's Surgical, had a good deal to say about them when she got down to her meal.

'A nasty pair,' she informed Eloise. 'I've got them in the two-bedded ward opposite the office—they're laid low at the moment and there's a member of the force with them, thank heaven, but I don't envy the day staff. How's yours?'

Eloise told her, gobbling rice pudding, her mind already hours ahead, working out how she could best catch up with the night's work before the morning was upon her. 'Someone gave me a pineapple,' she informed the table at large, and added apologetically: 'I would have brought it down with me, but I thought it would have been nice to take home...'

There was a chorus of assent; everyone there knew that Eloise lived in a poky little flat behind the Imperial War Museum—true, it was on the fringe of a quite respectable middle-class district, but with, as it were, an undesirable neighbourhood breathing down its neck. It had been all that her mother could afford after her father had died, and now, several years later, they both knew that she had made a mistake, giving up their pretty little house in the Somerset village and coming to live in an alien London. At the time it had seemed a good idea; Eloise had just started her training as a nurse, and if she lived with her mother there would be more money to eke out Mrs Bennett's tiny pension, and if her mother had stayed in Eddlescombe, then Eloise would have been hard put to it to find the fare home, even for an occasional visit.

Accordingly, when her sister-in-law had suggested that she might be able to find them a flat near St Goth's, Mrs Bennett had been delighted. Surprised too; her elder brother's wife and now widow had never liked them overmuch; she had paid an occasional visit, turning up her long nose at the smallness of the village house, sneering at the small country pleasures they enjoyed, wondering, out loud and in a penetrating voice, how they could exist without central heating, colour TV and the amenities of town life. But after Mr Bennett's funeral she had stayed on for a few days, full of suggestions as to their future. And at the time they had been grateful, for it had seemed a way out of their difficulties, but now, sadly, with the wisdom of hindsight they knew that they had made a mistake.

Mrs Bennett had never settled in London and although they lived more comfortably now that Eloise was trained and had more money, it was still hard to make ends meet. Besides, her aunt, now that her first enthusiastic efforts had palled and she had seen them settled in their new home, had rather washed her hands of them, not that Mrs Bennett would have accepted any help from her. A small, rather timid woman, sheltered all her married life by her husband and then by his daughter, she had nonetheless a good deal of pride which made it unthinkable to rely on any form of charity, especially from her sister-in-law, so she lived uncomplainingly in the hideous block of flats, her treasured furniture around her, and looked upon with good-humoured tolerance and casual affection by her neighbours, while she, for her part, was ever ready to babysit, read aloud to the bedbound and offer a ready hand when it was needed.

Eloise hated it too, but the hate hadn't soured her. She had done well during her training, been the gold medallist for her year and was well on the way to a Sister's post—Junior Night Sister first, the stepping off point for promotion, and then the chance of a ward of her own—and when that happened, and it wouldn't be all that long to wait, she had made up her mind to find a home for them both, in or near Eddlescombe. She would be earning enough to do that, and although she would hate living in the hospital, she would be able to go home fairly often and at least have the satisfaction of knowing that her mother was happy.

She was thinking about it as she went off duty in the morning after a tiring night, culminating in Mrs Fellows' shocking behaviour when she had wakened at six o'clock. Little Mrs Peake had died in the early hours of the morning, as gently and quietly as she had lived, and Eloise and her nurse had done what they had to do in a sad silence, for there had been no one to mourn the dear soul; as far as anyone knew she had no family and very few friends. They made up the bed with silent speed and went back to their endless little jobs until the first of the operation cases woke, to be instantly made comfortable for the day, sat up, given a drink, and where necessary, another injection. They had all the poorly ones settled by the time the rest of the ward roused itself and the mobile patients began their self-appointed task of handing round the early tea.

It was in the middle of this cheerful bustle that Mrs Fellows had made herself heard; she refused in no uncertain manner to drink her tea, take a bath and put on her theatre gown; she had refused loudly, rudely and at great length, so that Eloise, called from the re-packing of dressings, changing of drips and filling in charts, was hard put to keep her patience and temper—something Mrs Fellows' neighbours didn't do. She was told to belt up, shut up and invited to buzz off, their advice given in the pungent, forceful language of the cockney, with strong recommendations to mind what she said to Staff. 'For yer don't know yer luck,' declared one old lady, still without her teeth but none the less a force to be reckoned with. 'She's a h'angel, she is, an' yer jist wait till ter-night, yer won't 'arf be glad she's 'ere ter look after yer.'

The chorus of agreement was uttered in so menacing a tone that Eloise had intervened, begging everyone in a calm voice to hush a little: 'Don't forget the ladies at the other end,' she reminded her belligerent supporters, 'they're not feeling too bright and most of them have just had injections.'

She had pulled the curtains round Mrs Fellows' bed then, while that lady muttered abuse at her. It would have been nice, she thought tiredly, if she could have muttered back at her; the night had been a heavy one and she was dog-tired, and going off duty presently, with the prospect of a lot more of Mrs Fellows when she came on again that night, did nothing to cheer her. She had sent her junior nurse on ahead while she went back to say a final farewell to Mrs White, and then, with her bag, bulging with the knitting she hadn't had a chance to do, and the pineapple clasped under one arm, she had set off for the canteen, a vast, dreary place in the basement.

Women's Surgical was on the second floor and nurses were supposed to use the stairs; in any case both lifts were in use. Eloise started off running down the stone steps, late and tired and a little cross. She had reached the ground floor and had begun to traverse the back lobby in order to reach the last, narrow flight of stairs, when she saw Sir Arthur Newman, the senior consultant on the surgical side, standing directly below the staircase she was tearing down, looking the other way, talking to a tall man with very broad shoulders, facing her. The man was good-looking—very, noted her tired eye, with fair hair and commanding features—and he was staring at her.

And no wonder, she thought peevishly; her hair was coming loose from its bun and her cape was hanging from one shoulder; all the same, he didn't have to look at her as though she were surrounded by winking lights or something. She frowned and lifted her chin because he had begun to smile a little, and that was a great pity, because she took a step which wasn't there and fell flat on her face. The knitting cushioned her fall, but the pineapple bounded ahead and landed with a squashy thump on the man's shoe, denting itself nastily.

The shoe's wearer kicked it gently to one side, surveyed his large, well-shod foot and bent to pick her up. The pair of them hauled her to her feet rather as though she had been a sack of coals, dusted her down with kindly hands and while Sir Arthur handed her her knitting, his companion bent to pick up the crushed fruit.

'So sorry,' said Eloise breathlessly, 'very clumsy of me…' Her eye fell on the pineapple and her face dropped. 'Oh, it's spoilt!' She lifted a worried face to his. 'And I did so want to…' She paused; this stranger wouldn't be in the least interested in her intentions regarding her gift. 'I hope it didn't hurt your foot,' she said politely.

'I have large feet,' he had a slow, pleasantly deep voice, 'and there's no harm done—only to this.' He handed over the battered thing. 'A present?' he inquired gently.

'Well, yes—you know, someone going home…so

kind…thank you both very much…breakfast… I'm late…' She smiled at them both, happily forgetful of her deplorable appearance, and nipped across the lobby and down the stairs, to be greeted by her friends wanting to know why she was so late and had someone dragged her through a hedge backwards.

She sat down with her plate of porridge and showered it with sugar. 'Well, I got off late, and then I fell down in the back lobby and Sir Arthur was there and picked me up.' For some reason she didn't want to tell them about the man who had been with him. 'I've ruined my pineapple, though.'

'Put it in the fridge,' someone suggested. 'Perhaps it'll harden up—you've got nights off after tonight, haven't you?'

Eloise fetched scrambled eggs on toast and began to devour them. 'And three weeks' holiday only two weeks away.'

'What will you do?'

'Stay at home—I expect we'll go out, exhibitions and things,' she observed vaguely; London at the beginning of October wasn't really the place for a holiday. Now, Eddlescombe would be lovely; bonfires in the gardens and falling leaves and long walks under an autumn sky… She pushed aside the rest of her breakfast, no longer hungry, and got herself another cup of tea. 'Does anyone want any stamps?' she asked. 'I've got to go to the post office on the way home.'

She went home by bike, on an ancient machine which creaked and groaned through the morning traffic and brought her finally to the block of flats where she and her mother lived. The building looked bleaker than usual as she wheeled it to the basement shelter and chained it up for the day before walking up two flights of stairs to the second floor, the pineapple, very much the worse for wear, secure on top of the knitting in her bag. It looked a bit second-hand by now, but at least most of it would be edible.

Second-hand or not, Mrs Bennett was delighted with it, making light of the damage. 'What a lovely surprise,' she declared happily. 'We'll have it at supper.' Her still pretty face creased into a ready smile, while her eyes, hazel like her daughter's, noted the tired white face.

'A bad night, love? Well, only two more nights before you get nights off—what shall we do with them? There's that exhibition of pottery—oh, and your aunt wants to come and see us...'

Eloise had cast off her outdoor uniform and was putting on the kettle. 'Oh, Mother, must she? She only comes when she wants something.'

'Yes, I know, darling, but this time she's bringing Deborah Pringle with her—remember I knew her years ago and we were always great friends—still are in a way, for we write regularly even though she doesn't live in England. I should like to see her again.'

She went back into the kitchen and made the tea and they went into the sitting room, small and rather crowded with the furniture they had brought with them from Somerset; all the same, it was a pretty room with a few flowers and some small pieces of silver on the sideboard. The pair of them sat down by the window and drank their tea and presently Eloise went off to have her bath and go to bed. Really, night duty was no life at all, she thought sleepily as she brushed her hair; here it was almost eleven o'clock and she would have to be up soon after five so that she could eat her supper in peace before going back on duty—there was no time to read or talk. 'Poor Mother,' she muttered, 'it's even worse for her.'

She went to say goodnight to her parent, busy in the kitchen, and then retired to take her night's rest in her topsy-turvy world. It had been a horrid night, she reflected gloomily as she curled up in bed. At least, not quite horrid, for there had been that nice man... She fell asleep thinking about him.

Her mother called her, as she always did, with a cup of tea and sat on the end of the bed while she drank it. 'You've not slept very much, have you?' she wanted to know.

'Well, once the children get out of school...' Eloise tried to sound cheerful because she knew that her mother worried about her wakefulness, and her mother nodded and went on:

'That pineapple, dear—was there something special about it?'

'Just a pineapple, Mother.'

'Yes, I know that—but a special delivery man called after lunch with a Fortnum and Mason basket, I opened it because all the man said was "name of Bennett", the way they always do—and it's crammed with fruit: three pineapples and grapes and those enormous pears and apples...there's a note.'

She handed an envelope to her daughter and didn't

say a word while Eloise opened it and read the brief note inside: 'Allow me to offer compensation for the damage done by my foot this morning.' The signature was unintelligible and it was addressed to the Pineapple Girl.

'Well!' said Eloise, and then: 'He must be nuts.'

'Who, dear?' Mrs Bennett's voice was casual, masking her seething curiosity.

'Well, there was this man…' Eloise related the morning's happening without trimmings. 'And my hair was coming down—I looked a perfect fright—you know…' She paused. 'Mother, have I ever reminded you of a pineapple?'

Her mother took the question seriously. 'No, dear. You're not a beauty, but you're not knobbly—your hair grows very prettily too, not out of the top of your head.'

'How did he know where I lived?'

'He only had to ask, presumably. Porters, or someone,' said Mrs Bennett vaguely. 'If he was talking to Sir Arthur Newman he must have been respectable, so of course they would have told him.'

Eloise looked at her mother with loving amusement. 'Yes, well…' She finished her tea and went along to the sitting room where the basket was displayed on the table. It was indeed a splendid sight, Eloise walked all round it, eyeing its contents. 'I can't thank him,' she observed at length. 'I haven't a clue who he is, have I? I could ask, I suppose, but I don't think I want to—I mean if—if he'd wanted to see me again he would have put an address or said so.' She glanced at her mother and said seriously: 'He was a very handsome man, he'd hardly lower his sights to me, you know. I expect he just felt sorry.'

She sighed; usually she didn't waste time pining for a beautiful face, but just for a moment she wanted most desperately to be absolutely eye-catching. 'Oh, well,' she said at length, and then: 'We've got enough fruit to open a shop, isn't it marvellous?'

It seemed only fair to take Mrs White's gift back on duty that evening, to be shared among her friends at their midnight dinner; it made a nice change from the creamed rice and jellied fruit which were on the menu night after night. But Eloise didn't get any herself; she got down late to her meal because Mrs Fellows had made the early part of the night hideous with her loud moans and complaints. She had been sedated early because the day staff had been hindered in their evening's work by her constant demands for this, that and the other thing, but that had worn off by ten o'clock, and although Eloise got the house surgeon on duty to come and look at her and write her up for further sedation, he had told her to wait until midnight before giving it.

'She's not in pain,' he declared, 'just determined to make life hell for everyone else—let's see, supposing we give her...' He wrote busily. 'That should keep her quiet until morning and you can repeat it at six o'clock if she's still rampaging.' He thrust the chart at Eloise. 'It was only an EUA, after all...not even surgery.'

Cycling home in the morning, Eloise reflected that the night had been awful—thank heaven there was only one more to go before her nights off.

And that night was so madly busy that she had no

time for her own thoughts at all; with operation cases to settle, two severe accident cases to admit, an emergency case for the theatre at two o'clock in the morning, and Mrs Fellows, due home in the morning, but still complaining loudly, adding her quota to the night's bedlam. Eloise, too tired to know whether she was coming or going, ate her breakfast in a trance, got herself home and fell into her bed after a quick cup of tea and a hot bath.

She had six nights off due to her and it was on the third of these that Mrs Bennett's visitors came. Her sister-in-law arrived first; a tall, commanding woman with a penetrating voice and cold good looks, she pecked at their cheeks, told them that they both looked tired, chose a chair with deliberation and loosened the expensive furs she was wearing. Watching her aunt, Eloise found herself wondering how she had come to marry her father's elder brother in the first place, although perhaps it wasn't so strange, as he had been successful; making money as easily as a good cook makes pastry, quite unlike her own father, content to work in his bookshop, specializing in rare books and engravings. That he had loved herself and her mother she had no doubt, but books were his real love and he had lived largely in a world of his own far removed from the more mundane life around him. Which had probably accounted for the fact that when he died very suddenly from a coronary, it was discovered that his insurances had lapsed for a number of years and that he had mortgaged the shop and house in order to find the money to buy the rare books he had coveted. As a consequence he had left his wife and daughter very ill provided for and although neither of them had blamed him in the slightest for this,

his sister-in-law had never ceased, on every possible occasion, to mention his improvidence.

The lady made just such a remark now, once she had settled herself, and went on in her bossy way: 'You need a change, both of you, and I have the solution.'

She held up a beringed hand to stop any questioning, although neither of her listeners had had any intention of speaking; they had long ago decided that the only way to treat their overbearing relation was to give every appearance of attention and then go their own way, but the lady went on, just as though she had received a gratifying murmur of admiration: 'But I shall say no more until Deborah Pringle arrives.' She frowned and glanced at her watch. 'She should be here now.'

As though Mrs Pringle had been given her cue, the doorbell rang and Eloise went to answer it. She had met Mrs Pringle a number of times and liked her; she was a small bustling creature with a kindly nature which never sought to boss others around and Eloise had often wondered how she had come to be a friend of her aunt's. She came in now, exclaiming cheerfully, 'I'm a little late, but the taxi couldn't find you and I'm hopeless at telling people how to get to places.' She gave Eloise a kiss and added warmly: 'Your lovely hair—how I do envy you, my dear. How's your mother?'

Eloise said dryly: 'Aunt says she needs a holiday...'

'And I daresay she does but she's not one to waste time pining for something—not if I know her, and I should do after all these years.' She smiled widely and whispered: 'What's the betting that I'm wearing the wrong kind of hat?'

She was greeted with pleasure by Mrs Bennett and more austerely by that lady's sister-in-law, who, sure enough, told her at once: 'That's not the hat for you, Deborah—far too young...'

'But I feel young.' Mrs Pringle sat down between her two friends and looked at them in turn, rather like a referee might look at two boxers before a fight. She said cheerfully: 'Well, Mary, it's delightful to see you again—a pity I don't come to England more often and when I do, it's almost impossible to get away; Cor likes me to be with him all the time.'

'He's not with you this time?' asked Mrs Bennett.

'He went back last week—simply had to...' And when her friend cast her an inquiring look: 'I wasn't allowed to travel; I came over here for an operation, nothing vital, but I have to stay for a check-up before I go home.' She changed the conversation then, and it wasn't until Eloise had fetched the tea and they had finished the sandwiches and homemade cake that she reverted to herself.

'I've a favour to ask,' she began a shade diffidently. 'You see, I met Maggie a short while ago,' she paused to smile at that forbidding lady, 'and I mentioned that I was going back home in a short time and wanted to take a nurse with me, just for a little while, you know, and so she telephoned you, Mary, meaning to ask if Eloise was free, and you told her that she had a holiday in a couple of weeks. Now that would be simply splendid if only she would agree to come with me.' She flashed a smile at Eloise. 'Nothing much to do, just a small dressing and my temperature and so on, and I promise her that she shall have plenty of time to do what she likes.'

Eloise found her astonished voice. 'How kind of you to think of me,' she exclaimed, 'but you see I can't leave Mother alone…'

'Ah,' Mrs Pringle beamed in mild triumph, 'it just so happens in the most extraordinary way imaginable that I met Mrs Plunkett last week—remember her at Eddlescombe? Well, she was asking about you, Mary, and said how much she would like to see you again and if only you were on your own she would love to have you to stay—you know she has only that dear little cottage with two bedrooms?' She paused and looked around her. Mrs Bennett was staring at her with rapt attention, Eloise's nice, ordinary face betrayed her suspicion that the whole thing was a put up job and her aunt looked vaguely irritated as she always did when someone else was doing the talking.

'I know it sounds too good to be true,' declared Mrs Pringle with a glance at Eloise, 'but that's exactly what happened, and I thought how marvellous it would be if Eloise were to come with me and you, Mary, could go and stay with Beryl Plunkett. What do you say?'

Eloise darted a quick look at the longing on her mother's face. 'I think it's a super idea, Mrs Pringle; I'd love to look after you, and if Mother's with Mrs Plunkett I should be quite happy about going. What do you think, Mother?'

Mrs Bennett smiled widely at no one in particular. 'Well, darling, it does sound delightful, but you're sure you…you'll have a lovely time… Eddlescombe will be heavenly at this time of year…'

Mrs Pringle smiled too. 'Then that's settled. Eloise, when does your holiday start? I planned to go down to say goodbye to Beryl. You could drive down with me, Mary, and I'll come back and collect Eloise on the following day.'

Mrs Bennett looked overwhelmed. 'You're really going down to Eddlescombe? It would be lovely to drive down with you—if Eloise could manage for a couple of days?'

'Easily, darling.' Eloise smiled at her mother. She hadn't seen that look on her face for a long time; even if she hadn't wanted to go with Mrs Pringle, she would have declared her delight at the prospect—and she did want to go, not only because it would give her mother the chance of a holiday; it would be fun to go somewhere different. Which reminded her. 'You know, I'm not at all sure where you live,' she told Mrs Pringle.

'Holland, my dear. We've lived all over the world, you know, but now Cor is permanently based there, and he being a Dutchman finds that very satisfactory—so do I; we live in Groningen, in the north and within easy reach of the city. There's a car if you care to drive it, and the country around us is delightful—quiet but not isolated. Cor is away a good deal, but he's always home at weekends and we have friends—I think you might like it.' She caught the questioning look in Eloise's eye and added: 'I'll tell you about myself later; one's little illnesses are always so boring for other people.'

She turned back to Mrs Bennett. 'That's settled,

then, and how very pleased I am. Shall I collect you in—two weeks, is it? We'll fix the exact day later—and Eloise will be free the day after you go to Eddlescombe, won't she? Nothing could be better.' She gathered up her gloves and handbag. 'I really must fly—can I give you a lift, Maggie?'

She so obviously expected her offer to be accepted that Eloise's aunt got to her feet quite quickly and with unusual meekness, and it was during their rather protracted farewells that Mrs Pringle said quietly to Eloise: 'You're back on duty in two days, aren't you? Could you manage to meet me one morning before you come home?'

There was no time to ask questions. Eloise said yes and named a day and time and wondered what she was going to be told, for obviously Mrs Pringle was going to tell her something; something which she didn't care to discuss with everyone; something to do with her op. Eloise reviewed her surgery and decided that it was probably a good deal more serious than Mrs Pringle had implied.

It was; sitting in the visitors' room in the Nurses' Home after breakfast a few mornings later, her visit disclosed quite simply that she had inoperable cancer; that there was little more to be done and that she and her husband had decided that she should return to Groningen and live out the rest of her life among her friends and in the home she loved. 'I have a simply splendid doctor,' she told Eloise cheerfully. 'It was he who sent me to Sir Arthur Newman in the first place—you've worked for him, haven't you, dear? I was in a nursing home, of course, though I should have been just as happy in hospital, but Cor insisted, bless him...' She smiled. 'So now you know—or did you guess?'

'Almost—I thought it might be more serious than you wanted us to think, and when you mentioned a dressing...'

'And you really don't mind coming? It's silly of me, I know, but I have to get used to the idea and I thought if I had someone I knew with me, just for a little while, then I can face it. They tell me I can expect six months, perhaps a little longer.'

Eloise got out of her chair and went to kneel by her visitor. 'You're brave, Mrs Pringle, and I'll do all I can to help you. Your husband must be very upset.'

'Poor dear, he is. Do you believe in miracles, Eloise?'

'Yes, and I think most nurses and doctors do; you see, now and then there is a miracle, and who knows, it might be yours.'

Her visitor smiled crookedly. 'Bless you for saying that! I believe we're going to get on very well together.' She got to her feet. 'Not a word to your mother, mind— no one knows, only you and Cor and Sir Arthur, and of course my own doctor.'

'Dutch?' asked Eloise.

'From Groningen.' Mrs Pringle looked vaguely speculative for a moment. 'I expect you'll get on well with each other; he's a mild sort of man. Now I'm going for you have to go home and go to bed. Will you tell your mother that I'll write to her within the next day or so? And I'll let you know at what time I'll call for you.' She leaned up and kissed Eloise's cheek. 'You're a dear girl.'

Eloise cycled home thoughtfully, only half her mind on the traffic. Mrs Pringle was indeed a brave woman, and the idea of leaving her alone again after a couple of weeks went against the grain. She frowned over the problem until she was brought back to the present by a bus driver alongside her, waiting at the traffic lights, asking her from his cab if she had taken root. He said it nicely, for she was in uniform, but it recalled her to her whereabouts. She made haste home after that and spent the next hour or so listening to her mother's delighted comments on her forthcoming holiday. 'I am looking forward to it,' declared Mrs Bennett for the hundredth time, 'and I only hope you'll enjoy yourself too, darling.'

Eloise gave her mother a hug. 'I shall enjoy every minute of it,' she assured her, reflecting that to do anything else wouldn't help Mrs Pringle at all. 'And now I'm off to bed, darling—I had a beastly night.'

Chapter 2

The fortnight went very quickly. The ward was busy for one thing, and for another, both Eloise and her mother had something to plan for. Refuting that wise but cautious saying about rainy days, Eloise took her mother shopping and persuaded her parent to invest in a good tweed suit, pointing out with rather muddled good sense that the garment in question would probably be twice the price by the time they could afford to buy it. Mrs Bennett, thus spurred on, found a dear little hat to go with it, had her good shoes re-soled and then turned her attention to her daughter. Eloise dressed well, considering she did so on a minuscule amount of money, but as her mother pointed out, Mrs Pringle very likely lived in some style, and she had to admit that her winter coat, although well cut and nicely fitting, was now about to see its third winter—moreover, she was heartily sick of it; something would have to be done to liven it up. This they achieved at a reasonable outlay by the purchase of an angora cap, scarf and gloves in a warm shade of honey which helped the dark brown of the coat considerably.

Eloise found a dress too of almost the same shade; one of dozens similar in Marks and Spencer, but as she pointed out, the chance of anyone in Holland knowing that was remote. It was simply cut, with long sleeves and a wide belt to define her small waist, and if the occasion warranted she would dress it up with a neck scarf or some beads. Sweaters she already had, and skirts and an elderly velvet dress the colour of a mole, bought in their more affluent days; no longer high fashion, but it would, at a pinch, pass muster. The two ladies went home, packed their cases and professed themselves well pleased with their purchases.

It had been arranged that Mrs Bennett should be fetched by Mrs Pringle's car—a hired one, and as she confided to Eloise, it would be a treat in itself just to be driven all the way to Somerset. 'Though Deborah always drove herself,' she remarked, 'and when I asked her why she had a chauffeur she said something about it being not like the old days and there was too much traffic. I must say I was quite surprised.' Which Eloise wasn't.

Her mother gone, Eloise combated loneliness with a great deal of housework, slept soundly and went on duty for the last time before her holiday. The tiresome Mrs Fellows had long since gone, but the ward was full and some of the patients were ill; she went off duty tired out

and with the good-natured wishes of her friends ringing in her ears she cycled home, thankful that she had
nothing to do but go to bed. She got up early, finished
her packing, cooked herself an early supper, washed her
hair and after touring the little flat to make sure that everything was in apple pie order, went back to bed again;
she would have to be up in good time in the morning,
as she was to be fetched at eight o'clock.

She woke to a bright day, the chilliness of autumn
masked by brilliant sunshine. The winter coat was going
to be a little heavy, but worn without a hat it would
have to do. She took extra care with her pretty hair,
made up her face carefully, collected her passport and
purse, went through her handbag once more, and sat
down to wait.

Mrs Pringle was on time; Eloise saw the car from the
window, gave a final look round and went downstairs.
She felt excited now and happier than she had been for a
long time, although she knew that the happiness would
be dimmed before long—Mrs Pringle had put a brave
face on things, but there were going to be days when
she wouldn't feel so good, when Eloise would have to
coax and encourage and somehow rekindle the spark of
hope every patient had tucked away inside them. And
there was always the possibility, however remote, that
Mrs Pringle might make a recovery—it could happen,
no one knew why, and it didn't happen often, but it was
something to bear in mind and work for.

Her patient was in the back of the car; if she were
secretly worried about herself, no trace of it showed on
her face. She told the driver to stow the luggage in the

boot, invited Eloise to get in beside her and exclaimed happily: 'I'm so thrilled at the idea of going home! I've been thinking of some of the things we might do together, but first I must tell you about your mother. I left her looking ten years younger and so happy—she sent her love and said you were to enjoy yourself. Such a dear creature and not changed at all, which is more than I can say for your aunt—how lucky she is to have you, Eloise. I always wanted a daughter. Of course it's lovely having Pieter, but he doesn't live at home.' She sighed. 'We always said that we would have six children.'

'Mother wanted a large family...'

'Yes. Ah, well, perhaps when you marry you'll make up for it and have a pack of them—that will please her, though it's not fashionable.'

'Pooh,' declared Eloise, 'who cares about fashion?' and just for a moment she saw herself, surrounded by several quite beautiful children, with a pleasant house in the background and an enormous garden, and somewhere close by, but regrettably vague, a husband. She might have elaborated on his appearance, only her companion was speaking again.

'We'll be met at Schiphol—Cor will be there with the car—this one is hired; as you know. It won't take long to drive home from there—it's less than a hundred and fifty miles. The village where we live is called Scharmerbloem—it's small, but then you like the country, don't you, dear? Just a few houses and a church. Groningen is only ten miles away, though.'

'And your doctor—does he live in Groningen?'

'Well, he has his consulting rooms there and beds in

the hospital, but he lives quite close by us, by the side of a charming lake called Schildermeer. The village is called Oostersum—it's as small as ours.' She paused, 'We do depend on our cars, of course, as although the main road isn't too far away, it's a good walk, though once you're there the bus service is good.'

They were threading their way through the London traffic towards the airport and Mrs Pringle glanced out of the window rather wistfully so that Eloise said quickly: 'Of course you'll be coming back in a month or so for a check-up, won't you? Sir Arthur would want that.'

'Yes, although he did suggest that he might come and see me—he's an old friend of our doctor and it would give him an excuse to visit him.'

'What a good idea! I expect your doctor knows everything there is to know about you, Mrs Pringle?'

'Yes, dear, and I've great faith in him; he's quiet and solid and sure of himself.'

Eloise decided silently that probably he was big-headed; quite likely he wouldn't take kindly to giving instructions to a foreign nurse. It was to be hoped that his English was adequate. She reflected uneasily that she had better get herself a dictionary and learn a few vital words of the Dutch language. In a way it was a pity that she wouldn't be wearing uniform; a nurse never seemed a nurse unless she was in an apron and cap. As though her companion had read her thoughts, Mrs Pringle observed, 'I've got some white dresses for you, dear—you don't mind? There's that dressing, and just in case I should have to stay in bed...'

'How thoughtful of you, Mrs Pringle. I'll wear uniform all the time if you want me to.'

Her companion was shocked. 'Good heavens, no, dear—you're on holiday, at least, more or less—besides, I don't want any of my friends to know about me. I shall say that you're the daughter of an old friend come to spend a couple of weeks with us—will that do?'

'Very well, I should think.' Eloise looked out of the window. 'We're almost there; I'm quite excited, I've not been in a plane before.'

Mrs Pringle was looking at herself in a pocket mirror. 'I hate them,' she said, 'but they're quick. The driver will see to our luggage and if I give you the tickets do you think you could cope?'

It was all a little strange but straightforward enough; Eloise coped and presently found herself sitting beside Mrs Pringle, watching the runway under the plane slide away at an alarming speed. She wasn't sure if she liked it, so she looked away and didn't look again until they had left the ground beneath them.

It was similar to travelling in a bus, she discovered, and once over her initial uneasiness, she peered down through the gaps in the cloud and saw that they were already over the water. It seemed no time at all before her companion pointed out the Dutch coast, flat and very tidy, far below them, the sea frothing endlessly at its unending sands.

Mijnheer Pringle was waiting for them and at first sight Eloise was disappointed; she hadn't met him before, but his wife had always spoken of him with such warmth that Eloise had formed a picture of a commanding man, handsome and self-assured. And here he was, short, middle-aged and a little stout, with a round cheerful face from which the hair was receding, and not in the least good-looking. Nor was he commanding, although the porter seemed to treat him with respect. He embraced his wife carefully as though she were something precious and porcelain and then turned to Eloise, to shake her hand with a surprisingly hard grip and bid her welcome in fluent English. 'The car's here,' he said, and took his wife's arm. 'Shall we go straight home or would you like to stop somewhere for coffee?' He looked anxious. 'Should you rest for an hour or two, Debby? We could go to a hotel.'

Mrs Pringle gave him a loving look. 'I never felt better, Cor.' She glanced at Eloise. 'We had a very quiet flight, didn't we, dear? And I'd love to go home...'

Mijnheer Pringle drove well, his wife beside him and Eloise in the back of the car. He kept up a steady flow of conversation, pointing out anything which he thought might be of interest to her and making little jokes. He was as brave as his wife, and she liked him. When he asked: 'Do you not wonder why I, a Dutchman, should have so English a name?' she said, surprised: 'Well, I never thought about it—but of course it is English, isn't it? I've always said Mrs Pringle, but that's wrong, isn't it? It's Mevrouw. But you're Dutch, Mijnheer Pringle, so why...?'

'My grandfather came here when he was a young man and married a Dutchwoman, and my father was of course born here and married a Dutchwoman in his turn, so that I am truly Dutch although I have married an Englishwoman—amusing, is it not?' He added: 'And my good fortune.'

Eloise saw him glance sideways at his wife and smile; it must be marvellous to be loved like that; the kind of love which would surmount illness and worse. Perhaps somewhere in the world there was someone like Mijnheer Pringle waiting for her. It would be nice if he were tall and handsome, but that didn't matter very much; it was being loved that mattered. She thought briefly of the very few young men who had shown any interest in her, and even that had been casual. She wasn't eye-catching and she hadn't been any good at pretending to love someone when she didn't; they had found her amusing but shy and old-fashioned, and mostly treated her in a brotherly fashion, before long telling her all about some wonderful girl they had met and asking her advice. It had been a little lowering.

They stopped in Zwolle and had lunch. They were about halfway, Mijnheer Pringle told her, and would be able to travel fast on the motorway for almost the whole journey. 'Although the last few kilometres are along narrow dyke roads—real country, pasture land mostly; with plenty of big farms although the villages are small.'

'It sounds lovely,' said Eloise, and meant it, for she was a simple girl with simple tastes; she had disliked London even while admitting its charm and she had done her best to overcome that dislike because as far as she could see she would have to stay there for the rest of her working days if she wanted a good job in a good hospital. She observed suddenly, thinking her thoughts aloud, 'A lot of English nurses work over here, don't they?'

'Indeed they do.' Mijnheer Pringle was scrutinising the bill with such intensity that she had the uncomfortable feeling that he might not have enough money to pay it. 'Perhaps you like the idea, Eloise?' he asked her kindly, counting out notes with care.

'Well, it might be fun, but there's my mother—she really wants to go back to Eddlescombe, you know.'

Mevrouw Pringle gathered up her handbag and gloves. 'Well, things do happen,' she remarked vaguely. 'I'm ready whenever you are.'

It was still afternoon when they reached Groningen and Eloise looked round her eagerly, craning her neck to see everything at once and quite failing to do so; she was left with a delightful hotchpotch of tall, narrow houses, canals, bridges, a great many cyclists and even more people hurrying to and fro, darting into the streets and disappearing round tantalising corners.

'You shall come whenever you wish,' Mevrouw Pringle promised. 'I don't care for towns much—I like to sit about at home, being lazy.' She spoke so convincingly that Eloise almost believed her.

Mijnheer Pringle had been quite right about the roads. They were narrow, made of brick, and wandered through the wide landscape, perched as it were upon the numerous dykes. And the villages were indeed small, each a neat handful of houses encircling a church, a caf and a shop, and lying around and beyond the villages she could see the farms, large and solid with great barns at their backs, their fields dotted with black and white cows. Looking around her, she began to wonder just where the Pringles' house might be, and had her answer almost immediately when they passed through a village much like the rest and then turned between high gateposts into a short drive bisecting the grounds of a house. It looked a little like a farmhouse, only there was no barn built on to its back, although there were plenty of outbuildings to one side of it. Its front door was plain and solid with an ornate wrought iron transom above it and the windows were old-fashioned and sashed, two each side of the door and five in the row above. There were flower beds, well laid out, and shrubs and trees carefully sited; it looked peaceful and homely and exactly what Eloise had hoped for. When Mevrouw Pringle said eagerly: 'Here we are—I do hope you'll like it here, Eloise,' she replied that yes, she would, quite sincerely.

Inside was like outside; the rooms lofty and light, furnished with large comfortable chairs and solid tables and cupboards. The carpets were thick underfoot and the curtains were equally thick velvet, fringed and draped, not quite to Eloise's own taste but nonetheless very pleasing. But she had very little time to examine her surroundings; her patient was tired now and made no demur when her husband suggested that perhaps an hour's rest would be just the thing. They all went upstairs, Mijnheer Pringle explaining as they went that Juffrouw Blot, the housekeeper, would be along with a tray of tea just as soon as his wife was on her bed. 'We guessed that you would be tired, my dear, and you can have a good gossip with her later on, when you're rested.'

Alone with Mevrouw Pringle, Eloise quietly took charge, changed the dressing deftly, took off her patient's dress and tucked her under her quilt.

'Your room, Eloise,' protested Mevrouw Pringle. 'There's been no time to show you…here's Juffrouw Blot with my tea, she can take you…and ask Cor for anything.'

Eloise made soothing little sounds while she tidied the room, was introduced to the housekeeper, a stoutly built middle-aged woman who smiled and nodded and talked to her for all the world as though she could understand every word, and then followed her obediently across the wide landing to the room which was to be hers.

It was a pleasant apartment, lofty like all the other rooms in the house, and comfortably furnished with good taste if without much imagination. Eloise unpacked her bag, tidied her hair and did her face, peeped in at Mrs Pringle to make sure that she really was asleep and went downstairs.

Mijnheer Pringle was lying in wait for her. 'She's all right?' he asked anxiously. 'Such a long journey, but she would insist…it is good of you to come…' He looked away for a moment. 'Her doctor will be coming this evening—our friend too. He will talk to you and explain…'

'Explain what, Mijnheer Pringle?' She knew the answer already, though.

'Well—Debby has had this operation, you will have

been told about that, of course. What you weren't told is that she is going to die very soon—weeks, perhaps less. She doesn't know that; they told her six months or more, got her on her feet and allowed her home because that was what she wanted...' He sighed, one of the saddest sounds Eloise had heard for a long time. 'She's to do exactly what she wants,' he went on, 'because nothing can make any difference now. I hope that if she needs you and your holiday is finished, there will be some way of keeping you here. She has taken a fancy to you, you know—she has always been fond of your mother.' He cleared his throat. 'I'm determined that she shall be as happy as possible for these last few weeks.'

Eloise swallowed the lump in her own throat. 'Of course, and if she wants me to stay, I think it could be arranged; you would have to contact the hospital, of course—her doctor could help there. And if there's anything I can do to help, will you let me know?'

He nodded. 'Thank you. Shall we go and have tea? It's been taken into the sitting room.'

There was no milk with the tea, drunk from small cups which held only a few mouthfuls. Eloise, dying of thirst, was debating whether to ask for a third cup and run the risk of being considered greedy when Juffrouw Blot opened the door, said something to Mijnheer Pringle and flattened herself to allow a visitor to enter the room. The man who had sent her the basket of fruit; her firm little chin dropped and her eyes rounded in surprise—a surprise which he didn't appear to share, for his: 'Ah, the pineapple girl,' was casual to say the least as he crossed the room to shake Mijnheer Pringle's hand.

'You know each other?' queried that gentleman.

'No,' said his visitor cheerfully. 'That is to say, no one has introduced us, although we have met.'

Mijnheer Pringle looked puzzled, but he was a stickler for good manners. 'Eloise, this is Doctor van Zeilst, our very good friend. Timon, this is Miss Eloise Bennett who has kindly consented to spend her holidays with Deborah.'

'I know.' The doctor grinned at her. 'News travels fast in hospitals, doesn't it?'

'Apparently.' She looked at him coldly, quite put out because he had shown no pleasure at meeting her again. 'I believe I have to thank you for your gift of fruit.'

'Healthy stuff, fruit.' He nodded carelessly and turned to Mijnheer Pringle. 'How is Deborah?' and then: 'No, I'd better ask Nurse that.'

He looked across the room, smiling faintly, but for all that she sensed that she was now the nurse giving a report to the doctor. She complied with commendable conciseness, adding: 'I know little about Mevrouw Pringle's stay at the nursing home, only what she has told me herself—I've had no instructions...' Her voice held faint reproach.

He must have heard it, for he said blandly: 'Done deliberately. Sir Arthur felt that in this case, the fewer people who knew the truth, the better. However, I'll go into the whole thing with you presently.'

He smiled nicely at her and with a word of apology began to talk to Mijnheer Pringle in their own language.

After a few minutes she was a little taken aback to hear him observe: 'You don't have to look like that, we're not discussing you.'

She lifted her chin. 'I didn't for one moment imagine that you were.'

'Splendid, touchy females stir up the worst in me.' He was smiling again. 'Shall we have our little talk now? It seems a good opportunity; Mijnheer Pringle has some work to do.'

When they were alone he sat down opposite her. 'You know Mevrouw Pringle well?'

'No, not really—she's my mother's friend—oh, for a very long time. She used to visit us when we lived in Eddlescombe, but I've not met Mijnheer Pringle before.' She added soberly: 'It's very sad.'

He answered her just as soberly. 'Yes, it is, but it would be a good deal sadder if Mevrouw Pringle were to linger on for months in discomfort and perhaps pain, and later spend the last inevitable weeks in hospital. I think sometimes the longing to be in one's home is worse than the pain. Her husband and I are only thankful that this won't be necessary in her case.' He crossed his long legs, contemplating his beautifully polished shoes. 'I'll outline the case for you.'

Which he did, clearly and concisely in his quite perfect English, pausing now and then to allow her to ask questions. 'So there you have it,' he concluded. 'The haemoglobin is going down fast and nothing we can give her will check it now; her spleen, her liver...' he shrugged his great shoulders. 'The opiate we're giving her is strong, you will have noticed that; don't hesitate to let me know if it doesn't give enough cover. I shall come each day and you can telephone me at any time.'

'Do you live close by?' asked Eloise, and went delicately pink because it sounded as though she were being curious.

'I can be with you in ten minutes.'

He could have told her a little more than that, surely, but he didn't, merely went on to discuss the various small nursing duties she would be called upon to undertake. 'And you will remember that no one—and that means no one, is to know about Mevrouw Pringle's condition.' It sounded like an order.

'I am not a gossip,' she assured him coolly, 'and you seem to forget that I'm a nurse.'

She was quite outraged by his easy: 'Yes, I find I do, frequently.' But before she could frame a suitable reply to this, he went on: 'Will you be lonely here? It is very quiet—there are plenty of friends around but no bright lights and most of the young men are bespoke.'

There was no end to his rudeness. 'I can manage very well without bright lights,' she told him crossly, 'and I'm not accustomed to being surrounded by young men, so I shall hardly notice their absence, shall I?'

He laughed softly. 'I say, you have got a sharp tongue, dear girl. Might one venture to suggest that if you took the edge off it the young men might be more prone to surround you?'

She said flatly: 'Young men like pretty girls.'

'Young men, yes.'

Absurdly she flared up. 'Are you suggesting that I'm only suitable for a middle-aged widower with a string of children…?' She stopped because he was laughing at her, and anyway the conversation had got completely out of hand.

His next question surprised her. 'What did you do before you trained as a nurse?'

'I helped my father—he had a bookshop, he sold rare books and engravings.'

'Straight from books to patients—no fun, then. How old are you?'

She had answered him before she had had time to think that it was no business of his. 'Twenty-three.'

He nodded his head thoughtfully. 'Just right,' he observed, and taking no notice of her puzzled look, went on in a practical voice: 'Now this is what we will do. Mevrouw Pringle is to do exactly what she wishes— shopping trips, visits to friends…do you drive, by the way?'

'Well, Father had a little van, and I used to drive that, but I haven't driven much since we moved to London.'

'You have your licence with you? Good; it will be best if you go everywhere with her and if you're driving she'll not suspect.'

Eloise said helplessly, not liking the idea: 'But it's years—besides, it's on the other side of the road…'

The doctor got to his feet, unfolding his enormous frame slowly, until he seemed to tower over her. 'We'll have ten minutes in my car now,' he told her. 'I'll soon see if you can cope.'

She found herself being led outside to where a dark grey Rolls-Royce convertible stood before the front door. She stopped short when she saw it. 'Is that yours?'

she wanted to know urgently, 'because if it is I can't possibly drive it.'

He didn't even bother to answer her, but opened the door and stood there holding it until she got in, then he settled himself beside her and said: 'Off we go.'

She went; there was nothing else to do anyway, pride forbade her from getting out again. She fumbled for a few minutes, not understanding the gears, terrified of accelerating too hard and shooting through the bushes on either side of them, turning on the lights—even blowing the horn. To none of these errors did he respond, merely sitting quietly looking ahead of him while she wobbled down to the gate, to turn obediently when he uttered a laconic: 'Left.' But on the road her terror gradually subsided; true, she was driving a Rolls and if she damaged it heaven only knew what its owner would do to her, even though the whole thing had been his idea. She gripped the wheel firmly; she would show him, after all, even if the van had been small and old, she had driven well. After a few kilometres along the quiet road she even began to enjoy herself.

'Very nice,' said the doctor, 'and perfectly safe. One doesn't expect to find a girl driving with such cool. On the rare occasions—the very rare occasions, when I have been persuaded to let a girl take the wheel, she has invariably flung her hands into the air and squawked like a frightened hen after the first few yards.' His sidelong glance took in the pinkness of her cheeks. 'Mevrouw Pringle has a Citroën, easy to drive and quite small. You'll be all right. Now stop, and we'll go back. I've several more calls to make.'

He didn't talk as he drove back, fast, relaxed and very sure of himself, and Eloise, in a splendid muddle of vexation at his manner towards her and pride at her prowess, didn't speak either.

At the house he opened the door for her and ushered her into the hall, saying quietly: 'If I know Deborah Pringle, she will be in the sitting room...' And he was right; she was, smiling from a white face while she greeted them, assuring him that she was rested and had never felt better and was already planning some amusements for Eloise. 'And Timon,' she begged, 'don't dare suggest examining me today.'

He laughed gently and took her hand. 'It's delightful to see you again, Deborah, and I've no intention of spoiling your homecoming—besides, I've two more patients to see on my way home and then evening surgery. How about tomorrow? In the morning before you get up—ten o'clock. Nothing much, you know, just a check-up.'

He said goodbye and wandered to the door. 'I'll see myself out.' He gave Eloise a casual nod as he went.

'Such a dear man,' murmured Mevrouw Pringle. 'You'd never think he was a doctor, would you? So relaxed—I always feel he should be sitting by a canal, fishing.'

'Perhaps he does when he's got the time,' suggested Eloise.

'He's too much in demand, and not only as a doctor. He's something of a catch, my dear, only no one's caught him yet, although there are one or two girls...' She paused, leaving Eloise to conjure up pictures of any number of raving beauties doing their best to snap up the prize. The idea made her feel a little low-spirited and she told herself it was because not being a beauty herself, she couldn't have the fun of competing with them, rather the reverse; she could see that their relationship was going to be strictly businesslike, excepting of course when he chose to find her amusing.

'I daresay he feels very flattered,' she remarked airily, and went on to suggest that her patient might like to have an early night, and how about supper in bed. She was glad she had suggested it, because Mijnheer Pringle threw her a grateful look and added his voice to hers, and she spent the next hour making Mevrouw Pringle comfortable for the night and then went downstairs again to sit and read in the drawing room while Mijnheer Pringle went to have a chat with his wife; he took a bottle of sherry and some glasses with him and Eloise applauded his action.

Presently he came downstairs again and they dined in the rather severe dining room on the other side of the hall, while her host kept the conversation to trivialities, concealing his true feelings with a flow of small talk which lasted until she felt she could excuse herself and go up to bed. She went to see Mevrouw Pringle on the way, to give her her tablets and warn her that she was to ring for her if she needed anything during the night, and an hour later, when she crept back to take another look, it was to find her patient sleeping quietly, so that she could go to her own bed with a quiet mind. It had been a long, eventful day, and surprising too. She had never expected to meet the doctor again, although she admitted to herself that she hadn't really forgotten him, only tucked him away in the back of her mind. It was a pity that he had no interest in her whatever, but then why should he? Especially if he could take his pick of all those girls her patient had hinted at.

Tired though she was, Eloise got out of bed and went to peer at herself in the dressing table mirror. It was a triple mirror and she had a good look at her face from all angles. Not even the most conceited of girls could have considered herself pretty; her nose was just a nose, her mouth far too wide, and she didn't care for hazel eyes. Her hair, long and shining and fine, she disregarded; it was all the wrong colour. 'Tint?' she asked herself. 'Something chestnutty?' and then giggled; it was doubtful if the doctor would notice even if her hair were pink. When he had looked at her it had been with the detached gaze of someone who would have preferred to be looking at something—or someone—else. She sighed, hopped back into bed, and went to sleep.

Chapter 3

Doctor van Zeilst arrived punctually the next morning, and the examination he gave his patient was meticulously thorough. When he had at length finished he sat back and said easily: 'You're a wonder, Deborah.' He glanced at Eloise, standing quietly close by. 'But will you promise me to do exactly what Nurse advises? Otherwise have all the fun you like.'

Mevrouw Pringle chuckled. 'I intend to, Timon.' She hesitated. 'I suppose there's no chance that they were wrong?'

He answered her gravely. 'No, my dear, and I would be a coward if I pretended otherwise. On the other hand, no one can say exactly how long—six months has so often turned out to be a year, two—even six.'

She brightened. 'That is what Eloise said, but I hardly dared hope…'

'Well, do. What excitements are you planning?'

'A dinner party—all our friends. I want them to meet Eloise, and besides, it will be nice for Cor, he's had a rotten time lately. You'll come?'

'With pleasure—when is it to be?'

'Soon. I'll ask the van Eskes and the Haagesmas and the Potters, and there'll be us and Eloise—and you, of course. Who would you like me to invite for you?'

The doctor allowed his gaze to rest upon Eloise, who, just for a few blissful moments, found herself in a state of unexpected excitement, but only for moments; he said almost at once: 'Oh, Liske, of course.'

Mevrouw Pringle hadn't missed the look on Eloise's face, nor its instant dousing. 'Pieter will be here for Eloise,' she stated. 'Now let me see, when shall we have it?'

'Why not within the next day or so?' suggested the doctor blandly. 'Liske is going away at the beginning of next week…'

'That settles it—I'll telephone everyone today and see if they can manage Saturday. Eloise, don't look so worried, everyone will speak English—besides, you'll have Pieter.'

Eloise murmured suitably and wondered if she wanted Pieter. Now if the doctor had…but he hadn't; she gave herself a metaphorical kick for being a fool; of course he would have a girlfriend; possibly a fiancée, even a wife, and why hadn't she thought of that before? And in any case, why was she getting so worked up about it? He had shown no interest in her, and she for her part had no interest in him. She made a point of repeating this to herself very firmly, composed her ordinary features into serenity, said what was expected of her when the doctor gave his instructions to her in the hall, and bade him a coolly friendly goodbye. Let him bring a dozen Liskes—she for her part couldn't care less. She tossed her head and went back upstairs to Mevrouw Pringle.

Later, rather nervous but determined not to show it, she drove the Citroën to Groningen, parked outside Mijnheer Pringle's office and walked with her patient to the nearby shops. They were bound for the grocer that lady patronised, armed with a list of comestibles for the dinner party. Juffrouw Blot had entered enthusiastically into their plans, and between them they had put together a menu which should satisfy the guests and bring nothing but praise for their hostess. It was as they were returning from this errand that Mevrouw Pringle suggested happily that they might explore the city together during the next few days. 'And we can take short trips in the car, too,' she continued with enthusiasm. 'There's such a lot to see, though I don't think I could manage the museums—you could do those on your own, or perhaps Pieter…' She left the sentence in mid-air. 'There's Menkemaborg Castle, that's only twenty miles away and a splendid example of our architecture, and Heiligeree, where they make the bells, you know.' She glanced at Eloise. 'I'm sure Pieter will love to take you out—there are some rather nice restaurants…'

For a second time Eloise found herself battling with

the feeling that Pieter would be a poor substitute for the doctor, and this time she managed to succeed. 'He sounds nice, your Pieter,' she observed, and was rewarded by her companion's happy smile. The rest of their outing was taken up with a eulogy of the young man—a paragon, by all accounts, although Eloise felt gloomily sure that when they did meet he would turn out to be a head shorter than herself and of a serious nature.

They passed the next day or two very comfortably. Mevrouw Pringle appeared to be very much the same. She slept a little, ate a little, and Eloise, ever watchful, could see no worsening in her condition, although her pallor at times was alarming enough.

Doctor van Zeilst called each day, joked gently with his patient, encouraged her to amuse herself in any way she wished and brought tickets for a concert in Groningen. 'Your favourite,' he pointed out, 'Shostakovich—in three weeks' time; I got them in good time; you know how quickly they sell out.'

Three weeks was a long way ahead. Eloise could see that her patient was thinking the same thing and getting a degree of security from it, just as the doctor had intended, she suspected.

'You'll come too?' asked Mevrouw Pringle, and Eloise pricked up her ears at his reply:

'Yes, Liske will be back. I thought we might make up a party and go back to my place afterwards.'

He spoke casually and Eloise could see that Mevrouw Pringle believed him, that she would feel well enough to do what he suggested, although it would be

quite beyond her strength. When he asked carelessly:
'What do you think, Nurse?' she answered cheerfully.
'It sounds delightful,' and wished heartily that he would
call her anything but Nurse, in that cold, professional
manner.

They went next day to see the bell factory, but Mevrouw Pringle was so weary by the time they got home
that Eloise trotted out a variety of reasons why they
should remain quiet the next day. 'Look,' she pointed
out diplomatically, 'if you have breakfast in bed as usual
and then stay in bed for an hour or so, we could get
all the details for your dinner party arranged in peace
and quiet; there are bound to be interruptions if you're
downstairs.'

It seemed to her that her patient was only too ready
to agree and although she was her usual merry self
when Doctor van Zeilst paid his visit, it was obvious
that she wasn't quite as well as she had been. But he
made no comment, only as Eloise accompanied him
to the door did he remark: 'Not so good, is it, Nurse?
But only what we expected. You're doing very well,
though. Try and keep her in bed for as long as possible
tomorrow, and see that she rests until the last possible
moment before the guests arrive. I've passed the word
around that she is still convalescing, so no one will stay
late.' He stopped at the doorstep and turned to look at
her. 'You are quite happy here?'

'Yes, thank you, Doctor.' Her voice held its usual
calm and she said no more than that, for she suspected
that he was being polite and at the same time making
sure that she wouldn't pack her bag and leave him to

find someone else to nurse Mevrouw Pringle. He surprised her by saying: 'I'm glad. Most girls would dislike the quiet.'

'Well, I like it. I like Mevrouw Pringle too.' When he gave a careless nod she went on rather tartly: 'I did tell you that she is an old friend of my mother, and I was born and bred in the country—I much prefer it to town life.'

He nodded again, staring at her. She thought he was going to say something more, but he didn't, only smiled briefly, got into his beautiful car and drove himself away.

It took all of Eloise's ingenuity to keep Mevrouw Pringle in her bed the next morning, but by dint of getting Juffrouw Blot to come upstairs and discuss the last details for the evening, as well as her husband's soothing company, she contrived to prolong it until midday, and by mid-afternoon Mevrouw Pringle was ready enough to rest once more while Eloise laid out her dress for her, fetched up a tray of tea and finally persuaded her to take a nap.

Pieter was to arrive some time after tea. He came just as Eloise, the tray in her hands, came downstairs, and it was just as she had feared; he was indeed a head shorter than she was, nice looking enough even if inclined to faint corpulence, and already going a little thin on top. He was dressed with almost finicky neatness; he would be the sort of man who poked around the kitchen to see if his wife had cleaned the saucepans properly... She dismissed the thought as unkind and smiled at him as he crossed the hall towards her.

'You must be Eloise.' He spoke good English with a marked accent. 'What a big girl!'

Eloise ignored that. 'How do you do?' she said politely. 'You must be Pieter.' She remained on the last tread of the staircase so that he was forced to look up at her quite some way. 'Mevrouw Pringle will be delighted to see you; she's sleeping at present.'

He said importantly: 'I couldn't get home before this; I have an important job. Where's my father?'

'I believe he's in the cellar, choosing the wine.'

She watched his portly back disappear through the door leading to the basement and went on her way to the kitchen. She hadn't expected a great deal from Pieter, but even with that, she was disappointed. He had shown a marked lack of interest in his mother, and besides, he had called her a big girl. She wondered if Doctor van Zeilst thought that too. She wandered back to the sitting room, where there was a vast mirror over the carved mantelpiece and standing well back so that she could see the whole of her person, studied her reflection.

'He was right,' she observed to the empty room, and was startled into a squeak of fright when Doctor van Zeilst asked from the door behind her: 'Who was right, and what did he say?'

She was still so indignant that she didn't stop to consider her answer, but even as she uttered the words she would have given a great deal to have taken them back; there was nothing to do but wait for his laugh. But he didn't laugh. 'A girl, yes—but big? No.' He put his head on one side and studied her at his leisure so that she drew in a sharp indignant breath, a tart retort on her tongue, but before she could voice it he went on with impersonal kindness: 'Most of the women in this part of the world are tall and generously built—a good thing too, for we men would look silly if our women didn't match us for size.'

'Oh, do you mean that? But I'm not Dutch.'

He said kindly: 'No matter, you're quite all right as you are.' He became all of a sudden businesslike. 'Mevrouw Pringle—has she been resting?'

'Yes, almost all day. Do you suppose she'll be able to hold out? I mean, everyone is coming at half past seven, supposing no one goes until eleven o'clock or later?'

'I've thought of that,' he told her easily. 'A phone call for me and I'll take Liske with me, of course, and offer a lift to anyone going our way—that should start the ball rolling...' He frowned in thought and Eloise asked:

'She doesn't know—or guess? You wouldn't tell her?'

His voice was silky: 'My dear young lady, you haven't much faith in my professional integrity, have you?'

'Of course I have, but surely doctors tell things to their wives.'

His brows rose. 'But I have no wife.'

'Oh,' said Eloise, breathless. 'I thought—that is, you talk about Liske...' She stopped because of the look on his face, sheer, wicked amusement.

'Fishing, Eloise?' he wanted to know softly. 'Should I be flattered?'

She felt her face grow red and said crossly: 'I'm not in the least interested in your private life, Doctor van Zeilst.

And now if you will excuse me, I'll go up to Mevrouw Pringle.'

She crossed the room in her stateliest manner, her nose so high in the air that she didn't notice the small woven mat, one of many strewn about the house and the source of great annoyance to everyone in it excepting Mevrouw Pringle. It slid from under her as she tripped on it and would have fallen flat on her face if the doctor hadn't plucked her on to her feet with a powerful arm. She extricated herself from his hold even while she was enjoying it and said, very cross: 'These absolutely beastly little mats!' and bounded through the door and up the stairs. The doctor's low chuckle added to her discomfiture.

The mole velvet, when she surveyed herself in her bedroom mirror some time later, dissatisfied her; it was well cut and the material was still good, but any woman would see at a glance that it was several years out of date. She eyed its simple lines with disfavour, wishing childishly that she were small and slender and wearing clinging pastel crêpe in the very latest fashion. Her jaundiced eye failed to notice that the cut emphasised her charming shape and the sober colour complemented her creamy skin. She tugged pettishly at its high neckline, fastened the gold chain which her father had given her years ago, and went along to Mevrouw Pringle's room, for she had dressed early so that she would have ample time to help her patient.

Mevrouw Pringle had chosen to wear sapphire blue silk. It matched her eyes and what was more to the point, was easy to get into. Eloise dressed her gently and without haste, sat her down before her dressing table and under Mijnheer Pringle's loving eye, did her hair and face for her and then stood back to allow him to put on the sapphire pendant he had brought home with him earlier in the day.

There were a few minutes to spare when Eloise had finished; she settled Mevrouw Pringle on a chaise-longue with due regard to the blue silk and slipped away with the suggestion that she should make sure that everything was in order downstairs. She went back presently, having admired the dinner table, eaten an olive or two and signified by sign language that Juffrouw Blot had made a super job of everything, to find the Pringles sitting hand in hand. They looked happy although they had little to be happy about, but perhaps, thought Eloise, when two people loved each other as they did, it kept them safe from fear and loneliness and grief.

For no reason at all she thought of Doctor van Zeilst, calm, always a little amused about some small joke she was never asked to share, but surely a man who would prove a tower of strength to anyone he loved. She sighed, not knowing that she did so, and said brightly: 'There's five minutes to go—shall we go downstairs and get you settled in your chair?'

The drawing room looked pretty with the fire lighted and the lamps switched on. Mevrouw Pringle expressed pleased satisfaction at its appearance and had just settled herself when the first guests arrived; Eloise thought that she looked like a happy child at a party as she greeted them; the Potters, old friends and older than the Pringles, a little staid perhaps, but charming. They made all the proper remarks about their hostess, joked a little with their host and were kind to Eloise, as were the Haagesmas and the van Eskes when they arrived, drawing her into their friendly circle, speaking English so that she shouldn't feel shy. They had almost finished their drinks when Pieter came in with the excuse that he had had to return to Groningen. His manner implied that it had been a matter of grave urgency which had taken him there and his audience murmured sympathetically; except for Eloise, who considered him too self-important by far.

It was a pity that he caught sight of her at that moment and started to make his way towards her just as the door opened once more; Doctor van Zeilst and his Liske, as eye-catching a girl as Eloise had feared, and contrary to the doctor's assurance, she was the exception to every rule; small and willowy, with guinea-gold hair and bright blue eyes, and as if that wasn't enough, she was wearing pastel silk cunningly draped and probably, Eloise guessed sourly, it had cost a small fortune to achieve such simplicity. The mole velvet became all at once the most hideous garment in the room and she herself exactly what Pieter had said—a big girl.

The doctor's companion shared her view—not in so many words, of course, but the blue eyes took in Eloise in one sweeping glance, and although the girl smiled and shook hands and murmured pleasantly, she was left in no doubt as to what her new acquaintance thought of her, for the delicately made up eyes were full of cold amusement and the pretty mouth wore a faint sneer.

The doctor, looming behind his pretty companion,

wished her a bland good evening, his eyes on her face, and then went to speak to the other guests, taking Liske with him and leaving Eloise to entertain Pieter, who had reached her side by now and in fact, she quickly discovered, needed no entertaining at all, as he talked about himself, pausing only now and then to allow her to murmur suitably. It was quite a relief when they all went in to dinner, even though it was short-lived, for he was sitting beside her. But Mijnheer Potter was her other neighbour, and after giving Pieter her attention for the whole of the soup, she felt free to talk to the older gentleman, who entertained her with a gentle flow of small talk which was a nice relief from Pieter's self-important utterances.

The table was a circular one and over the elborate centrepiece, she could see the doctor, Mevrouw Pringle on one side of him and Liske on the other. Once or twice he caught her eye, but his glance was brief and abstracted. Only towards the end of the meal did she find him staring at her again, and this time he smiled, a slow smile which sent her heart tumbling against her ribs and left her short of breath. She took care not to look that way again until, dessert eaten, Mevrouw Pringle suggested that they should all go to the drawing room for coffee. She cast Eloise a quick glance as she spoke, and Eloise, rightly interpreting it as a plea for help, made her way round the chattering guests and un-obtrusively gave her an arm with the laughing remark that she had hardly spoken to her hostess all the eve-ning, just in case anyone had noticed, and out of earshot for a moment she whispered urgently: 'Are you in pain? Do you want a tablet?'

Mevrouw Pringle shook her head. 'No dear—just suddenly tired, but only for a moment. It seemed a long way to the drawing room.'

Somebody had noticed. The doctor was beside them now. 'Tired?' he murmured. 'We'll each take an arm— no one has noticed, don't worry, Debby. Sit in your chair for the rest of the evening and Eloise shall stay with you and bear the brunt of any conversation.' He added in a cheerful, rather loud voice: 'I love that dress, my dear—I've not seen it before. Blue always suits you...'

He turned to include the Potters in this remark, for they had come close enough to overhear, but by then they had reached the drawing room and the doctor, settling Mevrouw Pringle in her chair, wandered off without a word or a look at Eloise. But he had told her to stay, so stay she did, managing to take Mevrouw Pringle's share of the conversation on to her own shoulders and refusing Pieter's offer to show her the conservatory, which annoyed him very much. He was a bore, she decided, and even if he had realised how ill his mother was, he could have shown a little more concern for her. It amazed her that two such nice people could have such a tiresome creature for a son.

Mevrouw Pringle's cheeks grew paler and Eloise longed for the doctor to do something, and quickly, and true to his word, he did. It was chiming ten o'clock when Juffrouw Blot entered the room and whispered in his ear. He went away with a muttered excuse and returned almost at once with the news that he was wanted urgently at a remote farm some miles away and would have to leave at once. He glanced at the clock as he spoke and added: 'Liske, I'm sorry, but I'll have to drop you off as we go.' His eye swept round the other guests. 'Can I give anyone a lift?'

He had been right; the Potters made a move to go too, and presently the others followed suit, making protracted farewells and offering plans for future meetings, so that it was almost eleven o'clock by the time the front door was finally closed and by then Mevrouw Pringle was looking quite alarmingly exhausted.

Eloise worked fast; her patient was tucked up in bed within minutes and Mijnheer Pringle went to sit with his wife while Eloise undressed, plaited her splendid head of hair, put on her elderly dressing gown and padded back to take his place. Mevrouw Pringle was asleep, but she decided to stay with her for the next hour or so, a decision which her husband at first contested and then agreed to, agreeing that if she were needed, Eloise would be on the spot. 'All the same,' he told her in a whisper, 'I'll not go to bed yet—there's plenty of work I can do. I'll be in my study.' He added wistfully: 'You think it was worthwhile? She enjoyed herself?'

'Indeed she did—and don't worry, I think she's exhausted, but a good night's sleep will put that right.' She knew that she was being over-optimistic, but her soft voice was reassuring and kind. He gave her a grateful glance and went away, leaving her to sit in the small easy chair drawn up to a dim lamp. There were books on the bedside table. Eloise turned them over idly while she thought about the evening. It had been a success from Mevrouw Pringle's point of view and that was what mattered. She didn't think anyone had noticed anything untoward and even Pieter had bidden his parents goodbye without appearing to notice his mother's pale face. She hoped that the doctor would come in the morning and persuade his patient to rest for a day or two. There had been talk of going to the Potters' house for lunch one day soon and the Haagesmas had suggested that they might all make up a party and dine at Menkemaborg Castle. Mevrouw Pringle would never manage that; a twenty-mile car drive to start with, probably a protracted dinner and then the drive back...

Eloise closed the book she had been holding and sat quietly, listening to her patient's breathing, while her thoughts dwelt on the doctor and his pretty girlfriend. The smallest sound behind her made her look round. He was there, within inches of her chair, still in his dinner jacket, immaculate and calm. He smiled as she stared and got to her feet.

'Good girl, I knew you would keep an eye on things.' He trod soundlessly to the bed and stood looking down at its occupant, possessed himself of the thin wrist while he took the pulse, laid it gently back on the coverlet and beckoned Eloise to follow him onto the landing.

'Well, she stood that well,' he said, soft-voiced. 'Try and keep her in bed until I get here in the morning, and go to bed yourself, Eloise.' His blue eyes raked her. 'You looked charming this evening and I liked that brown thing you were wearing.' He grinned suddenly. 'You look charming now, even though you're muffled to the eyebrows in flannel.' He put out a hand and gently tugged at the thick plait of hair hanging over her shoulder, then bent his head to kiss her on her astonished mouth.

'And now off with you,' he urged her, 'and don't worry, I shall stay for a little while and talk to Cor. I'll look in on Deborah before I leave and if there's anything for you I'll let you know. But I fancy she'll sleep till morning.'

'I gave her a tablet when I put her to bed.' Eloise tried to keep her voice matter-of-fact. 'I usually go along at six o'clock to make sure she's still sleeping.'

'Do that.' The hand still holding her plait dropped to his side and he stood aside to let her pass. 'Good night.'

She fastened her eyes on his waistcoat. 'Good night, Doctor van Zeilst.' Her voice sounded wooden in her ears as she slipped past him and went to her room and closed the door without looking back. She set her alarm clock for six o'clock, took off the unglamorous dressing gown and got into bed, quite certain that she would never sleep. She did, of course, within minutes.

Chapter 4

Eloise, wakened by her alarm clock, muffled herself in her dressing gown, and yawning widely, hair hanging anyhow around her shoulders, crept along to Mevrouw Pringle's room. Doctor van Zeilst was there, standing with his back to the curtained window, doing nothing. She swallowed a yawn half way, choked on it and with a glance at her still sleeping patient, asked urgently: 'What's happened?'

'Nothing, and you don't need to look like that, pineapple girl, you're dead on time—you said six o'clock, and six o'clock it is. I was called out on a case and it seemed a good idea to call in on my way back—Cor left the side door open.'

She rubbed her eyes like a sleepy child. 'Yes, but...'

He came closer to the bed and looked down at his

sleeping patient. 'We have been friends for a long time now,' he told her softly. 'The least I can do is to make sure that everything that can be done is done.' He added: 'I'm glad it's you with her.'

He bent down and took the flaccid hand on the coverlet in his own large one. 'She'll sleep for another hour, I think.' He glanced at Eloise and smiled, and she saw then how tired he was. His handsome face was lined and he needed a shave; moreover she noticed for the first time that he was in slacks and a sweater.

'How long have you been out of your bed?' she wanted to know in a careful whisper.

He left the bedside and caught her by the arm and walked her to the door. 'Since three o'clock—come down and make me some coffee, there's a dear girl.'

She allowed herself to be swept downstairs with soundless speed, but once in the kitchen with the light on, she said: 'You're very tired, aren't you? Haven't you been to bed at all?'

'Oh, a couple of hours. I shall do all right.'

She was putting on the kettle and searching for the coffee grinder.

'Well, you must go straight to bed the moment you get home—you could get an hour or two…'

He chuckled. 'I can't, you know. Surgery at half past eight, then a round of visits after lunch, and I've a teaching round at the hospital.'

She persisted doggedly. 'Well, you could go to bed early.' She was assembling milk and sugar on the kitchen table. 'Do you have an evening surgery?'

He was laughing at her. 'Yes, and I'm taking Liske out afterwards.'

Eloise had, for the moment, forgotten all about the girl; she said now rather lamely: 'Oh, yes, of course…'

'Of course what?'

She was watching the coffee percolate and didn't look up. 'Oh, just of course. It—it didn't mean anything, actually.' She fetched two mugs. 'Would you like something to eat?'

'Kind, thoughtful girl—yes, anything.'

She fetched bread and butter and a wedge of cheese and set them on the table with the coffee and watched him while he demolished almost all of them. Presently she said: 'Mevrouw Pringle wants to go to Groningen tomorrow, to buy some clothes.'

He held out his mug for more coffee. 'Let her; nothing will make any difference now and I want her to enjoy every minute…'

'She's such a nice person. Why should it happen to her, I wonder?'

'My dear girl, death comes to us all, does it not, and none of us knows when. Deborah is in her early sixties—not old, but she has had a happier life than many people I know, one mustn't lose sight of that.' He got up and wandered over to the sink. 'And don't think that because I say that that I don't mind her dying.'

He was nice, thought Eloise, watching him tidy away the remains of his meal, and strong enough to face up to things; he would be a tower of strength without appearing to make any effort at all. She went to the sink with her own mug and took a towel to dry the dishes and he said: 'I'm going home now, but I'll have another look on my way. Tell Cor that I'll telephone later.' He smiled at her. 'How old did you say you were?'

'Twenty-three—and you?' After all, what was sauce for the goose was sauce for the gander and she did want to know.

He didn't mind telling her. 'Thirty-seven. I'll be back some time today. You know where to find me if I'm needed.'

He was gone, leaving her to stand in the kitchen, the dishcloth in her hand, staring at nothing in particular.

Mevrouw Pringle slept until almost ten o'clock and when she wakened ate quite a good breakfast and signified her intention of going shopping as she had planned. She was dressed and sitting in the drawing room when the doctor called. He stayed only a few minutes and when he spoke to Eloise it was with a cool professional detachment which quite daunted her, it was quite a relief when he went, with the excuse that he still had one more patient to see on his round.

The afternoon was a success. Mevrouw Pringle spent most of it in a small, very expensive shop, deciding which of the dresses she was shown she should buy; in the end she bought two. 'Such a splendid excuse to go somewhere exciting so that I can wear them,' she confided to Eloise as they were driving back home. 'Amsterdam, perhaps—we could make up a party and go to the theatre, spend the night there and show you something of the city…a little outing would do Cor good. The green would do nicely, wouldn't it, dear? And then we might go to Hilversum for dinner one evening. The grey chiffon would be just right with that lovely pendant Cor gave me.' She glanced at Eloise. 'That was a pretty dress you wore last night, dear. Did you bring any more with you?'

'Well, no—I didn't know that I should be going out...' She had no intention of telling her companion that that was the only party dress she owned. Mevrouw Pringle was kind enough to rush straight back to Groningen and make her a present of half a dozen dresses, so she added lightly: 'I must do some shopping for myself,' and then, quickly: 'I like the green, it really suits you.'

It was a successful red herring which lasted all the way home.

It was difficult to make Mevrouw Pringle rest; she declared gaily that she felt marvellous. 'And if I do feel tired, I can't see that it matters,' she pointed out gently, 'and I've such a lot to cram into six months—it seems a waste of time to rest.'

Eloise kept her voice matter-of-fact. 'Yes, it must seem so to you, but you're doing so well, if you take reasonable care those six months could possibly stretch to another six.'

Her patient agreed happily. 'You're quite right, dear—you're such a sensible girl and such a dear companion. If I had someone gushing sympathy over me I wouldn't be able to bear it. Cor knows that, bless him, and so does Timon. So I'll take your advice. What a pity Pieter is so busy, you could have had some young company.'

'I'm quite content, Mevrouw Pringle—it's like a holiday.' Eloise made haste to change the conversation: 'I had a letter from Mother this morning. She's having a wonderful time; Mrs Plunkett's brother is staying in the village and takes her out most days. They knew each other years ago, didn't they? She says she's getting fat.'

Mevrouw Pringle laughed. 'I'll believe that when I see her, but I'm glad she's enjoying herself. I expect you were both glad to get away from London.'

Eloise had brought the car to a halt outside the house. 'Yes—we don't like living there, you know. It seemed the best thing to do at the time, but it wasn't. The moment I can get a Sister's job, I'm going to send Mother back to Eddlescombe—rent a cottage, or something. I'll have to live at St Goth's, but I shall be able to go home quite often.'

'You might marry, dear.'

'I'm not counting on it,' said Eloise flatly. 'I'm rather plain, you see.'

They had gone indoors and she settled her companion in a comfortable chair and declared that she would fetch tea for her. Doctor van Zeilst hadn't been yet, perhaps he would come in on his way back from seeing his afternoon patients. She found that she was looking forward to his visit. 'Although I can't think why,' she muttered as she crossed the hall on her way to the kitchen, 'he doesn't even see me.'

An observation which seemed true enough during the next day or so, for although he came each day, he exchanged only the barest civilities with her and the only occasions he sought her out were when he wished to discuss his patient's condition, and then, as usual, he was coldly professional.

Eloise told herself that it was silly to mind; after all, it wasn't as though they would be meeting each other for the rest of their lives. Sooner or later she would go back to St Goth's and that would be that. She entered wholeheartedly into Mevrouw Pringle's plans for each day, took great care of her in an unobtrusive way, and when Pieter was home, which wasn't often, fended off his over-confident advances.

It was almost a week after the dinner party, as she and Mevrouw Pringle were returning from having lunch with her friends the Potters, that Eloise noticed her companion's extreme pallor. It made her uneasy, although her cheerful: 'How about a rest for an hour or two?' as they reached the house gave no indication of that, and she kept up a gentle chatter while she eased Mevrouw Pringle on to a sofa in the sitting room and tucked her in cosily with a rug. Her manner was calm and unhurried as she did so, and when she had finished she said with just the right amount of casualness: 'I'm going to leave you for a bit. I'll come back presently with tea; we can have it here and talk over the day. It was such a lovely lunch—the Potters are such dears.'

Her companion's tired face was lighted briefly by a smile. 'You should see Timon's house—we haven't been...'

'Unlikely,' thought Eloise, and Mevrouw Pringle went on: 'I don't know when I've enjoyed myself as much as I have done these last few days. That's a splendid idea of the Potters, that we should all go to Utrecht.'

'It sounds smashing,' declared Eloise comfortably, holding back the urge to fly to the telephone and get the doctor. But that would never do; Mevrouw Pringle mustn't even begin to guess... She went unhurriedly from the room, but once in the hall raced silently to the study, dialled the doctor's number and waited what seemed to be endless minutes before she heard his calm voice. 'Van Zeilst.'

'Will you come at once?' she asked without preamble and forgetting to say who she was. 'We're just back from the Potters and Mevrouw Pringle doesn't look too good. I've put her on the sofa in the sitting room; she thinks she's just tired...' She added in a voice she strove to keep calm. 'Please hurry.'

'I'm on my way. Let Cor know.'

She heard the click of the receiver and dialled the second number, and when Mijnheer Pringle answered, said quietly: 'It's Eloise. Will you come home at once, Mijnheer Pringle? Your wife isn't well.'

She heard the sharp intake of his breath. 'At once,' was all he said.

Mevrouw Pringle was sleeping when she went back to the sitting room, her face pinched and milky pale. Eloise took an almost imperceptible pulse and waited.

She didn't have long in which to do so; she had left the front door open and it was only minutes before she heard the doctor's quick, firm tread.

He said nothing but went at once to bend over his patient, but presently he straightened up and asked quietly: 'When did this start?'

She told him, a precise report, just as though she were on a hospital ward. He nodded. 'She will probably regain consciousness, but only briefly, I'm afraid.' He glanced at his watch. 'Cor should be here.'

They heard the car as he spoke and Mijnheer Pringle came in a moment later, and as though she had known that he had come, his wife opened her eyes and smiled at him. He spoke in a perfectly normal voice. 'Hullo, darling, I thought I would come home early for tea.'

Mevrouw Pringle didn't answer, although she was still smiling. She didn't speak again.

The rest of the day was unreal. Eloise did what she had to do with the least possible fuss, saw that Mijnheer Pringle ate his meals, comforted the weeping Juffrouw Blot and made herself useful around the house and when asked to do so, sat down with Mijnheer Pringle in his study and ticked off names as he telephoned. He had remained very calm, but once or twice she had seen the look of utter disbelief on his face. Presently the truth would hit him hard and then, she felt sure, he would want to be on his own. It might be best if she returned to England as soon as the funeral was over—a decision substantiated by her mother when she was asked to telephone her. 'I shall come to the funeral,' her mother spoke with unwonted firmness. 'Poor Debby, I didn't know... Just a minute, dear.' Eloise heard her talking to someone with her before she went on: 'Mrs Plunkett's brother is staying here—Jack—I knew him years ago, he's offered to bring me by car. You can come back with us, darling.'

Eloise's calm forehead wrinkled with surprise. It was unlike her mother to be so decided about anything, and this Jack Plunkett must be a very good friend to offer to drive her such a distance. She was tempted to ask several questions, but there were other calls to make. She agreed hastily because there was no time to do anything else, and rang off.

Later, as she and her host sat over a hastily cooked supper, she mentioned it to him. 'Although I'll stay if you want me to, Mijnheer Pringle.'

But he refused her offer. 'I'm grateful, Eloise, you must know that, but there is little point in you staying and I think that it may be better if I'm alone for a time— besides, you have your job.'

And when Doctor van Zeilst joined them presently to drink the coffee Juffrouw Blot had brought, he agreed so readily that Eloise was conscious of a pang of annoyance. He sounded positively eager to see the last of her, his bland: 'What a good idea, nothing could be better,' left her feeling strangely forlorn, the forlornness turned to vexation when Mijnheer Pringle remarked that he needed the doctor's advice about something and the latter remarked briskly that she might like to go to bed early. 'I daresay you're tired,' he remarked, 'and there's no hurry for you to make your arrangements, is there?'

She almost heard him sigh with relief as she got up from the table. 'None at all,' she told him in a colourless voice, and wished the two of them goodnight before going to her room. She came downstairs again almost immediately. Juffrouw Blot would be in the kitchen all by herself, for the daily help went home at five o'clock; she might like a hand with the dishes. Eloise didn't much like washing up, but she was aware that she needed to do something to keep herself occupied; to lie in bed and think would do no good.

Juffrouw Blot was at the sink, washing up with grim determination and crying her eyes out. She had known Mevrouw Pringle for many years and Eloise realised with surprise that no one had told her that her mistress was suffering from an illness from which she couldn't recover, and the poor soul's grief was genuine—more so, thought Eloise, than Pieter, who had come home when he had been told the news, and gone again within the hour, with the excuse that his work wouldn't allow him to stay longer. She took a cloth and began to dry the plates, talking soothingly all the time, mostly English, of course, with a few Dutch words popped in at random and most of it quite unintelligible to her listener, but at least it gave some comfort.

Juffrouw Blot stopped crying presently and began to talk. She talked for a long time and although Eloise understood no more than one word in fifty, it did the poor woman good; she had had a lot to get off her chest, and now she was doing it. She tidied the sink, took the tea-cloths away from Eloise, went to a cupboard and returned with a bottle of port and two glasses. Eloise didn't much like port, but it seemed part and parcel of Juffrouw Blot's real efforts to overcome her grief. They sat down at the kitchen table and drank a glass each while the housekeeper continued to talk, and by the time they had finished she regained a good deal of her composure. She put the glasses in the sink and the bottle back in the cupboard and held out a hand to Eloise, saying in a watery voice: '*Dank U*, Miss,' and Eloise, feeling quite inadequate said: 'Not at all, Juffrouw Blot,' and added hopefully: 'Bed.'

The housekeeper nodded, shook hands once more and made for the back stairs, and when she had reached the top, Eloise turned off the lights and went back through the narrow passage which led to the hall. She was closing the door gently behind her when the doctor strolled out of the sitting room. She hadn't expected to see him and she could think of nothing to say; she gave him a little nod and crossed to the staircase, only to be intercepted on the way.

'I thought you had gone to bed,' he observed mildly.

She paused to look up at him. 'Probably you did, Doctor, but just because you told me to go to bed it doesn't mean that I did so. It is barely ten o'clock.'

He leaned forward suddenly and gave a rumble of laughter. 'You've been at the port,' he said.

That magnificent nose of his must be very sharp. She looked down her own unimportant little nose and said austerely: 'It really is none of your business, but I went to see if I could help Juffrouw Blot. She's very upset, it was a shock for her, you know, and she was devoted to Mevrouw Pringle. It must have been hard for her to go on with her day's work, cooking meals and clearing them away...' Her voice faltered. 'She offered me a glass of port and I had one while she talked.'

'Did you understand what she was saying?'

'Of course not, but that didn't matter—she just wanted to talk.' She added for no reason at all: 'I don't care for port.'

He looked down at her gravely although there was

a gleam in his blue eyes. 'You're a very nice girl.' He
dropped his hands on her shoulders and kissed the top
of her head. 'If I ask you very nicely, will you go to
bed? It's been a hard day for all of us.'

She went upstairs at once with a muttered goodnight. He was being kind to her, just as he would be
kind to anyone who needed kindness, but the ridiculous feeling that she would like to throw her not incon-
siderable person on to his chest and bawl her eyes out
would have to be firmly squashed. She was more tired
than she thought and sad besides. It had, after all, been
a dreadful day even though it had been inevitable and
they had been prepared for it, but that didn't make it
any the less sad; she cried all the while she got ready
for bed and she was still sobbing quietly when from
sheer weariness she fell asleep.

Her mother arrived two days later; two long-drawn-
out days during which Mijnheer Pringle had gone
through the motions of leading a normal life, talking
pleasantly about various topics, discussing the daily
news, receiving visitors with unfailing good manners.
It was only occasionally that Eloise caught a glimpse of
the grief he was concealing with such great efforts, and
he confirmed this by telling her just before the first of
his wife's friends arrived: 'You will understand, Eloise,
that I shall be relieved when all this is over. I must have
time to think, to adjust… I was of course prepared for
Deborah's death, but even so it is difficult. I shall never
be able to thank you enough for being of such great help
to us both during these last weeks.'

Eloise had said quietly: 'Oh, but I did nothing, you

know, but if I did help a little, then I'm glad. I hope you'll write to me in a little while and tell me how you're going on.' She had hesitated. 'You are sure that you want to stay here—just with Juffrouw Blot, I mean—with no friends?'

He had smiled at her. 'Quite happy, Eloise. Besides, I have Timon, and he's a tower of strength, and Pieter will be going to Curaçao very shortly and I think that I may accompany him—he will be working for most of the time, but I have old friends there. I can look them up.' He had added in a rather toneless voice: 'I won't pretend that he feels his mother's death as keenly as I do, but he is our son and we get on well enough.'

Her mother arrived just before lunch, driven by Mr Plunkett in his elderly, beautifully kept Rover. She was naturally subdued but glad to see Eloise again, and besides that, she was quietly happy about something. It took Eloise just half an hour to discover that the something was Mr Jack Plunkett. She had rather liked him when they had met; he was tall and thin and stooping a little and his grey hair was balding; he had blinked at her with kindly blue eyes through his spectacles when they had been introduced, and he treated her mother as though she were something precious. She and her parent were in her bedroom putting on their outdoor things to go to the funeral when Mrs Bennett said: 'I know it's not the right time to talk about being happy, darling, though Deborah would have been the first to want it... Jack Plunkett wants me to marry him, and I'm going to.' She hurried on: 'I know it's ridiculous;

we've only just met after years and years, but I think we shall be very happy.'

The unconscious wistfulness in her mother's voice brought home to Eloise how unhappy her companion had been all the while they had lived in the horrid little flat in London, so that she said warmly: 'Darling, I had a feeling... I'm very happy for you—both of you. He looks a poppet; marry him just as quickly as you can. Where will you live?'

'Well, there's a cottage in the village—do you remember old Mrs Shaw's little house at the other end of Eddlescombe? Well, she's gone to live with her daughter and Jack's got first refusal...you could come too, love.'

Eloise was putting on her gloves. 'What a dear you are, Mother, but I won't, thank you. I'm almost sure to get a Sister's post within the next few months. I'll live in and we can give up the flat and send the furniture down to Eddlescombe. I'd be able to come home for my weekends, though.' She hugged her mother and added warmly: 'Mrs Pringle would have loved to know about you and Jack,' and then: 'We'd better go down, dear.'

There were a great many people and most of them came back to the house later. They left slowly, leaving the place empty at last save for Mijnheer Pringle, Eloise, her mother, Mr Plunkett and Doctor van Zeilst. Eloise had caught glimpses of him from time to time, although they hadn't spoken; indeed he had made no effort to seek her out, although, as she pointed out to herself, there was no reason why he should. He was standing now, talking to Mr Plunkett while her mother sat beside Mijnheer Pringle, talking to him in her gentle way.

Eloise wandered off to the kitchen to see if she could give any help there, but the daily girl was there, sitting at the table drinking coffee with Juffrouw Blot, so she wished them goodbye, for she was leaving with her mother within the hour, and then strolled into the garden.

It was late afternoon and the days were drawing in, although the weather was still fine. She stood in its peace and quiet and the thought of London made her feel sick. She supposed that her mother would go back to Eddlescombe with her Jack as soon as they had dropped her off at the flat—she would have to set about the business of giving it up. Her thoughts, not very happy ones, wandered on. She would have to wait for the Sister's post, of course, but in the meantime she would ask if she could have a room in the Nurses' Home. The prospect, even with the chance of promotion and a good deal more money, seemed dreary enough. She leaned her elbows on the old stone wall which bordered the lawn and cupped her chin in her hands. She didn't hear the doctor crossing the grass, coming from the other side of the house, so that she jumped at his: 'There you are—why did you wander off?'

She glanced at him briefly. 'Well, Mother and Mijnheer Pringle, and you and Mr Plunkett—besides, I had some thinking to do.'

'A pity Pieter had to go back to Groningen.' He frowned a little as he spoke and she thought that if he had been in Pieter's shoes he wouldn't have gone, pressing work or not. Come to think of it, what had happened to the doctor's own work—his afternoon surgery, his patients…?

She observed clearly: 'I liked Mevrouw Pringle, and I like her husband, but I don't like Pieter. What did you do with your patients this afternoon?'

He looked faintly surprised. 'Oh, I have a partner—two in fact, we stand in for each other from time to time. Are all your plans made?'

'Yes.'

'You will stay at St Goth's after your mother and Jack Plunkett marry?'

'Well, yes.' She sounded despondent without knowing it, and he said abruptly: 'But you don't really want to.'

She answered too quickly: 'Of course I do,' and almost choked on the lie, suddenly quite certain that it was the last thing she wanted to do. She wanted to stay in Holland and see Timon van Zeilst every day, preferably all day, for ever and ever. It was astonishing and rather absurd that she should discover, at this late hour and just as they were going to part, that she loved him. It was also quite hopeless, common sense pointed out, for had not the beautiful Liske already captured him? She said in a wooden voice: 'I should be going, I think—Mr Plunkett wants to leave before it's really dark.'

'Ah, yes—I almost forgot to mention it. The plans have been changed; you are all coming back with me for dinner and the night. Cor can't be left alone. Juffrouw Blot is going to the village with friends, and Mr Plunkett assures me that he can leave just as easily in the morning.'

Eloise said: 'Oh,' inadequately and thought how nice it would be to see Timon's home before she went; besides, she would see him for just a few more hours.

They set off presently, Mijnheer Pringle driving himself, Mrs Bennett with Mr Plunkett and Eloise, neatly plucked from the back seat at the very last moment, sitting beside the doctor in his Rolls.

He made gentle conversation during the drive, not seeming to notice her rather abstracted replies; she had a great deal on her mind, and most of it was him.

They hadn't gone back to the main road but had continued along the side road which ran past Mijnheer Pringle's house. It led to a village before long and then wound its way through fields to another, smaller village. The doctor slowed on the cobbles as they passed the first neat cottages, and when he reached the small square turned past the austere red brick church in its centre and drove down a lane on the further side. The lane wandered on into the fields again with nothing much to see save a double row of tall trees some way ahead, at right angles to the road, and when they reached them, the doctor swept the car through the massive gateposts on either side and driving faster now, entered an avenue where the trees were reinforced by shrubs and bushes so that Eloise could see very little of her surroundings. 'Where are we?' she wanted to know, peering around her.

'Home,' said her companion laconically as he drove round a sharp bend. And there before them was the house—old, magnificently ornate, with wrought iron balconies, shutters at its enormous windows and a steep tiled roof crowned by a circular dome.

'My goodness me!' exclaimed Eloise, and felt her heart drop into her shoes. The doctor, already out of reach, seemed even further away now by reason of possessing such a palatial home—although it might not be his. She brightened at the thought as she accompanied him up the shallow steps and in through the vast front door, only half hearing his formal welcome.

The entrance hall was large, square and light because of the glass dome above their heads, several floors away. The staircase, massive oak and intricately carved, ascended from the back of the hall, curving at the top to join the gallery on the floor above. There were black and white tiles under their feet, with a generous scattering of silky rugs upon them and two great wall tables, flanked by two equally massive chairs, cushioned in crimson velvet, faced each other from either wall. And coming to meet them through this magnificence was an elderly man, very spry, his white hair and whiskers framing a solemn face.

The doctor said something to him as he came to a halt before them, and the elderly face broke into a smile. 'We are delighted to welcome you to Huis Zeilst,' said the personage with tremendous dignity, addressing himself to Eloise.

'Bart,' explained the doctor, 'knows more about the family than I do myself; he's been with us man and boy and is our trusted friend as well as the world's best butler.'

Eloise stopped herself just in time from saying 'My

goodness me!' again and said sedately: 'Oh, how nice,' which upon reflection sounded even sillier. She went a faint pink and stole a look at the doctor, to be instantly reassured by the blandness of his expression.

The whole party crossed the hall, Bart leading the way to throw open double doors and usher them into a vast room, the magnificence of which rather took Eloise's breath. Its walls were white, picked out in gilt and lighted by crystal wall chandeliers. The ceiling was painted a rich mulberry pink, a colour repeated in the brocade curtains and the covers of the chairs and sofas arranged about the room. The floor was polished wood, covered for the most part by a needlework carpet in muted pinks and faded blues, and the great hooded hearth was flanked by glass-fronted cabinets, full, she had no doubt, of any number of treasures. She took in these delights within the first few moments; it was only as she brought her gaze back to the group of chairs arranged at one end of the room that she saw Liske, rising gracefully to her feet and coming forward to meet them with all the welcoming charm of the perfect hostess.

Chapter 5

It was a pity that Eloise wasn't looking at the doctor's face, for a surprise as great as her own was on his handsome features, to be instantly concealed behind a bland smile. Before he could speak, however, Liske had reached his side and tucked a hand into his arm, and Eloise couldn't help but see the sidelong glance directed at herself as she did so; as plain to her in its meaning as a neon sign flashing 'hands off!'

'I telephoned,' explained Liske prettily, 'and I made that silly old Bart of yours tell me what was happening.' She pouted charmingly. 'If you had told me, Timon, I would have come over sooner—you never mentioned that you were having guests for the night.'

The doctor gave her a look which could have meant anything at all: 'I have an excellent housekeeper,' he pointed out suavely, 'and Bart, being neither silly nor old, is perfectly capable of carrying out my orders and wishes. You had no need to—er—put yourself out, Liske. You'll stay to dinner, of course?' He turned to his guests. 'What about a drink before dinner? And then perhaps the ladies would like to see their rooms.' He smiled at Mrs Bennett and ushered her to a comfortable chair, ignoring Eloise completely.

He was a good host; despite the sombre occasion he contrived to keep the talk trivial and interesting enough to keep his guests talking easily among themselves, although Eloise, for her part, had very little to say. She was feeling annoyed that she should feel a little overawed by her surroundings and it annoyed her even more that Liske should be so at ease, almost as though she were already mistress of the lovely impressive house. It was a relief when her host got up to tug a thick silk bell rope by the hooded fireplace, and when Bart came, requested him to fetch someone to take the ladies of the party upstairs.

Eloise mounted the staircase beside her mother, Mevrouw Metz, the housekeeper a few steps ahead of them, and the sight of the wide gallery at its head, with its many corridors and little passages leading from it, caused her mood to become even more despondent. Even while admitting to herself that she loved Timon van Zeilst, she had at the same time almost, but not quite, squashed any romantic notions about her future. She was a very ordinary girl, she considered, and he had money, presumably, and good looks, a combination which allowed him to pick and choose—and he had picked Liske… All the same, until that moment she had cherished a faint hope, rapidly fading at the sight of so much wealth—and that wealth so taken for granted. He was in another world from hers.

She stopped as the housekeeper opened one of the doors in the gallery and smiled an invitation to her mother.

'Me,' said Mrs Bennett, happily ungrammatical. 'I expect you're next door, darling.'

Eloise smiled absently and allowed herself to be ushered into the neighbouring room, and Mevrouw Metz, her tall, stately figure quite at variance with her nice, placid face, sailed away with more smiles and murmurs.

Her room made Eloise sigh with delight—maplewood, the inlaid bedhead matching the dressing table with its triple mirror and the tallboy between the long windows, curtained in a flowery chintz. The floor, unlike the rooms downstairs, was close-carpeted in a thick cream-coloured pile which would show every mark—but how lovely it looked. There was an enormous fitted cupboard behind the first door she opened, the second one revealed a bathroom, which in turn opened into her mother's room.

Their overnight bags had been unpacked, so there was nothing to do but explore their surroundings before tidying themselves and going downstairs again. Eloise, applying lipstick, felt that anything she might do to her face would be of no use in competition with Liske. She screwed up her pretty hair in a severe fashion which called forth her mother's protests, and arm-in-arm with her parent, went back to the drawing room.

Sitting up in bed some hours later, Eloise mulled

over her evening. It had been surprisingly pleasant in a subdued way and the doctor had led the conversation quite deliberately round to Mevrouw Pringle, talking easily and quite naturally about her, so that very soon everyone else was doing the same, remembering earlier days, recalling holidays and meetings and parties, and watching Mijnheer Pringle, she had seen that that had been exactly what he had needed, to talk freely of his wife instead of trying to hide her away in his mind— probably he would sleep soundly for the first time since she had died. And Liske—she had had no chance to centre interest upon herself, although she had tried hard enough; in the end she had become sulky and soon after dinner declared that she would have to go home. The doctor had raised no objection to this, although he had gone out of the room with her and seen her into her car; he had been so long about it that Eloise imagined them quarrelling—or perhaps he was coaxing her back into a good humour. There was nothing in his face to offer her a clue when he returned to the drawing room and he didn't mention Liske during the whole of the evening.

It was when the party had broken up for the evening that she had come upon Bart coming from the dining room with such a miserable expression on his face that she, alone for the moment, had stopped to speak to him.

'You speak English, don't you?' she had asked, and when he nodded: 'Then will you tell me what is the matter? You look unhappy—are you ill? Can I do anything to help?'

He had answered her with great dignity. 'No, miss— you are kind to ask.'

She forgot it was none of her business, anyway. 'But there's something wrong. You're upset—look at your hands shaking. If you could tell me it might help—I won't tell anyone else.' She hesitated. 'Shall I find Doctor van Zeilst for you? Perhaps he…'

He looked shocked. 'Oh no, miss. He must be the last person to know.'

Eloise sat higher against her pillows and hugged her knees and shivered a little, remembering how the doctor, speaking very softly behind them, had surprised them. 'And what must I not know?'

She had been clumsy and interfering, she knew that now, for she had said quite sharply: 'Bart isn't well— or he's upset—can't you do something?'

The doctor had looked down his nose at her and remarked blandly: 'Certainly—if I may know what has upset him.'

They had both looked at Bart then, and the poor man, had muttered something in Dutch to which the doctor had replied briskly in English: 'You will tell me, Bart— we have known each other too long to have secrets.'

And Bart had cast her a reproachful and yet thankful look as he replied. 'It was only something which Juffrouw Haakema said—it is not important.'

'But it makes you shake like a leaf when you think about it, Bart. Out with it!'

Bart had broken into Dutch then and Eloise hadn't understood a word, which was perhaps just as well, for the doctor had looked angry, though not, fortunately, with Bart, for he had put a hand on the old man's shoulder and spoken to him in such a kind voice that Eloise had guessed that it was something for which Bart couldn't be blamed. She had longed to ask, but neither man seemed to remember that she was still there; after a minute or two she had gone away very quietly, upstairs after the others.

She lay down at last. Probably she wouldn't see the doctor in the morning; they were to leave immediately after breakfast and surely he would have a surgery to take. Not to see him again was terrible, but certainly the best thing if she thought about it sensibly. Only she didn't feel sensible; she closed her eyes on threatening tears and after a while fell into a troubled sleep.

But she was to see him again. When she got down in the morning, there he was, sitting at the head of his splendid mahogany table in the dining room with no company at all but for an Old English sheepdog she hadn't seen before. She had expected everyone else to be there too and after a moment's hesitation at the half open door, began a silent retreat. But he must have had eyes at the back of his head, because he said pleasantly: 'Do come in, Eloise—the others won't be down just yet.'

He got to his feet as he spoke and turned to look at her, so that she really had no choice but to go to the table. 'Good morning—I thought you said that breakfast was at eight o'clock. I'm sorry, I couldn't have been listening…'

'But I did say that, although I told everyone else half past the hour. I wanted to speak to you alone.'

Eloise went a delicate pink. 'Oh—about yesterday evening.' She was talking so fast in order to get it over with quickly that she didn't pause for breath. 'I'm frightfully sorry; it was frightfully interfering of me, I had absolutely no right…it wasn't any of my business. You and Bart must simply hate me for it—I…'

He interrupted her as she took a much needed breath. 'My dear girl, Bart doesn't hate you—on the contrary, he considers you to be one of the nicest young ladies he has ever met. You wanted to help him just when he was utterly miserable—he will dote on you for the rest of his life.'

The pink deepened, and Eloise, hating it, stared down at the snowy tablecloth. 'Oh, well—how kind, though I didn't do anything.' She added defiantly: 'He's a dear old man.'

The doctor agreed gravely. 'Indeed he is. I would have given a great deal not have him so upset—as I told you, he is a friend as well as a trusted servant. But I've dealt with the matter and he is reassured, but it is you I have to thank—he would never have told me. Indeed, thinking about it, I am beginning to wonder if there have been other occasions…'

Eloise, still engrossed in the tablecloth, fought a strong inclination to ask what occasions and why had Bart been upset, anyway, since it was obvious that she wasn't to be told.

'Eloise,' said the doctor, and she looked up to see him smiling at her. 'You know, I'm inclined to agree with Bart,' and he pulled her close and kissed her soundly before she realised what he was going to do and then, while she was still staring up at him, he let her go and asked in a perfectly normal voice: 'Will you have tea or coffee?'

She drew a steadying breath. 'Coffee, please,' and she took the chair beside his because he was holding it for her. It would help the situation a great deal if someone else came down to breakfast, but on the other hand she wondered what he would say next if they were alone for a little longer.

He handed her her coffee. 'Bacon? Eggs? Kippers, perhaps—or a boiled egg?'

How could he talk about kippers when only a moment ago he had been kissing her as though he really enjoyed it? 'Bacon and eggs,' said Eloise; if he could eat a hearty breakfast and do a little kissing on the side, so could she.

It was vexing of him to observe as he handed her a plate: 'How nice to find a girl who eats properly and doesn't nibble at various diets.' He sat down again and helped himself to toast. 'No weight problems?' he wanted to know, kindly.

Eloise sugared her coffee. 'None.'

'I must say you're very satisfactory as you are. I don't care for skinny women.'

Eloise choked. 'Are you suggesting that I'm fat?'

'Just right, dear girl. Why did you drag your hair back so savagely yesterday evening?'

Really, he was a most difficult person to converse with! 'What can it matter to you what I do with my hair?'

His voice was silky. 'Ah, now wouldn't you like to know? Here come the rest of us.'

And after that there wasn't a chance to speak to him alone. Mr Plunkett declared himself ready to leave the moment they had finished breakfast, and Mijnheer Pringle had to go to Groningen, although he had consented to stay another night or two at his friend's house.

Eloise made her goodbyes quietly, this time receiving nothing but a handshake from her host and the careless, conventional hope that they might meet again at some time. It was Bart's dignified goodbye which warmed her. 'I thank you, miss,' he said with a sincerity which she found touching, 'and I shall remember you with pleasure always. I hope that we may meet again.'

A sentiment the doctor, beyond his casual remark, didn't echo. She had hoped, right until the last minute, that he might say something—anything—to her, but he didn't. It was only too obvious that she didn't matter at all. She summoned a cool smile as she got into the car behind her mother and Mr Plunkett, and she didn't look back.

'Such a nice man,' commented her mother as they turned out of the gateway into the road, and looked round at Eloise.

'Yes, isn't he?' She knew that she had spoken too quickly and too brightly by the look on her mother's face, and before that lady could embark on a gossip about him, Eloise added: 'We haven't had a chance to talk about you—do tell me your plans. It's so exciting—when are you going to get married?'

The subject kept them occupied for hours, with Mr Plunkett putting in a sensible word or so every now and then. They were to marry quite soon, and their home would be hers whenever she liked to visit them. The banns had been read already and they had thought in about a couple of weeks' time, provided Eloise could get a day or two off for the wedding.

'And what about you, darling?' asked Mrs Bennett.

'Well, we'll give up the flat, won't we, and I'll get a room in the Nurses' Home as I suggested. Could you come up to London for a couple of days so that we could pack up? Could Mr Plunkett bring you?'

He begged her to call him Jack and agreed to do anything within reason, adding a number of helpful suggestions, so that by the time they were in England again, driving at his sensible pace up the motorway to London, everything had been more or less settled.

The flat looked terrible after the subdued splendour of the doctor's home. The three of them went up the stairs without speaking and Mrs Bennett unlocked the door and they followed her into the narrow hall. When they were all inside, she said soberly: 'I don't know whether to laugh or cry—this, after all that...'

Mr Plunkett put an arm round her shoulders. 'Well, my dear, I'm afraid the cottage isn't all that grand.'

'It's perfect,' protested his future bride, 'and it's all I want, Jack.' She gave him a happy smile and looked at Eloise. 'And you, darling—are you sure this is what you want to do, leave here and live in?'

Eloise allowed herself a moment's reflection on what she did want; to live with Timon van Zeilst in his lovely house, and rear a family of tough little boys and small girls with blue eyes like their father... 'Quite sure, Mother.' She made her voice cheerful. 'It all fits in so well, doesn't it? I'm sure to go back on night duty and the Junior Night Sister leaves in a month—if I'm lucky enough to get the job they'll give me a very nice bed-sitter, and I can come home and see you quite often—I might even afford a car.'

She smiled lovingly at her mother; it was lovely to see her looking so happy again. She had always been a pretty woman, now she positively glowed; Jack Plunkett was exactly right for her; calm and rather quiet and fond of her in a nice, speechless way—they would be very happy. Mrs Pringle, thought Eloise, would have been delighted. The thought saddened her, but she didn't allow it to show. 'I'll get the beds ready,' she declared, 'and make tea—we don't want anything to eat after that gorgeous meal we had on the way, do we? Mother, why don't you and Jack take a look round and decide what you want packed up and sent down to Eddlescombe? I've not quite finished my holiday, you know, I could get this place emptied. There's that man down the street who does small removals—he'd fix everything up and anything we don't want he'll buy, I daresay.'

The rest of the evening was spent making lists, measuring furniture to see if it would fit into the cottage, and deciding what to discard, and in the morning there was no time for anything at all, for Mr Plunkett wanted to make an early start. When they had gone, Eloise made another pot of tea and sat down in the silent kitchen to drink it. It was fortunate that there was so much to do, otherwise she might have moped.

It was something of a relief to go back to St Goth's a day or two later; the flat was no longer home with her mother gone and some of the unwanted furniture already sold. Mrs Bennett was to come up in a week's time and do the final packing and Eloise, when she was off duty, would help her. The money from the furniture already sold would be more than enough to buy her mother's wedding outfit. 'And a dress for you, too, darling,' she had insisted over the telephone. 'We'll have a lovely day shopping.'

Eloise had gone back to her packing cases, resolutely keeping her mind on the new dress, burying the persistent little niggle that there was really no point in trying to look chic. There would be no one—and by no one she meant Timon, of course—to see.

She was put straight back on night duty when she reported back. It was also intimated to her that if she wished she might apply for the Junior Night Sister's post. For the time being, she had decided not to ask to live in; there were still three weeks of their month's notice to leave the flat and it would be better, if she got the new job, to wait until she was made a Sister, so that she could move straight into the Sisters' Wing of the home. Everything, she told herself with hollow cheerfulness, was turning out splendidly; her mother happy and living in her beloved countryside again, and she herself with an assured future; it was ridiculous that she should feel like crying whenever she thought about it.

Women's Surgical was full and busy, and over and above that, it was take-in week. For the first few nights Eloise worked unceasingly with meals snatched when she could get them, and came off duty in the morning too tired to do more than cycle home to the unwelcoming flat and sleep.

But it was better when her mother arrived, excited

and bubbling over with delight at seeing her again. They sat in the now sparsely furnished sitting room, discussing the future, and several times Mrs Bennett led the conversation round to Timon van Zeilst, hinting wistfully that it would have been nice if Eloise could meet him again.

Eloise managed to preserve her usual matter-of-fact front. 'Well, Mother dear, we didn't get on all that well, you know, and it isn't as though I were a raving beauty. Besides, there was that girl—Liske, he's going to marry her, I believe.'

'I disliked her,' declared Mrs Bennett with unwonted venom, 'wanting attention all the time. She didn't care a button about Deborah—all she did was make eyes at Timon.'

'I daresay he liked it,' said Eloise dryly. 'Now, love, where are we going to do our shopping?'

It was fortunate that Eloise had nights off; the packing up of the flat was almost done now and they could easily spare a day or two to go in search of something pretty for Mrs Bennett. She forgot, for the time being, about the doctor while they embarked on a lengthy discussion about clothes.

They had a splendid day; they hadn't been able to let themselves go in such a fashion for years, and Mrs Bennett, rendered quite rash after a period of pinching and scraping, fitted herself out with a pale blue outfit. 'For,' as she confided to Eloise, 'Jack likes me in blue and he's given me a mink stole and they will go splendidly together.' She bought a frivolous hat too, and gloves and shoes. But Eloise didn't find her shopping quite so easy; for one thing, she had decided prudently that whatever she bought would have to be worn during the forthcoming winter, so it would have to be a colour she wouldn't get heartily sick of within a few weeks, but she found something at last; a dark green wool coat, and although she almost never wore a hat, she bought one to please her mother—a velvet tammy which matched very well. It was pure good luck that she saw a jersey dress in a paler green. Not spectacular but very wearable, and even in her own modest opinion, the outfit suited her.

The wedding was only a week away now; she would travel down to Eddlescombe on her nights off and spend a day or two there, staying with Jack's sister until after the wedding. It would be lovely to see the village again and meet old friends, and when she got back to London she would fill in her application form and take it to the Principal Nursing Officer and ask at the same time if she could move into the Nurses' Home.

Jack hadn't been able to come up to London to fetch her mother back. Eloise put her on to the train and went back on night duty, where work drove all other thoughts out of her head.

The wedding was a quiet affair, but happy, too. Mrs Bennett looked pretty and happy and at least ten years younger than she was, and Eloise enjoyed every minute of it. She had been taken round the cottage the evening before and seen how well the furniture from the flat suited it. There was a dear little walled garden too, with a low arched door leading to a small paddock where, her mother told her proudly, they were going to keep

chickens, and last of all, she had been shown the little
bedroom set aside for her visits. 'And never forget that
this is your home, darling,' her mother had said.

The village had been kind too, welcoming her into
the homes of people she hadn't seen for years, and all
of them delighted that her mother was marrying again.
Her mother was going to be happy; Eloise went back
to the cold little flat, satisfied that her parent's future
would be an untroubled one—not very exciting, perhaps...she sighed as she hung away the new outfit and
went into the kitchen to get her supper. Tomorrow night
she would be on duty again, but before that she would
fill in the application form and go along to St Goth's
and hand it in in the morning. Lying in bed later, she
told herself that she should be perfectly content with
her own future, too. It was as safe and assured as her
mother's. And much, much more dull, added a small
voice in the back of her head. She stayed awake a long
time thinking about Timon van Zeilst, a fruitless exercise which ended in a sleepless night until she dropped
into a heavy doze about five o'clock.

She was roused barely two hours later by the door
bell, its strident peal bringing her half awake, her wits
addled by its din and her lack of sleep. The milkman,
she guessed crossly, and turned over, pulling the blankets over her head. But the awful noise was repeated,
so that she was forced to get out of bed, wrap herself
in her dressing gown and make her sleepy way to the
door. If it was the milkman she would give him a piece
of her mind! She flung the door open in a pettish manner and was confronted by the doctor, his large person

elegantly clothed in a car coat over a dark grey suit, his calm face freshly shaven, his blue eyes clear and alert.

She had no words and it was he who said: 'Hullo, Eloise,' and added blandly: 'I see I'm a little too early to be welcome.'

She stopped scowling then and opened the door wide. She had no notion of telling him that he would be welcome at any time, day or night, and all she said, rather primly, was: 'Not at all, Doctor van Zeilst. I didn't sleep awfully well, and I dozed off…do come in. I'll make some tea.'

He squeezed past her into the narrow hall and glanced around him without saying anything, and she added defensively: 'I'm moving out in a day or two—the furniture has gone down to Eddlescombe.'

He nodded casually. 'Of course. Go and put some clothes on, dear girl. I'll make some tea.'

Eloise started for the bedroom and then paused. 'How did you know that I was here, and why have you come? Have you been over here long? And…'

'What a busy little tongue! I had your address from Cor Pringle—he asked me to come and see you.'

Eloise swept her wealth of hair over her shoulders, conscious of bitter disappointment. So he hadn't wanted to come—he'd been asked to look her up; doing a good turn, nothing else. She became conscious too that he was staring down at her, smiling.

'I want you to come back with me, Eloise. Cor needs someone with him, and he likes you. Will that do to go on with?' He sighed gently. 'I've only just arrived in England.'

Her mind seized on that. 'Travelling all night? You must be tired and hungry. Would eggs and bacon do? Wait while I put on some clothes.'

'So kind,' he murmured, and took off his coat. 'I'll put the kettle on.'

She flung herself into slacks and an old sweater she had been wearing while she cleared up the flat, and didn't bother about her hair or her face, only washed the latter and tied the former back with a handy ribbon, not bothering to look. He had the tea made by the time she got back to the kitchen, with the one cup and saucer and a mug on the table and a half full bottle of milk. He poured their tea while she assembled frying pan, eggs and the last of the bacon.

'It's rather primitive,' she apologised as she laid the table with the odds and ends of crockery it hadn't been worth packing, and cut bread for toast.

'I am a primitive man,' he observed blandly, and went on looking bland when she laughed. He added: 'How did the wedding go?'

'Perfectly. Mother looked so sweet, only she was a little sad because of Mrs Pringle.'

'We are all a little sad—Deborah was much liked.' He buttered the toast she gave him. 'Eloise, Cor Pringle is just about at the end of his tether, and that son of his hasn't helped. He's shunning everyone because he thinks they will be embarrassed if he talks about Deborah to them, and that's just what he wants to do at the moment. He talks to me, but I'm not always available, and then the other day he told me that he was sorry you had gone home because you would have understood and he could have talked to you. So I said I'd fetch you.'

'Just like that?'

'Just like that. I don't like to see a good man go to pieces. Oh, he'll get over it, but he has to blunt the first sharp edge of his sorrow and it helps to talk.'

She dished up three eggs and several slices of bacon and put them on his plate. 'Eat it while it's hot,' she advised him. 'Look, I'd like to help, but I haven't any more holidays due and I've been offered a Sister's post— I was going this morning to hand in my application form.' She added soberly: 'You see, I should have a secure future…'

The doctor buttered more toast and handed it to her. 'I see—well, there was no harm in asking.'

Eloise stared at her plate. 'Mind you, I don't give a jot about a secure future and even if I said I'd come I don't know how to set about it; you must see that I can't just walk into Miss Dean's office and tell her I'm leaving to look after someone in Holland—there's a month's notice too…'

He was staring at her hard. 'And if that could be arranged? If you were allowed to leave at a moment's notice, would you come?'

She took her eyes off her plate and met his blue gaze and heard herself say yes.

'Splendid. Is there any more toast?' And when she reached for the loaf: 'Bart wished to be remembered to you, by the way.'

'Oh, does he?' She smiled widely. 'I like him. You

must be so happy to have someone like that in your lovely home.'

'You found it lovely?'

She popped two more slices under the grill. 'Oh, I did—so lovely it's hard to talk about it.'

'I'm glad. Have you a telephone?'

She shook her head. 'It's been cut off—there's a call-box at the corner of the street. Do you want any more toast?'

'No, thanks. I'll wash up while you dress and then go and telephone.'

Eloise eyed him, wondering if she would seem inquisitive if she asked who he wanted to speak to at eight o'clock in the morning. She had just decided that it was when he observed: 'Let me allay your curiosity—I'm going to telephone Sir Arthur Newman.' He swept the dishes off the table and began to wash up as though he had done it all his life, and Eloise, restraining herself from saying anything at all, went along to dress.

He was in the only chair left in the sitting room when she went into it, reading a newspaper, but he put it down at once and got to his feet. 'Ready? We've got five minutes.'

She gave him a vexed look. 'Well, really, you might have warned me! And we can't possibly get to St Goth's in that time—if that's where we're going.'

'Care to bet on it?' He hurried her down the empty flights of stairs and out of a side entrance and popped her into the Rolls, discreetly parked where it shouldn't have been. They were halfway to the hospital before she asked: 'Why have we only got five minutes?'

'Sir Arthur was going to telephone your Nursing Superintendent or whatever she's called; he suggested that we should be there at half past eight because that's the time he was making an appointment for us.'

'Us?'

He gave her a sidelong glance. 'Having disorganised your plans, the most I can do is to smooth your path.' He shot the car into the hospital forecourt and hurried her inside. Glancing at the clock as he swept her along, Eloise was glad she hadn't accepted his bet; there was half a minute to go.

'It's down this passage,' she told him.

'I know. I've been here before. We'll just have time to state our case before Sir Arthur comes.'

She looked at him round-eyed. 'You're going to an awful lot of trouble…'

He had stopped outside Miss Dean's office. 'Ah, but you're worth a lot of trouble, Eloise.' He kissed her quite gently on her half open mouth, tapped on the door and pushing her ahead of him, went in.

Chapter 6

Afterwards, walking soberly back to the hospital entrance with Doctor van Zeilst and Sir Arthur on either side of her, Eloise wondered just what magic had been wrought by the two gentlemen, neither of whom looked capable of such unprofessional practice—indeed, peeping at them in turn, she decided that she had never seen two better examples of learned men going about their dignified business.

'I hope, dear boy,' boomed Sir Arthur over her head, 'that you will be out of the country before our worthy Miss Dean finds the time to figure out that masterly rigmarole you offered her. I almost shed tears at this young lady's plight—forced, if I remember right, to remain in this hospital just because its rules could not be bent.'

Doctor van Zeilst inclined his head and looked smug. 'I

thought it quite a good effort myself.' His self-satisfaction decided Eloise that it was about time that she bore a part in the conversation.

'I'm not quite clear…' she began in an uncertain voice, and both her companions stopped to look at her, so that she hurried on: 'Has Miss Dean given me the sack, or am I borrowed, or what?'

'Not sacked,' observed Doctor van Zeilst in a shocked voice. 'You have resigned for urgent personal reasons, with the option of applying for the Night Sister's post which you seem so anxious to have, when you return—provided it isn't filled in the meantime.'

She almost wrung her hands. 'But of course it will be by then—I'll be a staff nurse for ever! Oh, I wish I'd never…'

'Tut, tut, you weren't listening. Cor Pringle is going to Curaçao in two weeks' time—I surely mentioned that? There will be plenty of time to apply for the job if you're still bent on carving a career for yourself.'

They began to walk on again, and Eloise perforce with them. At the entrance Sir Arthur bade them goodbye and bon voyage and murmuring that he was already late for his ward round, went on his dignified way. When he was out of sight, Eloise, her temper frayed by uncertainty and the nasty feeling that she had been rushed into something she didn't know about, snapped: 'Well, what do I do next? You tell me.'

'Coffee, I think, don't you?' Doctor van Zeilst smiled at her with great charm, and although her heart beat so fast at the sight of it that she almost choked, she said firmly: 'That won't help in the least.'

'Oh, it will. We need a little time while I tell you what we're going to do.'

'We? Do what? Look, you must explain...' Her voice was shrill with the beginnings of temper. 'You rush me along to see Miss Dean and cook up a story I'm sure she doesn't in the least believe—and however did you get her to allow me to resign and then apply...'

'Charm.' His voice was all silk. 'And I must add, a good deal of spade work on the part of Sir Arthur. It's amazing,' he reflected gravely, 'what one can achieve when one really puts one's mind to it.' He suddenly became businesslike, almost urgent. 'Eloise, Cor Pringle really does need someone. Oh, he's got Juffrouw Blot, but although she's a splendid housekeeper, he can't talk to her. I had to think of some way of getting you back without falling foul of hospital rules.

'I imagine Miss Dean is fully aware that they are being bent, but why not when it's in a good cause? If you were ill for two weeks, someone would take your place, would they not? I know you're worried about resigning, but she promised that you might apply for that job, didn't she? Will you stop worrying and listen to me?'

'I've been listening.'

They had been walking down the narrow, shabby street behind the sprawling hospital. Now he stopped outside a neat little caf half way down it, much patronised by the hospital staff. There weren't many people inside and they sat down at a table in the window, and after a minute or two the proprietor ambled over, gave the table an extra rub up with his cloth, took the doctor's order for coffee, and went away again. It wasn't until it arrived, hot and strong, that the doctor broke the silence between them. 'We'll go first to Eddlescombe, on our way home...'

Eloise put down her cup. 'But it's miles out of our way!'

'Let us not exaggerate; it is a couple of hours' driving from here, perhaps a little more.' He looked at his watch. 'We could be there by mid-afternoon, stay the night if your mother would be so kind as to invite us, and journey on the following morning.'

Eloise's wide mouth curved with delight. 'How super! Could we really?'

He took a lump of sugar from the bowl and crunched it up. 'We could and we will—after all, you deserve some small reward. And now if you have finished your coffee, shall we go round to your flat? You can pack and do whatever is necessary—would an hour be long enough?'

It was obvious to her that she wasn't going to be given more than that. She nodded. 'Yes, provided you do some telephoning for me—the gas and electricity— oh, and the landlord.'

The doctor lifted a finger for the bill. 'My practical Eloise! Let us get started by all means.' He swept her out into the street again and walked her back the way they had come to where the car was parked in the hospital forecourt. A few minutes later they were at the flat.

And later still, with London's outskirts already behind them, Eloise found herself driving down the M3, with the doctor, peacefully asleep, beside her. It seemed a good opportunity to explore her thoughts; there was very little traffic and the Rolls purred effortlessly ahead. She didn't know if she were coming or going, all she was sure of was that her companion knew, and that because she loved him and trusted him she was quite content to leave her immediate future in a muddle in order to please him. Common sense told her that she was being a fool; later on she would come to her senses and probably bitterly regret allowing him to rearrange her life for her.

She sighed, remembered the instructions he had given her when she had taken over the driving, and slowed the car's pace as they approached Wimborne Minster. She had driven rather less than a hundred miles at a steady, fast speed, mostly on the motorway, but she didn't feel tired as she drove carefully through the little town and stopped in its square outside the King's Head. It was time to wake her companion, but when she turned to him it was to find him awake, his eyes fastened on her. 'Nice driving,' he murmured. 'You handle her very well.'

She thanked him primly and asked if he had slept.

'Soundly, thanks to you. Shall we have lunch—it's getting a little late, but I daresay they'll serve us.'

They ate roast beef and Yorkshire pudding and followed it with treacle tart, washed down with claret. They were drinking their coffee when the doctor remarked: 'I'll drive the rest of the way—it's not far now, is it? Just over twenty miles to Dorchester and take the Milton Abbas road—you'll have to direct me. Who taught you to drive?'

'My father.'

'He did it well, though I think you're a naturally good driver.'

Eloise said thank you once more and then allowed her tongue to run away with her. 'Do you let Liske drive your car?' she wanted to know.

His eyes became very blue and cold. 'No, I do not—why do you ask?'

Perhaps it was the claret, but she felt reckless. 'Well, I thought she might...'

'And what makes you think that?' His voice was silky.

'Well, she...she was at your house when we went there, and from what she said, I thought...she seemed very at home...' Her voice petered out under his cold stare.

'Well?' he repeated, still silky, and she could see that she wasn't to be allowed to leave the matter there.

'As though she...as though you both...' She tried again. 'I thought perhaps she was going to marry you,' she finished gamely, her voice small.

He smiled in what she considered to be a very nasty manner. 'You may think what you wish,' he told her blandly. 'Shall we go?'

Excepting for giving directions when it was necessary, Eloise preserved silence for the remainder of their journey, spending her time trying out numerous apologies to herself, none of which were really satisfactory. And as for her companion, he was silent too, although from time to time he whistled softly to himself, for all the world as though he were in the best of humours—which he quite obviously wasn't.

But when they arrived, no vestige of ill-humour was allowed to show. He got out of the car, came round to open her door and then waited while she went up the path to the cottage's front door, where she thumped the knocker, tried the handle, and when she found it open, called, 'Mother, it's us!' unaware of the doctor's reluctant smile at her words.

She was answered by the opening of a window above her head and the appearance of her mother's neat head thrust out. 'Darling, what a lovely surprise—and Doctor van Zeilst, too! Come on in, I'm on my way down.'

They had barely got inside when she joined them, running down the staircase with the lightness of a girl, to fling her arms round her daughter's neck and hug her before shaking hands with the doctor.

'Oh, isn't this just lovely!' she exclaimed. 'Jack will be pleased—he's in the garden making chicken houses. Have you come to stay? I do hope so.'

'We're on our way to Holland,' said Eloise quickly. 'We wondered if we could spend the night.'

'As many as you like, you're both very welcome.' Her mother smiled at her second guest and asked guilelessly: 'Why are you going to Holland? Or rather, why did you come to England—or mustn't I ask?' She tucked a hand into his arm. 'Come into the sitting room and sit down and tell me before I fetch Jack.' She opened a door and ushered them into the comfortable little room, bright with firelight, and said: 'Let me have your coats—now do tell...'

'There's nothing much to tell, Mrs Bennett.' It was the doctor who answered her, for Eloise seemed to have lost her tongue for the moment. 'Cor Pringle isn't too well—depressed, not eating, lonely. He told me that he wished Eloise had still been with him because she understood how he felt and he felt he could talk to her— she has very kindly agreed to go and stay with him until he goes to Curaçao in two weeks' time.'

If Mrs Bennett felt disappointment at this explanation, she concealed it admirably, only darting a look at her daughter's composed features and smiling faintly. 'How did you get away from St Goth's?' she wanted to know.

'Doctor van Zeilst and Sir Arthur Newman talked to Miss Dean,' Eloise told her flatly. 'I've resigned, but I'm allowed to apply for that job I told you about when I get back—if it's still going,' she added snappily.

Her mother ignored the snappiness. 'How sensible,' she declared. 'I'm sure Cor will be glad of your company— I thought it was a mistake staying on in that house by himself. Now he can talk as much as he wants to about Deborah. You can't just turn your back on years of happiness with someone without talking about it—the trouble is, other people tend to shy away from just that because they think it makes you miserable—such a mistake.' She looked at the doctor. 'Not you, of course, Timon—you don't mind if I call you that?—I thought you coped beautifully.' She got to her feet. 'I'm going to fetch Jack, then we'll have tea. Did you get any lunch?'

Eloise answered this time. 'Yes, thanks, dear—in Wimborne. But we'd love tea—I'll give you a hand.'

She sent her mother such a beseeching look that that lady said instantly: 'Oh, yes, do, dear,' and the doctor, sitting in his chair watching them, allowed his eyelids to droop over the amused gleam in his eyes.

Jack having duly welcomed them and taken a chair opposite the doctor, the two ladies went off to the kitchen, a surprisingly roomy place, a trifle old-fashioned, but as Mrs Bennett declared, just how she liked it. They set about getting tea; scones and butter and jam and a large fruit cake as well as muffins. It was while Eloise was putting cups and saucers on a tray that her mother asked: 'Did you two quarrel all the way here, darling?'

Eloise choked. 'Mother! Not until we got to Wimborne. I drove most of the way and he slept—he's been up all night.'

'That accounts for that bland expression; I've noticed it before—lack of sleep,' she went on vaguely, 'or perhaps it was something else?' She turned to look at her daughter, who was slicing cake savagely.

'I expect he was thinking about Liske,' muttered Eloise bitterly.

'That's what you quarrelled about?'

'Mother, you can't quarrel with him—he won't. He just—just silences you. Shall I take in the tray?'

Tea was quite enjoyable. The doctor, tired or not, was the perfect guest and Jack was a good host, and if Eloise and the doctor took care not to address each other directly unless it was absolutely necessary, their companions appeared not to notice. They sat around the fire after tea, until it was time to get supper; a sizzling macaroni cheese with a sustaining soup first and beer for the men, and then once more round the fire while they drank their coffee. They didn't stay up late, although it was very pleasant sitting there talking about nothing much, but as Mrs Bennett pointed out, they kept country hours and besides, Timon would be tired. She wished him goodnight, told her husband not to keep their guest up late, and whisked Eloise upstairs with her.

'It seemed a good idea,' she told her as they gained the small landing. 'Only one bathroom, you see, though there's plenty of hot water—you'll have time to get a bath.' She kissed Eloise gently. 'Dear child, things take so long to happen sometimes.' With which obscure remark she took herself off to her own room.

It was raining when Eloise woke in the morning, and not quite light. She got up and crept downstairs and made tea, then took a tray up to her mother's room before going back to the warm kitchen to sit in her dressing gown by the Aga to drink her own. She had decided against taking the doctor a cup. He could come down for it; if she took it, he might think that she was trying to get into his good graces. 'Monster!' she muttered crossly, filled her cup for the second time and curled up in the elderly basket chair; she would sit there in peace and quiet for ten minutes.

A plan instantly shattered. The back door opened and the doctor came in, very wet. He looked at her without surprise, wished her good morning, remarked that he had taken the car to the village garage to get filled up and asked, very politely, if he might have a cup of tea.

Eloise uncurled herself, conscious that she looked pretty awful; the dressing gown she had borrowed from her mother was too small, too short and faded, and her hair was a wild tangle down her back. She wished him good morning a little belatedly and went to fetch a mug. 'You're very wet,' was all she could find to say.

'It's raining,' he commented mildly, and took off his car coat and opened the door again to shake it before draping it over a chair.

She passed him the sugar. 'I hope you slept well?'

'Excellently, thank you.' He looked at her searchingly as he spoke, almost as though by studying her tired face he could see that she had stayed awake far too long, thinking about him. 'Shall you be ready to leave after breakfast?'

She nodded and got up once more. 'Yes. We're having it at eight o'clock—we can be away by half past. I'll go and dress. There's plenty more tea in the pot if you like to help yourself.'

He only smiled in reply and went to open the kitchen door for her, which was absurd of him, but nice all the same considering what a fright she looked.

It rained all day, with leaden skies and a nasty gusty wind which Eloise hoped would stop blowing before they got to Dover. Her companion was at his most amiable, although there was little warmth in his manner. She decided that he had made up his mind to be polite at all costs, maintaining a desultory conversation about this and that and being careful not to introduce any personal element. She replied suitably, and from time to time, feeling that it was her turn to bear the burden of polite talk, made observations about the weather, their journey, the countryside and the charms of Eddlescombe. Only as they sat down to lunch at the Wife of Bath in a small village just outside Ashford did she come to a halt. She sat studying the menu without really seeing it and presently, aware that his eyes were on her, said, quite against her inclination: 'I'm sorry if I annoyed you yesterday.'

She looked at him as she spoke and saw his brows lift slightly. 'Annoy me—you make me very angry, you frequently do.'

Any desire she might have had to apologise melted away into thin air. 'Well, you had no reason to be,' she told him roundly. 'I hadn't meant to pry, I only—well...' She stopped, rather at a loss for words, and he supplied them for her in a silky voice: 'Put out a feeler?' he suggested. 'Tried a little guessing? That will get you nowhere with me, Eloise.'

Nothing would get her anywhere with him. She ignored the snub and said haughtily: 'I think that I have made it quite clear to you already that I have no interest in your affairs.'

'No? I'm disappointed.' He smiled and his whole face changed. 'Shall we bury the hatchet for the moment? One day—not too far off, I hope, I shall do my best to interest you in what you so airily describe as my affairs. And now what shall we eat?'

She sighed. He was holding out an olive branch, but only as a gesture, and probably more for his own satisfaction than any intent to please her. She ate the delicious food he had ordered, and plunged once more into polite nothings by way of conversation, thinking how very foolish it was to love someone who barely tolerated you, and that with a remote civility which set her splendid teeth on edge—a reflection which bore her up for the remainder of their journey.

But she forgot her own grievances when they arrived at Mijnheer Pringle's house and she saw the pleasure on his face. He seemed to have aged a good deal in the short time since she had seen him, but his welcome was sincere, so that she knew then that she had done the right thing in coming. And an equally delighted Juffrouw Blot took her case up to her room before taking her downstairs again to join the men for a drink.

And later, when she had gone upstairs and unpacked and changed her dress, she found that the doctor was staying to dinner. She sat between the two men, one at each end of the table, and ate whatever was put before her, taking part in the talk when she was directly addressed while she wondered if and when she would see Timon again.

Not soon, she surmised, for she heard him tell his host that he couldn't stay for coffee because he had an appointment later that evening. Liske would be waiting for him, she supposed, and she wished him an austere goodnight in consequence, coupled with even more austere thanks for bringing her to Holland, although, now she came to think about it, she had no reason to do so; he had been the one who had insisted on her coming in the first place. It was mortifying to hear him say, just as though he had read her thoughts: 'You really have no reason to thank me, Eloise. It was I who persuaded you to come in the first place, and that for my own good reasons.'

She had nothing to say to that and he left very shortly

after, leaving her to sit with Mijnheer Pringle and drink more coffee while he talked about his Deborah. They sat up quite late although she was tired enough to have gone to bed hours earlier, but she had her reward when he told her: 'I shall sleep tonight, Eloise; I can talk to you about Debby—there is so much I want to remember and say, and Pieter won't allow that. He says it's morbid; he thinks that I should shut her away and think of other things, but that I cannot do, and I think that you understand that. If you will bear with me for a week or two...'

'There's no question of bearing with you, Mijnheer Pringle.' Eloise's voice was gentle. 'I like to talk about Mevrouw Pringle too as well as listen to you—besides, why should you shut her away? She will always be in your head, won't she—you can't shut her out. And I think I know how lonely you are.'

'You will make some man a good wife one day, my dear. I have been depressed and perhaps too sorry for myself—Timon knows that, but now that you are here by some small miracle, I promise you I will take up the threads of my life again.'

Eloise got to her feet. 'Well, your wife would want you to, you know. She was a happy person and she would want you to be happy too. Will you remember to take your sleeping pills or shall I get them for you?'

'I will remember.' He was on his feet too. 'And I have kept you from your bed, for which I am very sorry. To-morrow I will start afresh.'

'The garden,' suggested Eloise. 'You must keep it looking just as it always did—we could clear the leaves and light a bonfire.'

He smiled. 'That I shall enjoy—after breakfast?'

'After breakfast.'

She was even more tired than she had thought; she had intended to work out some plan for seeing Timon again, but she went instantly to sleep.

She and Mijnheer Pringle were busily engaged in building the bonfire when the doctor drove up. Eloise, sweeping leaves across the lawn at the side of the house, saw him coming up the drive and pretended not to have done so. She was muffled in one of Mijnheer Pringle's old raincoats, with a scarf over her head because the day was damp and chilly, and for a moment the absurd idea crossed her mind that he might not recognise her, an idea instantly dispelled by his loud: 'I like the outfit—are you intending to crown the bonfire?'

She shot him a cross look and said peevishly: 'Certainly not. I don't happen to be a girl who fusses over her appearance, that's all.'

'Meaning that Liske does?' he wanted to know blandly.

'Meaning no such thing,' she declared, and uttered the lie with conviction. 'And why bring her up?'

He smiled his nasty smile. 'I like to annoy you, my dear.'

He turned away and walked to where Mijnheer Pringle was happily forking the leaves and debris into a pile and the two men stood talking for a few minutes before Timon went back to his car, with nothing but a nonchalant wave as he passed her. 'Good riddance to bad rubbish,' muttered Eloise, and poked at her pile of leaves with such venom that they scattered all over the lawn again.

They were having their lunch when her host remarked: 'Timon asked us for dinner this evening and of course I accepted.' He didn't wait for her to reply, but went on: 'Shall we finish the garden this afternoon, or are you tired? We have made splendid progress.'

'Let's finish it,' suggested Eloise, her mind busy on what she should wear that evening—she hadn't anything, she concluded, and abandoned the idea of competing with Liske, who would certainly be there too. Aloud, she said: 'Have you been to see any of your friends? When the garden's finished would it be a good idea to call on them all—you won't see them for a bit if you're going to Curaçao.'

He liked the idea. 'Of course, that is a good idea—we will do that, but we must remember that Pieter is coming for the weekend.' He added with pathetic cheerfulness: 'We shall be quite gay.'

Eloise tried to imagine being gay with Pieter and her mind boggled. 'How nice—I expect he's looking forward to his trip.' She gave her companion another cup of coffee and deliberately led the conversation back to his wife.

Later, going through her scanty wardrobe in a rather hopeless way, Eloise decided to wear a grey jersey dress; indeed, with the exception of the dress she had bought for her mother's wedding, there was no other there; a variety of slacks and woollies and a skirt or two, but none of those would do. It would have to be the grey. She put it on without much enthusiasm, piled her hair into a shining topknot, did her face with care, and went downstairs to find Mijnheer Pringle. So far the day had been successful; they had been busy in the garden until dusk, and he looked better for it, although now he looked a little tired; perhaps it would be a better idea if they went visiting the next day and gave the garden a rest—she put the idea to her companion as they drove to the doctor's house.

·There were welcoming lights shining from the ground floor windows as they arrived. Eloise, getting out of the car, wondered just how much it would cost to maintain such a magnificent home; a small fortune, probably. The doctor must be a rich man—another good reason why she must forget him as quickly as possible. She sighed and then smiled widely at Bart's welcome, pleasure at seeing her again lighting up his elderly face. He took their coats and led them across the hall to the drawing room where Timon was waiting for them. He was standing at the other end of the big room, staring out into the dark grounds from the french windows, but he turned round when he heard Bart's voice, and Eloise had the impression that he had been so deep in thought that he hadn't heard their arrival, although his face was impassive and he seemed his usual unruffled self as he poured their drinks, wanting to know how they had spent their day and what their plans were for the days ahead. Eloise sipped her sherry, hating the grey dress and making polite answers to her companions' remarks. She wasn't surprised when Timon said casually: 'Liske should have been here long ago—probably she has been delayed.'

Doing what? Eloise asked herself silently, and answered her own question. Making up her mind which of her many dresses to wear. She peeped at the doctor and came to the conclusion that he was either angry or worried about something; the blandness was so very pronounced. But there was little change in his expression when Liske at last joined them, and Eloise, studying his face closely, could see no sign of the delight a man in love would surely show the object of his affections. True, he crossed the room to greet her and when she threw her arms around him and kissed him, he didn't appear to mind.

Eloise looked away quickly before Liske could see her watching them and chatted airily to Mijnheer Pringle until Liske came over to say hullo with what she considered to be a smug smile, but then she would have felt smug herself if she could look gorgeous in a silver lamé suit, with blonde hair bouncing on her shoulders, delicate wrists loaded with gold bracelets which tinkled and clashed each time she moved her useless, pretty little hands. She was all charm and friendliness towards Eloise, who feeling that at the moment she possessed neither of these attributes, was aware of being at a disadvantage. Indeed, she suspected that the horrid girl had deliberately engaged her in talk so that their companions could have ample opportunity to appreciate the vast difference between them. Certainly Eloise's tall, well built person served to emphasise the grace and daintiness of Liske.

Bart announced dinner almost at once, but Liske lifted a shoulder and said in a little-girl voice: 'But,

Timon, I've only just got here—I couldn't possibly swallow my drink so quickly.'

He smiled across the room at her. 'You're very late,' he pointed out. 'I'm afraid you'll have to leave the rest of your drink. Shall we go in?'

Liske pouted, tossed off the contents of her glass and went to join him while Eloise got up more slowly, conscious of her size and the inadequacy of the grey jersey. It surprised her when the doctor came towards her, saying casually: 'Cor, look after Liske, will you?' and took her arm.

'I can see that Cor is feeling better already,' he said quietly. 'Thank you, Eloise, you are just what he needed, you know.' He began to walk unhurriedly to the door, his hand still on her arm. 'Have you any plans for the next few days?'

'I wondered if we were to call on some of his friends? There's a lot to do in the garden, but I think he's tired, and if we gardened every day he'd get quite exhausted.'

He nodded agreement. They were in the hall now, with Bart watching them from the dining room door. 'Sunday,' mused the doctor, 'supposing we go over to my sister's place. I don't think you've met her; she was at the funeral, but there were so many there. I'll come for you and Cor about ten o'clock—we'll go for lunch.'

She felt a pleasant warmth underneath the despised jersey; he was only being kind and thoughtful, of course, but a day in his company would be something to treasure.

Dinner was delicious; thin soup, roast duckling with cherry sauce and a creamy pudding of great richness.

Eloise ate with healthy appetite, enjoying every morsel, while she pondered the fact that food, served on exquisite china and eaten with solid silver, tasted so much better. They drank claret with the duckling and a delicate white wine with the sweet, and Liske, who had behaved very prettily until the mouthwatering dish was presented to her, remarked rather pointedly that she didn't dare touch a morsel of it. 'For I should hate to get fat,' she trilled, and glanced across the table at Eloise, about to lift the first morsel to her lips. You couldn't answer rudeness like that, she decided furiously, and defiantly had a second helping.

They had coffee in the drawing room and Timon talked about Deborah Pringle in such a natural, unselfconscious way that presently Cor Pringle joined in, relaxing more and more as the evening wore on, but Liske, not in the least interested, wandered about the lovely room, picking up the trifles of china and silver lying on the little tables, doing her best to change the conversation, until she declared that she had a headache and would go home.

The doctor rose, sympathised with the headache and went with her into the hall, leaving the drawing room door half open, and although Liske was speaking Dutch, Eloise had no difficulty in guessing that she was furiously angry about something. The doctor's voice, on the other hand, sounded calmer than ever. He came back presently, looking quite inscrutable, and rang for more coffee, declaring that it was far too early to break up such a pleasant evening, so that it was an hour before Mijnheer Pringle suggested they should really go home otherwise Eloise would be asleep on her feet. So she got to her feet too, though reluctantly. She had enjoyed sitting there, listening to the two men talking quietly, joining in herself from time to time and loving the peace and quiet of the room. It was while Timon was helping her into her coat that he said softly: 'You look exactly right sitting in my drawing room, Eloise, in that pretty grey gown—you're a very restful person.' He lifted her hand and kissed it and she could only goggle at him. 'No bracelets,' he murmured, 'to drive a man insane.'

She managed to find her tongue at last. 'Oh—well, I haven't any, you know.'

He smiled down at her. 'Thanks for coming this evening,' and then in a brisker tone: 'Remember to be ready on Sunday. I shall look forward to it.'

So would she, but why, she pondered on their way back, should he look forward to it? Because he had quarrelled with Liske and wanted to teach the tiresome girl a lesson? Or perhaps she was coming too—she hadn't thought of that. It worried her all the way home and long after she was in bed and should have been asleep.

Chapter 7

Eloise and Mijnheer Pringle spent the next two days visiting, first the Potters, where they stayed for lunch, then on to the van Eskes, where they remained for tea and drinks before they went back home, and on the second day to the Haagesmas, who insisted on them remaining for both lunch and dinner. And all of them, Eloise was delighted to find, talked their fill of Deborah Pringle; perhaps the doctor had primed them, she wasn't sure, but of one thing she was certain, that Mijnheer Pringle was a happier man than he had been when she had arrived. They spent the next day in the garden, in windy rainy weather, and played chess in the evening, at which game Eloise showed herself to be possessed of some skill, for her father had taught her as a child.

And the next day was Sunday. Without going too

deeply into her reason for doing so, Eloise put on the grey jersey again, wrapped herself in her new winter coat and went downstairs to join Mijnheer Pringle. She barely had the time to brush him down and find his hat before the Rolls purred to a standstill at the front door and they were joined by Timon.

Liske wasn't with him; that was the first thing Eloise saw as they went outside. She was ushered into the back of the car, sharing it with Bluff the dog, who made much of her and then, at a quiet word from his master, retired to his corner. She sat, a hand on his woolly neck, as the doctor, with Mijnheer Pringle beside him, drove out of the gates and took the road to Groningen. 'It's not a long drive,' he told her over his shoulder, 'north of the city but well out in the country.'

Which meant very little to her without a map, but she was content to watch the countryside, bare with the beginnings of winter, while the two men talked quietly together. The villages all looked rather alike, small and compact, clinging to their churches in the centre, but away from them the great farmsteads squatted in wide meadows, their enormous barns, their pristine paintwork and well ordered gardens bearing witness to their prosperity. There were horses in the fields too, great powerful beasts, standing about in Sunday idleness, but the cows were indoors, kept warm against the chilly wind.

The road wound through the fields, occasionally plunging into a small copse, and it was in the middle of one of these that the doctor turned the car into a rough lane at right angles to the road. It was lined with trees, bare now, but the thickets on either side were dense enough. A little further on, when they reached an open gate, the track changed to a well kept brick surface which in its turn curved into a sweep before a roomy house with a great many windows, each crowned with eaves and embellished with small balconies. The front door was wide and lofty and reached by a short flight of steps, and there was a verandah running round the house on either side. It looked a pleasant, homely place and as Eloise got out she could hear dogs barking and children's voices. They all came tumbling out to meet them; a small boy, two little girls and a young woman with a baby under one arm, and behind her, the master of the house with a couple of golden labradors. For a few minutes they stood in a group while she was introduced; the dogs gavotting round them and the children tugging at their uncle's hands and then Eloise was whisked away to take off her coat by her hostess, a pretty girl, a good deal younger than her brother, who begged her to call her Juliana and hoped with the same breath that she liked children: 'For we have four, as you can see, and we like to have them with us as much as possible—Bram is away all day—he's an anaesthetist at Groningen hospital, and says he never sees enough of them.' She paused for breath and then went on before Eloise could speak: 'Yes, I can see exactly what Timon meant when he told me about you.'

Eloise paused in the tidying of her hair. For the life of her she couldn't stop herself asking: 'Oh? What did he say?'

'That you weren't pretty but that you had beauty.'

Eloise turned to stare at her hostess, her mouth open. 'He said that? Well, he must have been joking.'

'I think not, I believe he might be vexed if he knew that I had told you. Shall we go down?'

The rest of the morning was an unqualified success; they drank their coffee in a comfortable sitting room with the children, mouselike, eating biscuits, and later they had lunch, a leisurely meal taken in a room over-looking a beautiful garden. And after lunch, lulled by the wine she had drunk and the gentle stream of con-versation around her, Eloise sat with her hostess, the two little girls on either side, answering her questions. It wasn't until much later on that she realised that she had told Juliana almost all of her life's history.

But presently she found herself alone with the doc-tor while the others went to the greenhouses to inspect some plant or other. Juliana had dumped the baby in his lap, where it lay with its legs kicking the air, held fast by one large gentle hand. The two little girls and their brother were on the floor beside Eloise, who, a pack of cards in her hand, had offered to build them a card house, but she paused in her building to look at the doc-tor. His eyes were closed, his face calm—he really was very good-looking, but it wasn't his looks she loved, it was him. She was still looking when he opened his eyes a little so that they were mere slits and inquired: 'Why do you stare at me?'

'I don't know.' And then, her tongue getting the bet-ter of her once more: 'I quite thought that Liske would be here too.'

'I wonder why?' He sounded lazily uninterested.

'Well...' She glanced at him again very quickly; he was tickling the baby's chin and making it chuckle. 'I thought...as you were going to get married...'

'Am I? What makes you think that, Eloise?'

She snapped with a touch of peevishness: 'Nothing you've told me—you never answer any of my questions. The evidence of my own eyes, I suppose.'

His lids had drooped. 'You wish to see me married?'

She wouldn't look at him. 'Yes, if it made you happy.'

'I don't contemplate marrying for any other reason. And with half a dozen children besides?'

She added a card to her house with great care. 'Yes.'

'I hardly think that Liske would agree with you there— and it is her you have in mind as my—er—future wife?'

Eloise bit her lip, wondering how best to answer him. His voice had sounded silky and there was a note in it she didn't quite like. She was saved at the last moment by the return of the other three, who didn't come right into the room immediately but stood at the french windows, cheerfully arguing among themselves. There was time enough for her to hear the doctor say softly: 'Do you know, I have very nearly made the biggest mistake of my life, Pineapple Girl. Now I have to put it right.'

It was a pity that she had no time to ponder this remark before the other three joined them.

They stayed to dinner and she didn't speak to him alone for the rest of the evening, and on the drive back she shared the back of the car with Bluff. And when they reached Mijnheer Pringle's house, the doctor, although he came in with them, didn't stay above a couple of minutes and his goodbyes, although friendly, held nothing in them for Eloise alone.

Pieter came the next day and she wondered afresh why such nice people as Cor and Deborah Pringle could have had such a self-opinionated young man for a son. He had a good deal to say about the forthcoming trip, ate an enormous lunch, talking about himself for most of the time, and when later he sought her out and told her that he was taking her out to dinner that evening, she was very inclined to refuse. For one thing he seemed to take it for granted that she would be overwhelmed by his attention, and for another she didn't relish his company overmuch. But she could see no way of refusing him without hurting his father's feelings, and beyond an attempt, nipped in the bud, to get Mijnheer Pringle to join them, she could do very little about it.

Father and son wanted to talk after lunch, which left her free to potter in the garden before engaging Mijnheer Pringle in their daily game of chess, although this time she had Pieter breathing down the back of her neck. She knew that he longed to advise her on every move, which made her so reckless that she lost badly. It didn't help at all when he said heartily: 'That was bound to happen, Eloise. You should have...' He launched into a lecture on the basic rules of the game until she was able to escape to her room to dress.

She wasn't going to wear the grey jersey; Timon had liked her in that. She put on the green dress she had had for the wedding and went back to the sitting room to find the doctor, very much at his ease, standing before the fire. His 'Hullo, Eloise,' was briskly friendly and nothing more. He was staying for dinner, she was told, and he showed no signs of disappointment when he learned that she wouldn't be there; rather, he wished them a hearty goodbye, adding something about young people going out and having fun together, a remark which set her teeth on edge.

Pieter took her to a restaurant in Groningen and almost as soon as they had sat down made a fuss over the wine, so much so that the wine waiter's face assumed a wooden expression which barely concealed his contempt; it quite spoilt her dinner, although she quickly discovered that she had no need to entertain her host, since he was perfectly content to talk about himself, pausing only long enough for her to utter admiring comments. Eloise, who liked variety in her conversation, began to feel bored, although she strove to take an interest in what he was saying. But however hard she tried, it was Timon who held her thoughts.

He had gone when they got back and after sitting for half an hour with father and son, she thanked the latter prettily for her dinner, and went to bed.

It was two days before she saw the doctor again. She and Mijnheer Pringle had paid more visits, driven round the countryside, and enjoyed a visit to Franeker in order to view the planetarium. She had enjoyed that, listened carefully to the guide's careful explanation in his almost perfect English and then gone up the little staircase to study the cogs and wheels above the ceiling. It proved a good source of conversation all the way home and Mijnheer Pringle admitted that he had enjoyed it so much, they must plan another expedition as quickly as possible.

They were in fact discussing this over their dinner that evening when Doctor van Zeilst walked in. He had been out to a patient, he explained, and was on his way back to the hospital to confer with his Registrar there. He looked tired and remote, but when Mijnheer Pringle offered him coffee and something to eat, he accepted with alacrity.

The conversation was casual while he devoured soup, an omelette and the remains of one of Juffrouw Blot's desserts, but presently he sat back with a sigh while Eloise poured his coffee. 'When did you last have a meal?' she wanted to know.

'Oh, I've had a busy day—there was an accident on one of the farms very early this morning and I had a teaching round at the hospital; besides, it's the time of year when the waiting room is always full.'

'Your partners?' she prompted.

'Both away for a couple of days.'

'So when did you last have a meal?' she persisted.

'Er—an early breakfast, Eloise.' He passed his cup for more coffee, spooned in sugar lavishly and drank it with enjoyment. 'And don't look so concerned. Bart and Mevrouw Metz will be hovering with bowls of hot soup and heaven knows what else the moment I put my key in the lock.'

'I am not in the least concerned,' Eloise told him coldly, but he only grinned and began to discuss his host's trip, now only three days away. 'I'll give you a check up before you leave, Cor,' he suggested. 'You've had all the jabs you need, haven't you? Going in the afternoon are you? And you?' He had turned suddenly on Eloise. 'When do you go?'

The very thought of it made her feel sick. 'On the same day as Mijnheer Pringle—in the morning.' She left it at that.

'Plans all made? Job settled?'

'No.'

'Holidays, perhaps?'

'No.'

His eyes gleamed. 'Being inquisitive and not minding my own business, aren't I?'

She looked up from the coffee cup she had been studying with all the rapt attention of one who had discovered a priceless treasure. For lack of anything more suitable, she said 'No,' once again.

'It's like trying to open a tin with a knitting needle,' he informed the room at large, and continued cheerfully: 'You must come over and say goodbye to Bart and Mevrouw Metz—Bluff as well. Let me see…not tomorrow, I think, I have a date with Liske. The day after; I'll come for you before dinner. You too, of course, Cor.'

Mijnheer Pringle smiled faintly, watching them both. 'Of course, we shall be delighted, shan't we, Eloise? Shall we have an opportunity of seeing Liske?'

Timon was at his most bland. 'I think it unlikely, but I'll convey your good wishes.' He added: 'From you both, naturally.'

He went soon after that, leaving Eloise a prey to all kinds of surmise. Why, for instance, didn't he want her to meet Liske again? It must have been apparent by now that she and Liske didn't get on, but that didn't mean to say that they couldn't spend an evening in each other's company without saying a word out of turn. Perhaps Liske didn't want to meet her again and had told him so. In a way, she decided, it was a relief to know that she had seen the last of the girl.

But that wasn't to be the case. She and Mijnheer Pringle spent the whole of the next day in the north of Groningen, lunching with the Potters and then going back home at their leisure to dine early so that Mijnheer Pringle could do his packing. He was remarkably cheerful, she was pleased to note; his lassitude and lack of interest in life around him were almost gone. True, he was an unhappy man and would be for a long time yet, but he was coming to terms with that life once more and had even talked once or twice of going back to his work as soon as he returned from Curaçao. Eloise watched him go upstairs and with a motherly injunction to call her if he needed help, took herself off to the sitting room.

She was sitting doing absolutely nothing when she heard the front door bell and Juffrouw Blot's rather heavy tread in the hall, and despite herself, she couldn't resist turning round to look at the door; there was no reason why it should be Timon. Had he not made a point about going to see Liske? All the same, her heart bounced as the door opened.

It wasn't Timon, it was Liske. She came quickly into the room and without a word of greeting demanded: 'You are alone? I wish to speak to you.'

'I'm quite alone,' said Eloise in a steady voice, and waited to hear what would come next.

Liske threw off her splendid fur coat, revealing an elegant wool dress exactly the blue of her eyes, and sat down opposite Eloise. But only for a moment; she was up and pacing round the room again so that Eloise had to turn her chair round in order to keep her in view.

'What's the matter?' she asked, determined not to let the prowling figure worry her.

'I will tell you—you have turned Timon against me, that is what is the matter! You—a silly fat girl with no looks and dowdy clothes. How dare you? But you will not succeed, do you hear? I, Liske, will not allow it. He is mine, do you understand, I wish to marry him...' She paused to take a dramatic breath and Eloise asked quietly:

'Do you love him?'

'What has that to do with it? He has money—a great deal of it—and his lovely house and cars and an old honoured name. Besides, I wish to be his wife.'

'If he'll have you,' observed Eloise softly. 'And why on earth have you come to tell me all this? If he wants to marry you—if he loves you, do you suppose that anything I could say or do would make any difference to him? Don't be silly!'

'Silly—silly, you say!' Liske's girlish voice was shrill. 'It is you who are silly. He does not care a jot for you, you know—has he ever said so? Sought you out? Been attentive to you?' She paused to look into Eloise's face and went on in triumph: 'No, I can see that he has not. He is bewitched, to tell me that I mean nothing to him, that he has no wish to marry me, that I have dreamed things which he has never said…'

'And did you?' asked Eloise with interest.

Liske gave her a nasty look. 'I am a beautiful girl,' she declared with a self-assurance Eloise envied. 'If I wish for something, I have it, you understand. I shall have Timon, for I am quite beautiful and any man can be made to fall in love with me.'

'You're labouring under a misapprehension,' said Eloise, then, 'I've done nothing, nor do I intend to do anything. After all, if he had wanted me, he had only to say so, had he not? And he hasn't.'

'That I do not believe. There must be something you have done or said which has made him speak to me in this way.' Liske pounced on her coat and flung it on, looking so very beautiful that Eloise could only sit and admire her. 'I am angry,' she said loudly and quite unnecessarily, and rushed through the door, across the hall and outside to where, presumably, she had left her car.

Eloise sat where she was, her mind in a turmoil. Just what had Timon said? Had he used her as an excuse to get himself disentangled from Liske? As he had never given her any reason to suppose that he was interested in herself, she supposed so. He had made that strange remark at his sister's, that he had almost made the mistake of his life, but he could have meant anything, and nothing in his subsequent manner towards her had encouraged her to think otherwise.

She was disturbed from her rather unhappy reverie by Mijnheer Pringle calling from the landing above. 'Eloise? Who was it? Did I not hear voices?'

She got up and went into the hall. 'It was Liske. I'm not quite sure why she came; I think she's had a quarrel with Ti... Doctor van Zeilst. She went again—she's rather angry.'

He had joined her in the hall. 'She is a bad-tempered girl. It would have made Debby very happy if she had known that Timon wasn't going to marry her.'

'They are engaged, then?' She didn't care what questions she asked now; she was going so soon and afterwards it wouldn't matter.

'Certainly not. They have known each other for a long time, and it is possible that Timon has at some time or other considered her as a wife. She has so much, you see—youth and beauty and the same circle of friends—but there again,' he wrinkled his forehead in thought, 'she has so little also, no love to give to anyone but herself, no interest in his work and a great impatience with his good old Bart and Mevrouw Metz. She is also selfish and greedy; she wishes for all the good things of life and is not prepared to give anything in return. Debby never liked her, you know.'

'I don't either,' said Eloise flatly.

He gave her a perceptive look. 'No, I don't suppose you do, my dear.' They went back into the sitting room and sat down by the fire. 'It was she who upset Bart, did you know? So cruel a girl to taunt him with his age, and he a devoted servant and friend of Timon. Timon was angry about that.'

He got up and went to the cabinet where the drinks were kept. 'We will have a drink. You have had a trying evening and I am tired of packing my cases, they can wait. We will have a glass of Courvoisier, Debby always liked it.'

They sat companionably sipping their brandy and presently he said: 'Of course we go tomorrow evening as already arranged—Timon said that Liske would not be there.'

'I'm not afraid of her,' said Eloise, fired by the brandy.

'No, I don't imagine you are. Shall we wait and see? I often think that that is the best course when one is not sure what is going to happen next.' He got up and took her glass. 'Now I have some work to do in my study. Go to bed, my dear, and don't bother your head about Liske.'

So she went to bed, to dream fearful dreams of Timon waving her goodbye with Liske hanging on to his arm, wearing a fur coat and a wedding veil and laughing at her. She woke in a bad temper and didn't sleep again.

She got up in the morning with a splitting headache and the temper no better; somehow she got through the day, anxious now to get the evening over and done with; she didn't care if she didn't go, she told herself. All the same, she found herself putting on the grey jersey dress. She was sitting quietly in the sitting room, puzzling out the headlines of the *Haagsche Post*, when the doctor arrived, and although she greeted him pleasantly she made no attempt to sustain his attention and nor did he seem to wish it, embarking at once upon a conversation with Mijnheer Pringle about the weather. 'Which reminds me,' said the older man, 'talking of weather, it is just possible that I may have to return here later this evening. Pieter wanted some figures from me before we go; he was going to telephone—if he does so I've told Juffrouw Blot to let me know and I'll go back.' He paused. 'I have no car.'

'There's the Mini or the Bristol, you can borrow either, Cor,' said the doctor easily. 'A pity to spoil the evening, but if these figures are important, then you must return, of course. Are we ready?'

Bluff was in the car. Eloise got close to him and flung an arm round his woolly shoulders; he was a nice comforting creature, which was more than could be said of his master, who had barely looked at her.

The doctor's cook, his treasured Magda, had excelled herself. The table, its silver and glass winking in the soft glow of the wall sconces, was decorated with a great bowl of roses and the food was superb: if Timon wanted her to remember his home and the luxury in which he lived, thought Eloise, he had gone the right way about it. Would she ever forget the salmon mousse, the roast pheasant, the great silver dishes of vegetables, the sauces? Nor for that matter would she fail to recall the luscious bombe glacé which followed them. They had drunk champagne, but she had had only one glass; she wasn't used to it, she told her host gravely, and people said that it went to your head. He had agreed with her in the nicest possible way.

It was while they were sitting in the drawing room that the doctor was called away to the telephone and at the same time Mijnheer Pringle received a message from his own home, which left Eloise sitting alone. She curled up more comfortably in the armchair by the fire and reflected that if history were to repeat itself, Liske should make a dramatic entrance at that very moment.

Which she did. There was no ring at the door, nor was the great knocker thumped. She came in quietly, and even as Bart, crossing the hall on some errand, saw her, shut the double doors of the drawing room in his face.

One didn't need glasses to see that Liske was beside herself with rage. 'You're here—I knew it would be so! You—you harpy, you…' she paused to think, 'designing trollop!'

Eloise laughed. It was of course quite the wrong thing to do, but she couldn't help herself and it was better to do that than burst into tears or go running to Timon. She said in a reasonable voice: 'I'm not, you know. Mijnheer Pringle and I were invited to dinner, that's all.'

'Bah, I do not believe you! Where is his car if he is here, and I do not see him, nor do I believe you—you are here alone with Timon.' Her voice had risen. 'I have told him… I will not allow…'

Eloise got out of her chair. 'Oh, do be quiet,' she begged. 'How you do carry on… Timon is a man to do exactly what he wants and when he wants to do it nothing you say is going to make any difference to that. You really are a little fool.'

The other girl turned to face her across the lovely room. 'I am no fool, and that you will discover! Timon will believe anything I choose to say to him. I shall tell him…never mind that… I shall marry him also, and you can go back to England and stay there.'

Eloise wanted very much to shout back at the tiresome girl, but she managed to keep her voice low and steady. 'No, I don't think I'll do that,' she said slowly. 'I think I shall stay here and make sure that you don't have him. You are a petty, selfish girl, you deserve nothing and no one, because I don't think you have any idea what loving means. You're something under a stone…' She stopped because the look on Liske's face was pure triumph, and before she could turn her head, the girl had broken into Dutch, her voice sweet and coaxing now, and Eloise had no idea of what she was saying, although she could hear that it was eloquent and pleading and appealing.

When she did turn her head at last, Timon was there, standing by the door, leaning against the wall, his hands in his pockets. There was no expression on his face, but she knew that he was angry, although when he spoke his voice was level and quiet. 'Did you really say that, Eloise?' he asked, and when she didn't answer:

'That Liske was a trollop?' His mouth twitched a little. 'And a harpy? That she is cruel and selfish and something under a stone?'

'I said that she was something under a stone; she's got the rest wrong. I'm the harpy and the trollop…'

He ignored that. 'Why should you provoke her? She is upset, you can see that for yourself, you who are usually so sensible. And in the circumstances, that is natural enough. You should not have added to her distress, you had no need to be cruel, nor,' his voice was cold, 'did you need to interfere in my affairs—I prefer to manage them for myself.'

Eloise watched him cross the room and proffer a handkerchief to Liske. She wasn't at all sure that she knew what he was talking about—why should Liske be distressed anyway? The girl was putting on a splendid show, sobbing in a picturesque manner and throwing herself into his arms. Eloise would have liked to have done that herself.

He said over his shoulder, 'You could have waited, Eloise; I would have explained, for I have a great deal to tell you, but you can see for yourself that at the moment that is impossible. Could you not have been generous?'

Eloise was standing with her mouth open, trying to understand, watching the doctor's face. Her eye caught a faint movement from Liske as he was speaking; the girl wasn't crying at all, she was smiling at her over his shoulder. Eloise felt sick. She went through the door like a breath of wind, whisked her coat from the chair where it had been cast when she had arrived, and opened the front door. To get away, and fast, was the only thought in her mind. She closed the heavy door behind her and plunged down the drive, only then realising that it was drizzling with rain and the wind was blowing a gale.

But it would have taken more than bad weather to send her back now. Let Timon console Liske; he deserved her—she swallowed tears. He hadn't minded that Liske had called her names. Perhaps he hadn't believed her; he hadn't wanted to know her side of the horrid little affair, he had even asked her to be generous. 'He's mad,' she shouted above the wind, 'and I hate him!' The strength of her feelings carried her down the drive and out into the lane.

Chapter 8

The wind had become a mini-hurricane, tearing over the rolling countryside, hitting at her with giant hands, flattening her against its strength. For a moment she considered going back, but then the wind would be at her back and she would be bowled over—besides, she never wanted to see Timon again. She kept plodding on, tears, of which she was quite unconscious, pouring down her sopping cheeks. What, she asked herself, did it matter if this vile wind knocked her down, concussed her, even broke a limb—a leg or an arm, she decided, for then she would remain conscious to see Timon's remorse, although on second thoughts he wasn't likely to show remorse at all, only rage at the inconvenience, or worse than that, indifference.

She paused to gather some of the breath being bludgeoned out of her body. He had a nasty temper, but she could have managed him—she smiled a sad little smile through her tears and fought her way into the wind once more. It would be pitch dark soon; it was dark now and she felt sure that the sky she could no longer see was thunderous, but she reckoned that she was more than halfway to the main road by now and surely once there, there would be a bus. Luckily she had her purse in her coat pocket. Where she would go didn't seem important at the moment. She looked around her, although there was nothing to see by this time, just the faint glimmer of the road before her. She wasn't a nervous girl, but she had a nasty feeling that something was going to happen.

A moment later there was an uncanny lull in the wind, prelude to a flash of lightning which almost stopped her heart and a peal of thunder which crashed and banged round the wide horizon until she was deafened. And as though that wasn't enough, it began to rain in good earnest, a hard, cold deluge which soaked her in seconds. She came to a standstill; she had always hated storms, and now, alone in the dark and with no place to hide, she panicked. It was silly to shout for help, because who would hear above the howl of the returning wind and the noise of the rain? But shout she did, to no effect at all, for the wind took the sound the moment she opened her mouth. The roar of it filled her ears too, so that when she was caught roughly by the shoulders and swung round to be held fast in Timon's fierce grip, she screamed at the top of her voice. Another flash of lightning did nothing to reassure her either; what did bring her to her senses was the vigorous shaking the doctor was giving her. She couldn't see his face, but his already strong grip became iron-fast as he turned her round again and, by the light of his torch, hurried her off the road, over a narrow stone bridge, to squelch over a muddy field which, for all she knew, might be full of fierce bulls.

She was half running in his hold, terrified out of her wits still and still finding time to marvel that he was there. Now she could stop being frightened, although from the cruel grip with which he was holding her, he was probably just as much to be frightened of as the storm. He was going at a fine pace, seemingly oblivious of the fact that Eloise was now really running to keep up with him. He seemed to know where he was going, though, as indeed she discovered very shortly when a building of some sort was lighted by his torch; she couldn't see precisely what it was; only when Timon had swung back its still solid door did she see that it had once been a cottage, a very humble one, with the thatch above their heads in a sorry state and great cracks in its walls, but still blessed shelter.

Timon banged the door shut, shone his torch around the place and then turned it on to Eloise. 'Little fool,' he said furiously, 'have you run mad? Take off that wet coat—how anyone could be so…' He muttered in Dutch and she was glad that she couldn't see his face as she meekly struggled out of the sopping garment.

There was a fireplace of sorts against one wall. He walked over to it, turned over the ash and charred wood in it with one foot and looked around him. There was wood enough; one or two broken chairs, a smashed table, a couple of boxes—Timon collected them, broke up the boxes and kindled a fire with his lighter, and without looking at Eloise once, began breaking up the wrecked table and chairs. Surprisingly, the table, once on the fire, blazed merrily, sending light if not warmth round the miserable little place, defying the violent flashes of lightning flaring at the broken window.

Eloise, out of her coat, squelched over to the fire. She was wet through to her skin, with chattering teeth and a tear-stained white face which luckily she couldn't see. She steadied her teeth long enough to say: 'How clever of you to make a fire so quickly,' and at once had her head snapped off with: 'Clever? If I were clever I would shake you until your teeth rattled!' He smiled thinly and broke a chair leg over his knee and threw it on to the fire with a force which she supposed he would have liked to have used on her, remarking silkily: 'They're rattling now, aren't they? And serve you right!'

She could only see his profile, sharp with his rage. 'How dared you?' he asked.

'It's none of your business what I dare,' she snapped. Her nerves were fiddlestrings by now and her whole shivering chest trembled with its weight of unshed tears.

He peeled off his Burberry and tossed it into a corner, taking no notice of her words at all. 'Have you any idea of the trouble you have caused? Bart is beside himself, so is Mevrouw Metz, and the maids are snivelling in corners—just because you chose to walk out into the storm for some childish reason or other.'

Her white face had gone even whiter. He had called hers a childish reason, and that meant that he didn't care at all that Liske had called her names; a designing trol-lop, she remembered. Perhaps he thought of her like that too. She edged a little nearer the fire and wished with all her heart that she had managed to reach the main road and was on a bus, miles away.

'Why did you come after me, then?' she asked wood-enly.

He gave the fire a savage kick and said in a goaded voice: 'My dear girl, with the entire staff incapable of behaving sensibly until you were found, I had no choice.'

'Did Liske…was she worried too?'

He shot her a surprised glance. 'Liske? Surely you don't expect her to worry about you? She went home before I left the house.'

It was annoying of him not to say more, for she wanted very much to know just what had happened after she had left. She could imagine Liske weaving some pretty tale in which she was the injured, innocent party. Eloise unpinned her hair and started to wring it out in a hopeless sort of way. It really didn't matter what Timon thought of her now. Liske was determined to have him and if he was silly enough to be taken in by the wretched girl, then good luck to him. Eloise scowled horribly, choked on something which sounded very much like a small sob and said meekly: 'Oh, I see,' which meant just anything, and then asked: 'What shall we do?' She let out the ghost of a scream too at an extra vivid flash of lightning.

'Stay here, of course, until the storm has worn itself out sufficiently for us to get back.'

'Will that be long, do you think?'

'Probably all night.' They were standing side by side, steaming before the fire.

'If you want to go back,' she offered in a small voice, 'I shall be quite all right here.'

He looked down at her. 'My dear Eloise, should I return without you, I should be torn limb from limb; you seem to have cast a spell over the lot of them.' He put out a hand and touched her cheek lightly. 'Why did you have to behave as you did? Why did you have to interfere?'

She wanted to tell him that she hadn't interfered; that she hadn't behaved badly at all, but what would be the use? He was hardly likely to believe her. Oh, he would answer her courteously enough, no doubt, but she would have no chance against Liske's clever lies. And what was she supposed to be interfering about? Coming between him and Liske? Trying to turn him from her? Liske would have told him that, of course. She tried to forget the touch of his hand on her face and said crossly:

'Well, what did you expect? I have an interfering nature.'

'Yes, I know that,' he remarked surprisingly, 'but that makes no difference. But it didn't seem like you, to be unkind and ungenerous.'

He gave her a questioning look and it was on the tip of her tongue to ask him to start from the beginning and explain, but pride wouldn't let her; she stared back at him, her ordinary features screwed into defiance, so that he looked away presently, saying blandly: 'Well, for the moment there is nothing more to be said, is there? Take off your shoes and stockings and put them before the fire.' He added, almost irritably: 'Why do you not plait your hair? It would at least be out of the way.'

She obeyed without a word and then went to pick up their coats and arrange them close to the fire before sitting down on a rickety stool he had found in some corner or other. There seemed no more to be said. She sat silent, gradually getting warm once more, and presently, her hands clasped round her knees, she let her tired head drop and dozed off.

She was awakened by his hand on her arm. His voice, calmly impersonal, pierced her brain, clouded with sleep. 'The storm's over and the wind is a great deal less. We're going back, Eloise.'

She struggled into her shoes and stockings and put on the still damp coat and tied a bedraggled scarf from its pocket over her hair without saying a word. She had no idea how long she had been asleep. Not that it mattered—really, nothing mattered. She watched him stamp out the last few embers of the fire and went with him to the door, where she discovered that the wind was only a little less than it had been, although the rain, still falling, had turned to a drizzle again. She thanked heaven that they would have the elements behind them as they returned and then winced at a pale flicker of lightning on the horizon. The doctor didn't speak at all but took her arm, and with the torch in his hand strode along, taking her with him, and big girl though she was, she had a job to keep up with him.

They seemed to walk for a long time and when they reached the lane it was almost as mushy underfoot as the field had been. But Eloise was past caring; she hardly noticed the windblown drizzle trickling down the back of her neck, her scarf was long since sodden once more, but she didn't notice that either; she was far too busy wondering what would happen next. She would be going to England in the morning, anyway, presumably under a cloud and with the memory of the doctor's anger remaining with her for the rest of her days. She had no liking for women who burst into tears for little or no reason; she told herself this as tears began to run down her cheeks; she hadn't cried so much in years, but since the gale blowing them along was quite deafening, there was no need to check them. She sobbed gently, sucking in her breath like a small child, catching the tears with the tip of her tongue and sniffing from time to time, feeling a great relief from it. By the time they reached the house she would be herself again and able to face whatever was going to happen next.

What did happen next took her quite by surprise. Her companion came to an abrupt halt, swung her round to face him and stared down at her frowningly through the dark, shouting above the wind: 'What are you crying for? You have been sniffing and sobbing for the last five minutes—I find it disturbing.'

She gave a watery snort. 'Then don't listen.'

He had produced a spotless and dry handkerchief from a pocket and begun to mop her face. 'Tomorrow,' he told her, suddenly gentle, 'we will have a talk—there is a great deal I have to say to you. You must see that being cruel to Liske was impossible. I have already been cruel enough...'

He kissed her suddenly, put the handkerchief away

and walked her on once more, faster than ever. She was still gathering her wits when they turned in at the gates and started up the drive. As they rounded the curve she could see that almost every light was on in the house, and someone must have been watching for them, for the great door was open long before they reached it, with Bart on the porch and Mevrouw Metz hovering behind him.

Eloise was a little hazy after that; a great many people surrounded her, shook her hand, patted her shoulders, poured out long speeches in Dutch and took her wet things from her. They were only stopped by the doctor's voice telling her to go upstairs with Mevrouw Metz. She pulled herself together then, protesting that she had to go back to Mijnheer Pringle.

'You'll stay here, have a hot bath and go straight to bed. I'll telephone Cor now. And just for once, do as you're told, Eloise,' begged the doctor in a voice which didn't beg at all but expected to be obeyed. She was considering a retort to this when she sneezed, a signal for her to bustle up to the room where she had slept before, undressed and put into a steaming bath, clothed in a voluminous nightie of Mevrouw Metz's and popped into bed with a glass of some hot, pungent mixture which the housekeeper offered her with encouraging clucks and nods. The haziness returned after that and merged almost at once into sleep.

She awoke the next morning feeling none the worse for her adventure. True, her head ached and she had the beginnings of a sore throat, but she had no intention of telling anyone about that, and when Mevrouw Metz brought her breakfast tray, Bart, hovering discreetly in the doorway, informed her in his careful English that the doctor had gone out to an emergency case and wished her to remain where she was until he returned.

'But I'm going back to England later this morning,' she protested.

Bart nodded smilingly. 'Yes, miss, but the doctor wishes you to stay; he has, I understand, something important to discuss with you.'

No 'will you' or 'do you mind', reflected Eloise crossly. Well, she wasn't going to play doormat for anyone, and why should he wish her to stay in the first place? So that she might apologise to Liske who had been treated so cruelly? Well, she wouldn't, but to refuse point-blank wouldn't do; she had only to look at the two elderly faces looking at her so intently. 'Oh, well, in that case,' she told them airily, 'there's no more to be said, but I simply must go to Mijnheer Pringle's house and get some clothes; I've nothing fit to wear. Do you suppose I might borrow the Mini and drive over for them? I'd better go myself because I know where they are.'

She felt mean when Bart said at once that of course she was to do exactly what she wished. He would see that the car was at the door when she wanted it. 'The doctor doesn't expect to get home until late this afternoon,' he volunteered, 'there's an outbreak of food poisoning in two of the local schools and he expects to be fully occupied.'

'Nasty,' commented Eloise. 'It might take a little while to clear up, too.' And by the time it was, she would be miles away and probably forgotten.

After Mevrouw Metz and Bart had gone, Eloise gobbled down her breakfast, bathed and dressed again in her ruined clothes and went downstairs still feeling mean, although she reminded herself repeatedly that one man's poison was, in her case, her meat; it would be more than unkind to feel pleased at the outbreak of food poisoning, but it would undoubtedly keep Timon fully occupied until she was safely away. At the door, wishing Bart a guilty '*Tot ziens,*' she asked: 'Juffrouw Barrema, is she expected to call today?'

Bart gave her an inscrutable look. 'I really couldn't say, miss.' She had a feeling that he could have told her more than that, but at least she had the satisfaction of knowing that if Liske did come, she wouldn't be there to offer apologies she didn't mean.

She got into the car, waved once more to Bart, and drove quickly to Mijnheer Pringle's house.

She hadn't stopped to consider what she would say to that gentleman when she saw him, and she was spared that worry by finding him from home. Juffrouw Blot, made aware by some means or other of her last night's adventure, found nothing strange in Eloise's awkwardly expressed statement that she was returning to England at once, for she had known that she would be leaving on the same day as Mijnheer Pringle. She went away to fetch Eloise's case and then to make coffee while Eloise tore into another dress and coat, quite frightened that Timon might have returned home unexpectedly and be even now on his way to fetch her back.

The taxi she had asked Juffrouw Blot to get was at the door by the time she got downstairs; she scribbled a hasty note to Mijnheer Pringle, wishing him good-bye and a pleasant trip, aware that it was quite inadequate but unable to think of anything better, exchanged a warm embrace with Juffrouw Blot, and jumped into the taxi.

It wasn't until they were in the crowded streets of Groningen that she began to feel safe. She paid off the taxi at the station and bought herself a ticket to Schiphol. The fare was quite frightening, but she paid it recklessly, telling herself that it was a small price to pay for getting away so easily and ignoring the small voice at the back of her head telling her persistently that she didn't want to get away at all—never to see Timon again, to have to think of him married to Liske; she would make him a terrible wife... She stood on the platform waiting for the train and wished she were anywhere else but where she was.

She had plenty of time for reflection once she was in the train; it was a quite lengthy journey and once at Amsterdam she had to find her way to the KLM terminal and board the bus for Schiphol and once there arrange a transfer to an earlier flight; the one she had booked wasn't due out for another two hours, too long a time to wait. She toyed with the idea of telephoning Mijnheer Pringle and dismissed it. He would only tell Timon and the whole object of her flight, to disappear decently with no fuss, would be defeated. She would write when she got back to the hospital; she had the address in Curaçao. She sat through the short flight with an empty mind which refused to cope with any plans for the future, it was enough that she had returned without difficulty. She closed her eyes and tried to sleep but instead found herself thinking of Timon.

She was expected at St Goth's, that at least made life more normal; she went to her room and put away her things and sat down to decide what to do. Her application form, already filled in, was in the drawer where she had left it; she supposed that she should go at once to Miss Dean's office and hand it in. It was really a little awkward; she was actually no longer on the staff even though she had been allowed a room until she returned from Holland. Presumably if she got the Sister's post, she would be given a bedsitter in the Sisters' Wing. The prospect left her indifferent; a secure future, a chance to climb to the top of the nursing profession, a steady income with a pension at the end of it…anything but that!

She went downstairs and asked for an appointment with Miss Dean early the next morning and presently went to supper, where she ate nothing at all, pushing the food round her plate while she answered her friends' questions about her stay in Holland. She telephoned her mother later, telling her almost nothing, allowing her to believe that she would accept the post of Night Sister if she should be offered it. Time enough to let her know her plans for the future when she knew them herself. She then went to bed and cried herself to sleep.

She got up in the morning resolved not to shed another tear, and made her way to Miss Dean's office. That lady received her kindly, inquired after Mijnheer Pringle's health, hoped that Doctor van Zeilst had been satisfied with her services as a nurse and then waited, hands clasped before her on her desk, for Eloise to speak.

She could have been no more surprised at Eloise's next words than Eloise herself; she heard her own voice, quite calm and unhurried, telling her superior that she had decided against applying for the Night Sister's post, indeed, against hospital work of any sort, at least for the time being, and as this decision had only at that very moment entered her head, even though she had known since the night before that she wasn't going to apply for the job, she could only gape when Miss Dean inquired with well-concealed surprise if she had any idea what she was going to do.

Eloise uttered the first thing which entered her head. 'I want to go a long way away,' she stated clearly, 'and look after children or babies—but it would have to be in the country.'

Miss Dean, a practical woman even when confronted by the unlikely situation of one of her most promising nurses apparently without her wits, answered immediately: 'In that case, Staff Nurse, since you are not technically on the staff, I am free to make a suggestion. Should you wish for a temporary post while you reconsider your position, I may be able to help you. My brother is headmaster of a boys' prep school in Cumbria—near Buttermere, but rather remote. He telephoned me only yesterday and mentioned that the school matron had a nasty attack of shingles and was desperate for a substitute. About two or three weeks, I believe, probably less. If you are interested, I could recommend you.'

'I should like that,' said Eloise without stopping to think about it. 'It's just what I want.'

Miss Dean reached for the telephone. 'And of course,' she went on smoothly, 'if you feel differently at the end of your stay there, I will consider your application to rejoin the nursing staff. It would have to be as a staff nurse, you understand, but there will be other Sisters' posts.'

Eloise said: 'Yes, Miss Dean,' but she wasn't really listening. Cumbria was a long way off and no one would know that she was there. By no one she meant Timon, of course; not that he would want to know, although it would be wonderful if... She came back to her surroundings with a jerk to find Miss Dean speaking on the telephone and looking at her in a questioning manner. 'I asked,' said that lady patiently, 'if you could travel up there today? There is a train about noon and you would have to change at Lancaster for Keswick where you will be met—there is a car journey of half an hour from there. Your expenses will be paid and you will receive a salary *pro rata*.'

'That will do nicely.' Eloise watched her boats burning behind her and didn't care at all.

Miss Dean spoke into the telephone, put down the receiver, asked: 'You have enough money, Staff Nurse?' and when Eloise said yes, she had: 'Then I suggest that you go and pack a few things for your new job.' She smiled nicely. 'And I hope to see you again shortly.'

Eloise said: 'Yes, Miss Dean,' which could have meant anything, and wasted no time; there was her mother to telephone, there was a case to pack and the warden to see about her room; she should by rights give it up instanter, but since Miss Dean had left a loophole for her, surely she would be allowed to keep it for another week or two, in case she came back. But she wouldn't do that, she knew that for certain now; she would have to find a job as far away from London as possible, something which would keep her so busy that she would have little time to remember. She told herself bracingly to be thankful that things had turned out so well, gave her mother the bare bones of the matter in an over-bright voice which disturbed her parent very much, packed a case with suitable clothes for the Lake District in early winter, bade brief goodbyes to such of her friends as she could conveniently find, and took a taxi to the station.

The journey was uneventful, but throughout its length she didn't allow herself to think deeply; she speculated on the job ahead, took a close interest in the scenery, and read several newspapers from cover to cover without taking in a single word. It was a relief to reach Lancaster at last and catch the local train to Keswick. The country was worth looking at now, and Keswick, when she reached it, looked charming. She got out of the train eagerly, anxious to get the journey finished with now, for it seemed hours since she had left London and it was as though she were in a different country. There weren't many people on the platform and she spotted the man who had been sent to meet her almost at once—one of the housemasters, Miss Dean had told her, and here he was, looking the part; tall and thin and stooping. Just for a moment she thought she had been mistaken, though, for he stood lost in thought, not looking about him at all, but then, apparently remembering where he was, he gazed around him, saw her and came at once, peering at her through pebble glasses.

'Miss Bennett? Ah—welcome. I'm Carter—John Carter. You have no idea how glad we shall all be to have you with us—our Miss Maggs is laid low and we are lost, completely lost without her.'

If they were all like him, thought Eloise, that seemed very likely. She wished him a brisk how do you do, exchanged a few banalities about the journey and accompanied him outside the station to where a Landrover was drawn up to the kerb.

Mr Carter put her case in the back and opened the door for her to get in beside him. 'The school's rather remote,' he explained, and set off at a pace which rattled the teeth in her head.

They left the town behind them quickly enough, taking a road which led them through the hills, already only dimly to be seen in the dusk, and after the first mile or so Eloise quite saw why Mr Carter drove a Landrover, for they turned off on to a side road presently, which dipped and twisted over rough ground, its own surface none too smooth. Mr Carter drove badly, with the manner of a man who hated doing it, any way and he spoke little, answering Eloise's questions with a minimum of words, so that presently she gave up trying to hold a conversation with him and sat staring into the dark, wishing that it was Timon sitting beside her.

It was a relief when they arrived at a very small village and her companion stated: 'The school is another mile along this road—there's a drive on our left.'

As indeed there was, marked by two very small

lodges, built apparently for dwarfs. The drive ran, straight as a ruler, to the imposing pile of the school, standing well back from the road, lights shining from its windows. Eloise, who was hungry, was glad to see it at last.

Mr Carter drove round to a side door, stopped the Landrover with a frightful jolt, took her case inside, muttered something about putting the car away, gave a great shout for someone called Mrs Emmett, and went away, leaving Eloise standing uncertainly in a gloomy passage wondering what to do. She didn't have long to wait, however. A small, round woman with grey hair and pale blue eyes appeared through a door, talking as she came. 'You'll be the new matron—you'll want a meal and see your room, I'll be bound.' She picked up the case and opened another door for Eloise to go through. There was a staircase in front of them, and with Mrs Emmett toiling ahead of her, Eloise went up it, heartened by the thought of supper. Her room was close by the stairs, and comfortable enough with a small electric fire and an armchair drawn up close to it.

'Bathroom's down the passage,' Mrs Emmett told her, 'supper's in half an hour; I'll be back for you in twenty minutes so's you can see the headmaster first.' She smiled and trotted off, leaving Eloise disappointed; she would have liked a cup of tea, but it seemed she wasn't going to get one, so she explored her room, unpacked her case, inspected the white uniform and little caps someone had thoughtfully provided for her use, did her hair and face and sat down to wait for Mrs Emmett.

'You're the housekeeper?' she inquired when that lady reappeared.

'Yes, Matron—and a busy woman I am, too. If you would just come with me, Dr Dean will see you now.'

They went back the way they had come and down another passage which brought them out into the main hall where the housekeeper tapped on a door, opened it, gave Eloise's name, and disappeared, leaving Eloise to get herself into the room and cross its vast carpet to the desk where the headmaster was standing.

He looked stern, but perhaps he had to because of the boys in his care, but he wasn't as old as she had expected, although a beard did add to his age. He greeted her in a no-nonsense fashion, thanked her for stepping into the breach, begged her to take a chair and gave her, very briskly, a sum of the tasks which she would be expected to perform.

'You have had no experience of school nursing?' he wanted to know. 'Miss Maggs, our regular Matron, has of course spent a lifetime at it and is naturally an expert at her work.'

And she would need to be, Eloise fancied, if she performed half the jobs the headmaster had rattled off so glibly. He resumed: 'This is only a temporary post, as you know. We hope that Miss Maggs will be back before long. Meanwhile, we are very grateful to you for filling in for her.'

It was obvious that these gracious words marked the end of the interview. Eloise got to her feet and he marched to the door beside her and opened it, saying:

'Please feel free to come to me if there are any problems.'

There were dozens, and the most pressing one was where did she go for her supper. She was standing in the hall wondering which door to open when a youngish man came into the hall. 'Lost?' he asked. 'You're the temporary Matron, aren't you? Come with me and I'll show you where we have supper—with the boys, I'm afraid, but don't let that affect your appetite.'

Nothing would affect it. She followed her guide along a long passage to double doors which opened on to the dining hall, a vast, lofty place and very draughty. It was filled with long tables, lying parallel to each other and presided over, as it were, by another table raised on a platform at one end of the hall. Evidently this was where the staff sat; she could see Mr Carter standing behind a chair, looking down at the boys waiting to sit, presumably when he said so. Her companion hurried her along, introduced her to such of the staff who were within speaking distance, indicated a chair and went to stand at his own chair. Mr Carter must have been waiting for them, for he said a lengthy grace and everyone sat down. Eloise, sitting between two learned, grey-haired gentlemen, found herself facing the boys below her; there seemed to be an awful lot of them; she had forgotten to ask how many—some of them seemed quite small and she supposed that they sat in houses, for at the top and bottom of each table there were older boys sitting, but she didn't waste much time on speculation; a maid was bringing round plates of soup and that interested her far more.

Supper was a substantial meal and she enjoyed it, as she enjoyed the conversation of her neighbours. They all stood through another long grace, in Latin this time, and with her original guide to show her the way, went back to her room. 'There's no one sick at the moment,' he told her, 'but if you like to go to the end of this passage you'll find the sick bay; it might help if you were to explore it.' He grinned at her. 'My name's Sewell, by the way, Dick Sewell.'

'And mine's Eloise Bennett—thanks for showing me around.' She bade him goodnight, and did as he suggested, to discover that the sick bay was ten-bedded, well equipped and cheerful. There was a small treatment room leading from it as well as an isolation ward with one bed in it. She pottered round for half an hour or more, discovering where everything was, and on her way back to her room met Mrs Emmett.

'Miss Maggs and me usually have a cup of tea about now,' said the housekeeper pleasantly. 'I wondered if you would like one with me?'

'Oh, please—and perhaps you could tell me one or two things—what time to get up and if there's a sick parade, and do I go to the hall for breakfast…'

'We'll go to my room, Matron, and have a little chat.' Mrs Emmett led the way downstairs and ushered Eloise into her own sitting room, crowded with old-fashioned furniture and with a great many photos in frames arranged on every available surface, but it was homelike and the tea was hot and strong and there were biscuits with it. Eloise sat by the old-fashioned fireplace and toasted her feet while her companion gave her a bird's

eye view of what her day would be. A long one, by all
accounts, starting at half past seven in the morning and
ending after supper, and taking in the checking of the
laundry, the inspection of the boys' clothes, the sick parade, the attending to any minor injuries and the care
of any boy in the sick bay. Eloise went to bed presently,
trying to remember everything she had been told, all
the same, it was of Timon she was thinking when she
finally went to sleep.

She got through her first day's work very well. There
were several boys with cut fingers, chilblains, sore
throats and boils, but once she had dealt with them she
was free to work her way through the laundry, piled
high and not attended to since the unfortunate Miss
Maggs had been carried off sick. She inspected the
dormitories too, a little vague as to what was expected
of her, and after lunch she had an hour or two to herself. It was a clear, chilly day, so she wrapped herself
up warm and went for a brisk walk down to the village
where she bought a few odds and ends at the only shop
and then telephoned her mother.

Mrs Bennett sounded worried. 'It sounds a long way
away,' she observed. 'Is it hard to find, darling?'

Eloise told her and then extolled the scenery, the size
of the school and the comfort of her room, and finally
her mother observed: 'Well, dear, it sounds quite nice.
Are you going back to St Goth's?'

'No—I don't know. I—I thought I'd make up my
mind while I'm here.' And with that her mother had
to be content.

The days passed quickly enough. There was plenty to

do but none of the work was arduous, and after a little while Eloise began to get to know the boys, the little ones especially. Privately she considered that an eight-year-old was too young to send away from home and judging from the number she discovered were homesick, she thought that quite likely she was right. There was a certain amount of bullying, of course, and at least once a day, a fight about something or other, but as various masters hastened to assure her, boys would be boys and they had to expend their energy on something or someone, and they were taught to fight fair. She quickly learned to deal with a black eye or bruised knuckles without asking too many questions, although it seemed to her that one or two of the boys came off worst every time. One especially, an undersized, spectacled boy of eight or nine years, Smith Secundus by name, for he had a much older brother in the school. Eloise came across him on several occasions getting roughed up with what she considered to be quite unnecessary violence, so much so that on one particular morning she had waded in to rescue him and taken the names of the three much older boys who were plaguing him—Tomkins, Mallory and Preedy, they had told her rather defiantly, and had refused to tell her why they so frequently set about Smith Secundus.

'Well, I shall find out,' she told them sternly, 'and if it doesn't stop I shall see your housemasters about it. Smith Secundus, come to the treatment room and have that nose-bleed dealt with.' She had marched him away and done her best to worm out of him why he was so unpopular.

He told her finally, his voice muffled against the cold compress she was holding to his small nose. 'They don't like me because I'm small and I like lessons.' He added proudly: 'I'm very good at maths, Matron.'

Eloise gave him a comfortable pat. 'Good for you, and you'll grow, my dear, and in a little while when they understand maths too, you'll all be friends and laugh about it.'

He hadn't believed her. 'I shall do something desperate,' he had told her rather importantly as she had tidied him up and sent him back to his class.

Chapter 9

Eloise kept an eye on Smith Secundus for the next day or two, but he seemed to have settled down; at least she saw no signs of bullying, and any fighting there was was the cheerful give and take of boys enjoying a rough-house together. She had become quite fond of them all, although she wasn't sure if she could manage the older boys, who tended to regard her as someone of their own age. All the same, she had settled down during the two weeks in which she had been there, and if she wasn't happy, at least she was learning to live with the prospects of never seeing Timon again. She resolutely stopped herself from thinking about him and that made her feel empty and sad, but that, she felt sure, would pass in time, and in the meantime she must make up her mind what she wanted to do once the school no longer needed her.

Miss Maggs had returned that very morning, and Eloise realised anxiously that she had really made no plans at all. Her mother wanted her to go home for a holiday and she was tempted to do that, although it wouldn't solve her problem. Perhaps she should go back to St Goth's after all, and supposing she did? What if Timon should turn up one day? After all, Sir Arthur Newman was a friend of his—it would be like turning a knife in a wound if she had to see him again. She thought about it until her head ached, and came to no conclusion at all.

She finished her work earlier than usual that afternoon and Miss Maggs was closeted with the headmaster. It was a fine, cold day, with a decided nip in the air; she got her coat and started off for a walk; exercise was what she needed. She went a long way and the afternoon was failing as she took the little path which ran alongside the drive. The school looked rather spectacular from where she was, the fading light warming its stone walls. She stopped to admire it—and then suddenly began to run towards it. There was someone on the balustrade which ran right round the attic floor of the house, standing out on the narrow ledge between the sewing room and the attic where the luggage was stored. She knew who it was, too—small and black-haired and rigid. Smith Secundus.

She ran well and she made light of the stairs to the top of the house. The sewing room door was open and she made herself slow down and go in quietly, taking off her coat as she went. At the open window she leaned out. 'Hullo,' she said cheerfully, 'what are you doing out there?'

His voice came to her in a whisper. 'They called me a dwarf—they said I wouldn't grow—Mallory and Preedy and Tomkins... I'll make them sorry...' Eloise could hear the rising hysteria in the treble voice and stretched herself a little further out of the window. 'I'll jump,' said Smith Secundus.

'Well, yes, dear,' she spoke soothingly, 'but that wouldn't be of much use, would it? I mean, the boys would get a nasty shock if you did, but what would be the point of that if you weren't there to see?' She swung a shapely leg over the sill and tried not to look down to the ground far below. 'It would be a frightful waste.'

She saw that the good sense of this remark had struck him and added in a voice which shook only very slightly with fright: 'I'll come out on to the ledge with you and stretch out my hand—I think you'll be able to reach it and catch hold, then you can edge back...'

He turned a face stiff with terror towards her. 'I can't—Matron, I can't. I'm going to fall.'

'Of course you can, Smith Secundus.' Eloise spoke with brisk authority, but her heart sank as she saw that the rest of him was stiff with terror too. He looked as though he were carved in stone and just as hard to budge.

'I'm going to fall,' he repeated.

'Pooh, don't be silly!' She was still brisk, quite sure that she would fall herself before very long; heights had never been her strong suit, but it was not time to be worrying about that. She swung the other leg over the sill as she spoke, murmuring vague prayers as she did so, and stood upright on the ledge, a hand clutching at the parapet behind her. Gingerly she turned until her back was pressed hard against it, one hand still clinging to it as though she would have soldered it there, the other stretched out to the boy. There was still a gap between them and she moved sideways, refusing to allow her mind to dwell on the fact that the ledge was barely a foot wide.

'Catch hold,' she told Smith Secundus, 'and come towards me, my lamb—sideways like a crab, and don't look down. We'll go back together.'

It sounded easy and she was proud of her steady voice even though she was silently screaming her head off for help. And that was futile, she knew; the boys would be back from their paperchase by now and in the dressing rooms behind the gym changing their clothes and making more than enough noise to drown a dozen screams. There was no help.

There was. Her terrified eyes, much against her will, had looked down; coming up the drive with smooth soundlessness was a silver-grey Rolls-Royce. It stopped precisely outside the entrance a little to her left and Timon van Zeilst got out. Even from that distance and angle he looked reassuringly large; the epitome of security. Eloise whispered his name and then, in a remarkably squeaky voice, shouted it. He was already strolling towards the porch, but he stopped and looked up, saw them at once and then before she could get another sound out of her dry mouth, disappeared inside.

The minute that passed seemed like a year; Smith

Secundus was crying now and his hand felt cold and clammy in hers. She had pulled her gaze away from the ground once more and was concentrating on clinging to the parapet with all her strength—they only had to hang on a little longer…

Without turning her head, for she dared not, she knew that Timon was at the window, one leg, indeed, already over its sill. His voice, reassuringly matter-of-fact, sounded quite placid. 'Boy—you'll do exactly as I say. Step sideways towards Eloise, and when I tell you, step past her—there's room enough if you press close to her. You'll be perfectly safe; she's holding you and I'm holding her.'

Eloise felt his large firm grasp round her hand and its reassuring squeeze and heard, incredibly, his laugh, and Smith Secundus said in a wobbly voice: 'Yes, sir— but it's Matron, sir.'

'Is that what they call you, Pineapple Girl? Anyone less matronly…' His voice became brisk and commanding once more. 'Now boy, come along.' And Smith Secundus came, with a heart-stopping stumble or two, pressing his bony little body against Eloise so that her bones ached with the effort to keep steady while he wormed his way past her. After what seemed an age she heard the doctor say: 'Good man—very nicely done. Over the sill with you and into a chair, and stay in it. You can leave go of my hand now.'

Eloise felt his hand tighten on hers. 'And now, my pretty, you'll do the same—it will be easier this time; you're nearer and I'm right here beside you. All you have to do is move sideways—don't look down and don't hurry.'

'I'm so much bigger,' she pointed out shakily.

'And so much braver—and not so big that I can't hang on to you easily enough with one hand if I have to. Come on.'

She was too scared to do anything else—indeed, she was beyond thinking for herself any more. With a few cautious, terrified steps she found herself beside the doctor's reassuring bulk and then whisked with surprising strength across him and tossed through the window. She landed untidily on the window seat and was barely on her feet when he was beside her.

'My poor girl,' he said in a kind voice, and caught her close. She looked up into his face and was surprised to see how white and drawn and somehow older it was. 'Timon, oh, Timon!' she mumbled, and heaven knew what she might have said if he hadn't released her almost at once and said in a matter-of-fact voice: 'You both need a cup of tea. Is there anyone…?'

Eloise did her best to sound as matter-of-fact as he did. 'Yes, there's Miss Maggs, she's the School Matron—she came back today, actually I was on my way to have tea with her when I saw… Smith could come with me…' She looked anxiously at him. 'We don't need to say anything, do we?'

He stared at her thoughtfully, sat her down in a chair and went to sit on the arm of the boy's chair. 'I came to see the headmaster about another matter—I think I could explain to him—he will have to know.' He put out a hand and ruffled Smith Secundus' untidy hair. 'Don't

worry, boy, we'll get it sorted out. And you, Eloise—
er—Matron, could you explain over the tea-cups; the lad
can fill in the gaps.' He looked down at the boy. 'Why
did you do it, Smith?'

It all came pouring out once more while the doctor
listened gravely and then remarked simply: 'We all do
silly things now and then. I shouldn't think anyone need
know other than the headmaster and your housemaster—
and the lady Matrons, of course.' He grinned suddenly
at Eloise, who frowned.

Unimpressed by the severity of her expression, he
got to his feet. 'Shall we go, then?'

Eloise went to the mirror above the old-fashioned
grate and straightened her sadly battered cap. It was
heaven to see him again, but he needn't suppose that
she was going to behave like a meek doormat... She
took her time and, her headgear once more arranged to
her satisfaction, asked: 'Why are you here?'

He looked wicked. 'Interested? I seem to remember you saying that you didn't care if you never saw
me again.'

'Well, and I don't.' She spoke mendaciously and
much too quickly.

'Your mother seemed to think otherwise.'

'Mother?' she stared at him round-eyed. 'She's not
here?'

'At Eddlescombe. I went there after I had been to St
Goth's—looking for you, Eloise.'

She had gone to stand by the boy, putting a comforting arm round his narrow shoulders. 'Why?'

'That will have to wait for the moment. Supposing we go, as I suggested, and find Miss Maggs.'

The School Matron was sitting at a small table in her neat sitting room, carefully repairing some small boy's coat. If she was surprised to see a very large man open the door in answer to her 'Come in', and stand aside to allow her colleague and Smith Secundus to enter, she didn't betray it. She smiled at Eloise, gave the boy a quick, all-seeing glance and turned her attention to her visitor.

'Doctor van Zeilst,' said Eloise breathlessly.

Miss Maggs' blue eyes twinkled nicely at him. 'Ah, yes, of course,' she murmured in a pleased way, 'the headmaster did mention...' They exchanged a look and she went on smoothly: 'Will you join us for tea?'

'Thank you, no, Matron—I have an appointment with Dr Dean and I believe that I am already a little late.' Timon turned round to look at Eloise. 'And you, Matron, could perhaps discuss what is best to be done while you have your tea.' He smiled suddenly. '*Tot ziens*, dear girl.' He shook hands with Miss Maggs, ruffled the boy's hair once more and at the door turned to say: 'They had rather a nasty experience, Miss Maggs, but I'm sure that I leave them in excellent hands.'

He had gone. Eloise stared at the gently shutting door, unable to believe that he could have walked off in such a casual manner; without even bothering to in-quire how she—or Smith Secundus, for that matter—felt. She frowned fiercely to check the tears she would have liked to shed and said too brightly: 'Well, that's done and finished with—we'll feel fine when we've had a cup of tea.'

Miss Maggs was a wise woman; she looked at the boy's white face and Eloise's cross one and allowed them to drink two cups of tea and empty the bread and butter plate before she interrupted her gentle flow of small talk to ask: 'An old friend of yours, my dear?'

Eloise went bright pink. 'No—yes, that is we knew each other just for a little while in Holland.'

Miss Maggs nodded her severely coiffed head. 'And he came all this way to see you. I have been wondering why a nice girl like you should wish to bury yourself in such a remote part. Still, he's found you now.'

'He wasn't looking for me,' said Eloise gruffly, 'he's going to marry a Dutch girl—she's fair and slim…' She glanced down at her nicely rounded person and sighed.

Miss Maggs remained unruffled by this statement. 'There's many a slip…' she quoted mildly. She was a woman who liked her proverbs, and what was more, believed in them, too.

'Timon doesn't make slips,' declared Eloise gloomily, and Smith Secundus, who had been allowed to get up from the table and look at Miss Maggs' photograph album of old boys, said unexpectedly: 'No, he didn't, did he, Matron? He walked along the ledge just as though he was on the ground and he felt like a great big tree. Why does he speak English if he comes from Holland?'

'He's a very well educated man,' supplied Eloise gloomily. 'And now we'd better tell Miss Maggs all about it, hadn't we—right from the beginning.'

Miss Maggs, her placid face set in comfortable attentiveness, listened, popping in a question here and there when Smith Secundus got too involved or excited and saying at the end of their joint recital: 'Well, Smith, it was a foolish thing to do, wasn't it? How fortunate Matron was close at hand and brave enough to come to your rescue, or you might still have been out there, catching dear knows what kind of a cold. I hope you intend to thank her properly for coming to your aid, and as for the doctor who rescued you, nothing less than a letter of thanks in your best handwriting will do.'

'Shall I have to see Dr Dean?' asked the boy unhappily.

'Naturally, and so will Matron, but as to punishment I imagine that he will consider that you have had enough of that, standing out there on that nasty ledge. There's no more to be said about it now; I'm only thankful that it didn't turn out worse than it was. You'll go to bed after you have seen the headmaster and I shall come and take a look at you later, just to make sure that you're all right...' She was interrupted by a knock on the door and the entrance of one of the school prefects. Eloise was required in Dr Dean's study, and Smith Secundus was to go to his housemaster's room.

Eloise put up a hand to tuck away a stray end of hair. Her appearance wasn't as pristine as she could have wished, but really that hardly mattered. She got to her feet, caught sight of the look of dread on the small Smith's face and said bracingly: 'We'll come at once, thank you—don't wait; I'll take Smith Secundus along as I go.'

There was no one about in the long corridor outside Matron's room. Eloise took her small companion's hand and when they reached his housemaster's room, knocked on the door and went in with him.

Mr Sewell, the housemaster, was standing before the gas fire, warming himself, and he turned a stern face to them as they entered.

'Thank you, Matron—it is Smith Secundus I wish to see.'

'Oh, I know that,' agreed Eloise, who hadn't quite learned how to be a school Matron. 'I just popped in to warn you that this boy has had a very nasty fright. He was very good and brave though, once he saw how silly he'd been. I'd be proud of him if he were my son.' She smiled warmly at the glowering housemaster. 'I shouldn't be surprised if he doesn't grow up to be a fine man,' she assured him, and then to the boy: 'You have no need to be afraid now; Mr Sewell is going to explain just how silly you were, my dear, but you don't need to be afraid of him, and if you're punished, mind you take it like a man. I'll see you at supper.'

She smiled warmly at them both and Mr Sewell actually smiled back.

The headmaster looked stern too, but not frighteningly so. He offered her a chair and said without preamble: 'Doctor van Zeilst has told me about this unfortunate incident, Matron...' He paused and Eloise glanced quickly round the room. Timon wasn't there and she was aware of bitter disappointment, although there was no reason why she should; he had shown a lamentable lack of interest in her. She swallowed the knot of tears which had been in her throat ever since she had climbed on to that awful ledge, and gave her attention to the learned gentleman addressing her.

'I must thank you, Matron, for your presence of mind and courage—it could have been a serious accident, even tragedy. After discussion it has been agreed that the boy has been sufficiently punished, and I hope that you concur. I shall of course speak very severely to those boys who caused him to take such a drastic course.'

'Good—I detest bullies, and he's only a little boy and he showed plenty of pluck.'

'So Doctor van Zeilst assured me.'

She couldn't resist asking: 'He's a friend of yours, Headmaster? I mean, it seemed so strange to see him here, it's rather off the beaten track...'

'So he himself observed. No, Matron, I have not had the pleasure of meeting the doctor before. A fine man, if I may say so.'

She hoped that he was going to say more than that, and looked at him encouragingly, but he merely smiled, remarked that he didn't wish to detain her and got to his feet once more, a sign that the interview was over.

There was plenty to keep her busy that evening. She had supper with Miss Maggs, who didn't mention the doctor once but talked a great deal about Eloise's departure, something Eloise didn't much want to discuss. Once she had left the school she would have severed the last slender link with Timon—a good thing; general opinion had always had it that a clean break was the thing. But it wasn't. She had done that once and what good had it done? The moment she had set eyes on Timon getting out of his car she had come alive again.

She sorted sheets after supper, dosed one or two boys with colds, peeped in on the sleeping Smith Secundus and took herself off to bed, where she was at last able to cry her eyes out in peace and quiet.

She was to leave, it was decided in the morning, in two days' time. Everyone had been very nice, had praised her lavishly for her part in rescuing Smith Secundus, wished her a pleasant future, and beyond Miss Maggs, had shown no further interest. That lady, however, made up for that by displaying a lively curiosity as to where she would go. 'I know you came here on a temporary basis,' she observed, 'and of course, it's none of my business, but have you another post to go to?'

Eloise shook her head. 'Well, no—I thought perhaps I'd have a short holiday and then perhaps go abroad for a while.'

Her companion gave her a shrewd look and said nothing to this, so Eloise felt bound to add: 'I've always thought I should like to…'

'Australia?' queried Miss Maggs. 'It's a long way away, but I hear from all counts that there are excellent prospects there. You hadn't thought of getting married, I suppose?'

Eloise gave her a goaded glare; she had thought of nothing else, quite pointlessly, for some weeks now. 'No, I haven't.' She put down the neat pile of shirts she had been folding. 'Shall I go along and take young Adams' temperature? He looked feverish to me this morning when he reported a cold—I thought I'd look him over for spots.'

'A sensible suggestion,' agreed her senior, 'half term, you know, a week or so ago, and if there's anything catching about, you may be sure one of the boys will bring it back with him.'

Adams, a small, plump boy with spiky hair and round blue eyes, had a temperature, he had spots, too. Eloise cast a professional eye over him, reported her findings to Miss Maggs with the observation that it looked like chickenpox to her, and set about transferring the patient to the isolation ward and telephoning the school doctor.

The rest of the day was nicely taken up with this exercise and the careful scrutiny of any small boys who had been in contact with the victim; there were any number of them, but they all looked, for the moment at least, remarkably healthy. Miss Maggs, over their evening cup of tea, expressed the fervent hope that Adams would be the only case, and that a light one.

He was well covered in spots by the following morning and a little pale and lethargic, but Doctor Blake pronounced himself quite satisfied with him, and left Eloise to make the boy comfortable for the day, observing as he went: 'I hear that you are leaving us, Matron—I'm sure we shall all be sorry to lose you. I believe Miss Maggs has arranged for a nurse to take over tomorrow, if you would be good enough to keep an eye on him today.'

Eloise didn't believe in beating about the bush; she went straight to Miss Maggs and asked: 'Why don't you want me to stay on, Miss Maggs? You know I haven't a job to go to. I could have easily stayed another week, or at least until Adams is better, it would have made no difference.'

The Matron looked uncomfortable. 'Well, dear, nothing would have pleased me more, but Dr Dean told me quite positively that arrangements had already been made and that you were to be free to go in the morning. In fact, I hear the nurse is arriving this afternoon, directly after lunch.'

Eloise felt quite bewildered. 'Is she? But why…?' and then, suddenly rather cross: 'In that case she can take over straight away; it won't take me a minute to pack and I can leave this afternoon just as easily as tomorrow. In fact, I could go now—this minute…'

Miss Maggs looked, if that were possible, even more uncomfortable. 'Oh, I'm not sure…'

'Well, I am. Someone could have told me—all this secrecy—if they want me away why didn't they say so? Wild horses wouldn't keep me here. For two pins I'd walk out this very minute!'

Her superior's agitation was quite alarming. 'Oh, my dear, don't do that—at least…' She glanced at the clock. 'If you could just change Adams' bed for him first—it wouldn't take more than half an hour—and there are all those sheets and pillowcases… I'd do it, but I've all these forms to see to.'

Eloise was cross and hurt, but neither of these feelings had been caused by Miss Maggs. 'Yes, of course I'll do that,' she promised, and put down her coffee cup. 'All the same, I shall go just as soon as the nurse arrives.'

Miss Maggs made a soothing sound and looked at the clock again and when Eloise had taken herself off, allowed herself a sigh of relief.

Eloise had Adams sitting in a chair, wrapped in a blanket, and was smoothing the bottom sheet, when the door opened and Timon came in. At the sight of him her heart missed a beat, turned over and leapt into her throat so that the only sound she could manage was a small choking breath.

'Hullo,' said Timon, and smiled at her.

The smile played even more havoc with her heart, but she ignored that. 'Have you had the chickenpox?' she demanded in a severe voice. 'This boy's in isolation.'

He had strolled right into the little room, to lean against a wall and watch her. 'I have indeed, abundantly, at the age of six.'

She had a sudden vivid picture of a small spotty Timon, probably refusing to stay in bed; he would have been a lively small boy… 'Oh, well— Have you lost your way? Did you come to see the headmaster again?'

'I came to see you, Eloise.'

Her heart did a somersault, but she replied coldly. 'That's too bad; I'm leaving in about half an hour.'

His eyebrows rose. 'Indeed? I understood you to be going tomorrow morning.'

She began: 'Well, I…' and then: 'How did you know that?' She mitred the corners of the top blanket very precisely and invited the spotty Adams to jump back into bed.

'Oh, I arranged it with the headmaster.' His voice was bland. 'Miss Maggs, however, had the good sense to telephone me and tell me your change of plans.'

'You arranged it…you must be joking… I've never heard…' She stopped to draw an indignant breath.

'No, dear girl, I don't joke about it; I don't joke about something which matters to me more than anything else in the world. And of course you have never heard, for I have never told you, have I?' He smiled at her with such tenderness that she went pink and then quite pale. 'Is Adams now safely tucked up? Could he be left to his own devices for a little while?'

'Well, yes, I suppose so. But I have the sheets to put away. I said I would do that before I go.'

He held open the door without a word, waited while she made sure that the invalid had all he wanted, and ushered her out into the passage.

'The linen room,' directed Eloise, strangely short of breath, 'and really I can't think why you should want to see me.'

She was brought to a standstill by the simple expedient of having her waist clamped by his two hands and then turned round to face him. But she would look no higher than his chin. 'After all,' she reminded him, 'you walked off without…' Her voice became indignant at the very remembrance of it. 'You didn't even ask how I felt.' She glanced briefly up at his face, to encounter blue eyes which gleamed so brightly that she lowered her own in panic. 'Besides,' she went on, quite unable to stop herself now, 'when I left Holland you didn't m-mind—not in the least.'

'Did I say that, my Pineapple Girl?'

She said a little pettishly: 'No, you didn't, you just looked down your nose at me.'

'Shall I tell you what I really wanted to do?' His voice was full of laughter and something else, so that she said hastily and much against her inclination: 'No, I have to see to the sheets.'

He made no attempt to release her. 'Damn the sheets,' he observed mildly. 'I'm sure that Miss Maggs will be delighted to deal with them; I've not come all this way to watch you count linen.'

Eloise wriggled a little and his hands tightened. 'Well, why have you come?'

'To marry you, of course.'

Her eyes flew to his and this time she didn't lower them. 'Marry...?' she managed. 'But you've not asked me.' She added without conviction: 'Besides, I don't want to.'

He sighed loudly. 'My darling love, is that true? I do hope not, for I have the licence in my pocket and the parson waiting.'

'The parson...' Eloise's unremarkable features had assumed beauty as she assimilated this news; she felt a pleasant glow sweeping over her, but all the same she damped it down just for a moment. 'I'll not marry you until you explain about Liske. Besides, you let me go...'

He bent his head then and kissed her so that she really didn't care about his answer, but presently he said: 'I could hardly tell you that I loved you until I had made it quite clear to Liske that any feeling I had had for her was quite gone—and there never was much, you know, my dearest, and what little there was melted away when you fell in a heap at my feet and flung a pineapple at me.' He kissed her again. 'I told the Reverend Mr Culmer that we would be at the church by half past one.'

Eloise didn't know whether to laugh or cry. 'But it's long after twelve o'clock, and look at me...'

She shouldn't have said that, for he wasted quite a few minutes doing just that before observing: 'Very nice too, my darling, and something I shall never tire of doing.'

She gave his arm a little shake. 'Timon, darling Timon, you don't understand—I'm in uniform and I've got to pack and no one knows...it'll take ages to explain...'

'Don't fuss, woman.' He had stopped her by kissing her once more. 'I've already explained—why do you suppose I wanted to see Dr Dean in the first place? And you can change in ten minutes. If you can't pack in that time it really doesn't matter; we can stop somewhere and get what you need.'

She blinked at him, smiling gloriously. 'All right. You—you are sure, aren't you?' She wasn't given the chance to say more than that, though. Presently she said in a voice muffled by his shoulder: 'Will you tell me where we're to be married and where we're going?'

'In the village church, of course—I arranged that yesterday. I was on the way to see the headmaster when I looked up and saw you. I've never been so frightened in all my life, dearest; to have found you and then to see you teetering wildly on the parapet far above my head.' His blue eyes searched hers. 'I died a dozen times before I reached you.' He pulled her closer and pulled the cap off her head. 'Such pretty hair. Once we're married we're going to drive over to Buttermere—they're expecting us at the inn there—we can have a late lunch.'

'Expecting us?' asked Eloise sharply. 'You were sure, weren't you?'

He answered her placidly. 'Yes, my darling, I was, just as you are sure—and we've wasted too much time already.'

'I'm sorry, Timon, of course I'm sure. I've loved you for—oh, ever since I first saw you, I suppose. Are we going to stay at Buttermere?'

'For a few days, then I'll take you to Eddlescombe before we go back to Holland.' He let her go reluctantly. 'Go and put on something pretty while I go and thank Miss Maggs. I'll wait for you there.'

She took rather less than the ten minutes Timon had given her; it was wonderful what one could do when one had a sufficiently good reason to do it. She was out of her uniform and into the green outfit, and had her hair and face done, her velvet tammy nicely arranged, well within that period, and time to spare to search for her best gloves and handbag, urged on by her happiness and excitement.

The rest of her packing was done in a careless manner which would have revolted her normally, but now nothing was normal; it was a dream come true, so wonderful that she couldn't quite believe it.

The next few minutes was a confusion of goodbyes and good wishes which she hardly heard; nor did she realise that she was in the car until they were driving away, out into the narrow road which led to the village. But the dream became glorious reality when they walked side by side up the churchyard path and Timon opened the old, creaking door and took her hand in his and kissed her very gently. 'This is where our life begins,' he said tenderly.

She kissed him back, for she had no words.

* * * * *

SPECIAL EXCERPT FROM

H HARLEQUIN®

SPECIAL EDITION

Former soldier Nick Garroway is in Wedlock Creek to fulfill a promise made to a fallen soldier: check in on the woman the man had left pregnant with twins. Brooke Timber is in need of a nanny, so what else can Nick do but fill in? She's planning his father's wedding, and all the family togetherness soon has Brooke and Nick rethinking if this promise is still temporary…

Read on for a sneak preview of
A Promise for the Twins,
the next great book in Melissa Senate's
The Wyoming Multiples *miniseries.*

If the Satler triplets were a definite, adding this client for July would mean she could take off the first couple weeks of August, which were always slow for Dream Weddings, and just be with her twins.

Which would mean needing Nick Garroway as her nanny—manny—until her regular nanny returned. Leanna could take some time off herself and start mid-August. Win-win for everyone.

A temporary manny. A necessary temporary manny.

"Well, I've consulted with myself," Brooke said as she put the phone on the table. "The job is yours. I'll only need help until August 1. Then I'll take some time off, and Leanna, my regular nanny, will be ready to come back to work for me."

He nodded. "Sounds good. Oh—and I know your ad called for hours of nine to one during the week, but I'll make you a deal. I'll be your around-the-clock nanny, as needed—for room and board."

She swallowed. "You mean live here?"

"Temporarily. I'd rather not stay with my family. Besides, this way, you can work when you need to, not be boxed into someone else's hours."

Even a part-time nanny was very expensive—more than she could afford—but Brooke had always been grateful that necessity would make her limit her work so that she could spend real time with her babies. Now she'd have as-needed care for the twins without spending a penny.

Once again, she wondered where Nick Garroway had come from. He was like a miracle—and everything Brooke needed right now.

"I think I'm getting the better deal," she said. "But my grandmother always said not to look a gift horse in the mouth." Especially when that gift horse was clearly a workhorse.

"Good. You get what you need and I make good on that promise. Works for both of us."

She glanced at him. He might be gorgeous and sexy, and too capable with a diaper and a stack of dirty dishes, but he wasn't her fantasy in the flesh. He was here because he'd promised her babies' father he'd make sure she and the twins were all right. She had to stop thinking of him as a man—somehow, despite how attracted she was to him on a few different levels. He was her nanny, her *manny*.

But what was sexier than a man saying, "Take a break, I'll handle it. Take that call, I've got the kids. Go rest, I'll load the dishwasher and fold the laundry"?

Nothing was sexier. Which meant Brooke would have to be on guard 24/7.

Because her brain had caught up with her—the hot manny was moving into her house."

Don't miss
A Promise for the Twins *by Melissa Senate,*
available July 2019 wherever
Harlequin® Special Edition *books and ebooks are sold.*

www.Harlequin.com

Looking for more satisfying love stories
with community and family at their core?

Check out **Harlequin® Special Edition**
and **Love Inspired®** books!

New books available every month!

CONNECT WITH US AT:

Facebook.com/groups/HarlequinConnection

 Facebook.com/HarlequinBooks

Twitter.com/HarlequinBooks

 Instagram.com/HarlequinBooks

Pinterest.com/HarlequinBooks

ReaderService.com

**ROMANCE WHEN
YOU NEED IT**

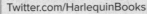

SPECIAL EXCERPT FROM

Love Inspired®

*Paralyzed veteran Eve Vincent is happy with the
life she's built for herself at Mercy Ranch—until her
ex-fiancé shows up with a baby. Their best friends died
and named Eve and Ethan Forester as guardians.
But can they put their differences aside and build a
future together?*

Read on for a sneak preview of
Her Oklahoma Rancher *by Brenda Minton,
available June 2019 from Love Inspired!*

"I'm sorry, Eve, but I had to do something to make you see how important this is. We can't just walk away from her. It might not be what we signed on for and I feel like I'm the last person who should be raising this little girl, but James and Hanna trusted us."

"But there is no *us*," she said with a lift of her chin, but he could see pain reflected in her dark eyes.

The pain he saw didn't bother him as much as what he didn't see in her eyes, in her expression. He didn't see the person he used to know, the woman he'd planned to marry.

He had noticed the same yesterday, and he guessed that was why he'd left Tori with her. He'd been sitting there looking at a woman he used to think he knew better than he knew himself, and he hadn't recognized her.

"There is no *us*, but we still exist, you and me, and Tori needs us." He said it softly because the little girl in his arms seemed to be drifting off, even with the occasional sob.

"There has to be another option. I obviously can't do this. Last night was proof."

"Last night meant nothing. You've always managed, Eve. You're strong and capable."

"Before, Ethan. I was that person before. This is me now, and I can't."

"I guess you have changed. I've never heard you say you can't do anything."

He sat down on a nearby chair. Isaac had left. The woman named Sierra had also disappeared. They were alone. When had they last been alone? The night he proposed? It had been the night she left for Afghanistan. He'd taken her to dinner in San Antonio and they'd walked along the riverfront surrounded by people, music and twinkling lights.

He'd dropped to one knee there in front of strangers passing by, seeing the sights. Dozens had stopped to watch as she cried and said yes. Later they'd made the drive to the airport, his ring glistening on her finger, planning a wedding that would never happen.

"Ethan?" Her voice was soft, quiet, questioning.

He glanced down at the little girl in his arms.

"What other option is there, Eve? Should we turn her over to the state, let her take her chances with whoever they choose? Should we find some distant relative? What do you recommend?"

He leaned back in the chair and studied her face, her expression. She was everything familiar. His childhood friend. The person he'd loved. *Had* loved. Past tense. The woman he'd wanted to spend his life with had been someone else, someone who never backed down. She looked as tough, as stubborn as ever, but there was something fragile in her expression.

Something in her expression made him recheck his feelings. He'd been bucked off horses, trampled by a bull, broken his arm jumping dirt bikes. She'd been his only broken heart. He didn't want another one.

Don't miss
Her Oklahoma Rancher *by Brenda Minton,*
available June 2019 wherever
Love Inspired® books and ebooks are sold.

www.LoveInspired.com

LIEXP0619

Love Harlequin romance?

DISCOVER.

Be the first to find out about promotions, news and exclusive content!

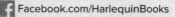 Facebook.com/HarlequinBooks

Twitter.com/HarlequinBooks

Instagram.com/HarlequinBooks

Pinterest.com/HarlequinBooks

ReaderService.com

EXPLORE.

Sign up for the Harlequin e-newsletter and download a free book from any series at **TryHarlequin.com.**

CONNECT.

Join our Harlequin community to share your thoughts and connect with other romance readers!
Facebook.com/groups/HarlequinConnection

 **HARLEQUIN®**

**ROMANCE WHEN
YOU NEED IT**

HSOCIAL2018

Reward the book lover in you!

Earn points on your purchase of new Harlequin books from participating retailers.

Turn your points into **FREE BOOKS** of your choice!

Join for FREE today at
www.HarlequinMyRewards.com.

Harlequin My Rewards is a free program (no fees) without any commitments or obligations.